Praise for Anna Durand's Books

"[*Insatiable in a Kilt*] smokes from the very first pages. [The] plot works on a number of levels, giving this story suspense and drama as well as sizzle, and her characters are well-defined and credible. Durand's Hot Scots family saga just keeps on getting better."
Readers' Favorite

"[*Notorious in a Kilt*] is the book I have been waiting for! A great second-chance romance and one of my favorites in this series."
The Romance Reviews

"I loved the Scottish in Ian and the strength of Rae, but the love of one little girl makes [*Notorious in a Kilt*] something to behold."
Coffee Time Romance

"*Gift-Wrapped in a Kilt* is a marvelous continuation of the author's Mac-Taggart family saga. Durand's story has an entertaining plot, and her steamy interludes are well-written...a celebration of healthy relationships between loving adults written in a tasteful and compelling manner."
Readers' Favorite

"I have enjoyed this whole series, but Emery and Rory [from *Scandalous in a Kilt*] have stolen my heart and are now my favorites!"
The Romance Reviews

"[*Scandalous in a Kilt*] is beautifully written with a heavy emphasis on the actual romance and sensuality experienced by [the] two characters. [...] I've found each of the [Hot Scots] books to have entertaining and original plots and marvelous characters."
Readers' Favorite

"An enthralling story. [...] I highly recommend the writing of Ms. Durand and *Wicked in a Kilt*, but be warned you will find yourself addicted and want your own Hot Scot."
Coffee Time Romance & More

"*Dangerous in a Kilt* by Anna Durand delivered! [...] It was the journey, characters, and smoking hot sex scenes that kept me turning the pages."
The Romance Reviews

Other Books by Anna Durand

Insatiable
IN A KILT

Hot Scots, Book Six

ANNA DURAND

JACOBSVILLE BOOKS JB MARIETTA, OHIO

INSATIABLE IN A KILT

Copyright © 2019 by Lisa A. Shiel
All rights reserved.

ISBN: 978-1-949406-13-9 (paperback)
ISBN: 978-1-949406-14-6 (ebook)
ISBN: 978-1-949406-15-3 (audiobook)
Library of Congress Control Number: 2019909809

Manufactured in the United States.

Jacobsville Books
www.JacobsvilleBooks.com

Publisher's Cataloging-in-Publication Data
provided by Five Rainbows Cataloging Services

Names: Durand, Anna.
Title: Insatiable in a kilt / Anna Durand.
Description: Lake Linden, MI : Jacobsville Books, 2019. | Series: Hot Scots, bk. 6.
Identifiers: LCCN 2019909809 | ISBN 978-1-949406-13-9 (paperback) |
     ISBN 978-1-949406-14-6 (ebook) | ISBN 978-1-949406-15-3 (audiobook)
Subjects: LCSH: Man-woman relationships--Fiction. | Scots--Fiction. |
     Americans--Fiction. | Highlands (Scotland)--Fiction. | Extortion--Fiction. |
     Family secrets--Fiction. | Billionaires--Fiction. | Romance fiction. | BISAC:
     FICTION / Romance / Contemporary. | FICTION / Romance / Romantic
     Comedy. | FICTION / Romance / Billionaires. | FICTION / Romance /
     Later in Life. | GSAFD: Love stories.
Classification: LCC PS3604.U724 I67 2019 (print) | LCC PS3604.U724 (ebook) |
     DDC 813/.6--dc23.

Chapter One

Keely

I sipped my tea and gazed out at the view of the Eiffel Tower framed between the buildings on either side of the narrow street. Golden-orange lights illuminated the Tower's body, while white lights flashed so fast the structure seemed to sparkle. It looked majestic and ethereal at the same time, like a specter of the past enlivened by modern technology. Sometimes I felt like something past its prime, though I hadn't been given new life by technology or anything else. Tonight, I felt old.

Snap out of it, I chastised myself. *Forty is not old.*

I relaxed back into my chair, returning my attention to the outdoor cafe I'd chosen as my first stop after checking in at my hotel. People ambled by on the street, some as couples holding hands. One pair paused to share a sweet kiss.

My throat went thick. I peered down at my teacup, reflecting on how I had come to be here. Alone. In the most romantic city on earth. The simple answer was my boss had sent me to attend a conference in his place because he'd had an emergency appendectomy. The more complicated answer involved two ex-husbands, one former live-in boyfriend, and lots of bad judgment on my part. My second divorce had been finalized on my fortieth birthday three months ago. *Happy birthday to me.*

I picked up the brochure I'd set on the table and flipped through it for the fifth time. The Approach the Future Summit promised workshops and round-table discussions about cutting-edge technologies, as well as a keynote speech by the man my boss insisted I had to speak to before leaving the conference. Vic Bazzoli had vowed he would force me to listen to polka music all day every day for a week if I failed to introduce myself to Evan MacTaggart, the twenty-nine-year-old CEO of an up-and-coming tech company. Vic lusted after MacTaggart's spy gadgets and wanted them in our store. What people in our small Utah city needed with spy gadgets, I had no clue.

The brochure did not include a photo of Evan MacTaggart. I would find out what he looked like in two days when he gave his keynote speech. Until then, I'd have to settle for imagining what a twenty-something billionaire might look like—or be like.

I set the brochure down on the table. How did one approach a filthy-rich twenty-something? I didn't have a clue.

My phone rang, and I knew who was calling.

"Hello, Serena," I said when I answered the call. "No, I am not moping in bed while eating ice cream and watching sappy old movies."

"Good, but are you getting your ooh-la-la on?"

"Excuse me?"

"Are you having fun? That's what I asked."

"Having fun? Sure."

She made a rude noise. "Keely O'Shea, I've known you for twenty-five years and you can't fool me. You're probably sitting in a romantic little cafe drinking tea alone."

Damn. Serena Carpenter knew me too well. Being friends since high school had its perks and its downsides. I couldn't hide much from her.

"Maybe you're right," I said, "but I need to rest up for the big conference."

"Ugh. Two days of boring tech stuff. All the more reason you need to get over the Bryce shit and get yourself a hot young Parisian man."

"Please. A boyfriend is the last thing I need." Could a forty-year-old still call a man her boyfriend? It sounded strange.

"I should have sneaked into your house and erased your computer. Why didn't you unfriend Bryce ages ago?"

"Never thought about it. You know I rarely go on social media except to maintain the store's page."

This morning before I left for the airport, I had logged in to check for any notifications about the business where I was assistant manager, Vic's Electronics Superstore. Just my luck, the second I'd logged in I'd been presented with a notification about my ex-husband. Three days after our divorce was finalized, Bryce had married his twenty-two-year-old mistress. The notice I'd seen this morning announced she was pregnant.

For our entire seven-year marriage, eight years including the year-long separation, Bryce had insisted he never wanted children. He'd also claimed he could never want anyone else.

I snatched up my tea and swigged it. Hot liquid scorched my mouth. I gulped it down and spluttered.

"Are you okay?" Serena asked.

"Never guzzle hot tea. I just learned that lesson."

"Did you hurt yourself? Maybe you should stick to water."

"I'm fine. No harm done."

"Good. Now get out there and dazzle someone. You are too hot and amazing to sit there by yourself."

"I'm saying goodbye." I held the phone away from my face, hearing her voice even as I reached for the red symbol on the screen to disconnect the call. "Goodbye, Serena."

Placing the phone on the table, I took a gentler sip of my tea. Eyes closed, I savored the sweet flavor with a touch of creaminess from the milk I'd added. The voices of other patrons drifted around me, most speaking French, their voices soft and melodic. I'd always loved the French language and the way native speakers let the words roll off their tongues even when they spoke fast. Until tonight, I'd mostly heard the language in movies and in French pop music, and I hadn't had a chance to learn much of it before coming here.

A chair scraped on the concrete patio of the cafe.

Sighing, I opened my eyes to gaze at the newcomer who had taken a seat at the table across from mine.

The tall, muscular man seemed to overflow the chair. He fidgeted as if trying to get comfortable, his mouth crimping briefly before he relaxed into the seat. His blond hair framed a face with smooth, elegant features. The glow from the cafe's lantern-like lights sparkled in his eyes, though I couldn't make out their color. Thick biceps strained the fabric of his long-sleeve, cobalt-blue shirt. His jeans hugged his powerful thighs.

His attention swung in my direction, and his lips curved into a soft smile. As his gaze swept up and down my body, his smile warmed.

Something about him intrigued me. Maybe it was his smile or angelic good looks or his well-built body—well-hung too, based on the bulge in his pants. Then again, maybe it was something more indefinable.

What had Serena said? *Get yourself a hot young Parisian man.*

I couldn't. I wouldn't. Ogling him was one thing, but speaking to him…

His smile had turned positively sizzling.

Sitting up straighter, I smoothed my dress, glad I'd worn a sexy one. My inner critic had warned me not to bother with sexiness since I had no interest in men, but I'd suffered an irresistible impulse to wear the dress I'd bought on a whim last week. The deep, lush green fabric complemented my eyes. The backless design featured spaghetti straps, a low neckline with

a knot between my breasts, a skirt that flared out around my thighs, and a
hem that stopped a good six inches above my knees. When I sat down, the
hem rode up a little higher. The strappy stilettos I'd worn gave my ankles a
nice curve. I loved the decadent sensation of a breeze caressing my bare back
but going without underwear felt scandalously indecent.

The man sitting across from me could see all of the dress, all of me,
thanks to the fact I was positioned sideways to him. His tongue slipped out
to moisten his lips. His gaze landed on my face.

My pulse sped up, and every hair on my arms and my nape tingled and
stiffened.

He gestured toward my table and the vacant chair beside me. "May I
join you? It's too bonnie a night to drink coffee alone."

What was that accent? Scottish, I decided. His sexy voice made a new
tingle rush through me. Forget finding a hot Frenchman. A hot Scot was
even better.

Not interested in men, remember?

Sure, but I could play at being interested. This man looked young, maybe as young as my ex's new bride. Maybe I should find out why men liked
younger women by experimenting with a flirtation with a younger man.
What happened in Paris stayed in Paris. Or was that Las Vegas?

Who the hell cared.

"Please do," I said, patting the empty chair beside me. "I'd love some
company."

He moved into the chair beside me, his big body filling it and then some.

With him so much closer, I got my first good look at his eyes. Dark-
blue rings encircled blue irises so pale that they almost appeared silver. The
combination of his eyes and his blond hair, along with that beautiful face,
lent him the aura of an angel who'd come down to earth in disguise. But
that body, all muscles and strength, made him seem more like a fallen angel
destined for sin and designed for pleasure.

His chair scraped on the concrete as he turned it slightly toward me.
Resting an arm on the table, he focused his attention on me.

Only me. Even when a gorgeous young mademoiselle in a dress far
skimpier than mine sashayed by, he did not even glance at her or her perky
breasts.

"What is a beautiful woman doing alone in Paris?" he asked in a deep,
silky voice. "Or are you waiting for your lover?"

"You think I would sit with another man while waiting for my boyfriend?"

He lifted one shoulder. "This is Paris."

"I wouldn't do that."

"So, you are alone." He leaned toward me just a touch. "I'm glad to hear it."

"Why? Are you hoping to make time with me?"

"Ahhh," he purred, "I would love to make time for you. Tonight. Alone."

The way he kept his gaze exclusively on me had my body rousing, warming, softening in ways it hadn't done in a very long time. What was I doing? Flirting with a stranger, a very young stranger, in a foreign country. Maybe I'd gone insane, but I didn't give a damn.

He dragged his chair closer and draped his arm across the back of mine. "You are the most enchanting woman I've ever laid eyes on, and your dress shows off every curve of your sensuous body."

I lost the power of speech, dumbstruck by his brazenness but also stunned by my body's reaction to what he'd said and the heated look in his eyes. When had a man last spoken to me like that? Never, that's when.

"Are you in Paris for business or pleasure?" he asked.

"Business."

One of his fingers traced slow circles on my naked back. "A woman like you should find nothing but pleasure in Paris. It is the City of Love after all."

"Not interested in love."

"I meant the physical sort." He slipped that finger under the strap of my dress. "You're alone. I'm alone. Seems a pity to waste a sultry summer's night on business."

Sultry summer's night. The way he'd spoken that phrase had my breaths going shallow and my breasts tightening.

"May I kiss you?" he asked.

Those silvery irises lured me in until I could see nothing else. A damp ache between my thighs had me fighting the urge to squirm. Common sense urged me to reject his request, but the rest of me yearned to feel his lips on mine. Kiss a stranger? Like he'd pointed out, this was the City of Love.

I leaned toward him, touching my fingertips to his chest. "Yes, you may."

He tipped forward, slowly, deliberately, until his lips brushed mine.

My breath caught in my throat. My pulse revved up. Those eyes, silvery and mysterious, captured my focus even as his lips feathered over mine, back and forth, in leisurely sweeps. I splayed my palm on his chest, loving the decadent softness of his shirt and the sensation of strong muscles beneath it.

He pressed his mouth to mine, licking at the seam of my lips.

I opened for him, and my lids drifted shut.

The stranger flicked his tongue out to tease mine.

A throaty moan resonated through me. Had I made that lustful noise? Oh God, I had. I wanted this man like I'd never wanted anyone or anything in my entire life. I'd met him seconds ago, didn't even know his name, and yet I craved him.

He tunneled a hand into my hair to cradle my nape and plowed deep inside my mouth, his tongue gliding over mine, every movement measured and designed to whip me into a frenzy of need. And damn, it worked. My nipples hardened, and the sensation of my dress whisking over the sensitized peaks made me moan again, deeper and hungrier.

The stranger withdrew, though his hand lingered at my nape. "Ahm wanting to make love to ye all night."

I roused from the sensual spell he'd cast little by little, my lids easing apart, my mind swimming in a haze of desire. "What?"

"Tonight," he said, rubbing his thumb over my bottom lip. "I want ye tonight. My hotel is two blocks away."

Blinking several times, I struggled to make sense of...anything. I had made out with a total stranger. In a cafe. With other people nearby.

And I wanted more.

I gazed into those unearthly eyes. "Who are you?"

"A man who wants to give you pleasure." He slid his hand across my shoulder and down my arm. "Please come with me to my hotel. We can learn each other's names in the morning. For tonight, I want to learn every dip and swell of your body."

He dragged a finger down the slope of my breast.

I wanted to go with this man—anywhere he wanted, for as long as he wanted. The new me, who'd awakened here with this stranger in Paris, had no qualms about it. The old me couldn't quite bring herself to say yes.

But if I said no, he'd probably leave.

His fingertip tickled my breast.

I sucked in a big breath, exhaled it slowly, and said, "Yes."

A thrill chased over my skin, warm and electric. I'd agreed to spend the night with a complete stranger.

He rose, offering me his hand. "Come, lass. Tonight, you belong to me."

I dug some euros out of my tiny but fashionable purse, slapped them on the table, and slung the purse over my shoulder. "Let's go."

We hurried down the street hand in hand. My companion seemed anxious to get to his hotel, and I understood the need. It burned inside me, making me a little lightheaded.

That was probably why I tripped.

I teetered on my stilettos for a split second before I toppled.

My companion caught me in his brawny arms and pulled me snug against his body. "Careful. You might hurt yourself."

Speechless, I stared at him.

"Are ye all right?" he asked.

I nodded.

We had stopped near the entrance to an alley, a dark space between the buildings. Behind him, the Eiffel Tower glowed with ethereal golden light. He really did seem like an angel, with a brilliantly lit tower in place of a halo.

"Cannae wait," he hissed. "Not one more second."

He rushed into the alley, his hand clamped around mine, hauling me in his wake. Before I had time to process what was happening, he'd backed me up to a smooth wood door set into a brick wall and pinned me there with his body. A delicious excitement shivered through me. Caged by his body, I felt the outline of every muscle beneath his clothes and the way they flexed with the slightest movement. His erection was a hard line against my belly.

I glided my hands up his chest, breathless and on fire in the most intimate ways. Maybe I should've run, but I'd been seized by an overpowering need to shed my every inhibition and give in to anything this man wanted to do to me.

He towered over me, several inches taller than my five eight. Only my stiletto heels gave me enough height to link my hands behind his nape. I toyed with his short hair, swirling my fingertips in the silken strands, loving the sensation of our bodies melded in an intimate embrace. He bent his head to lick a path up my throat, groaned, and tugged my hips into his erection.

I tipped my head back.

My companion took advantage, scraping his tongue back down my throat and nibbling at the underside of my chin.

And then he kissed me.

Rough, hot, demanding. Our tongues tangled, our teeth bumped against each other, and our hands groped as wildly as we devoured each other. He rasped his thumb over my nipple and palmed my breast, pinching it.

I gasped into his mouth.

He pulled his hips back, separating our bodies by a sliver, though he never broke the kiss. With my eyes shut, I sensed only sounds. The ripping of foil. The *zzt* of a zipper. He shoved a hand under my dress and pushed up the skirt and jammed a knee between my thighs.

Thoughts? None. Worries? None. My inhibitions? They'd flown away the second I'd seen him in the cafe. My awareness centered on him, our tangled bodies, the roughness of his palm on my skin and the smoothness of his slacks on my inner thighs. My companion seized my knee and hoisted it up, hooking it over his hip. I gripped him with my leg, and the heel of my stiletto dug into his ass.

The whole time he never stopped kissing me.

I flung my arms around his neck.

He plunged his cock inside me.

The swift and powerful thrust made me gasp into his mouth again. I clutched at him with my hands and with my leg hooked around his hip. I held on while he pumped into me, fast and hard, our bodies slapping and my dress flapping. The cool wood of the door behind me frisked over my bare back as I rebounded from every thrust of his shaft, the excitement mounting within me with such strength and speed I lost any semblance of sanity. He ravished my mouth and my body, his fingers digging into my ass, and I clung to him.

I came like a bomb detonating, my strangled cries muffled by his mouth. Every spasm in my sex made me feel his thrusts even more, feel the thick length of him penetrating deep into my body. I threw my head back, tearing my lips away from his, the breath trapped in my lungs.

He plowed into me with even more strength and held stone-still, his cock buried inside me. His chin fell to my shoulder, and with his mouth grazing my skin, he let out a long, guttural groan of intense pleasure. We were both breathing hard. The weight of him crushed me to the door.

My companion stepped back and zipped his pants. He tossed the used condom into a nearby trash can I hadn't noticed before, blinded by a carnal need too powerful to deny.

I stood there paralyzed, shocked by what I'd done even as a new excitement tingled to life inside me at the thought of spending all night with this man.

He tugged my dress down and pressed a hand to his cheek, his gaze aimed at the ground.

"Are you okay?" I asked.

My companion raised his head, his expression blank. His brows crinkled, and he stretched out a hand to touch his fingertips to my cheek.

I opened my mouth to speak.

He grabbed my hand and towed me back down the alley to the street. We collided with a group of laughing girls who shouted French curses at us. I assumed the words were curses based on the gestures and expressions that accompanied the phrases, though I had no idea what anyone had said.

My companion halted at the curb, released my hand, and flung out an arm to hail a taxi.

Somehow, my purse had stayed on my shoulder throughout this...experience. I gripped the purse's strap. My heart pounded, adrenaline burned in my veins, and I still couldn't summon a coherent thought.

The stranger yanked open the door of the taxi that had pulled up to the curb in front of us. He waved for me to get inside.

Dazed, I climbed into the vehicle.

He slammed the door shut.

I stared at him through the window.

The stranger stared right back at me, rubbing his jaw. He whirled away and stalked off down the sidewalk, swiftly vanishing into the Parisian night.

The taxi driver rattled off something in French. Deciding he wanted to know where to take me, I mumbled the name of my hotel. As the streets of Paris whizzed by in a blur, I reached a solitary conclusion. What I'd done in Paris would stay in Paris. No one would ever know, not even Serena.

The next day, I went to the Approaching the Future conference only to learn the mysterious Evan MacTaggart had canceled his speech. Another CEO took his place. I attended every workshop and round-table discussion, scribbling notes for the report I would write for Vic. All the while my thoughts kept rewinding to my first night in Paris and an even more mysterious man who had tempted me to be wild and reckless.

Chapter Two

Evan
Ten months later

I leaned against the tall windows in my office, one foot braced on the sill, surveying the view beyond the glass. This building, my building, stood high above the tops of the shorter structures clustered around it. In the distance, the dark ribbon of the River Ness snaked through the city, out into Loch Ness, and further out to the rest of the Highlands. My roots lay out there in the village of Ballachulish, surrounded by mountains and lochs and fields of heather. I'd grown up in the countryside on the outskirts of the village, but I hadn't gone back there in a very long time. I visited my cousin Iain, who lived near the neighboring town of Loch Fairbairn, but I stayed away from Ballachulish.

Too many memories there.

With one finger, I pushed up my glasses. Other memories had distracted me this morning. For ten months, I'd had frequent flashbacks to a sultry night in Paris and the sensual woman who had captivated me. The woman I'd fucked in an alley. The woman I'd abandoned without any explanation. I hadn't bothered to learn her name, but I remembered every exquisite detail of our brief time together. That body. Those green eyes. The dark hair that had brushed my skin, silky and soft.

The intercom on my desk buzzed.

I turned away from the windows and approached my desk. It was, I admitted, too bloody enormous. The mahogany monstrosity hulked in the center of the room, three meters wide and one meter deep, like a mountain barricading me from whoever sat in either of the two chairs opposite the desk. Why had I bought such a boulder of a desk? It had seemed appropriate at the time.

Stopping at the desk's edge, I hit the intercom button. "What is it, Tamsen?"

"Miss O'Shea is here. Should I send her in?"

A business meeting. I used to love those, but ever since Paris, I'd been less and less interested in growing my company. Keely O'Shea had flown all the way from America to meet with me, so I had to see her. I hoped the lass hadn't been confused by my executive assistant and her English accent. Miss O'Shea might wonder if she'd stumbled across the border by mistake.

With a sigh, I pressed the intercom button again. "Send her in. Thank you, Tamsen."

I dropped into the leather chair behind my desk, the oversize one that matched the desk in scale but made me feel like a bairn. I straightened my jacket and tie, rolling my chair up to the desk so I could settle my arms on it. Playing the part, I was. The billionaire CEO of an international corporation ought to appear professional at all times.

Bod an Donais. I was fair sick of being professional.

My mother would've smacked my erse for mentioning the devil's penis, or anyone's penis, even in Gaelic. Mother. Just thinking the word made my jaw tense. Why did I curse my life, anyway? I'd never known how to do anything except work. Nothing had changed.

But everything had.

The door swung inward, and a woman walked into my office.

Not just any woman. All the blood drained out of my body. That's how it felt at least. While I gaped at the woman, the office door clicked shut.

She saw me and froze, her striking green eyes flaring wide.

I should have stood up, to be polite and professional, but I couldn't move. We contemplated each other in silence for a moment that grew more and more awkward with every passing second. I couldn't look away. Was I hallucinating? No, I would've imagined her in that green dress, not in businesswoman clothes. Even without my glasses, I'd gotten a clear, up-close view of her face on that night.

She held a leather binder in one hand, and a purse hung from the other shoulder. Her raven hair was pulled back in a crisp bun. She wore a beige skirt suit and modest heels of the same color, but the skirt fitted to her body in a way that accentuated every curve. Her white blouse dipped low but not too low, making her ensemble an enticing combination of sexy and professional.

And those legs. I flashed back to the alley in Paris and her leg wrapped around my hip while I drove into her.

Clearing my throat, I swerved my gaze away from her and waved toward the chairs. "Have a seat, Miss O'Shea."

I resisted the urge to clean my glasses and comb my hair. My glasses were clean, and my hair was too short to need much combing. Why did I feel the urge? It was nonsense.

Miss O'Shea fiddled with her purse strap, biting her lip, then squared her shoulders and shuffled to one of the chairs. As she settled her shapely erse onto the seat, she set her purse on the floor and clasped her hands over the top edge of the binder that rested on her lap. "I take it you're Mr. Mac-Taggart."

Her voice was calm and level.

I tried to exude a similar calm. It should've been easy. Studied composure was my specialty, until the moment she'd walked into my office.

"Yes," I said. "And you are Keely O'Shea, vice president of Vic's Electronics Superstore LLC."

Why in the name of heaven was I reciting her title?

"Vice president?" she said with the barest hint of a laugh. "I guess Vic must've told you that. Probably thought it was more impressive than assistant manager, but that's my real title."

"Nothing wrong with being an assistant manager. Mr. Bazzoli trusts you enough to let you negotiate a distribution deal with me, so you clearly deserve to be called vice president."

"Do you call everyone by their last name? Vic tells everyone to call him Vic. Besides, you've been talking to him on the phone for two weeks. Getting pretty chummy by the sound of it."

Vic Bazzoli was gregarious and exceptionally cheerful. During our conversations, I might have given in a wee bit and let him call me Evan. Sometimes it was more expedient to make a concession, especially when I liked the other person.

"Formality," I said, "is a show of respect. I ask for the same courtesy in return."

"Yes, your executive assistant told me I should always call you Mr. Mac-Taggart." Keely crossed one leg over the other, making her skirt slide up enough to reveal a tantalizing glimpse of her thigh. "But we're negotiating a deal with your company, not you personally."

"There is no difference. I am the company." The statement sounded arrogant even to me but seeing her again had done something to me. I could not hold my tongue no matter how hard I bit down on it. "It's called Evanescent Security Technologies Limited. *Evan*-escent."

She regarded me blankly for one point five seconds, as gauged by my watch, before she leaned back and shook her head. Her mouth crimped as if she fought off a smile. "Oh, I get it. You are the company because you named it after yourself in a kind of clever way."

Kind of clever? I wanted her to see me as more than slightly intelligent. I wanted her to be as captivated by me as I was by her.

We both fell silent, watching each other like we each needed to size up the opposing side.

The woman I'd dreamed of for ten months tapped her nails on her leather binder. "Are we going to pretend we haven't met before?"

"No, I could never forget you." I linked my hands on the desktop. "At least I know your name now. Keely O'Shea. A name as bonnie as the lass who bears it."

"Evan MacTaggart doesn't suit you." She bobbed her foot, the heel of her shoe popping free. "You should be called Don Juan."

"Afraid that one's taken by my cousin Aidan. He used to be known as Don Juan MacTaggart." I dragged my focus away from her leg and all that creamy skin, forcing myself to meet her steady gaze. "Maybe we should discuss what happened in Paris."

"What's there to discuss? You screwed me in an alley, shoved me into a taxi, and took off."

"I didn't take off. I walked away…rather swiftly."

"Bolted is more accurate."

Her foot kept bobbing. Her lovely ankle stretched with each downward swing.

I wanted to fall to my knees at her feet and lick my way up her ankle, up her entire leg, until I reached that sweet spot between her thighs. I remembered with vivid detail how it felt to thrust my cock inside her and make her come, but I had no idea what she looked like without clothes. My mind conjured an image of me stripping her naked and laying her across this desk so I could bury my face between her legs.

Her curt voice snapped me back to reality.

"Just to be clear, I do not have sex with strangers. Not ever." She wriggled in her seat even while maintaining a cool expression. "Except for that one time with you. Maybe we shouldn't talk about this after all."

"Please let me apologize."

She straightened, her hands clasped primly on her lap. "Go on, if you must."

"I am sorry for the way I behaved, more than you can imagine. Every day since, I've regretted it and wished I could see you again to tell you that."

"You've told me. Thank you." She dropped her foot to the floor. "Let's keep to business and move on."

Business? I'd focused on nothing else for six years. Longer, actually. All my life, I'd focused on goals and accomplishments in school and in business. Here with her, just like in Paris, I could think of nothing except having her. Ten months ago, I'd wanted to make love to her. Today, I wanted more than sex.

"Have dinner with me," I said.

She stopped blinking for two point eight seconds. Her lids fluttered, and she smoothed her fingers over the leather cover of her binder as she recovered her professional demeanor. "Thank you for the offer, but I don't date anymore."

Of course she didn't. I'd never wanted a relationship with a woman until today, so naturally, the only woman I wanted to date would have none of it.

I pulled in a deep breath, exhaled it slowly, and leaned back in my chair. "Why don't you date?"

Keely resumed bobbing her foot. "I'm here on business, Mr. MacTaggart. My personal life is irrelevant."

Mhac na galla. I suppressed a groan. Son of a bitch was right. I had a long road ahead of me to earn her trust and get her in my bed—and in my life. If I had learned one lesson, it was to never give up on what I wanted.

"You'll need to eat at some point," I said. "Why not do it with me?"

"Business, Mr. MacTaggart. Please."

Her schoolteacher tone made my balls ache. I'd never let a woman boss me around, but I would've let her do anything she wanted. The fact she managed to be polite while commanding me to stop pestering her for a date impressed me.

And turned me on.

Keely retrieved a pair of reading glasses from her purse and put them on so they perched near the end of her perfectly shaped nose. The rims of her glasses were a golden shade of tortoiseshell. She opened her binder and plucked out a sheet of paper. "You asked Mr. Bazzoli to present you with a sample contract to start off the negotiations."

"I thought he preferred to be called Vic."

Her eyes sparkled with a humor she seemed to be trying very hard to repress. "I'm in your office, speaking to you, and Mr. MacTaggart prefers formality."

I grinned like a bloody eejit. "You are wonderful."

The spot above the bridge of her nose wrinkled in the most endearing way. "Because I'm following your rules? Tamsen was very specific about how I should behave in your presence. I'm simply showing the deference you require."

Deference? I shifted in my seat, unable to get comfortable when I felt on the verge of developing a raging erection. No one had ever reminded me of my own rules. Certainly not in that calm, patient schoolteacher tone she kept using. My fantasy about spreading her over this desk naked began to change. Now, I was the one naked and sprawled over the solid-wood surface while she slapped a ruler on her palm and recited my rules.

While calling me Mr. MacTaggart.

Keely arched her delicate brows. "Are you all right, Mr. MacTaggart?"

Christ, she'd called me that again. And it made my cock twitch.

I coughed into my fist. "Call me Evan, please."

"Tamsen said—"

"Never mind that. I'm making an exception for you."

"Okay," she said carefully, eying me with a hint of suspicion. "Could we talk about the contract please, Evan?"

That was worse. My name, spoken in her sexy voice, sounded erotic.

I grinned like an eejit again.

That spot above her nose wrinkled again.

Keely O'Shea turned me into a stark-raving bampot, in Paris and here in my office. If I didn't calm down and start acting like myself, like the businessman she'd expected to meet today, Keely would run from me this time.

I punched the button hidden on the underside of my desk. A wall panel slid open ten feet to the left.

Keely jumped and twisted sideways to peek at what had been revealed. "You have a secret wet bar in your office?"

"I find a wee dram can grease the wheels during negotiations. Would you care for a drink?"

Bloody hell, I needed one.

She faced forward and straightened, reassuming her professional demeanor. "Thank you, but no. I don't drink before dinner, much less before noon."

It was still morning. The back of nine, by my watch. And I'd offered the woman a drink. She must've thought I was a drunk as well as a lunatic.

"You're right," I said. "I'm sorry. That was an inappropriate suggestion. I don't normally drink at nine a.m. either."

She waved the paper she still held in her hand. "The contract—"

"Let me give you a tour of my headquarters first."

"That's not necessary."

I sprang up from my chair and marched around the massive desk.

Keely's eyes widened for a fraction of a second. "You're wearing a kilt?"

"Aye, of course. It's Monday."

Her mouth fell open, but she clapped it shut swiftly. "Are you saying you wear a kilt to work every Monday?"

"Yes."

Her gaze lowered to my legs. Her tongue slid out to wet her bottom lip.

I approached and offered her my hand. "Come, lass. Let me show you my kingdom."

She swung her attention up to my face. "I'm too old to be called a lass."

"No woman is ever too old for that."

"I'm forty-one, which makes me definitely past the 'lass' age." Her gaze flicked down to my kilt again. "How old are you?"

"Thirty."

Her mouth opened again, but she seemed incapable of speech. "Oh."

Why was she shocked by my age? Women could be strange about numbers, whether they referred to age or bank account balances.

I thrust my hand toward her. "Come."

That was exactly what I wanted her to do, but not at this specific moment. I needed to regain my equilibrium. Nothing calmed me faster than focusing on work. Taking Keely on a tour of my headquarters would give me time to recover from the shock of seeing her again. What were the odds the woman I'd shagged in Paris, whose name I had never known, would walk into my office ten months later? Maybe my cousin Iain was right, and fate did exist.

Bullshit.

Then again, I was standing in my office with the woman I'd dreamed about for nearly a year.

Keely grabbed her purse and took off her glasses, dropping them into the bag. Rising, she hooked the purse over her shoulder and slipped her hand into mine. "After the tour, we discuss the distribution contract. Vic will be very upset if I don't come home with a signed deal for us to sell your spy gadgets in our store."

"They're not spy gadgets. My company produces security and surveillance devices for personal and business use."

Ah, back to my comfort zone.

"Right," she said. "Sorry. I didn't mean to insult your doohickeys."

She smiled a little, her eyes glittering in the light coming through the windows, and I knew she was teasing me.

I couldn't help laughing softly. "Doohickeys? You really are a wonderful lass."

Before she could inform me again that she was too old to be a lass, I guided her toward the door. Her hand felt warm and soft. She smelled like pure woman, a scent no man could describe but we all recognized instinctively. I wanted to push her up against the door and kiss her mindless. Instead, I gave up the feel of her delicate palm in mine and set my hand on the doorknob.

"Are you ready to meet the heads of every department in this company?"

"Sure, but is that necessary?" She picked at the seam of her leather binder, which she held tucked under one arm. "This is a distribution deal, not a corporate merger. And our company is minuscule compared to yours."

"I don't judge businesses by their size. The character of the owners matters far more to me than how many locations they have or the size of their workforce." I swung the door open and waved for her to exit. "Bonnie lasses first."

She shook her head, trying not to smile. "Are all billionaires as strange as you?"

"No idea. I've never met another one."

Miss O'Shea squared her shoulders and marched out the door.

I watched her swaying hips and the way her round, taut erse moved as she walked. Good thing I'd worn shorts today or the erection sure to form any moment would've tented my kilt. My employees did not need to know I was deeply in lust with Miss O'Shea.

When I passed Tamsen's desk, my executive assistant raised her brows at me.

"We're away on a tour," I told Tamsen. "Miss O'Shea will be meeting everyone, so please call ahead and let the department heads know."

"Meeting everyone?" Tamsen said, her brows lifting even higher.

I never introduced clients, much less prospective distributors, to all of my top-level employees. Tamsen had good reason to be surprised.

"Yes," I assured her. "Everyone. Quit gawping and make the calls, please."

Tamsen nodded and snatched up the phone on her desk.

I caught up to Keely, placed a hand on the small of her back, and ushered her down the hall.

Chapter Three

Keely

*I*f I'd thought I might understand Evan MacTaggart by spending time with him, my delusion was shattered after three hours with the man. In his office, I'd wondered if he was drunk or strung out on illicit substances. Once we'd left his office, his personality switched into corporate-tycoon mode. He was courteous to everyone, friendly even, though he didn't ask personal questions. Evan introduced me to so many people, all heads of various departments, that their names and faces began to blur in my memory. I knew the names of every employee at Vic's Electronics, knew their children's names too. We had twenty-five employees. Evan's company seemed to employ all of Scotland and half of England, probably a good segment of Wales and Cornwall too.

Our journey through Evanescent's headquarters failed to improve my understanding of the man behind the company. In his office with me, he'd been...odd, to say the least. He grinned and joked and refused to discuss the business at hand. Out in the wilds of his corporate offices, he adopted a completely different demeanor. He walked with purpose and self-assurance, his posture straight and his head held high, his gaze always scanning his surroundings. I couldn't imagine any other man would be capable of pulling off wearing a kilt at work, but he made it seem natural. He didn't simply wear a kilt, he owned the kilt.

After three hours with him, I'd come to know that kilt like I knew the contents of my own underwear drawer. The tartan pattern featured stripes of light blue and green mixed with black and laced with reddish-orange lines. The fabric shifted with every purposeful stride he took with those well-muscled legs. I couldn't see his thighs, but his calves were taut and muscular, dusted with hairs a shade darker than the hair on his head. His thighs must've been equally strong. My mind couldn't resist replaying the moment when he'd hoisted my leg up and strapped it around his hip right before he pushed inside me.

With a jolt, I realized I was staring at his crotch.

Snap out of it, I admonished myself. *You are way too old to lust after someone so young.*

In Paris, I'd liked the idea of hooking up with a younger man. But thirty? Had he been twenty-nine back then? I'd forgotten about the conference brochure that said how young he was. Jeez, I was turning into a cougar. This was all Serena's fault for encouraging me to land myself a hot young lover.

I shook off my thoughts of muscles and thrusting, choosing to focus on his face. His glasses obscured his eyes somewhat, but I'd had an unimpeded view of them in Paris. Why he hadn't been wearing glasses then was on my list of questions to ask him later. His eyes couldn't be as pale and unearthly as I remembered. My memory must've exaggerated things.

Not everything. It hadn't exaggerated his body.

The man towered over everyone. Whenever he gestured to emphasize something he'd said, his biceps flexed inside his suit jacket and his shirt stretched tight over the muscles of his chest. His hands fascinated me and looking at them had me flashing back to the sensation of those fingers gripping my ass.

Oh for heaven's sake. Had I regressed to high school? I was a twice-divorced forty-one-year-old woman, not a virgin desperate to get laid for the first time. Memories of that night in Paris were keeping me off balance and out of my head.

To bypass the lust circuits in my body, I resorted to what Vic Bazzoli called my "woman on a mission" mode. When Evan introduced me to someone new, I charged right in to ask questions—about the business, yes, but also about the people. I got to know the names and ages of everyone's children, not to mention their parents and siblings and pets. Maybe I went overboard in my determination to get involved, but it did prevent me from ogling Evan.

Mostly.

Plus, I got to know a lot of nice people and learned a lot about Evanescent Security Technologies Limited. The techno stuff, I didn't get. I understood enough about technology to get by in my position as assistant manager, but Vic hadn't hired me for my tech skills. He'd needed someone to handle everything else, the boring business stuff that had to be done.

Evan had lots of people to do lots of things for him. They all seemed to genuinely like him, with one possible exception. During our visit to the accounting department, Evan introduced me to Ron Tulloch, the head of the department. The man was a foot shorter than Evan, and his salt-and-pepper hair suggested he was older too. He smelled of cigarette smoke. Whenever he met Evan's gaze, Tulloch squinted his eyes. Though he spoke polite words, something about him made the hairs on my arms stiffen.

"That guy doesn't like you," I murmured to Evan as we left the accounting department. "What's his problem?"

"I'm not aware of any problem."

"Be careful around him. He gives me the itchy feeling that always means I shouldn't hire someone."

"Tulloch had a canary a few weeks ago, but he's generally a good worker."

I stopped ten feet from the elevator. "He had a what?"

Evan smiled. "A canary. It means he had a tantrum. It happened because he asked for a pay rise and I said no."

"You said he's a good worker. Why not give him a raise?"

"He had one six months ago. Besides, his department's efficiency has declined."

Tulloch gave me the creeps, but this wasn't my company. I let it go and followed Evan into the elevator.

After we'd greeted the last department head, Evan and I boarded the elevator. Rather than punching the button to take us to the top floor and back to his office, he hit the lobby button.

"I thought the tour was over," I said. "Where are we going now? To meet the janitorial staff?"

"No, we're going to lunch."

"Lunch?" I folded my arms over my chest. "This had better not be a stealth date."

He chuckled. "I don't know how I would take you on a date without you realizing it, but that's not my intention. I'm fair starved after all this walking and talking."

My stomach chose that moment to grumble loud enough for him to hear it.

Evan glanced at my belly and smirked. "I gather you're hungry too."

"Yes." I wagged a finger at him. "This is not a date, young man. We are business associates having a working lunch. We can talk about the contract while we eat."

He groaned and rubbed his forehead. "I'm needing a break from blethering. This morning, I've spoken to more people than I do in an average month. May we please eat without discussing business?"

"Sure. My voice needs a rest too."

We did talk while we ate lunch at the cafeteria on the main floor, but the conversation was intermittent and of the "nice weather we're having" variety. Evan insisted on buying me dessert. While he scurried away to get whatever secret concoction he had in mind, I called home.

"Keely, how's Scotland?" my dad asked when he picked up on the third ring.

"All I've seen so far is the Inverness airport, the inside of my rental car, and every room in the headquarters of Evanescent Security Technologies Limited."

What a mouthful that was.

"The business stuff is just today, right? Your vacation in the Highlands starts tomorrow." He paused briefly, then added in his stern dad voice, "Right, Keely?"

Okay, I couldn't blame him for the sternness. I hadn't taken a vacation...ever. Not even for my honeymoon at the start of marriage number two nine years ago. Had it been that long? Nine years. *Time flies when you're trapped in a dead-end marriage.*

"Keely?" Dad said. "Everything okay?"

"Yes, everything is fine."

"What's the billionaire like?"

Odd, gorgeous, confusing, sexy. "Evan MacTaggart isn't what I expected. He's...personable."

A voice in the background interrupted the call. I couldn't make out the muffled voice, but it wasn't hard to guess the other person's identity.

Dad cleared his throat. "Uh, Serena wants to know if this guy is hot, and if so, what's his hotness quotient."

I snorted in my attempt to thwart a laugh. My dad did not like talking about this sort of thing, but my best friend who doubled as his home care nurse would insist on getting an answer. "Tell her Evan MacTaggart is 'whew, get out the firehose' hot."

My father grumbled but relayed the message. "Serena says—Cripes, tell her that yourself."

Shuffling indicated he was shoving the phone at Serena.

"Hey, sweetie," she said in her always-cheerful voice. "Glad to hear the Scot is a scorcher. When's the wedding?"

Serena and I were the same age, but she often acted like a twenty-something on the prowl. With her fourteen-year-old son, she acted her age. I didn't begrudge her a little immaturity now and then. She'd earned it after the gut-wrenching grief she had suffered when her husband was killed in combat in Iraq ten years ago.

These days, she was determined to find me a boyfriend. When I'd told her I was far too old for a boyfriend, she'd assured me, "Well, we can at least get you laid." As far as she knew, I hadn't slept with anyone for more than two years. The thought of sharing my Paris experience with her had gotten my stomach tied in knots. Anonymous sex was not my thing. The fact I'd had anonymous sex in a Parisian alley was definitely not shareable information.

I sighed into the phone. "Serena, you know how I feel about dating and sex. I'm done with all of it."

"Bryce was a douche, I get it. That's no reason to give up. You deserve to be happy."

"I am happy."

"Sure, but you could be happier." She lowered her voice to a whisper. "I won't tell anybody if you tap that Scottish booty."

"There will be no tapping of anything. After today, I will never see Evan MacTaggart again."

"Right," she said with a disapproving tone. "Tomorrow you start your solo vacation. That's just about the most depressing thing I've heard in my life."

"Baloney. So, how's Dad? Is he doing his exercises?"

"Honestly, girl, your father doesn't need a home care nurse anymore. He gets around fine all on his own."

"I feel better knowing you're there."

"Yeah, but I feel guilty taking your money for not doing anything. The accident was three years ago. Gary's all recovered."

"I guess."

"Oh, your brothers called. They're jealous you're in Scotland, but Gary ordered them not to pester you while you're on vacation." She adopted an overly chipper tone when she added, "That means you'll have no one to interrupt you while you're getting it on with your hot Scottish lover twenty-four seven."

"Please get your mind out of the gutter, Serena." I looked up to see Evan heading for our table carrying a tray. "Gotta go. Tell Dad I'll call him tomorrow."

"Sure thing." She hesitated, then said, "At least make out with this guy before you leave Scotland. How many chances will you get to lock tongues with a billionaire?"

"Goodbye, Serena."

I hung up and dropped the phone back inside my purse.

Evan set his tray on the table and reclaimed his seat opposite me. The tray held two banana split sundaes, each topped with whipped cream and a cherry. A spoon was wedged inside each bowl with the handles sticking up. He placed one sundae in front of me and the other in front of himself.

I studied the dessert.

"Were you expecting something Scottish?" he asked.

"Guess I was."

"The cafeteria makes the best sundaes." He scooped out a spoonful of his dessert and slid it into his mouth. His lips closed around the concoction, and he slowly pulled the spoon out. His jaw worked as he chewed and swallowed. "I'll take you out for something more authentic tonight."

"No, you will not." I stabbed my spoon straight through the cherry on my sundae. "We are not dating."

"Consider it a professional courtesy."

I gave him a look I hoped conveyed my skepticism. "You have a strange definition of professional courtesy. In your office earlier, you were grinning and acting like a crazy person."

"Not that bad, was I?"

"Okay, maybe crazy isn't quite accurate." I stuffed a spoonful of ice cream and fudge sauce into my mouth, chomping on the cherry embedded in it. "You were acting strange, though."

And yes, I'd spoken with my mouth full. Since this was not a date, I didn't need to worry about whether my eating habits disgusted him.

Evan watched me chewing, his lips quirking into a slight smile. "I love a woman who eats with enthusiasm."

The eerie sensation of being watched prickled at my nape. I surveyed the area but saw only people eating their lunches and ignoring us, until I spotted a familiar figure. Ron Tulloch was hunched at a table by himself picking at a plate of food, his gaze trained on Evan. When he noticed me noticing him, he got up and left.

"Everything all right?" Evan asked.

"Yeah, fine."

He reached across the table to wipe something off the corner of my mouth. Ice cream, I saw when he lifted his finger in front of my lips. He moved his finger closer, waggling it. Did he actually expect me to lick his finger?

I sat back, dropping my spoon in the bowl.

Evan sighed and leaned back in his chair. He thrust his ice-cream-smeared finger into his mouth and sucked. After wiping his finger off with his napkin, he leaned forward to speak in a low and rumbly voice. "Maybe you'd rather suck on a different part of me."

"No, but thanks for the offer." I shoved a spoonful of sundae into my mouth and wiped away the dribbles before he could do it again.

Evan swirled his spoon in the caramel sauce on his sundae. "You were staring at my dick all morning."

I froze, the ice cream melting into a soup in my mouth. Swallowing, I set my spoon on my napkin. "Not all morning. I'd stopped by the time we got to the sixth floor."

"Donnae mind. I was admiring your erse and your breasts."

"My erse?"

"Your sweet little derriere, lass."

I made an impatient noise. "Stop calling me 'lass.' I've already explained I'm too old for that."

"You're no *cailleach*."

"Huh?"

"I'm saying you aren't an old woman. You are not too old for anything, Miss O'Shea." He devoured another mouthful of ice cream. "Are you not married, then?"

"No, I'm not."

"Have you been married?"

I tried not to frown, but really, he was pushing the limits of what he'd called professional courtesy. "I'm divorced. You?"

"Never been married." He tilted his head and scrutinized me like he was considering how to reverse engineer me. "Why are you Miss O'Shea if you've been married?"

"I went back to my maiden name after the divorce. Can we please get back to business?"

"Aye, if you insist."

His questions had unnerved me for some reason, but I didn't want to analyze why. I wolfed down my sundae to avoid talking anymore. He didn't seem to care. After we finished our desserts, we returned to the top floor. When we exited the elevator, one of his employees waylaid Evan with urgent questions about manufacturing protocols or some such technical stuff.

I wandered over to the desk occupied by his executive assistant, Tamsen Spurling. Since we gals had already bonded while I waited to be summoned into Evan's office this morning, I felt comfortable propping my hip on the edge of her desk.

"How was the tour?" Tamsen asked.

"Interesting." I considered how to ask a question tactfully. "Is Mr. MacTaggart always so cheerful?"

"Cheerful? He's friendly to everyone if that's what you mean."

"Well, not exactly." I checked over my shoulder to ensure Evan was too far away to hear before I leaned closer to Tamsen. "Does he usually grin and crack jokes during business meetings?"

The pitch of her voice kicked up a few notches. "Grin? Evan? No, I've never seen him do that."

"Do you know him well? He lets you call him Evan."

Her posture and her expression softened. "I've been with Evan since the day he founded this company six years ago. And since I'm five years older, I've become a sort of surrogate mother figure."

Jeez, I was eleven years older than Evan. If a five-year difference made Tamsen a mother figure, what did eleven make me? A dirty cougar, that's what. An older woman on the prowl for some sweet young tail. Not that I planned on "tapping" that tail.

I swung my foot, letting the heel of my shoe dangle free. "Does Evan take every potential business partner on a tour of the building?"

"Never." Tamsen tipped her head to the side. "He lets you call him Evan?"

I held up my hands. "Tried to stick to the rules, honest. He insisted I call him by his first name."

"How odd." She studied me like I was a bizarre new form of human being. "Only I call him Evan, because we've been together for so long. If he wants you to use his first name..."

She shook her head, seeming unable to comprehend the implications.

Evan strode up to Tamsen's desk and handed her a file folder. "Send this to Robert at the factory."

"Of course." She took the folder. "I'll take care of it right away."

He moved to the door and pushed it open, his hand on the knob. "In my office, Miss O'Shea. If you please."

I waltzed past him into the office.

Evan slammed the door and pushed me back against it. His mouth covered mine, the kiss brutal and hungry. His tongue pushed inside my mouth, and I sagged against the door, opening for him, devouring him as greedily as he devoured me. Our tongues lashed and thrust, licked and scraped, while he plastered his body to mine and I shoved my hands inside his suit jacket to clutch at him for support. My knees felt wobbly, my head floaty.

He tore his mouth away.

I fought to catch my breath, my body pressed into the door to keep from falling into him.

Breathing hard, he braced his arms at either side of my head. "Been needing to do that since you walked into my office this morning. After watching your bonnie erse all day, I couldnae wait anymore."

"That was completely unprofessional."

He smirked. "Better tell that to your tongue. It wouldn't let mine go."

"Don't you worry I might accuse you of sexual harassment?"

"No, you wouldn't do that." He rubbed his erection against my belly. "Besides, you want me as much as I want you. And since you were obsessed with my cock all morning, I think I'd have as good a chance at winning a lawsuit as you might."

I couldn't refute that logic.

"Kissing," I said, "does not mean we're dating or romantically involved in any way. We should stick to business from here on."

"That'll be right," he said with unmistakable sarcasm. He brushed his lips over mine, making my breath hitch. "Give me one good reason why we shouldn't be involved."

"I'm eleven years older than you."

"That's not a good reason. I don't care about your age."

"Stop being so pigheaded. I am way too old—"

He mashed his mouth to mine.

I held perfectly still, waiting for him to pull away, but he kept his mouth crushed to mine for so long I couldn't prevent my body from responding. It slackened, and I slumped against the door again. My lips relaxed too, parting just enough for him to forge inside.

But he didn't.

He pulled away, his arms still braced against the door, and gave me a smug smile. "Doesnae matter how old ye are, Keely. Ye want me, and ye cannae hide it." He moved one hand to my hip. "Every time you tell me you're too old for me, I am going to kiss you senseless."

"No man's kiss does that to me."

"Mine will."

I made a scoffing noise.

He crushed his lips to mine yet again and leaned in until his entire body was molded to mine, pinning me to the door. A decadent heat bloomed inside me to suffuse my entire body, though it settled heavily in my lower belly. God, I did want him. Too much. Way too much.

I shoved my hands between us and pushed.

With one hand still on my hip, he straightened his other arm to create a gap between our bodies, though I doubted my pushing had much to do with it. With all those muscles, he could've outmaneuvered me. He hadn't, and I could admit I appreciated that.

Nevertheless, I aimed a chastising look at him. "Behave, Evan."

"Why would I do that?" One side of his mouth inched upward. "I love it when you reprimand me in that schoolteacher voice."

A man with a schoolteacher fetish. *Wonderful.* Well, if he wanted to be reprimanded…

I barred my arms over my chest. "Do I need to call your mother?"

Every muscle in his body stiffened. He gritted his teeth, a muscle pulsing in his jaw. "That won't be necessary."

His flinty tone cut into me as sharply as his gaze.

Spinning on his heels, he stalked across the room, behind his desk, and jerked the chair out. His big body dropped onto the seat with a thud. He wheeled the chair up to the desk, his hands flat on the surface. "The contract, please. Now."

Okay, he had mommy issues and a schoolteacher fetish. Even if I'd been inclined to date him, I would've paid attention to the alarm bells his behavior had set off.

I took a seat across the desk from him and wondered for the hundredth time who Evan MacTaggart was.

Chapter Four

Evan

Keely slapped the paper down on my desk right under my nose. I'd been staring down at the large calendar on the desktop, wondering what the bloody hell was wrong with me. Why did I get angry when Keely mentioned my mother? I knew why in the general sense, but she couldn't know about the problems between me and my mother. I'd been the moron who mentioned how much I liked her schoolteacher voice, and Keely had responded in kind.

She tapped the paper with one fingernail. "Here it is, Mr. MacTaggart. As you commanded."

The woman was furious, and she was right to be.

I scratched the back of my neck. "I'm sorry, Keely. I shouldn't have shouted at you."

She leaned forward. "You didn't shout. Snarled, maybe."

"I acted like a daftie."

"Not sure what that means, but I'm guessing it's not good."

"Means I've been a fool." I slouched into my chair. "I am sorry."

She seemed to appraise me for a moment while she absently ran her fingertips along the smooth surface of the desk's edge. "Why did mentioning your mother make you fly off the handle?"

I straightened and plunked one finger on the contract she'd laid there for me, spinning my finger to twirl the page. "I don't have a good relationship with my mother. It's very complicated, and I'd rather not talk about it."

"Okay." She rested her hip on the desk and bent her knee. "On to the contract."

"Yes." I spun the paper so it faced me the right way, grabbed my pen, and prepared to sign at the bottom of the page.

Keely slanted toward me to stay my hand with her own. "Don't you want to read it first? Negotiate the details?"

"You drafted this contract, yes?"

"I did."

The warmth of her hand lingering on mine was distracting, but I managed to speak in a measured voice. "You are a clever and honest person. I trust you."

"You don't know me."

"I trust my instincts." Shaking off her hand, I moved my pen closer to the paper.

Keely stopped me again with her soft hand on mine. "I'm not comfortable with you signing the contract without even reading it."

"Doesn't bother me."

"Read it, Evan, please. Humor me."

I set down the pen, leaned back, and folded my hands over my belly.

Keely planted her hand on the desk near the paper and leaned into it. She tapped her fingers. "I flew all the way to Scotland so we could negotiate this distribution deal. You commanded it. Why make me come all this way if you're going to sign the contract without so much as glancing at it?"

"You're implying I deceived you, but I didn't know the woman I had a meeting with this morning would be you." I rocked my chair back, never looking away from her piercing green eyes. "If I had known, I would've met you at the airport. But you wouldn't let me send a car for you, so I doubt you would've agreed to me picking you up."

"Send a car?" She gave me that chastising look again, the one that made my balls tighten. "You wanted to send a limousine and set me up at a five-star hotel."

"I treat all my clients and potential business partners the same way. Again, I did not know you were the woman in question." I couldn't help admiring her cleavage, the way her blouse stretched tight over her breasts when she leaned in. "You didn't know who I was either. Why wouldn't you let me treat you like a VIP?"

"Because I'm not a VIP, I'm the assistant manager of an electronics store. One store. We don't have a chain. The VIP treatment would be over-kill." She straightened and swiped her hands over her skirt, avoiding my gaze. "Besides, I planned on taking a tour of the Highlands after this meeting today. I needed my own car for that."

This trip was a holiday for her? I sprang forward, hit with a brilliant idea. "How long are you staying?"

"I leave Saturday." Her gaze flicked to me, and something on my face must've told her I had a scheme in mind. Her eyes narrowed, and she wagged her finger at me. "Oh no, Evan. No-no-no-no-no. I'm taking a solo vacation. In case you're in doubt about the meaning of the word solo, it refers to something done alone."

"Say no-no-no again in that schoolteacher voice. I love it."

Keely sighed, her mouth tight. "You have a schoolteacher fetish, don't you?"

"Only since you walked into my office." I rested my elbows on the desk and petted its surface with two fingers, imagining I was petting her. "I've been fantasizing about you slapping a ruler on your palm while telling me to behave."

"Keep your fantasies to yourself, Mr. MacTaggart."

Hearing her call me Mr. MacTaggart again brought my brilliant idea back to me. "I meant to give you a tour of my factory this afternoon, but we should—"

"Factory? I didn't realize you had one of those. I thought your company designed the doohickeys."

She was teasing me with that word, but she seemed genuinely unaware of the scope of my business. Despite the fact she'd interrupted me, preventing me from sharing my brilliant idea, I explained anyway. "I have five factories in the UK. Two in Scotland, two in England, and another in Cornwall."

"Most companies as large as yours outsource to China or India or at least Eastern Europe."

"If and when we need to expand production, I'll open more factories here. Outsourcing does not appeal to me. I want to create jobs where I live. Besides, I can't keep a close eye on production standards if the factories are a world away."

She looked me up and down, seeming satisfied with what she found. "That's an admirable attitude. A rare one, in my experience, when it comes to big business."

"You might've noticed I'm not like most businessmen."

"No, you are definitely one of a kind."

I liked hearing her say that.

Keely slid off the desk, strolled around it to my chair, and perched on the desk's edge again. "What do I have to do to get you to read and sign the contract?"

This woman was dead brilliant, and she didn't even realize it. She'd given me the perfect opening to share my idea.

I settled back in my chair, propping one ankle on the other knee. "Spend your holiday with me."

She closed the fingers of both hands over the beveled edge of the desk. "I've told you more than once I am not interested in dating or relationships."

"Yes, I heard you every time. I'd meant to show you the Inverness factory this afternoon, but let's delay that until tomorrow. I want to show you my favorite parts of the city." I let my gaze wander up and down her body, tracing every voluptuous curve. "If you're afraid ye cannae keep from ravishing me, I willnae hold it against ye."

"Don't worry about me. My willpower is at full throttle." She squinted at me. "That sounds an awful lot like a date. There will be none of that, Mr. MacTaggart."

I grinned. "I love it when you're disciplining me in that voice."

"Forget your fetish for one minute and try to focus on what I said." She lifted a finger, most likely to wag it at me again, but crimped her mouth as if she'd realized I would like that. She withdrew her finger. "No dating."

"I understand, Keely. My brain works very well." My cock tended to override my brain in her presence, but I decided to keep that fact to myself. "Think of it as sightseeing, and I'm your tour guide."

"Sure, every tourist gets the CEO of an international corporation as their guide."

"Call it a professional courtesy."

"There you go again with professional courtesy." Her lips tightened. "I appreciate the offer, but I can't accept it. Not when you refuse to behave."

"You mean because you can't put the hems on me."

"Are you speaking English? It's not like any version of it I've heard."

"I gather you've never been to Scotland before."

"This is my first trip to the UK."

"What I said," I explained, "means you can't control me. I refuse to follow your orders, and that clearly fashes you."

She made a frustrated noise. "You explain one phrase and throw another at me."

"Fash means bother."

"Maybe it does bother me." She shifted her attention to the windows, her expression faintly pinched. "I've been told I'm bossy and that it's not an attractive quality."

"Who said that?"

"My—" She met my gaze again, rubbing her arms, and I swore I noticed a hint of vulnerability in her eyes. "My two ex-husbands and the man I lived with between husbands, not to mention nearly every man I've ever dated. Some of them tolerated my bossiness, but none of them liked it."

Her frank confession stopped me. I searched her eyes, suddenly feeling like I understood why she kept insisting we should not date. All I'd wanted since the moment she'd stepped foot in my office was to wine and dine her. Well, that and shag her mindless. Mostly, I wanted to get under that soft, creamy skin of hers and get to know the real Keely O'Shea.

A frank confession of my own seemed in order.

"I told you I've never been married," I said. "Haven't dated much either. Women confuse me. Before I became wealthy, most girls wanted nothing to do with me because I didn't speak unless I had something worth saying. I wasn't shy, though other people thought so. I didn't see the point of blethering. Still don't. Once my company took off, women only wanted me for the thrill of fucking a billionaire. I gave up on dating."

"I assumed you were a Casanova."

"You want to think the worst of me, don't you? I've had sexual partners, even after I stopped dating. But I've been celibate since Paris."

"Celibate? I don't think the worst, but you could have any woman you want. Why give up on sex?"

"Because I don't want just any woman." I touched my fingertips to her thigh, gliding them along the hem of her skirt. "I want you."

She gripped the desk with enough strength to make the sinews on the back of her hand visible.

"Ever since Paris," I told her, "I've wanted no one else."

"That's...flattering, I suppose. But it doesn't change my mind about anything. No dating."

"Have it your way." I tickled the back of her knee, making her squirm. "This time."

"I'm sure my schoolteacher charm will get on your nerves eventually."

"You are bossy, but only because you know what you want and you aren't afraid to ask for it." I slid my fingers under the hem of her skirt to caress her inner thigh. "I like that."

Her lips ticked upward. "That's because you are a lunatic."

"I'm certainly insane with lust for you." I moved my fingers higher, earning a wee gasp from her. "I'm beginning to think your problem is that you choose the wrong sort of men. Weak men will let you boss them around, but they'll start to resent you for it after a while. They haven't got the *bagais* to handle a woman like you."

"*Bagais?*"

I tickled her thigh, making her gasp again. "Balls, lass. The men you've been with obviously didn't have the balls to handle you."

She huffed. "I do not need a man to handle me."

"No, you need the right man. The sort who knows what you need." I spread my hand over her inner thigh, pushing upward until my longest finger grazed her mound and the silky panties that covered it. The fabric felt like lace. "I know what you need."

She frowned at me, but the expression lacked vigor, which might've had something to do with my finger teasing her flesh. "You are the most arrogant—"

I pulled my hand away. "Lift your skirt, Miss O'Shea."

"Excuse me?"

"I said lift your skirt. Let me see those lace panties."

She locked her arms under her breasts, the action pushing them up, and slanted toward me. "No."

I chuckled.

Her brows knit together over her nose, carving out that sweet little dimple I'd seen before. She seemed thoroughly confused by the shift in our discussion.

This was the most fun I'd had in years.

"What's your game?" she asked. "I'm not into that BDSM stuff."

"Neither am I, but you need this. You need a man who stands up to you, challenges you, understands what you need and gives it but doesn't give in to you at every turn." I steepled my fingers. "Lift your skirt, Keely. I won't say it again. Hike it up or I'll do it for you."

She squinted at me again, the way she had earlier. "I don't take orders."

"You want to do this as much as I want you to do it." I skimmed my fingers over her knee, up to her inner thigh, and curled my hand around it. "So go on and do it."

Chapter Five

Keely

I couldn't tear my gaze away from his, spellbound by his sudden turn into domineering territory. Spellbound and shocked. All day, he'd been flirtatious. This was something else. Maybe I shouldn't have been surprised since he had dragged me into an alley on that infamous night in Paris. Either he had multiple personalities, or our unexpected reunion had stunned him as much as it had me.

First, he offered to be my tour guide. Now, he ordered me to hike up my skirt.

Heat had rushed through me when he spoke those words. *Lift your skirt.* My body betrayed me at every turn, softening and warming, tingling and shivering, awakening to every touch of his fingers. Even a glance made my sex ache with an emptiness only he could fill. And when he smiled the way he had a moment ago, right before issuing his directive, a hot slickness had drenched my panties. A mature woman over forty should not respond this way. A twice-divorced woman really shouldn't. I was done with dating and romance.

But maybe I could have sex with him.

A week with Evan MacTaggart, getting naked and having spectacular orgasms, sounded like exactly the kind of vacation I needed. Either that or a recipe for disaster.

"Last chance," Evan said, "before I push up your skirt and rip those panties off."

My clitoris throbbed. I wanted him to do that. Wanted it badly. He'd left me with three choices—obey his command, walk out the door, or let him shred my panties.

I slid off the desk and hiked up my skirt.

"The panties too," he said, his voice deeper and huskier.

Excitement shivered through me, raising the hairs on my arms and instigating a new rush of cream in my sex.

I pushed my panties over my hips and let them fall to my ankles, then kicked them off but kept my shoes on.

He plucked my panties off the floor, lifted them to his face, and inhaled deeply. His eyes drifted half shut. A satisfied smile curved his lips.

"*Bod an Donais,*" he half growled. "Ye smell so good."

Wetter. Hotter. Achier. Everything inside me craved his touch, his mouth, his body.

"What does that mean?" I asked, flailing for anything I could use to prolong this heart-pounding anticipation. "The thing you said first."

"*Bod an Donais* means the devil's penis. It's a curse, like shit or damn."

"I see."

"No more talking." He set my panties on the desk near his computer, took off his glasses, and rose up from his chair. "It's time to show you why I'm a billionaire."

"Because you're smart and ruthlessly determined to always get your way."

"That obvious, is it?" He grasped my hips, massaging the hollows with his thumbs until I sucked in a sharp breath. A slow, naughty smile slid across his lips as he glided his hands down to my thighs. "On the desk again, like before."

I hopped up to rest the edge of my buttocks on the desk, the heels of my shoes elevated off the floor.

He crouched between my legs, easing my thighs apart with his hands.

Oh shit. In a flash, I understood his intention.

"Here in your office?" I blurted out, instantly wishing I hadn't.

"Aye," he said in that husky voice. "Here. Now. Got to feast on ye or I'll go mad."

"What if someone walks in?"

"No one enters my office without an explicit invitation."

While he peppered kisses along my inner thigh, I struggled to hold on to my sanity. Never in my entire life had I done something like this. Let a man pleasure me in his office? A billionaire, no less. A man used to getting what he wanted. A man who wanted me, and I'd relinquished myself to him without a second's hesitation.

And God, I'd loved giving in to him.

"Someone might hear," I whispered.

With his mouth glued to my thigh, he peeked up at me through his thick lashes. His lips vibrated against my skin when he spoke. "Be quiet, then. That's a command."

My clit pulsated. I was on the verge of orgasm, and he hadn't even touched the most sensitive parts of me.

He raised his head. "Should I stop?"

"Don't you dare." I spread my legs wider. "Head between my thighs. Now."

The arrogant man laughed loud enough anybody outside the office door could've heard it.

He lunged his head between my thighs and fastened his mouth around my clit.

And I stopped breathing.

Suckling my taut bud, he whisked his tongue around and around it while his fingers clutched my hips, pulling me closer to his mouth. He worked my flesh like an expert, like a man who knew how to give a woman incredible pleasure and who loved doing it. I gripped the desk and let my head fall back. He raked his tongue down my cleft and licked his way up one side and back down the other, all the while massaging my ass with his strong fingers. I moaned when he dived his tongue inside my entrance, and I had to clamp my lips between my teeth to stifle a louder moan when he dragged his mouth back up to my nub and began to lap at it.

I pried one hand away from the desk and thrust it into his hair.

Lapping became rasping. Rough, hungry strokes of his tongue that had me choking back a gasp. He tore one hand away from my hip to plunge his finger inside me.

"Evan," I gasped, desperately fighting not to make a sound. "Yes, Evan, yes."

A second finger thrust inside me while he suckled my nub like a man starved for the taste of me. My body bowed forward, every muscle going rigid, and I grasped his head with both hands. Soft, whimpering cries bubbled out of me.

I came so hard my leg twitched and kicked him in the side.

The intercom buzzed.

Evan hissed a curse under his breath with his head still between my legs. He flopped into his chair and punched the intercom button. "What is it, Tamsen?"

He sounded grumpy, and I couldn't blame him. Even the folds of his kilt couldn't conceal the bulge of his massive erection. He must've been wearing briefs since it didn't tent his kilt.

Damn, I burned to lift his skirt, tear off those briefs, and mount him.

Instead, I reached for my panties.

Evan snatched them away.

"Bad news, I'm afraid," Tamsen said through the speaker. "Someone at the factory ordered the wrong parts for the AS190, and the London supplier can't send the proper ones until Thursday."

"What?" Evan leaped up from his chair. "Those goddamn eejits. Find out who ordered the wrong components and let me know before I leave. I'll be away in—" He checked his watch. "Ten minutes."

Evan punched the button to cut off the intercom feed and shoved his glasses on again.

"Sounds like an emergency," I said. "We can discuss the contract tomorrow."

"No." He crumpled my panties in his hand. "You will come with me to the factory. After I sort this mess, you'll have your tour. Tomorrow, we'll start the sightseeing."

"Evan, no."

"It's settled, Keely." He sniffed my panties, his lips sliding into a sensual smile. "I'm not leaving you alone to change your mind about the sightseeing."

"Never agreed to that in the first place."

"Yes you did." He fondled my panties some more. "Your agreement was implied when you let me feast on you."

Straightening out his misconceptions could wait until later since it seemed like he was urgently needed at the factory.

"What's an AS190?" I asked.

"A miniaturized listening device that looks like a stud earring."

"Sounds handy." I held out my palm. "May I please have my underwear back?"

He rubbed my panties on his cheek. "Maybe I'll hold on to them."

"Sure, if you want me to think you're a lunatic and a pervert."

"I can live with that. But if you agree to go sightseeing with me, I'll let you have your underwear."

"Fine, you can be my tour guide."

Taking one last whiff of my panties, he tossed them to me.

I pulled them on and tugged my skirt down. "Why do you have to go to the factory? If they don't have the right parts, you can't make the components magically appear."

"You'd be surprised what I can do." He snared my hand. "We're away."

"No, we're both right here. We can't be away from where we're standing."

"It means we're off, we're leaving, we're—"

"Yeah, I get it."

I barely managed to grab my purse and binder as he hauled me out of the office.

Chapter Six

Evan

The evening breeze wafted over the balcony of my apartment, warm but cooling as the sun dipped lower and lower toward the horizon. I leaned my hip against the railing and gazed out at the view of the River Ness with the waning sunlight dancing on its surface. If I'd mentioned to Keely that I lived along the River Ness, she probably would've asked me about Loch Ness and the supposed monster. Most Americans did. Then again, Keely O'Shea was not an average American or an average woman.

I lifted my whisky glass to my lips, sipping the single malt, letting it slide down my throat. Whisky had never appealed to me until my cousin Rory introduced me to Ben Nevis. Over the past year, I'd made an effort to be friendlier with my cousins. Unfortunately, they all lived in and around Ballachulish. Just thinking about the village made my hand tighten around my glass and my jaw tense.

Did I have any right to bring Keely into the mess I'd made of my life? Maybe I didn't have the right, maybe I shouldn't pursue her, but I couldn't stop myself. She had haunted my dreams, day and night, for ten months. Now that I'd spent time with her, I wanted her even more—a relationship with her, not just sex. Spending more time with her, getting to know her, might prove to me we had no future together. I wouldn't know unless I tried.

What did I know about relationships?

My phone chimed, indicating a new text. I dug the phone out of my pants pocket and swiped the screen to activate it.

The text consisted of three words: *We need you.*

It came from a blocked number, but I knew who had sent it. With my thumbs, I typed a response: *No.*

Not your choice. We have a job for you.

Find someone else.

Several seconds ticked by before the response came: *Consider the alternative.*

An image appeared below the message, a photograph of a bonnie woman in her forties with gray hair and blue eyes.

Cold swept through me. My hand tightened around the phone. The picture was of my mother. She stood outside her cottage near Ballachulish, in front of a window box filled with pink blossoms. My mother hadn't planted pink flowers in years, as far as I knew. But then, I'd barely spoken to her over the past eighteen months.

I texted Duncan Hendry. *How is the weather?*

A minute ticked by, then another, before his reply appeared. *Clear as a bell.*

No dark clouds?

All's well. Relax.

I thanked him and ended the conversation. The weather code had been Duncan's idea to make sure no one else would understand us, in case anyone bothered to hack my phone. "Clear as a bell" meant everything was fine at my mother's house. The bodyguards she didn't know she had reported no problems.

Someone took a picture, I typed.

Four seconds elapsed.

My phone rang.

I answered, but before I could say anything, Duncan's gruff voice said, "What picture?"

"Someone texted it to me. It's of my mother outside her house."

"The code, Evan, remember to use the code."

"Forget the bloody code. How did no one see a stranger taking a picture?"

"Send it to me. I'll have a look. Could be they used a telephoto lens to take it from a distance, outside our perimeter. If you'd let us tell your mother we're here…"

"No."

"I'll examine the picture and talk to my team."

"Thank you."

I hung up and texted him the photograph of my mother, then dialed her number.

"*Gràidh*," she said instead of hello, picking up the call on the second ring. My number was programmed into her phone, so she would've seen my name when it rang. "What a lovely surprise to hear from you."

How could she sound pleased to hear from me? After the things I'd said to her the last time we saw each other. She'd even called me darling in Gaelic.

I kept my tone measured as I said, "How are you?"

"Fine. You'd know that if you called me more than once every three months." She hesitated. "I heard you've been out to see your cousins quite a bit."

Her voice conveyed no anger, only a hint of dismay. She adored her nieces and nephews, but we both knew I'd visited them instead of visiting her. *You're a bastard, Mr. MacTaggart. No wonder Keely doesn't want you.*

I cleared my throat. "Have you planted flowers in the window box?"

"Aye, ye know I do that every year."

"What color?"

"Pink."

"Did you plant pink flowers last year?" I asked, praying she would say yes.

"No, dearie. They were purple last summer."

My chest constricted, the pressure like a heavy foot pressing down on me. I gripped the balcony railing. Pink flowers. The picture was recent.

She hesitated again as if uncertain of whether to speak her mind. When she did speak, her tone was cautious. "Are ye all right, Evan?"

"Yes, I'm fine. I have to go."

"But I've hardly spoken to you. It's been months since you called and longer since I've seen you. My son bought Loch Fairbairn, but he won't come home."

"I didn't buy Loch Fairbairn. I own property in the village."

"Aye, it was kind of you to step in after Rhys Kendrick was arrested and all his tenants were about to lose everything. If you hadn't bought those businesses, the village might have died." She sniffled, and a slight quiver infected her voice. "You're good to everyone but your own mother."

I scratched my neck, afflicted with a sudden itch that wouldn't let up. "You know why I haven't been back to Ballachulish. Until you answer the question I asked last time I visited, we have nothing to say to each other."

"Answering willnae help, Evan. And you've known all your life I donnae want to talk about your father. The truth won't make you feel better."

"I'm not a child anymore. I deserve to know—about my father and about why you leave the country every summer."

She fell silent for several seconds. "Leave it alone, Evan, I'm begging you."

After all these years, she still wouldn't trust me to deal with the truth. Until she did, I couldn't deal with her. "I'm sorry, but I can't talk right now. Take care."

"Evan, please, tell me how you are."

"I told you I'm fine. Busy but fine. Goodbye."

I disconnected the call and examined my hand, turning it side to side. It was shaking. Not much, but enough. I fisted my hand.

A text appeared on my phone's screen: *You know the stakes.*

Yes, I typed, *I am aware.*

Details sent. Confirm receipt.

A new message appeared, this one with a file attached. I saved the file and typed my confirmation. *Details received.*

You have until three p.m. tomorrow.

I understand.

Maybe no one else would understand why I let anonymous strangers I'd never met or spoken to control me. I had no choice. Their threats were not empty. I knew this from hard experience, from having ignored them the first time they contacted me. After eight months of not hearing from them, I'd hoped they had given up.

Of course I wasn't that lucky. After the things I'd done, I hadn't earned any luck.

How did these blighters know all my weaknesses?

I stuffed the phone in my pocket and glared out at the river. The sun had nearly set, and darkness crept in behind it to consume the sky. Lights burned in the houses that hugged the riverbank. Maybe my enemies hid inside one of those structures. Maybe they worked for my company.

Maybe I could drive myself mad wondering.

No amount of wattage could chase away the darkness in my life. The brightest light I'd ever seen didn't illuminate a house or twinkle in the sky. It burned inside Keely O'Shea.

I raced through the apartment, nabbing my keys off the kitchen island, and slammed the front door behind me. Pursuing Keely might've been a mistake, a selfish and reckless act, but I didn't care. I couldn't care. I needed her light to dispel the shadows. If she believed in me, maybe I could become the kind of man she deserved. First, I needed to redeem myself in her eyes.

Might as well have decided to climb Mount Everest while blindfolded and handcuffed.

Chapter Seven

Keely

Lying on the bed in my hotel room, I counted the acoustic balls on the ceiling and tried to make sense of what I'd experienced today. Evan Mac-Taggart was an enigma, for sure. He'd acted giddy and almost nutty when we first met, but later, he'd been the personable employer who introduced me to his employees. Tamsen Spurling treated Evan like a surrogate son, though she was younger than I was. At lunch, Evan had flirted. After lunch, he'd coaxed me into spreading my legs for him right there on his desk.

What on earth had I been thinking? He short-circuited all my good-sense wires. Once he'd started issuing directives, I'd given in without hesitation. No man had ever ordered me around. My exes had never cared enough to express an opinion, much less take charge. Did I like being bossed around by a sexy billionaire? No, it wasn't his money or his company that made me dissolve for him. He had…something. I couldn't define it. Didn't understand it.

But I wanted him to do it again.

Evan was impossible to deny and difficult to pin down. His factory was the cleanest, most efficient operation I'd ever seen. His employees seemed genuinely happy in their jobs, and they smiled when he walked into the factory just like the people who worked at his headquarters had done when he approached them. Everyone seemed to like the boss.

He hadn't been kidding or exaggerating when he'd told me I would be surprised at what he could do. Got the wrong components? Never mind that, Mr. MacTaggart will manufacture them himself. I'd watched in awe as he took apart other devices to scavenge parts and recreate the components needed to finish the AS190. Clients and partner companies had already placed orders for the new model, and Evan's company had promised to deliver them this week. They had to be completed and shipped by tomorrow.

At most of the jobs I'd had, prior to working for Vic Bazzoli, the bosses would've thrown a fit if an error like this had occurred. Evan stayed calm and pleasant, assuring his employees one misstep did not mean someone would get fired. When I'd asked why he had seemed angry when he first heard about the mistake, he'd said, "Because I wanted us to have a poke, not go to the factory."

Yes, he'd needed to explain that a poke meant sex.

The way his fingers moved, manipulating tiny electronic parts, it was impressive to say the least. I'd never imagined the billionaire CEO of any company would get hands-on like that to solve a production issue. Evan was the most unusual man I'd ever met.

Once he'd finished his work, I'd told him, "That was amazing, how you jury-rigged those components and saved the day."

His mouth tightened. "The components are not jury-rigged. They're manufactured to the same high standards as any other components we use in production."

"I didn't mean it as an insult. You overlooked the part where I said I'm impressed. There's nothing sexier than a man who can build things with his hands, whether those things are made of wood or wires and circuits."

His mood had improved after that compliment, and for the rest of the afternoon, he'd shown me the inner workings of the first factory his company had ever built. It now had four siblings. Evan had slyly offered to show me all of those sites too, which would've required me to stick around for two weeks instead of one. Oh, he was a genius at negotiation. His offer intrigued me, because he intrigued me, but I declined. If I spent too much time with Evan, I might begin to want more than sex. No more dating, no more relationships.

If I needed to repeat that to myself, I might have a problem.

A knock at the door surprised me out of my reverie.

I sat up, acutely aware I was dressed in a white terrycloth robe and nothing else. My hair, still wet from my shower, had dampened the pillow and the shoulders of the robe. Who would be calling on me at ten o'clock?

The visitor knocked again, and a familiar voice said, "Keely?"

Evan.

Jumping off the bed, I cinched my robe's belt tighter and padded to the door. I swung it open, not at all surprised to see him but stunned by his casual demeanor. He wore cargo pants and a blue polo shirt that complemented his eyes. A pair of well-worn leather hiking boots covered his feet. His short hair managed to be mussed like he'd run his fingers through it too many times.

He leaned against the doorjamb. Gone was his air of confidence and determination. Tonight, he seemed like an average guy who'd knocked on the door of a woman who refused to date him.

He looked sexy as hell.

"Did I wake you?" he asked.

"No, I was up."

His gaze traveled down my body and back up to my face. "You're wet."

That was all it took to make his statement true. My hair was wet, but other parts of me had gone slick in ways that had nothing to do with cleanliness. "I got out of the shower a few minutes ago."

"Fresh and clean. I bet you smell good too." He pushed away from the jamb. "May I come in?"

"It's late, Evan."

"Are you sleepy?"

Not in the slightest, especially since I'd opened the door and seen him. My body awakened in his presence, and the rest of me followed suit.

He stuffed his hands in his pants pockets. "You don't trust me because of Paris. I understand that, but I'd like a chance to make it up to you."

"Make it up to me?"

"Please, Keely, let me come inside and I'll explain."

Let him into my hotel room? Ten feet from a bed? That sounded like a very bad idea.

Oh for heaven's sake, we were both adults. I could control my lust for the five minutes it might take him to apologize again or say whatever it was he intended to tell me.

Sure, like I'd controlled my lust in his office this afternoon.

"You can slam the door in my face," he said, "but I'll wait out here until you let me in. I'm persistent, in case you hadn't noticed."

"I've noticed." What the hell, I told myself. The worst that might happen was we had sex. Serena kept insisting I needed to get laid. So, I swung the door wide and spread an arm in invitation. "Come on in."

Evan walked past me, halfway to the bed, and stopped.

Shutting the door, I approached him. "Well? What is it you wanted to say?"

"I'm sorry, but I've told you that already." He ran a hand over his cheek. "I want to show you I'm not a bastard. What I did last year, that was an aberration. Let me prove it to you."

"Not sure how you can do that tonight. It'll take time."

"Whatever it takes, I'll do."

"Answering a few questions might be a good start." I clutched the collar of my robe with one hand. "Why did you run away? Why did you skip out on the conference? And why weren't you wearing your glasses that night?"

"You're referring to Paris. I took my glasses off when I saw you but before you saw me. It was a vain impulse to hide the fact I'm not perfect." He ducked his head, kicking at the carpeting with the toe of one boot. "As for the rest, I'd never done anything like that before. Meant to take you to my hotel, but I couldn't wait that long, I had to have you. Once it was over, I realized what I'd done and I…needed to get away so I could think and figure out why I'd done it. Still don't know the answer. As for the conference, I couldn't think about giving a speech when all I wanted was to find you. Couldn't do it, though. Without knowing your name or even where you were staying, I had nowhere to start."

What might've happened if he had found me? He'd told me women confused him, and he seemed genuinely baffled by his own behavior too—in Paris and in his office this morning. From what I'd seen today, he was the most self-contained person I'd ever met. I could believe he honestly didn't know why he'd done the things he'd done with me.

He moved closer, and his voice turned sultry, soft, and rough. "I made you a promise in Paris. Tonight, I mean to keep it."

"What are you talking about?"

"I promised I'd make love to you all night."

Excitement sizzled through me at the mere thought of it. Evan. In bed. Naked and gorgeous, determined to spend all night proving himself to me with steamy sex.

No, I couldn't.

Maybe if he understood the parameters, understood this did not mean we were dating or otherwise involved in a romantic way…

He took my face in his hands and pressed his lips to mine.

My whole body slackened. I parted my lips, all but begging him for more. His tongue slipped inside, gently stroking and exploring, inciting me to plow deep into his mouth.

Evan broke the kiss. "Should I leave? If I stay, I will be making love to you all night."

Tell him it's just sex. Tell him quick.

My vocal cords had a mind of their own. "Stay."

He untied the belt of my robe, letting it fall away, and slid his hands inside the terrycloth to push the robe off my shoulders. It flumped to the floor. He drank in the sight of my naked body, muttering words I didn't understand, possibly another Gaelic oath.

"You are perfect," he said. "Breathtakingly beautiful."

Even if I'd been able to speak, I had no clue what I would've said in response. My body knew what to do. It softened and warmed even more, angling forward to get closer to him.

He picked me up and carried me to the bed, laying me down on it. "I always keep my promises, even if it takes me ten months."

My voice had abandoned me. I lay there watching him undress, my rapt attention focused on his every movement as he whipped his shirt off over his head, kicked off his shoes, and shed his pants. He removed his glasses, setting them on the bedside table.

"No underwear?" I asked while he removed his socks.

"Only wear them when I'm at work. On my own time, I prefer to go without."

"So, if I see you wearing a kilt after hours, you'll be buck naked underneath it."

"Aye."

I had no chance to absorb that fact. The sight of his naked body mesmerized me. Evan was the most beautiful man I had ever laid eyes on, from his broad shoulders and thick biceps to his muscular chest and defined six-pack abs. I roved my gaze down his belly to his hips and those well-developed thighs, and further to his strong calves and large feet. Sandy hair dusted his legs, and on his chest, the hairs tapered down to a tantalizing trail that led straight to his dick.

My mouth watered. His cock was thick and long, the skin sleek—and velvety smooth, I imagined, though I'd find out soon enough. His rigid length curved up toward his belly, the tip already rosy. I swallowed, my throat suddenly tight and dry. He'd said he wanted to make love to me all night. Make love. It implied things I didn't want to think about, things neither of us could feel yet, but things that made my tummy flutter and trickled unease through me.

Evan swung his leg over my body to straddle me on all fours.

"Listen to me," I said, "this is not—"

He covered my mouth with his own, holding his lips against mine for several seconds. When he peeled them away, he did it little by little. "Shhh, lass. Let me show you who I really am."

I'd known him for one day, and I would leave at the end of the week. He didn't need to show me anything or prove anything to me. Maybe I should've told him to leave, but our encounter in his office this afternoon had left me wanting more.

More sex. That was all.

I reached down to close one hand around his shaft, sliding it up and down. Oh yes, velvety smooth.

Evan grasped my hand and pried it away from his flesh. "Not yet. I'm in charge tonight."

A shiver whispered through me, warm and sensual, erasing all my doubts. I wanted this. I wanted him. I wanted to relinquish control to the beautiful, naked man hovering over me.

"Do it," I said. "Command me."

Chapter Eight

Evan

I kissed her again, softly, tenderly, painting lighter kisses on her cheek and jaw as I worked my way down to her slender throat and lower to her chest. Her skin tasted clean and delectable, fresh from her shower, but she smelled of desire—musky, sweet, more tempting than any woman had a right to be. I wanted to bury my face between her thighs and gorge myself on her until she came apart beneath me, her body dissolving into the sheets and her cries echoing off the walls. She was luscious in every way, a decadent feast I hadn't gotten enough of in my office this afternoon. I needed more of her, all of her, with a lust so all-consuming I couldn't fight it even if I'd wanted to try.

Make love to her, that's what I'd promised to do. What the bloody hell did I know about making love to a woman? I fucked them. They knew not to expect more. I didn't stay the night or contemplate the curves of their bodies or get drunk on the scent of them. But for the second time, I'd told her I wanted to stay with her all night.

This woman deserved more than I knew how to give. From what she'd said about her exes, she needed to be with a man who would treat her like a treasure instead of an albatross around his neck. I would've gladly let her wrap those legs around my neck, though, while I coaxed her into the first of several climaxes. She would come for me until I let her stop, and I would do that only when she'd surrendered everything to me, spent and satisfied in every way.

Her skin warmed my lips as I traced a path down between her breasts. Her nipples had already puckered and swollen into taut peaks I hungered to devour. I grazed my mouth over her skin, following the swell of her breast until I found the tip. I flicked my tongue out to tease the areola, dancing it in leisurely circles around her nipple without ever brushing it, relishing the way her breaths quickened and her back arched like her body was begging for me to swallow her nipple.

"Mmmm," I hummed against her skin, my mouth hovering over the dusky tip.

She wriggled. "Suck on it, please."

I chuckled, my breaths reflecting off her skin. "At least you say please when you're telling me what to do."

"I'm bossy, you know that. This shouldn't be a surprise."

"Not surprised." I nipped her skin. "Enchanted. But you agreed to let me control this, control you."

"Shut up and make me come."

I slapped her hip. "Behave, Keely."

"You're stealing my line."

She squirmed, and her hips lifted just enough to give me a stronger whiff of her arousal. I dragged in a deep breath, savoring the scent of her, knowing she would taste even sweeter. My cock rubbed against her belly when she wriggled again. The feel of her soft, heated skin on mine was almost too much to take, and I couldn't wait any longer.

"Donnae worry," I murmured. "I'll give you what you need. In my own time."

Her impatience was my opportunity. I caught her nipple between my teeth and tugged, then raked my tongue over the peak.

She gasped.

I sealed my mouth around her nipple, suckling it gently until her back bowed up into me again and she shut her eyes, her lips parted. The pleasure on her face made me harder—impossibly, painfully hard—but I kept suckling and licking until I knew she was on the edge. She fisted her hands in the sheets, her head thrown back and her neck arched.

A long, deep moan resonated through her.

I surged up to plant an open-mouth kiss on her throat, feeling her pulse throbbing beneath her skin. I dragged my lips lower and lower until my face was between her breasts, lower still to skim my lips over her navel and keep traveling down and down until the hairs of her mound tickled my chin. She writhed beneath me. I feathered kisses over her skin, tracing a line over her hip even while my hands wandered down her thighs to slip between them and I eased her legs apart.

"Yer skin's so soft," I murmured against her flesh. "And yer scent makes me starved for the taste of ye."

She panted softly like she couldn't take in a whole breath. I tasted and caressed every inch of her skin that I could reach, determined to give her all the pleasure I'd denied her in Paris. I crawled backward along her body and dipped my head between her thighs.

"Oh God," she groaned. "Screw me already or get the hell out of here."

"Donnae worry. When I command ye to come, ye will."

"You're so full of it. Nobody orgasms on command."

"Ah, but you will." I nuzzled the curly strands on her mound.

She thrust her fingers into my hair. "Then say it. Please."

I sealed my mouth around her stiff nub, lapping and nipping even while I hooked my hands under her knees and urged her to bend them.

She thrashed, gripping the pillow, her teeth clenched from the urgency to find release.

I sat back on my heels, kneeling between her legs.

She scowled at me. "You stopped."

"Very observant of you." I coasted my hands up her calves and over her knees, smiling when she huffed and twisted her leg to kick me in the erse. "Impatient?"

"Yes. Get back to it."

"No more saying please, eh?" I let my hands roam over her thighs, exploring her silken skin while she kept glaring at me. "You are the most demanding woman in the bedroom. I like it, but you'll need to learn a little patience."

She groaned in frustration. "Screw me and get it over with."

My hands went still. Did she expect me to do this like I had in Paris? Quick and dirty, then gone? No, not this time.

I patted her hip. "I'll let you rest and catch your breath for a minute."

"Don't you dare."

I bent to kiss her belly. "Relax, *mo leannan*. You're going to come for me so hard ye willnae be able to move or speak for at least five minutes after."

"Oh please. Nobody's that good in bed."

"Soon enough, you'll learn never to doubt what I say."

I leaned over the side of the bed to find my pants and get what I wanted. Straightening, I held up the condom packet between two fingers. "Almost ready."

She watched with slitted eyes, her cheeks pink and her lips pinched, while I covered myself with the condom. Keely O'Shea was the only woman I'd ever met who could look aroused and annoyed at the same time.

I cupped her with one hand, slipping my fingers between her folds, and held my hand there until she squirmed. Her tongue swept out to moisten her lips, and her breasts rose and fell with every breath. I pushed two fingers into her core, coaxing a moan out of her. She was wetter and hotter than this afternoon when I'd tasted her, so wet the scent of it drugged me. I closed my eyes to inhale the aroma of her.

She jerked her hips up, forcing my fingers deeper inside her body. "Do something."

"Not yet."

I pulled my hand away and licked my fingers one by one, slowly, savoring the flavor of her desire. Spread out beneath me, she was the most beautiful thing I'd ever seen, from her full breasts to her flat stomach to her bonnie little toes that kept wriggling. Her lips had darkened to a deep shade of rose, and the haze of lust shimmered in her eyes. How could I have ever run away from this woman?

"Please," she moaned.

"Well, since you asked politely..."

I hoisted her knees onto my shoulders and thrust into her.

She clenched the pillow, her mouth falling open.

The soft, slick heat of her felt so good around me I had to force myself to take deep, slow breaths. No repeats of Paris. This would last longer than a minute, as long as I could stand it before the feel of her pushed me over the edge. I braced my hands at either side of her body and pumped in and out, my pace deliberate, determined to show her I'd keep my promise.

She tried to lift her hips into my thrusts, but she couldn't get leverage with her knees over my shoulders. A frustrated noise burst out of her.

I rolled my hips into her, plunging deep with each push into her exquisite body and withdrawing almost completely with each backward motion. Pulling out of her was torture, but every time I sank deep into her hot sheath my eyes almost rolled back into my head. I'd never wanted a woman like this. What was she doing to me? I never lost control, never had to fight my own lust to make sure my lover got what she needed. The longer I fought to keep the pace unhurried, the more I wanted to go faster, punch harder, nail her to the mattress again and again until we both blew apart.

Keely gasped, whimpered, gasped again.

And the need to fuck her like a demon gripped me hard. *No, no, no, you goddamn eejit.*

I held still, half inside her, and took deep breaths.

"What's wrong?" she asked, her voice a husky whisper.

"Nothing," I grunted.

She grasped my upper arms. "Please."

The desperation in her voice made me want her even more. But I wouldn't let my cock command me. Only Keely was allowed to do that, when I decided to let her.

I pushed her knees off my shoulders and lowered my body until all of me rested on top of her. I was still inside her, but now we were in full contact, body to body, skin to skin. I moved my hips in a steady, controlled rhythm, all the while kissing her neck and nibbling her earlobe, running my hands up and down her body.

"Evan, I—"

Whatever she'd wanted to say dissolved into a long, throaty moan.

"Shhhh," I murmured and pushed up onto my elbows so I could see her face. I bracketed her head with my hands, combing my fingers through her hair. "You're about to come. Let it happen and trust me to take you only as far as you can handle."

She choked back a cry, her neck arching.

Her body went rigid under me.

I levered my body off hers, my arms straight, and let go. She clamped her hands around my wrists, and I bucked into her again and again, any tatters of self-control I'd had left disintegrating under the crushing power of my need for her. Her breasts bounced. The mattress bounced. The whole bed creaked and thumped and bounced. Her body clenched me hard, and with the very first spasm of her climax, I came.

Two more thrusts and I was done—but she wasn't.

I shoved a hand between our bodies to rub her clitoris until her spasms faded and she stopped thrashing. Her skin was flushed, her cheeks too. Reluctantly, I pulled out of her sweet body and got rid of the condom.

She lay there not moving, seeming dazed while she tried to catch her breath.

I lay down on the bed beside her and turned onto my side to face her.

Keely held a hand to her cheek and let out a long, gusty breath.

Rushed it again, that's what I'd done. The woman drove me out of my mind. Luckily, I had the rest of the night to fulfill my promise.

I draped an arm over her belly. "Don't know about you, but I'm exhausted. Does this place have room service? A piece would get us both ready for the next round."

"Round of what?" She eyed me sideways. "And what's a piece?"

"A snack. A sandwich, usually." I drew curving lines on her belly with my finger. "And I meant the next round of making love to you."

"This hotel does not have room service." She wriggled, frowning slightly. "You're leaving, anyway."

"No, I'm not. I promised I'd stay all night, and that's what I mean to do."

"You have to go."

"Why? I know you like me, or I wouldn't be here." I raised up on my elbow to study her face, but I couldn't decide if she was annoyed, scared, or some combination of the two. "Let me spend the night with you."

"Not necessary. You've already kept your promise. We had sex for more than thirty seconds, and you didn't run away."

"But you're ordering me to leave."

"Yes." She sat up, rubbing her arms as if she were cold. "I'm sorry, but this is how it has to be. You need to understand the parameters. We are not dating, this is not a romance. If you want to keep having sex, we can do that until I fly home Saturday morning. But this is casual, only casual, and we are not involved in any kind of relationship beyond the physical."

She stared straight ahead at the door.

Her orders didn't cow me, but for once they didn't make me want to kiss her into a frenzy either. For reasons I didn't know yet, she was terrified of getting involved with me. If I walked out the door tonight, maybe she'd use this time to reconsider her opinion of dating. If not, I'd find another way to convince her I wasn't like her ex-husbands.

I got up, grabbed her robe, and placed it around her shoulders.

She glanced up at me, startled.

Had she been so deep in thought, in worry, that she hadn't noticed me moving closer? I doubted that. It was more likely she was surprised a man would want to take care of her. Her exes sounded like erseholes.

I crouched beside the bed to look her in the eye. "I'll go, but you need to understand a few things too. I'm not giving up. Sooner or later, you will realize this is more than casual sex. Every time we're together, I will be making love to you. It's personal and intimate and, if I have a bloody clue what I'm doing, it will be a romantic relationship. I've never wanted more than sex with any woman, but with you, I want everything."

Her shoulders sagged, and she clutched the robe over her chest. "You're sweet, Evan, but I'm damaged goods. You'd be better off finding a cute young lass your own age."

Damaged? I would never describe her that way. She was vibrant, sexy, intelligent, and bossy. Still, I couldn't change her mind tonight. Only time could do that.

Time with me.

I leaned in to kiss her.

She threw a hand up between our mouths. "No more kissing. This is not a relationship, which means we do not need to kiss."

"What about foreplay? That involves kissing."

"I'm sure you can be more creative than that."

"Maybe I can, but—"

She tapped two fingers on my mouth. "No kissing."

I would not agree with her command, but I wouldn't argue at the moment. I found my clothes and shoes and pulled them on, then retrieved my glasses and headed for the door. There, I hesitated with my hand on the knob. "I'll pick you up at eight and take you to my favorite breakfast spot."

"I'll meet you there. Text me directions."

My lips flattened, I blew out a sigh. "Keely."

"Either meet me there or forget it."

I blew out another sigh and grumbled, "I'll text you the directions."

"Good."

I walked out, yanking the door shut behind me.

Chapter Nine

Evan

From the moment Keely swept into the restaurant at five past eight in the morning, I realized something important had changed between us. Last night, she'd ordered me to leave. Today, she smiled when she caught sight of me and chose to sit in the chair right next to mine instead of the one across the table from me. We talked, about nothing important, and mocked each other with friendly taunts. I had trouble focusing on our conversation. I lost my train of thought every time I looked at her body.

Today, she wore a short-sleeve white blouse that clung to every inch of her torso. The neckline dipped low enough that every time she leaned in I glimpsed the swells of her breasts. The pale-blue skirt she wore hugged her hips but hung looser around her thighs, swishing when she walked. And those shoes. *Bod an Donais*, the heels must've been four inches high, and they gave her ankles a tantalizing curve that made me want to duck under the table and lick them. She'd lost the bun and let her hair tumble in loose waves around her face and shoulders. How she could look professional but still make me crave her mystified me.

After breakfast, I'd convinced her to not only go to the office with me but to ride in my car too. A minor concession, but one I celebrated silently. On the kissing front, she refused to relent. Five times this morning I'd tried to kiss her and five times she'd thrown a hand up between our mouths to block me.

Once we were inside my office with the door shut, Keely asked, "I thought we were going sightseeing today. What's so important we have to cancel our plans?"

I decided not to point out "plans" implied more than casual sex.

"Something urgent came up," I said. Urgent and of questionable legality, but I didn't want to explain that to her today. After I'd won her, then I'd confess my sins. Selfish? Aye. But I needed her in ways I couldn't explain or understand, and so I would do anything to keep her. "I'll have Tamsen show you our latest catalogs while I take care of this other business. She can help you place your first order too."

"I can order from home. I'd rather stay here with you."

"To do what? Watch me typing on my computer?"

She dug her phone out of her purse. "I can read a book on my phone."

I started to complain but then realized this was exactly what I'd wanted. She would rather sit in my office waiting for me to finish my work than handle business of her own. Keely wanted to be with me.

Casual sex? No romantic relationship? One day soon she would realize her claims were nonsense.

"Make yourself at home," I said. "If you'd like a drink, I have water in the wet bar. It's a bit early for a hard drink."

She patted my cheek. "Good boy. This morning, you know it's too early."

"I was in shock yesterday. My behavior then was not typical."

"A fact I recognize today."

While I settled in at my desk, Keely stretched out on the window ledge. She sat with her back against the window frame, her ankles crossed, and the phone cradled on her lap. Her gaze drifted to the landscape beyond the glass. The sunlight coming through the windows cast her in a heavenly glow, giving her the aura of a celestial being reclining on a mountaintop, too beautiful and ethereal to be touched by man.

I meant to touch her. Often. And kiss her, dammit.

Her lips curved in the faintest smile. She tipped her head back until it met the window frame and closed her eyes as if soaking up the rays of sunshine. She seemed more relaxed than yesterday and younger somehow, freer, less burdened by the past.

She might dismiss whatever this was between us as nothing meaningful, but her behavior this morning testified to the truth.

I should've started working on the task assigned to me by the thugs who seemed to own my soul. Why else would I do their bidding? To protect my family, that's why. My invisible masters might have tied their strings to me, but I was not their slave, bought and paid for, to do as they dictated. I'd never seen their faces or heard their voices. For all I knew, I was dealing with one person who had underworld resources and no conscience whatsoever.

Keely sighed, her smile deepening.

My chest constricted. I should never have brought Keely into my world, but my selfish need to keep her near me had overridden my common sense. I needed her. It was insane, but since the moment I'd first laid eyes on her in Paris, I'd known she was the only woman I could ever want for more than sex. And now she claimed to want only sex with me.

Frowning, I turned to my computer and tried to concentrate on my work. I prayed this task wouldn't harm anyone. As far as I knew, nothing I'd given them had caused harm, but I couldn't know for certain. I understood what the code did. I couldn't predict how these people might use it. If anyone got hurt because of me...

I gritted my teeth and squeezed my eyes shut.

"You okay?" Keely asked.

"Aye, fine." I forced my jaw to loosen and scooted my chair to the left so she couldn't see me around the computer monitor. "Are you sure you wouldn't rather sit with Tamsen?"

"Positive."

After a few seconds of silence, I rose partway to peer over the monitor at Keely. She was engrossed in the book displayed on her phone's screen. Her tortoiseshell glasses perched on her nose.

I dropped back into my chair and set to work.

The only sounds were the faint tapping of my fingers striking the keyboard and the occasional rustling of Keely's clothes as she adjusted her position on the window ledge. For twenty-two minutes and sixteen seconds, I avoided looking at her. I wasted another minute and ten seconds carefully cleaning my glasses and another fifty seconds after that rearranging the things on my desk. Finally, I could resist no longer and let my attention wander to Keely's curvy body stretched out on the ledge. She was smiling, her eyes sparkling. Whatever book she was reading must've been humorous. I itched to ask her about it, to engage her in conversation so she would aim those lustrous green eyes at me and grace me with a smile like the one her book inspired. But I had work to do.

I got back to it.

One hour and eleven minutes later, she excused herself to make a call. She'd asked me where she might find some privacy, and I'd told her to ask Tamsen to show her the conference room down the hall. No one was using it today. While she was gone, I called Duncan Hendry for an update on the security breach at my mother's home.

Before I could ask, he answered my question. "No one got close to the house or breached the property. Because of the trees and the terrain, there are only two ways to get a clear view of that window box. One is from inside the yard, not more than twenty feet away. The other is to stand on the hill about a hundred meters behind the house. My men don't patrol that far away from the house, and our thermal and motion sensors wouldn't pick up anyone at that distance."

I should've felt better hearing his explanation, but I didn't. If someone could take a picture of my mother from that distance, they could do something worse too—like firing a long-range rifle at her. "I'll send you our latest drone model. It's small and quiet and has built-in thermal imaging capabilities."

"We're not licensed for that."

"Don't worry. If you're arrested for operating a drone without permission from the government, I'll pay all your legal fees."

"Thank you, but I'd rather not tempt fate."

"I'll double what I'm paying you, and you can keep the drone."

After a few seconds of silence, he said, "If that's what you want."

"It is. I'll send the drone right away. Goodbye."

Soon after I'd ended my call to Duncan, Keely came back from making her own call. I wanted to ask her to whom she had spoken, but it wasn't my business. Not yet. Once she admitted we were dating, I could ask her personal questions.

And she would want to ask me similar questions.

How would she react if I told her the full truth? The things I'd done, what I was capable of. I had no right to keep her with me, but I couldn't let her go.

Selfish bod ceann, that's what you are. Maybe I was a dickhead, but I'd taken this thing with Keely too far to back out now. Being a selfish *bod ceann*, I realized that was an excuse but didn't care.

That niggling sensation in my gut had nothing to do with guilt.

A liar too, eh?

I leaned sideways to get a glimpse of Keely. She had kicked off her shoes, and her bonnie toes wriggled the way they had last night when I was stoking her fire. A yawn overtook her. She stretched her arms above her head, making her blouse tighten over her breasts to the point the buttons seemed about to pop free. My cock roused, liking the idea of her blouse springing open to reveal more of her delectable body. She was wearing a bra, I could tell that much. It seemed very low-cut, though. If I walked over there and helped those buttons along, ripping them away with my teeth, I could bury my face between her breasts and—

How could I concentrate with her in the room? I jerked my attention away from the sensual woman on the window ledge and back to the screen in front of me.

Somehow, I managed to focus on my task for another hour in spite of Keely traipsing around the room to inspect the furniture and the abstract artwork on the walls. I hated those paintings or drawings or whatever they were. The interior decorator had chosen them, insisting they created a mood of "serenity and comfort." Keely paused at each piece of art to examine it.

Precisely at noon, she approached my desk and leaned her bottom against it right beside my chair.

I glanced at her sideways. "Did you need something?"

She bent toward me. "It's lunchtime. Let's go eat, I'm starving."

Aye, so was I. Not for food, though my grumbling stomach disagreed. I hungered for her.

"Too busy," I said. The deadline was three hours away. "Go on and have lunch without me."

"Uh-uh." She angled in more, hands on her thighs. "You've been staring at your computer all morning. It's time for a break."

"I need to finish this."

"You need food too unless you're an alien that lives on coffee and cardboard."

Maybe I couldn't live on those things, but I was fair certain I could survive by nibbling on nothing but her.

"What are you doing that's so important?" she asked.

"It's technical," I hedged. "Do you know much about computer programming?"

"Nope."

"I'm not skilled at it, but I have to take care of this myself."

"How do you not know about writing code? You make technical doohickeys."

That word almost made me smile, until I looked at the screen again. "I design the devices, and I used to manufacture them myself too. Now, I have people to do that. I also have people to create the software for the devices. Even in the beginning, I knew I needed to hire a programmer to help me since I'm not adept at writing code."

Did my invisible masters know that? They must not or they wouldn't have blackmailed me into doing work for them—unless they liked forcing me to do something outside of my expertise. I couldn't see how that would benefit them.

Keely straightened, hands on her hips. "You are taking a lunch break, Mr. MacTaggart. That's an order."

Her schoolteacher voice and a bossy order. Did she have no idea what that did to me?

I slung an arm around her waist and hauled her onto my lap.

She yelped and blew hair away from her eyes. "What do you think you're doing?"

"Having lunch. Nothing I'd rather snack on than you."

"Evan, please."

"Begging?" I arched one brow. "Please what? Kiss you? Your command is my wish."

I moved in, aiming for her lips.

She shoved a hand between our mouths. "No kissing, remember?"

"Every contract is negotiable."

"Not after you've signed it."

"That was a verbal contract, and I never agreed to it, anyway." I tried again to steal a kiss, but she blocked me again. "You decreed we shouldn't kiss. I didn't argue, but I didn't consent to it either. I've gone along with your order for the time being because it serves my purpose."

"What is your purpose?"

"To get you to admit we're involved in more than a casual liaison."

Her lips compressed, and her eyes narrowed. For several seconds, neither of us said a word. She stared at me, and I stared at her—though I couldn't resist fondling her erse and licking my lips when I glimpsed her breasts.

"No kissing," she repeated.

"You can believe that's what you want if it makes you feel safer."

She squinted at me again with her lips puckered, though their corners ticked upward just enough to prove to me she was not annoyed. No matter how much she denied it, she liked having me around for more than sex. Why else would she loiter in my office all morning? Later, maybe I would bring that fact to her attention. For the moment, I was happy to have her on my lap.

Keely twisted around to look at the desktop.

I knew she was looking at the distribution contract. It lay right there, the sole document on my desk.

She tapped a fingertip on the paper, and her gaze rolled to me. "You're holding me hostage with this contract."

"Am I?" Of course I was, but I loved winding her up.

"Yes, you are." She bent her head close to mine, so close I tasted her breaths. "I can't go home without a signed contract. Vic would be devastated. That means I'm your hostage until you sign the damn thing."

I skated a hand up her back. "You've got it backward, *leannan*. I am your slave."

"Hah."

"You do realize you're close enough to kiss."

She pulled away and crossed her arms over her breasts. "Are you afraid I'll run away if you sign?"

"No, you like me too much to do that." I moved my hands from her back to her front, stroking the undersides of her breasts with my thumbs. "And you love the way I make you feel."

"There you go again, being arrogant."

I skated my fingers up to caress her breasts everywhere except her stiff little nipples. "I like you too, Keely."

"And yet you refuse to sign. You obviously think I'll take off once we seal the deal."

"We've already sealed one deal. What's another?" I reached around her body to grab my pen and scrawl my signature on the contract. Legally, the contract would need to be witnessed, but I could get Tamsen to do that later. Tossing the pen aside, I hugged Keely closer. "There. You're free."

She slapped a hand over my mouth, apparently thinking I'd meant to kiss her.

I had, naturally. Foiled again, I settled for kissing her fingers.

She withdrew her hand. "About lunch…"

"You go on. I'm far too busy."

She nibbled on her lower lip in a way that made me want to throw her down on the desk and ravish her like a wild animal.

"I'll go get our lunch," she said, "and bring it back here."

I couldn't help smiling, though it may have come off as a smirk. She wanted to have lunch with me. Keely O'Shea, the all-business-and-no-play woman, wanted to stay with me even after I'd signed the contract. She must've realized I was plotting various ways to steal a kiss.

Keely hopped off my lap.

I slapped her bottom.

She mouthed "behave" and marched off to get our lunch, retrieving her shoes along the way.

Forty-one minutes later, I had Keely on my lap and the remains of our lunch littered the desktop. She had eaten her sandwich while balanced on my thighs. I had eaten mine while gazing at her lovely breasts and her slender throat. Every time she took a bite of her food, I became fixated on her lips.

"Behave, Evan," she said, tapping my lips with one dainty finger. "I can tell what you're thinking."

"I want to kiss you."

"And I said behave."

"You know how I feel about you disciplining me." I tugged her closer until our noses almost touched. "Say it again in your schoolteacher voice."

"Thought you had urgent stuff to do on your computer."

Yes, I did have urgent "stuff" to do. As much as I would've preferred to play with Keely, I needed to get back to work. One hour and sixteen minutes until my deadline.

The picture of my mother flashed in my mind. Those thugs had tracked her down simply to take a snapshot and prove to me they could get to the people I loved anytime they wanted. As if I needed a reminder after the one and only time I'd ignored them.

"You've gone serious again," Keely said. "Like you did this morning. Are you sure you're okay?"

"I'm certain." That she cared if I was all right should've lifted my mood, but I couldn't shake my unease. "Go back to your reading."

"Need a break from that." She picked up the remains of our lunch. "Think I'll ask Tamsen to show me those catalogs after all."

She climbed off my lap, the lunch remnants in her hands, and dumped the lot into the bin beside my desk. Gracing me with a subdued smile, she ambled out of my office.

Fifteen minutes later, I'd completed my task and texted the file to the anonymous individuals who held me captive. Though I had released Keely from the one thing tying her to me, my captors showed no signs of intending to release me.

Once I'd sent the file, I stared at the door without seeing it. Keely wanted to control our relationship. I already had a master, and I didn't intend to let her pull my strings too. Not that she wanted to control me. She was afraid to care for me. I could see that plainly, and though I suspected her former lovers had something to do with it, she wouldn't tell me more until I convinced her what we had was more than casual. How could I do that while I let her write all the rules? Yesterday, I'd taken charge and she had liked it. I enjoyed her domineering side, but maybe it was time for another reminder that I was a man, not her sex toy.

I shoved my chair back and stalked toward the door.

Chapter Ten

Keely

This is our master catalog," Tamsen said, turning the three-inch-thick book toward me where I half sat on the corner of her desk. "It includes every device and bit of software we produce. We also have the surveillance catalog, the security catalog, the software catalog, and the catalog of services we offer in addition to the devices and software."

"Services?" I asked. "I thought Evan made devices only."

"In the beginning, he made only the devices and the software to run them." She pushed the catalog closer to me, then brought out another, slimmer one. "Since then, we've added services such as on-call technical assistance and twenty-four-seven monitoring. If a client's alarm goes off, our people are alerted and call the client immediately. We have call centers in sixteen cities throughout the UK, serving our clients in seventeen countries around the world. Our clients include government agencies, corporations, and museums, including the museum owned by Evan's cousin Rory."

"Wow, that's impressive." My thoughts spiraled back around to Evan, the way he'd deftly created the missing components for a tiny listening device and finally to his urgent work this morning. I asked Tamsen, "Guess you're in on the big secret this morning. You are Evan's right-hand woman."

"Big secret?"

"The urgent work he had to finish today."

Tamsen opened her mouth to speak but seemed unable to drum up any words for several seconds. At last, she regained her professional composure. "I wasn't aware Evan had an urgent project this morning."

"He probably forgot to tell you." Our encounter last night must have distracted him as much as it had me. "Anyway, it's the reason I'm hanging around here pestering you. We had to delay our sightseeing until later so he could finish his work."

Tamsen pursed her lips and appraised me. "Evan does not take days off, not even for the weekend except to visit his family. He definitely does not take a holiday for a woman." She turned her attention to stacking the catalogs on her desk. "He must like you very much."

"I think he's just being a gracious host."

"Evan MacTaggart does not take time off. This is unprecedented."

A throat clearing made us both look at the office doorway.

Evan's large body filled the open doorway. He wore a determined expression, his focus squarely on me. "If the pair of you are done debating my recreation habits, you and I have something more important to discuss."

"What is it?" I asked.

"Something I need to show you."

He strode up to me and threw me over his shoulder with my head hanging down his backside. One of his arms was locked over my thighs, securing me in place. His free hand settled on my rump. He carted me into his office, kicked the door shut, and stomped straight to his desk where he set me down on my feet.

"You've got some nerve," I said. "Have you regressed to caveman behavior?"

"Aye." He undid his tie and yanked it off. "You need a reminder that I'm not your lapdog."

"My what?"

He seized my wrists, holding them behind my back, and bound them with his tie.

An unreasonable thrill electrified me, from my skin down to the depths of my sex, and my tummy fluttered. I should not like this. He was being an arrogant caveman. And what did he mean about being my lapdog? I should ram my knee straight up into his groin. Why didn't I?

Oh, I knew the answer. I wanted to find out what he was up to, what he might do to me next. The memory of yesterday, when he'd commanded me to lift my skirt, replayed in my mind. My body reacted like he'd shoved his head between my legs again, heating and melting and aching for whatever he planned to do.

He backed me up to the desk, his body firm and warm against me, and slanted his head down until our mouths hovered millimeters apart. "No more of this nonsense about parameters and no kissing. I'm meaning to claim you for mine, starting with your mouth. But only after you ask me to kiss you."

"Why would I do that?"

The light glinted off his glasses when he canted his head. "Because you want me to kiss you as badly as I want to do it."

He latched an arm around my body, his hand spread over my lower back. The other hand dived into my hair, cradling the back of my head and tipping it at the perfect angle for the kiss he believed I wanted.

My lips tingled as if confirming his claim. "You agreed to my parameters."

"As I pointed out earlier, I never agreed to no kissing."

Right, he hadn't explicitly agreed. That didn't matter. "I told you what I want."

"No, you told me what you think you need because you're afraid of getting close to me." He pressed forward a little more, hugging me to his hard body. "Ask me to kiss you."

"Like hell I will."

He rocked his hips into me, his entire body rubbing on mine, chafing my nipples against the fabric of my bra. The sensation of his muscles flexing against every part of me made more than my lips tingle.

What was the point in arguing? We both wanted the same thing.

I pulled in an uneven breath. "Please kiss me."

He covered my mouth with his, plowing his tongue between my lips to force me to open and yield control to him. I surrendered, sagging into him, letting out a small, involuntary moan. The kiss grew wild and demanding as he whipped his tongue around mine, groaning and crushing me to his body. With my wrists bound and his arm behind me, I couldn't have struggled to get free even if I'd wanted to. But I didn't want to. His hand held my head in position—to stop me from turning away, I assumed—but he needn't have bothered. I'd burned for him to kiss me all day, trapped by my silly demand that he never kiss me again. I answered the swipes of his tongue with greedy strokes of my own, devouring the flavor of him and not even caring that I tasted the sandwich he'd eaten for lunch too.

My body melted into him. Everything inside me craved him. Craved more. Craved everything.

He ripped his mouth away from mine, undid the tie around my wrists, and took one step away from me.

Robbed of breath by our kiss, I slumped until my butt landed on the desk.

He looped the tie around his neck and tucked it under his shirt collar as if he were about to do it up again.

"Was that it?" I asked.

He shrugged one shoulder. "What else did you want?"

I wanted him. On top of me. Inside me. Driving me past the limits of reason and not stopping until I came apart in his arms. Unwilling to voice my need, I straightened my clothes and pushed away from the desk.

Evan pecked a kiss on my forehead. "I've finished my work. We still have time for a bit of sightseeing today."

Sightseeing? Was he insane? He'd gotten me all worked up, and now he expected me to admire the scenery. I hadn't even caught my breath yet.

He laid a hand on my cheek. "Take a moment, lass. When you're steady again, we'll be away."

My voice still wouldn't work, so I tried to glare at him. My heavy breathing and flushed skin probably rendered the expression ineffectual.

He bent over the desk to click the button under its opposite edge.

The wet bar emerged from the wall.

I blinked at the thing. "What's that for?"

He sauntered to the bar, poured an inch of amber liquid into a glass, and brought it to me. As he offered me the glass, he said, "A bit of Ben Nevis ought to revive you."

"Is that whiskey?"

"Aye. That's spelled with no E, by the way. I've learned Americans spell it differently."

"Didn't realize that." I accepted the glass. "I'm more of a rum girl, but I'll give this a try."

I took a sip. The rich, smoky flavor of the whisky glided over my tongue and slid down my throat. I noted hints of nut and chocolate chased with a flash of fruitiness. "Mmm, that is delicious."

"Never cared much for whisky until my cousin Rory introduced me to Ben Nevis. It's made in Fort William, a town southwest of here."

I sipped the whisky and moaned. "God, this is good."

He wrapped his hand around mine and raised the glass to his lips, tipping it so he could take a sip. His hand lingered around mine as he ran his tongue over his lips. "You taste better."

"Bet you taste better than whisky too." I shot a meaningful glance at his groin and the large lump inside his pants. "Love to find out for sure."

"Later. I promised to show you the sights today."

"Okay, sightseeing it is." I wriggled my hand free of his and downed the rest of the whisky in one gulp, shuddering as its full effect hit me. "Whew, that's potent. Thanks for the booze boost."

"My pleasure." He set the glass on the desk and clasped my hand. "Are we away now?"

"Let's hit the road."

He led me away, or maybe astray, but I didn't care which anymore. Damn, that whisky was good.

Chapter Eleven

Keely

Sightseeing with Evan MacTaggart turned into quite an experience and taught me more about the secretive billionaire. We rode in his Porsche SUV, a sleek blue-gray vehicle that I was sure cost more than the going rate for a college education. I considered asking him how much the vehicle cost but decided my head would fly off my body if I heard the answer.

Evan's knowledge of Inverness, its history and its current events, impressed me and I let him take me wherever he wanted to go. We visited Inverness Castle on the banks of the River Ness, and Evan explained some of the history of the nineteenth-century castle. When I'd asked if he studied history in college, he'd laughed softly.

"No," he said, "but my cousins Iain and Catriona are both archaeologists. My other cousin Rory and his wife own a castle they turned into a museum, and my cousin Jamie and her husband run it. Hard to avoid learning about history with them in the family."

"You've mentioned five cousins so far, including your reference to Aidan yesterday. How many cousins do you have?"

He gave me a teasing sidelong look. "Isn't that violating your parameters?"

"Maybe, but I'm curious. I have five cousins, but I never see them. They're basically strangers to me."

"I have too many cousins to count." He slipped an arm around my waist while we both gazed out at the view from atop the castle tower, where the river stretched out ahead of us with the city on both sides. "I used to be an outsider in the family, but last year Iain and his wife decided to bring me into the fold. According to them, I'm a recluse."

"Are you?"

He tipped his head side to side, screwing up his mouth. "Yes, I have been."

"But you're not anymore."

"I'm recovering, thanks to my meddling cousins."

"Meddling? That doesn't sound very nice."

"You have to know the MacTaggarts to understand." His smile was a touch melancholy. "Meddling is a family pastime, but it's done out of love. Iain keeps pestering me to go to family events. He's threatened to invite me to Thanksgiving dinner this year, which has become a tradition since several of my cousins married Americans."

"MacTaggarts like the Yanks, eh?"

Evan gave me a squeeze and turned his head to smirk at me. "I'm familiar with the appeal of a sexy American."

A knot hardened in my stomach. This was getting too personal. Why had I asked about his cousins even after he reminded me of my own parameters? I didn't need to know him, and he didn't need to know me. The way he'd made love to me last night had sent me into a near panic, though this morning I'd felt better than I had in a long time. What did that mean?

Nothing. It meant nothing.

If I'd expected him to stop talking about family, I should have known better. He might not want to discuss his mother, but he had no qualms about asking me about my kin.

"Are you an only child?" he asked.

"No, I have two brothers." Why didn't I tell him to mind his own business? Maybe it was the earnest look on his face that kept me from putting him off this line of inquiry.

"Are your brothers younger or older?"

"Two years younger. Before you ask any more nosy questions, Ryan and Grady are twins, they're both married, and they both have children."

His next question turned the knot in my gut into a cold ball of ice.

"Do you have children?" he asked.

"No."

"Why not?"

I pulled out of his hold. "Awfully nosy, aren't you? Two can play that game. What secret project were you working on today?"

He said nothing, his face a mask that concealed more than I cared to think about.

"Tamsen knows nothing about it," I said. "So, what are you hiding? Your private porn collection? An app that steals money from every bank account in the world? Or maybe you were running a background check on me."

"None of the above."

"Which is your way of saying it's none of my business." I faced the river, refusing to look at him any longer. "Same goes for your question."

"Keely." He settled a hand on my arm. "Let's not ruin our time together by arguing. You don't want a relationship, anyway."

"You claim to want more than sex with me, but you want to keep your secrets too." I spun toward him. "Secrets and relationships do not mix."

His shoulders sagged, and he nodded solemnly. "All right. I won't ask any personal questions."

For the rest of the day, we stuck to discussing the places we visited. If he mentioned a cousin, I ignored it. We stopped in at St. Andrew's Cathedral and shopped at the Victorian Market so I could buy presents for my dad, Serena, Vic, my mom, and my brothers. I'd have to mail the gifts to Mom and my brothers since she lived in Seattle and they lived in Spokane. I asked for Evan's advice about what I might buy for Tamsen to show my appreciation for her babysitting me while Evan finished his super-secret work. He suggested a scarf, so I picked a lovely one that would complement her skin tone and hair.

"Why are you buying my executive assistant a gift?" Evan had asked after I made my purchase.

"Don't you give her presents? You must make her work long hours because she swears you never take a day off, not even on the weekends."

"I work long hours. Tamsen arrives at eight each morning, takes an hour for lunch, and leaves at five every afternoon. She does not work weekends except in rare circumstances." He flashed me an irritated look. "I am not a tyrant."

"Never thought you were, but you clearly work very hard."

"So do you," Evan said. "Mr. Bazzoli told me you often stay late to get more work done. He also said his store was on the verge of bankruptcy when he hired you and that Keely O'Shea saved the business."

"Vic exaggerates."

"He swears you're a genius at marketing and at managing employees."

"The two of you sure talked about me a lot."

"Your employer is very fond of you. Now that I've met you, I understand why."

I didn't want Evan to be fond of me. Any affection between us would surely lead to a big, steaming-hot mess. To change the subject, I pointed out it was dinner time and that I was hungry.

Big mistake.

He took me to a romantic French restaurant where the food cost more than I spent on groceries in a week. I resisted the impulse to chastise Evan for trying to make this a date by choosing a fancy restaurant. He would've liked being chastised.

After dinner, I was exhausted. He took me back to my hotel and kissed me goodbye—on the cheek.

The next day, we went on the grand tour of Inverness and its vicinity. We walked along the River Ness to admire the landscape, crossing over a picturesque suspension bridge to reach the opposite bank. Only after fifteen minutes of walking did I realize we were holding hands. It felt so natural I hadn't noticed when he slipped his hand into mine. Even after that fact penetrated my brain, I let him go on holding my hand. Maybe I should've worried about why I liked the feel of his palm warming mine and his fingers laced with mine, but I was sick of worrying about everything. For this one week, I would enjoy spending time with a gorgeous and obscenely wealthy younger man.

We ambled through an art museum to appreciate its historic treasures as well as modern exhibitions showcasing local artists and artisans. I learned that Evan MacTaggart, a tech billionaire and sexy geek, was an art aficionado too. Listening to him explain what he loved about his favorite artworks gave me an odd pain behind my ribs. His love of art was disarming.

I didn't want to be disarmed by him. I needed my emotional weapons for self-defense.

For lunch, we had a picnic along the shores of Loch Ness. Evan laid out a blue plaid blanket for us to lounge on while eating our sandwiches.

While I peeled the crust off my sandwich, I asked, "Isn't this blanket the same color as your kilt?"

"Aye, it's the MacTaggart clan tartan." He tore off a mouthful of sandwich, crust and all, chewing and swallowing before he spoke again. "You don't eat the crust."

"Lots of people don't."

He chewed up another large bite of sandwich, studying me with keen interest, scanning his gaze over my entire body. "You're very proper, the way you eat and the way you hold yourself. Even when we're relaxing on a picnic blanket, you sit up straight. And you always wipe your mouth very daintily after you take a bite."

I set down my sandwich. "Are you calling me uptight?"

"No, you're ladylike. It's uncommon these days."

"Well, that's what you get when you hook up with a senior citizen."

He lunged forward to mash his mouth to mine, holding his lips there for a brief moment before he pulled away.

I waited for an explanation, but when he offered none, I had to ask. "What was that about?"

"Told you every time you say you're too old for me I'd kiss you."

"Actually, you threatened to kiss me senseless every time I said that." I grabbed a potato chip and chomped it noisily. "But I did not say I'm too old for you. I said you hooked up with a senior citizen."

"The 'too old' bit was implied. As for kissing you senseless..." He leaned toward me inch by inch, his eyes obscured by the glare on his glasses. "I always keep my promises."

I held up a hand. "I'm eating. And you probably taste like those hot peppers you insisted on having in your sandwich."

He retreated again, picking up his sandwich. "After I've brushed my teeth, I'll kiss you mindless."

The man did not lie. He always kept his word. After we ate and collected up our picnic stuff, we ducked into a tourist shop and he disappeared into the restroom. I bought a cute little statue of Nessie, wasting time until Evan returned. When he did, he rushed me out to the car and kissed me until I went boneless in the plush leather seat and the only sounds I could manage were little moans of pleasure.

He tasted like minty toothpaste.

A man who brushed his teeth for me. He was truly unusual.

For the afternoon, we visited the Clava Cairns to see the ancient stone burial structures. Evan knew all about those too, regaling me with the lore surrounding the Bronze Age inhabitants of Scotland. Maybe he'd learned that stuff from his archaeologist cousins, but I was enthralled listening to the animated way he described all of it. We strolled among the ruins of Urquhart Castle to take in the crumbling majesty of the thousand-year-old site, and of course, Evan described its history to me. He insisted we do more shopping because my family needed lots of gifts. I asked why, but he only shrugged and told me, "Because they do."

After that, he took me to another outrageously expensive restaurant for dinner.

We had just gotten into the Porsche again when he said, "You must be exhausted."

"Not really." I snaked a hand over the center console to massage his thigh. "We didn't have sex last night. I'm horny. Take me somewhere and do me for hours, please."

He stroked my chin with his thumb. "I love your enthusiasm for sex and the way you tell me what you want and then say please. Courteous and bossy."

"You are the only man I've ever been with who doesn't get annoyed about that."

"It's charming." He started up the engine and navigated out onto the street. "I'd like to take you to my apartment."

"Sure, I'd like to see it." I fondled the buttery leather of my seat. "This is hands down the fanciest car I've ever taken a ride in. How much does one of these go for?"

I was babbling, not expecting an answer—but he answered.

He had one hand on the wheel, the other on the center console, the picture of a relaxed and confident driver. "This is the Porsche Cayenne Turbo. It costs about one hundred thousand pounds."

"One hun—What?" I gaped at him, sure I must've been suffering from an auditory hallucination. "One hundred *thousand*? How much is that in American money?"

"About one hundred and twenty-five thousand dollars."

"Holy shit."

I surveyed the interior with a new appreciation for his wealth. Sure, I'd known he was a billionaire, but hearing it and grasping the full implications of the word proved to be vastly different things. Money didn't impress me in and of itself, but the idea someone could buy anything, truly *anything*, he wanted was staggering.

My brain at last processed all of what he'd said. "Did you do the currency conversion in your head?"

"Yes."

"I can't balance my checkbook without a calculator." I sank back into my seat, turning my head to continue gazing at him. The billionaire who wanted to date me. The much-younger man who wanted a relationship. The genius who built electronics with his bare hands and could do complex math in his head. "Drive faster or I'll have to climb on top of you and speed things up. That brain of yours turns me on."

A smug smile tightened his lips. "Only my brain?"

"I think you already know the answer to that question."

We arrived at his apartment complex ten minutes later. The building had that ultra-chic modern industrial look but somehow managed to blend in with the more traditional structures around it. The five-floor building occupied a prime spot along the River Ness, and an imposing old castle perched atop a nearby hill. Evan steered the SUV into the underground parking for the apartment complex, pausing to swipe his keycard at the entrance, and pulled into a reserved spot near the elevator.

He insisted I wait until he opened the door for me before I got out of the car. He'd done this constantly since I'd met him, though I'd thought chivalry flew out the window a long time ago. None of my exes ever opened a door for me.

I must've looked stunned when Evan offered me his hand to help me out of the car because he asked, "What's wrong?"

"Nothing. It's been a long time since anybody opened a door for me, much less offered me a hand getting out."

"My mother taught me—" He frowned, his forehead tightening into faint lines. He grasped my hand and led me toward the elevator. "It's common courtesy, that's all."

He still didn't like talking about his mother. I wondered what awful things she'd done to make him angry every time he mentioned her. How bad could the woman be? She'd raised one amazing man.

A few minutes later, we walked into Evan's apartment.

I stopped just inside the door. This was not what I had expected. A billionaire ought to live in a high rise with doormen and butlers and insanely expensive...everything. Evan MacTaggart lived in a very nice apartment, but it wasn't over the top. Like the building itself, the apartment featured a clean, modern design with white walls and white ceilings and beautiful wood floors in a light color, possibly oak. The dining table sat half inside the open kitchen, while sparse but comfy-looking furniture occupied the living area. No artwork or decorations adorned the walls. No rugs lay on the floor. In fact, I saw no evidence of any personalization—no knickknacks, no family photos, nothing except the utilitarian necessities.

On the far side of the living area, floor-to-ceiling windows revealed a large balcony with a table and chairs. The lights of the city glimmered all around and shimmered on the surface of the river.

Evan came up behind me, taking hold of my upper arms. "What do you think?"

"This isn't where I pictured a billionaire living. It's so...normal."

"Normal? I must've walked into the wrong apartment. Where are my obscene sculptures and torture devices?"

A laugh spluttered out of me.

He kissed my cheek. "I like making you laugh."

I liked it too, the way he made me feel. "Where's the bedroom?"

"This way." He clasped my hand, leading me across the living area toward the only hallway in the apartment. "I have a guest room too, in case you'd like to stay here instead of your hotel."

"I'm fine in my hovel."

"You have a phobia about letting anyone help you."

"No, but I don't like being beholden to anyone, especially someone I've known for a few days."

He halted us in front of an open door to a bedroom and pointed toward a closed door on the other side of the hall. "That's the guest room. Both bedrooms have en suite bathrooms."

"Interesting, but irrelevant since I am not staying in your apartment."

"We'll see."

"Not staying here, Evan."

"I'll change your mind." He guided me into the bedroom and made a sweeping gesture with one arm. "This is the room where I'll be ravishing you for hours per your instructions."

He loosened his tie, preparing to get rid of it.

"I won't be changing my mind," I said as I kicked off my shoes, "about staying in your guest room. And I will not be sleeping over in your bed either."

"Aye, you've made it clear that's what you think you want."

"Not what I think. What I know."

"I understand." He tossed his tie to the floor and shed his jacket, then started to work on the buttons of his shirt. "Plans can change."

"You are the most infuriatingly obstinate man on earth."

He grinned. "You haven't met my cousins yet."

"And I'm not going to. This is strictly a fling." Watching him unhook his buttons one by one with deliberate care was driving me crazy. I swatted his hands away, grasped his shirt with both hands, and ripped it open. While falling buttons ticked on the floor, I shoved the fabric off his shoulders. "Stop talking and get naked."

He obeyed my command.

I let him strip me because, oh, I loved the way he did it. Evan obeyed my other command too and spent two hours proving to me he was a genius with more than technology and very, very inventive. He talked me into staying for a bowl of ice cream before he drove me back to my hotel. He kissed me goodnight at the door to my room, kissed me until my knees quivered and I fought an almost irresistible urge to invite him to spend the night with me.

Two more days. After that, I'd fly home and never see him again.

"Good night, Evan," I said and shut the door.

Chapter Twelve

Evan

Thursday, we continued our sightseeing tour of the Inverness region, venturing out into the countryside so Keely could "see the real world, not just the city." I'd assured her the city was real, but she had patted my cheek and called me a "nice boy." I couldn't decide what that meant, but I was getting bloody sick of her implying I was too young to have a relationship with her. Those ex-husbands and ex-lovers of hers must have been responsible for her fear of trusting a man again.

I tried many times to coax her into opening up about her personal life, but the woman had nerves of steel when it came to refusing to answer questions. Her life outside of work remained a secret except for the occasional tidbit of information she would inadvertently share. I knew she had cousins she never saw. I knew she had brothers. I knew she'd been divorced twice and lived with a third man. I wanted to know everything about her.

No matter how I prodded, she would not share even a crumb of her life outside work.

Thursday night, we made love in my apartment again and she left afterward again, though she lingered longer this time. Progress? I couldn't decide. The night before, I'd tempted her to stay for a while by offering her ice cream. This time, she had wanted to cuddle in bed while talking about the sights we'd seen during the day.

I lay awake for an hour after she left wondering if I was cursed. As a lad, I'd had no luck with the lasses because they didn't like quiet boys who preferred tinkering with electronics to participating in pointless sports. I made useful devices, but teenage girls had valued muscles over brains. Things had not improved much at university or after that, before my company became a success. The women I met these days wanted to shag a billionaire, not have a relationship. My luck hadn't changed at all. I wanted a relationship with a woman who was terrified to go down that road again.

Our encounter in Paris didn't help my case. I'd panicked back then because Keely was not like any other woman I'd ever met. From the moment I'd seen her, I had known this was a woman to keep, not to enjoy for one night.

All wasn't lost. It couldn't be. My cousin Rory had gone from uptight and closed off to being married to a vivacious woman who turned him into a freewheeling and blissfully happy man. If Rory could win the heart of a good woman, I could change Keely's mind about love—and me.

How was I to do that? I had no idea how Rory's wife had turned him around.

I contemplated that mystery all of Friday. At lunch, Keely and I enjoyed another picnic, this time along the banks of the River Ness not far from my apartment. Keely had insisted on conjuring up a small feast for us, making use of my kitchen to create "authentic American fare," as she'd called it. I learned that meant fried chicken, potato salad, and apple pie for dessert. I told her I'd eaten these foods before, here in Scotland, but she waved a hand to dismiss my statement.

"Doesn't matter," she said, "this is American food because an American cooked it for you."

Reclining on the blanket, I watched her pluck the last shreds of meat from her piece of chicken breast. "I love the way you eat, and I loved watching you make this feast. Never realized cooking could be so erotic."

"It's not." She tossed the bony remains of her chicken breast into the picnic basket and wiped her hands clean with a napkin. "You are obsessed with sex, that's all. Everything is erotic to you."

"Only the things you do." I sat up to get closer to her, skimming my hand up and down her thigh, making her dress slide up. "You're the one who keeps ordering me to pull the car over so you can have your way with me."

"You are not the kind of man who follows a woman's orders blindly. You do it because you like me bossing you around."

"When it comes to sex, yes." I adjusted my glasses, which didn't need adjusting. "I'm getting fair sick of you ordering me to stop wanting more than a fling with you. Whether you want to admit it or not, we are dating. Picnics, romantic dinners, making love in my apartment every night. That's a relationship, Keely."

"No."

"Yes."

She narrowed her eyes. "You are too young to understand these grown-up issues."

I clamped my mouth shut, my lips stretched taut, determined to stop myself from showing the depth of my irritation. Sometimes I got the impression she wanted to make me angry so she'd have an excuse to run away.

Eyes half closed, she groaned. "I've become a cliché, a dirty cougar on the prowl."

"Cougar?" I frowned, confused by her statement. "What does a big cat have to do with anything?"

Her lips twitched, almost a smile. "A cougar is an older woman who dates younger men."

"What's the term for a man who dates younger women?"

"Lucky bastard."

I couldn't help laughing. "I suppose you're right about that. Men dating younger women is acceptable, even admired, but older women with younger men isn't."

"Exactly." She plucked a piece of crust off the half-eaten pie and chewed on it. "An older woman is a cougar if she's with a younger man. A wild beast. A predator. Yet men who snag younger women are heroes. And a woman who hooks up with a young man after her husband dumps her for a newer model…That's just pathetic."

At last, I'd gotten a glimpse into her mind. No wonder she was hesitant to call this a relationship or even dating. Her exes had wounded her deeply, and she felt like she'd become a joke in a raunchy movie.

"Keely, I—"

My phone rang.

I glanced at the screen. My cousin Iain was calling. I'd been on the verge of coaxing Keely into opening up about her fears. The last thing I wanted to do was talk to Iain or anyone else but Keely.

The phone rang twice more while I stared at the screen.

"Aren't you going to answer that?" Keely asked.

No, dammit, I did not want to.

"It's okay," she said. "Take your call. It's not like we were having a vital conversation."

Like hell we weren't.

When the phone rang a fourth time, I realized the moment had been shattered anyway. I might as well see what my cousin wanted. I swiped the screen to accept the call.

"What is it?" I said into the phone.

My cousin sighed melodramatically. "Is that how you greet everyone who calls you? No wonder you don't have a girlfriend."

I stole a glimpse at Keely. "What makes you think I don't?"

Why had I said that? Keely wouldn't want my family knowing about us.

"You have a girl?" Iain said with genuine surprise. "Who is she? When do we meet her?"

"Careful, Iain, you're starting to sound like your daughter. Incessant questions with no time to answer."

"Two questions is not incessant. Who is she, Evan?"

In the background of the call, I heard his wife's voice. "Evan has a girl-friend? That's wonderful!"

Ah, bloody hell. If Rae knew, then soon every one of the American wives would know, and soon after that, every MacTaggart in creation would know. But Keely was not my girlfriend.

According to her.

No, I couldn't use Iain's mistaken assumption to my advantage. That would be wrong. Then again, Keely needed some sort of kick in the erse to show her the truth. Still, it would be wrong. Very, very wrong.

"Yes," I said, grimacing at my horrible behavior. "It's not such a shock, is it?"

"No," Iain said. "We're happy for you, that's all. What's her name?"

"Ahhh...." My gaze flicked to Keely, who was watching me with a sweet expression and softness in her eyes, her raven hair shimmering in the sun-shine. I swallowed hard. "Too early to share that."

Iain laughed. "Too early? I asked for her name, not a complete back-ground investigation and medical history."

He was right, but I couldn't tell him her name without her permission. Keely would never consent to that.

"Forget it," I said. "Your nosiness is no excuse for invading the lass's privacy."

Keely pointed at herself and mouthed, "Me?"

Nodding, scowling, I grumbled into the phone, "Lay off it, Iain."

"At least show her to us."

"What?"

"A video chat, man. Point your phone at her."

"I—No, she wouldnae want that."

The flapping of Keely's hand drew my attention back to her. She mouthed, "What?"

"Hang on," I told Iain, then held the phone to my chest. "My cousin Iain has figured out I'm with a woman. He's irritatingly perceptive. If I won't tell him your name, he insists I show you to him with my phone."

She smiled, her lips sealed and her cheeks dimpling.

Was she—No, she couldn't want to have a video chat with my cousin. "It's okay," she said. "I don't mind."

Shock immobilized me for two and a half seconds—or thereabout. I'd forgotten to time it on my watch. "Are you sure?"

"Yes, Evan, I'm sure."

I turned on the video feed, and Iain's face appeared on the screen. I aimed the phone at Keely. "Here she is, Iain."

Keely smiled brightly and waved at him. "Hi, I'm Keely."

I couldn't blink or speak, my gaze riveted to her. She had introduced herself to my cousin. The woman who wanted nothing more than a fling had said hello to a member of my family. Voluntarily. Cheerfully.

"That's Iain," I said, pointing at the screen. "He's fifty-one years old, but he married a woman fifteen years younger. If anyone's a predatory beast, it's Iain MacTaggart."

"Predatory?" Iain said with a laugh. "And what's my age got to do with anything?"

"You don't look fifty-one," Keely said. "I'm forty-one, but Evan keeps telling me I'm not a cougar for being with him."

"Cougar," Iain repeated thoughtfully. "Oh yes, Rae has mentioned that term. Never mind labels, Keely. No one is ever too old for the right person."

A shadow seemed to descend over Keely, her happy expression dimming, and I knew she'd had enough of this conversation.

"We have things to do," I told Iain, angling the phone's screen toward myself. "I'll talk to you later. Say hello to Rae and Malina for me."

"Not the baby?"

"He's a wee bairn, too young to understand. Goodbye, Iain."

I hung up before my cousin could say anything else.

"Sorry about that," I told Keely. "Iain likes to push his nose into my business."

"That would be some of your family's well-meaning meddling."

"Yes." I studied her for a moment. "Why did you tell Iain your name? Why did you want to speak to him at all? You say this is a fling, so you shouldn't want to know my family."

She caught her bottom lip between her teeth and let it slide out slowly. "I'm not sure. My curiosity got the better of me, I guess, and I'm in the habit of introducing myself when I meet new people."

That sounded like an excuse rather than an explanation, but I let it go to avoid embarrassing her. She'd wanted to speak to my cousin. It had to mean she liked me as more than a sex partner.

Once we'd collected the remnants of our picnic, we strolled back to the Porsche.

Keely moved toward the passenger door.

I held up the keys. "Would you like to drive?"

"Me?" she said, pretending to be shocked. "You're going to let a woman drive your manly man car?"

"Aye. But it's not a manly man car. It's simply a means of transportation."

"Hmm. I don't think something that costs over a hundred thousand dollars is 'simply' anything." She stepped closer, eying the keys that dangled from the ring hooked around my finger. "Men don't usually like to let a woman drive their cars."

Another clue about her exes. I was beginning to well and truly dislike them.

"None of the men in the MacTaggart family mind letting their women take the wheel." I took hold of her hand, flipped it upside down, and dropped the keys into her palm. "Drive, Keely. I know how much you like being in control."

She closed her fingers around the keys. "Thank you."

While I climbed into the passenger seat, Keely marched around to the driver's side and settled in behind the wheel. She adjusted the seat and started up the engine, revving it while she stroked the wheel with both hands.

"Do you like driving?" I asked.

"I love it." She eased the Porsche forward, carefully pulling out into traffic. "I didn't get to do much driving until the last few years. My ex-husband would never let me drive. We shared a car since we worked, um, at the same office. After my dad was injured, I became his chauffeur."

A scrap of personal information? I wanted to press for more but didn't want to push too far again.

Instead, I tilted my seat back and crossed my ankles, folding my hands behind my head. "You don't have to leave tomorrow, you know. I can have you flown home on my jet anytime. Stay another week. Let me show you even more of my favorite places in Scotland. I'll take you to visit my cousin Iain and his wife and their two children."

"I appreciate the offer, but I'm going home tomorrow as scheduled."

"Think of all the fun things we could do together, in and out of the bedroom."

"Hot sex is nice, but it's not a valid reason to skip out on my responsibilities."

"The vice president can take a holiday without the whole business going under. I'm sure Mr. Bazzoli could handle things on his own for a bit longer."

"First of all, he really can't. I'm in charge of human resources, which means I deal with all the employees. Vic hates riding herd on them. He's too nice to give anyone a dressing-down even when they need it." She pulled one hand away from the wheel to gesticulate while she continued. "I also handle all the bookkeeping and marketing. Vic's an expert in electronics, but he knows nothing about the stuff I take care of. But I think you know all of that since Vic blabbed to you on the phone about me."

"One more week won't destroy the business."

"I have family responsibilities too."

"Tell me about those. Maybe I can help you. Hire people to fill in for you at work and at home so you could stay—"

"Stop it, Evan. I'm not accepting charity from you or anyone." She exhaled a long breath that seemed to ease the tension in her body. "Look, I appreciate that you want to help. It's kind of sweet. But I need to handle my responsibilities on my own. I told you from the start this is a fling, nothing more than an enjoyable distraction, and it will not go on past Saturday. I'm leaving tomorrow."

My mouth wanted to remind her of every time she'd done or said something that contradicted the "just a fling" idea, but I gritted my teeth to keep from speaking. I had less than one day to convince her to stay. Words wouldn't do the job. I needed to show her how good we were together.

We drove to the company headquarters so Keely could give Tamsen the gift she'd bought for her the other day. We'd been so caught up in sightseeing and sex that we'd both almost forgotten Keely wanted to hand deliver the gift-wrapped scarf.

By the time we reached my building, I'd made a resolution. Whatever it took, I would prove to Keely she could trust me and that we belonged together. I had never done anything of the sort in my life. Never before had I wanted to keep a woman with me for more than the occasional night. How did a man prove to a woman they had something more than sex between them? I had no bloody idea. Unless I figured out the answer, I'd lose her. Failure? No, I hadn't gotten where I was by giving up. Keely O'Shea hadn't seen even half of my obstinate side.

Time to show her the rest.

While she pulled the car into a parking space, I said, "Next week, I'll show you my other factories."

"No, you won't. I'm leaving tomorrow morning."

"You don't have to."

"I told you I have responsibilities."

"Fate brought us together. Don't run away from that because you're afraid."

She shut off the engine and twisted to face me. Her eyes were squinted in that analytical way she adopted whenever she was about to reprimand me in the tone that made me want to tear off her clothes. "Fate? Are you seriously claiming destiny brought us together? That's hogwash."

"No, it's a fact." I twisted toward her too, laying an arm across the back of her seat. "How do you explain the way we met in Paris? And how you turned up in my office on Monday? It was meant to be."

"Bullshit. I don't believe in fate."

"Neither did I until I experienced it." I drilled my gaze into her sparkling green eyes, willing her to accept the truth. "What were the odds the woman I approached at a cafe in Paris ten months ago would turn out to be the woman sent to Scotland to negotiate a distribution deal with my company?"

"That does not make it fate. Coincidence, yes. Not fate."

I hadn't expected her to agree with me the first time I mentioned the idea. A willful and practical woman like Keely would need time to digest the information. At least I'd introduced the subject.

What were the odds of coincidence? Zero point zero percent.

All my life I'd banked on facts and numbers and electronic circuits. Ten months of dreaming about the raven-haired beauty I'd met in Paris had forced me to reconsider the value of logic. All of my cousins had found their perfect matches via a series of supposed coincidences. Where was the line between luck and fate? I knew where. It was a bright red line drawn between me and Keely.

Sooner or later, I'd convince her to step over to my side.

Chapter Thirteen

Keely

I rested my cheek on Evan's shoulder, enjoying the sweet pleasure of post-sex tranquility. We sat naked on the bed entwined with me on his lap, my arms and legs wrapped around him. He held his arms around me too as he placed soft kisses on my shoulder. I closed my eyes, my cheek on his skin, and absently massaged his nape with my fingertips. He'd done it again. He had made love to me like a man who cherished the woman in his arms, but this time, I hadn't panicked afterward. The feeling of connection, the intimacy of this moment, had lured me into its spell.

His spell. The man must've enthralled me with sorcery.

Not that I believed in magic. It was hogwash just like fate.

Basking in the afterglow with him like this, I had trouble remembering why all that stuff was hogwash. If Vic hadn't sent me to Scotland to handle the distribution deal, I would never have met Evan again. If we both hadn't chosen the same cafe in Paris...

Not fate.

Sex made me loopy, that was all. I did not believe in destiny or the magical powers of Evan MacTaggart. Better to leave before things got too messy.

He brushed his fingers through my hair and caught my earlobe with his lips, releasing it slowly. "Stay the night."

The request, whispered straight into my ear, sent a warm shiver down my spine. I wanted to say yes, but I'd sworn I would not sleep with him. Have sex, yes. Sleep, no. Keeping to my parameters seemed less and less important every day. He'd already convinced me to give up my decree about no kissing. Did it matter if I spent the night with him? The fact that I wanted to, that I yearned to, answered my own question.

I wrapped my arms more snugly around him. "I'll stay."

He kissed a path down my neck to my shoulder, resting his forehead there. "Thank you."

"You don't have to thank me for something I want to do."

Evan went motionless, not quite tensing up. "You want to stay? I assumed you were saying yes to make me happy."

"I am, but staying will make me happy too."

He toppled backward onto the mattress and took me with him. I ended up sprawled half on top of him with his arms still around me. He tugged the covers over us and frisked his hands over my back. "You don't have to leave tomorrow."

"Yes I do." I snuggled into him, probably giving him the wrong idea. Or maybe it was the right idea. My desire to spend the night with him testified to some facts I didn't care to think about, tonight or ever. "This was always supposed to be a limited-time affair."

"If you're calling it an affair instead of a fling, you must not see it as casual anymore."

Damn. The hypnotic afterglow of intensely intimate sex had turned my brain to mush. With Evan, I didn't feel like a bossy forty-one-year-old woman who couldn't hold on to a man.

He was right. The word affair did suggest more than a casual thing.

"Can we enjoy sleeping together," I asked, "and worry about the rest later?"

"Aye."

We both fell silent, and before long I drifted off to sleep.

In the morning, I woke before Evan did and sneaked out of bed without disturbing him. Our clothes lay strewn across the floor where we'd tossed them when we undressed each other, driven by a burning desire to get naked. I found Evan's white dress shirt and slipped it on, hooking two buttons so the shirt covered my breasts. Last night, he'd insisted on changing into a suit to take me to a fancy restaurant, and I'd worn the most dining-appropriate clothes I'd brought with me, the skirt and blouse I'd worn the day he tied my hands behind my back and convinced me no kissing was a stupid idea.

Dressed in only his shirt, I ambled to the floor-to-ceiling windows and pulled the semitransparent drapes open so I could appreciate the view of the River Ness. My gaze was drawn to the old castle that hunkered atop a hill. Had I locked myself up in an emotional fortress no man could breach? Maybe I had, but I couldn't take a chance on letting Evan inside my walls. I knew so little about him.

You can change that, a voice whispered in my head.

If I hadn't insisted we not get to know each other, I might've learned more about him. He had cousins, I knew that. He had a problem with his mother, that I also knew. My curiosity prodded me to ask questions, to learn more. My heart warned me against doing that. It had been bruised too many times.

"Good morning."

He'd gotten out of bed and was stretching his entire body. His entire naked body.

Oh my, but I had wonderful memories of the ways he put all those muscles to work.

"Good morning," I said, leaning against the window.

He sauntered toward me and the huge windows that overlooked public places.

"You're naked," I said like he wouldn't know that already.

"Aye." He stopped near me, in clear view of anyone who could see these windows. "What would you like for breakfast?"

"You aren't at all concerned someone will see you through the windows. Stark naked."

He lifted one shoulder, then stretched again and sighed. "Tell me what you want me to feed you and I'll make it for you."

"You cook?" The realization distracted me from the issue of his nakedness on full display for the residents of Inverness to enjoy.

"I cook, yes. Don't look so surprised."

"Can't help it. I imagined a billionaire would have servants tending to his every need."

"Where's the fun in that?" In one big stride, he closed the gap between us and sandwiched me between his body and the window. "You know from personal experience I'm a hands-on man."

"That you are." I roved my hands up his torso to his chiseled pecs. "I love it when your hands are on me."

"Stay another week and I'll make sure to lay hands on you several times a day."

"We've been through this. I can't stay." I sucked in a breath when his cock jerked, stiffening against my belly. "My flight leaves in two hours. We don't have time for sex."

"Ah, but we do." He planted his hands on the windows at either side of my shoulders, pressing his entire body into mine. "If you let me fly you home on my jet."

"No, Evan. Commercial is good enough for me."

He rolled his hips, and his hard shaft rubbed against me. "I need you one more time, Keely. Miss that flight and take my jet."

My body had a mind of its own. My arms encircled him, my leg hooked around his, and my hips rocked forward as if seeking his erection.

One more time. To say goodbye.

My gaze flitted to the window behind me. "We can't do it here."

He pulled back a few inches. "Be wild, Keely. Let me fuck you up against these windows where anyone might see."

That husky request dissolved my willpower. I unhooked the two buttons I'd done up on the shirt I'd stolen from him, letting it fall open. "Let's do it."

Those silvery blue eyes zeroed in on my chest. "Christ, you have the bonniest breasts I've ever seen." He cupped my tits in his hands, flicking his thumbs over the peaks. "I love your body."

At least he hadn't claimed he loved me. We hadn't known each other long enough for me to believe it if he'd said those words. Not that I wanted to hear them. "I love you" meant nothing if he spoke the words just to make me stay.

Telling me he loved my body on the other hand…I didn't mind that at all.

"Love your body too," I said, moaning when he captured one nipple and scraped his tongue over it. He bent his knees until his face aligned with my groin. I grasped his chin to make him look up at me. "Enough foreplay. I'm ready, and I've got a plane to catch."

"Ye'll be taking mah jet."

"No, Evan. I'll be taking—unh." I couldn't produce any coherent sounds, not with his face planted between my thighs and his tongue forging between my folds to lap at my nub. I braced one foot flat on the window and turned my knee to the side, opening myself to him. "What was I saying?"

He chuckled against my flesh. "Nothing important."

No more talking. No more complaining. I let my head fall back against the window and grasped his head with both hands. My hips undulated while he licked and nibbled and sucked on my flesh. His hands gripped my buttocks. My breathing became erratic, and I slapped my palms on the window like I might glue myself to the surface to keep from flying away when I hit that blissful climax, the one that burned and tingled and tightened inside my body.

At the instant I came, he sprang up and dived two fingers into the breast pocket of the shirt that sort of covered me. He yanked out a condom.

My chest heaving, I glanced at the little packet. "Didn't notice that in there."

"Yer a randy lass," he purred. "Need one on hand at all times."

He ripped the packet open and covered himself. "Ahmno done with ye."

"More, please, yes."

Grinning like a predator who'd spotted his unsuspecting prey, he thrust into me in one long, smooth stroke. I gasped. He wasted no time on fondling my breasts or kissing me. No, he grasped my ass and pushed deeper inside me, setting a hard and fast pace that plastered me to the cool glass. In the back of my mind, I wondered if we could break this window with our passion. He shifted his hands down to clasp my thighs, lifting them, and I obediently locked my ankles behind his muscular glutes.

I was having sex in front of a window, on public display above the street and the river.

The idea of someone seeing us made me so slick I felt the moisture dribbling down my inner thighs. The orgasm I'd experienced a moment ago hadn't finished. It ramped up again, shuddering through me while my body milked his cock. I moaned and gasped his name, flung my arms around his neck, bucked my hips into every one of his thrusts, lost myself to the mind-shattering pleasure of this man inside me and this moment that I wished could go on forever.

He punched into me once more and let out a long, deep groan of pure satisfaction. His breaths gusted into my hair.

I unwound my legs from him and slid down his body until my feet touched the floor. "You sure know how to say goodbye."

"Not saying it yet." He peered over my shoulder at the view beyond the glass. "Look, a group of schoolchildren is down there watching us through telescopes."

I smacked his cheek without any real punch. "Not funny."

He assumed a grave expression. "I think we may have scarred them for life."

"Please tell me there aren't actually any children down there."

He kept up the seriousness with such conviction I almost started to believe him, until he grinned. "I'm having you on. No traumatized children, I promise."

"Asshole." I smacked his cheek again, though both the action and my words lacked any force.

"You're in Scotland. Say 'ersehole.' And then I'll slap your lovely erse."

I clamped my lips between my teeth.

"Since you won't make your flight on time anyway..." He swept me up in his arms. "Let's have a shower."

We did get into the shower with the water running, but we did not bathe. After that, we made inventive use of the vanity before we headed to the kitchen, having more fun there while Evan cooked me a delicious breakfast of omelets stuffed with veggies and sausage with toast on the side. He brewed up the tastiest coffee I'd ever had, observing with amused interest as

I poured so much cream into the coffee that it barely looked beige anymore and then dumped in four spoonfuls of sugar.

"Are you sure you like coffee?" he asked. "Maybe I should give you a mug of cream and sugar instead."

He drank his coffee black of course.

I was missing my airline flight, and I didn't care.

With one quick call, Evan arranged for his jet to ferry me home. Naturally, he tried to talk his way into accompanying me—talked, kissed, and fondled in fact—but I summoned what little willpower he hadn't already crumbled to dust and refused his offer. The fact that I wanted him to come along dismayed me less than it should have.

At the airport, he walked with me to the stairs hooked up to the jet.

I stopped at the bottom of the steps. "Nice plane. How much does one of these go for?"

Though I hadn't meant for him to tell me, he did. "About fifty million pounds."

"Fifty million? How much is that in American dollars?"

He opened his mouth to answer.

I raised a hand up to stop him. "Never mind, pretty sure I don't want to know."

"This is a GulfStream G650ER," he said as if I cared about the brand and model. "It has all the amenities you could want or need. You will be much more comfortable traveling this way than on an airliner, and you'll get home faster."

"Does it have a swimming pool?"

"Afraid not." He trailed a finger down my jaw. "Are you sure I can't change your mind about letting me escort you home?"

"I'm sure, but thanks for the offer." I scrutinized the jet, suddenly uncomfortable with accepting a ride on his plane. I'd told him I wouldn't accept charity because I didn't want to be beholden to him. Did appropriating his jet count as charity?

He bowed his head, scratching the back of it. "Would you stay if you had a job here?"

"I don't know. Since I don't have a job in Scotland, it doesn't matter."

He straightened and lifted his chin, assuming his CEO stance. "I'm offering you the position of vice president at Evanescent Security Technologies Limited."

The man must've been kidding, right? He wouldn't offer me a job solely to keep me within screwing distance. And he couldn't have feelings for me.

"You have a vice president," I reminded him. "His name is Stewart Atkins. I met him."

"I know who Stewart is. You would be vice president of client management."

A bewildered laugh bubbled out of me. "Have you ever had a vice president of client management before?"

"This would be a new position."

My laughter died. "Evan, you can't do that. Creating a job for me is weird. And how do you think your other employees will feel about it? The assistant manager of an electronics store in Nowhere, Utah, who has zero qualifications becomes a vice president."

"Donnae care what they think. It's my company."

I flapped my arms. "Come on, Evan. Can't you see what a horrible idea this is? You might as well call me the vice president in charge of screwing the CEO."

He pursed his lips, then scrubbed a hand over his face. "I suppose you're right."

For the first time, I realized how badly he wanted me to stay. Flattering as that was, I couldn't give him what he wanted.

"Let's say goodbye," I told him, "and end this on a positive note. I've enjoyed spending time with you, and you've made my first trip to Scotland a very memorable one. Thank you, Evan."

He took my face in both his hands, fixing his earnest gaze on me. "I don't want to say goodbye."

"You have to. We have to."

"I know." He touched his lips to mine, holding the contact for so long I began to think he would refuse to let me go by holding onto my face forever. When he finally broke the contact, he gazed at me with a solemnity that tugged at my heart. "Goodbye, Keely."

"Goodbye, Evan."

I slogged up the stairs into the jet, and the pilot shut the door.

Numbness overtook me as I shambled through the cabin. Though I noticed the furnishings, none of it impressed me the way it might have under different circumstances. The floor was carpeted, and a big-screen TV occupied a prime spot along one wall facing a long sofa on the opposite side. Beyond that, leather chairs offered more seating. I flopped onto the sofa, stretching out on my back.

Goodbye, Evan.

Did I miss him already? No, that was crazy.

The flight home took half the time it had on a commercial airliner. Though six and a half hours had elapsed, I arrived before I had left Inverness thanks to the seven-hour time difference. This meant I walked into the house at eleven a.m. feeling like it should be dinnertime. The jet lag hadn't caught up to me in Scotland, what with a sexy Highlander occupying my time and keeping me awake and energized with hot sex and scintillating conversation. The second I stepped into the house, weariness engulfed me.

My father rolled into the entryway, stopping his wheelchair a couple of yards away. He smiled with an enthusiasm I couldn't match. "Keely, you're home. We weren't expecting you for a while yet." Confusion deepened the wrinkles on his forehead. "Did your flight leave early? I've never heard of airlines doing that before."

"Uh, no." I set my bags beside the door and shut it. "Evan MacTaggart lent me his private jet."

"You mean like a little Cessna?"

"Not a turboprop, Dad. A jet. One that cost fifty million pounds."

He whistled. "Fifty million. How much is that in American money?"

"I don't know. A lot more, for sure."

Serena popped out of the kitchen doorway, her toffee-brown hair tied up in a ponytail on top of her head. She was drying her hands with a dish towel even as she smiled at me. "Welcome home, Keely. How was your Scot—I mean how was Scotland?"

The twinkle in her gray eyes assured me she had almost asked me how my Scot was and that her apparent flub had been done on purpose. Evan was not my anything. We had a fling, it was over, end of story. My real life needed me. Time to file away my fantasy in Scotland in the "pleasant memories" folder.

If I'd wanted to forget it, my irritating inner voice asked, why had I told Serena about Evan? She and I had talked every day when I called to check on my dad. I could have left out the parts of my day that involved Evan, but I hadn't.

"You must be exhausted," Serena said. "Why don't you catch a nap?"

"I slept on the plane."

Dad waggled his brows at Serena. "Keely traveled in high style on Evan MacTaggart's fifty-million-dollar jet."

"Fifty million pounds," I corrected.

"Oh," Serena said, her mouth forming a perfectly round O. "Well, you must be hungry. I'll whip you up a sandwich."

"Not hungry," I said. "I ate on the plane too."

"Okay, fine. I made brownies if you want dessert."

Dessert. Why did the word remind me of Evan?

I did not want to discuss Evan or his jet anymore, or the gourmet meal I'd enjoyed on the plane. Evan had hired a five-star chef to cook me a sumptuous meal in flight. Was he trying to impress me with his wealth? He couldn't believe flaunting his bank balance would make me change my mind.

He had told me he'd never been in a serious relationship, never had a genuine girlfriend either. Maybe he honestly had no clue how to navigate the treacherous waters of dating and relationships. Not that I was an expert. I'd need at least one success under my belt to qualify for that title.

I followed Serena and my father into the kitchen, where Dad and I headed for the round table. I pulled one chair away, tucking it in the corner so Dad could pull his wheelchair up to the table. We didn't have a fancy house with a kitchen island. Our house offered a table, chairs, and limited counter space. Evan's kitchen had been large, open, and gorgeous.

Serena brought a pan of brownies and three plates to the table. Once she'd settled into the chair across from me, she doled out the brownies and handed each of us a plate.

When I lifted my first bite to my mouth, Serena stopped me with a question.

"So, what was it like dating a billionaire?"

I set down my loaded fork. "We weren't dating."

"You went sightseeing together, you ate meals together, you had—"

"Lots of fun together." I'd cut her off before she could mention sex since I had no doubts she'd been about to do just that. The woman had no compunctions. None whatsoever. I added, "Evan is a nice man. I'm glad I got to spend some time with him outside of work, but that's all it was. Friendship."

Dad gave me his skeptical-cop look. "You can't fool me."

Serena wouldn't have told my father I was sleeping with Evan. Would she?

"It's okay," Dad said. "You don't have to be embarrassed about boffing a billionaire."

My gaze flew to Serena, and it was my turn to squint like a skeptical cop. "You blabbed, didn't you?"

"I did not," she said, appearing genuinely affronted. "I would never do that."

"She didn't blab," Dad told me. "Former police detective sitting here, kiddo. I figured it out all on my own."

Damn. Sometimes I hated having an ex-cop for a father.

"Not sure what it was," I said, "but it's over. I am never going to see or speak to Evan again."

"Why the hell not?"

"Because I don't date anymore. You know that."

He rolled his eyes, his mouth crimped. "I know you keep saying that, but it's bullcrap. You're too young to give up on dating." He bent forward to spear me with his cop stare again. "Who's the one who keeps pestering me to sign up on that dating website for old farts? Oh yeah, it's you."

"That's different. You and Mom divorced amicably."

"What's that got to do with the price of beans?"

"You're not—" I searched my brain for a way to say it without sounding self-important. "You didn't have the bad experiences I've had with marriage. Besides, I'm not pushing you to get involved with someone half your age."

Serena chimed in. "Evan isn't half your age unless you time-warped and came back sixty years old."

"He's thirty," Dad said. "Eleven years' difference ain't nothing. Billy and his lady have an eighteen-year difference, and they've been happy as clams for twenty-one years."

Oh yes, my father loved to use his ex-cop buddies as proof of whatever point he was trying to make about my life. When I'd announced I was done with dating, he'd told me about his pal Rocko who got divorced after thirty-two years of marriage and started dating again right away. Somehow that proved I shouldn't give up on romance. Rocko had initiated his divorce, though, because his wife wanted to move to Boca Raton and he refused to leave Utah. That hardly compared to what my ex-husband number two had done.

"Call the billionaire," Dad said in his stern-parent voice.

Was this how I sounded when I told Evan to behave? He'd called it my schoolteacher voice. He'd liked it, but I did not appreciate it when my father adopted that tone. It meant he was going to meddle and wheedle until I did what he thought I should do.

The tactic rarely worked. I was as stubborn as he was.

"Stop calling Evan 'the billionaire,' please," I said. "He's not an untouchable deity who lives in an ivory tower."

But he sure was a god in the sack.

"Oh no," Serena said in a sarcastic tone, "he's definitely not untouchable. You know all about that, don't you, Keely?"

"You like him," Dad said. "And you are not too old for anything."

I growled under my breath. "Could we please drop the subject of Evan MacTaggart?"

"Let's make a deal," Dad said. "I'll sign up on that dating website if you call Evan and invite him to visit you here."

"No, Dad. That's N-O spelled out in giant, flashing neon letters."

Resigned to never getting my loved ones off my back, I snatched up my brownie with my bare hand and tore off a massive bite. If I couldn't stop them talking, I'd stuff my mouth so at least I wouldn't snap out a sassy retort.

Invite Evan to visit? Never. I'd had two flings with the man, and that was my limit. In Paris, he'd bolted. In Scotland, he'd tried to convince me to jump into a relationship with him. Even if I liked him—okay, I did like him—I couldn't trust him not to take off again or hurt me in some other way I hadn't imagined yet.

No more dating. End of story.

Chapter Fourteen

Evan

For nine days, I tried to put Keely O'Shea out of my mind. Banishing her ghost proved harder than I'd thought, harder than seemed rational. What I felt for her was not rational, though, and it never had been. She'd entranced me in Paris. My desire for her had propelled me into a wild and reckless act of selfish need. I understood she had trouble trusting me after the way I'd run off that night. The moment she had strolled into my office dressed like a sexy librarian, I'd lost my mind again. When she told me to behave, I had needed all my self-control to keep from repeating my Paris mistake, this time by throwing her down on my desk and rutting with her like a sex-starved bull.

Hadn't I proved to her I was a decent bloke?

Clearly not. She went back to America, and I was left here in Scotland, alone, struggling to reassemble my wits. They were slippery buggers. I couldn't seem to sweep them all up.

I slumped in my chair, gazing at my computer monitor without seeing anything on the screen. What was I meant to be doing today? Writing some sort of report. The board of directors was convening tomorrow, and I'd promised them an update on my works-in-progress. Why the bloody hell had I ever created a board of directors? The interfering erses did nothing but annoy me.

Two weeks ago, I would've called them demanding but fair. Today, I wanted to strangle every one of them.

Keely had done this to me. Why couldn't she trust me?

Maybe she sensed I was the sort who fantasized about murdering my board of directors.

A long, miserable groan resonated in my chest. Keely. I couldn't work because I couldn't stop thinking about her. Missing her. Remembering our five and a half days together. Her smile. Her laugh. The softness of her lips. The way she appended "please" to the end of every command she issued. Most of all, I remembered the expression on her face when she came, and the way she held on to me through every spasm of her release.

No other woman had ever looked at me that way, in bed or out. She made me feel like I could do anything, be anything, have everything I wanted.

Everything except her.

The door shivered from three crisp knocks.

"Come," I called.

Tamsen stalked into the office and directly to my desk. "You are a bloody moron."

"Good morning to you too, Mrs. Spurling."

"Don't get cheeky with me, Evan. You know what I'm talking about."

I sat up, straightened my jacket and tie, and pulled my chair forward to rest my arms on the desktop. "My personal life is none of your concern."

"Like hell it isn't. I've been your employee and your friend for six years." She jabbed a finger in my direction. "And you are making a muddle of your life."

"What is it you claim I've done that qualifies as a muddle?"

She shook her head, her lips tight. "You let her get away."

"Keely wanted to leave. What would you have me do? Kidnap the lass and keep her in my apartment, bound and gagged?"

My mind flashed back to the day I'd bound Keely's wrists with my necktie. Her cheeks had been flushed, and her lips had been parted and waiting for the kiss she denied she wanted. I loved her fire. I loved it even more when she'd given in and admitted the truth. Only Keely could make giving in seem like a victory for her.

"Don't be an idiot," Tamsen said. "You're smitten with her. For the first time in all the years I've known you, Evan MacTaggart is head over heels for a woman. Go and get her."

"I can't. She said—"

Tamsen slapped her hands on the desktop, leaning in to fix me with her hardest glare. "Are you going to give up because she didn't beg you to go after her? Keely is as smitten with you as you are with her."

Was she? I'd thought so, but then she had fled back to America.

At the airport, right before she'd run up the jet's stairs, Keely's eyes had glistened with moisture.

I hissed a curse under my breath. Tamsen was right. Keely left because she was terrified of getting hurt again, not because she had no feelings for me. I hadn't achieved everything I had by giving up when things got tough.

"You're an angel, Tamsen." I leaped out of my chair and lunged forward to plant a firm kiss on her cheek. "Thank you."

Her eyes bulged. "You're—You're welcome, Evan."

"I'll need the jet as soon as possible."

"Where should I tell the pilot you're going?"

"Carrefour, Utah."

I glanced at my computer and the two sentences I'd typed. "Tell the board my report will have to wait. I have pressing business in America, concerning our latest distribution deal."

"Yes, sir."

Tamsen saluted, spun on her heels, and marched out the door.

I'd just shut down my computer when the door exploded inward, thwacking into the wall.

Ron Tulloch stormed up to my desk. His face was crimson, his eyes were wild, and he was breathing heavily.

"You bastard," he snarled. "I know what you're doing, MacTaggart."

"What are you having a canary about this time?" I gathered the papers on my desk and put them in a drawer. "If it's about your pay rise, I told you—"

"Pay rise? You're auditing my department. I demand to know why."

I rose from my chair with deliberate slowness, placed my palms on the desktop, and spoke in a level tone. "I talked to some of the people who work under you. They have concerns about how the accounts are being kept, so I hired an independent firm to perform an audit."

"Without asking me?"

Christ, I wanted to drive to the airport, not deal with Tulloch's nonsense. If he insisted on an answer, I'd tell him the truth. "It became clear that someone is overbilling all our clients by tiny amounts that when combined add up to a large sum."

Tulloch jerked like he'd been hit with a steel pipe. "You think I'm embezzling."

I'd expected him to take offense at the suggestion, but that wasn't the impression I got from his behavior. He shifted his weight from one foot to the other, over and over, and twisted his wristwatch. The man was on edge.

"Someone must be embezzling," I said. "We'll find out soon enough who it is."

He clenched his fists so tightly his hands trembled. "You've got a nerve, MacTaggart. First, you destroy my business, and now you're framing me for embezzlement."

"You ruined your own company, Mr. Tulloch. I had nothing to do with it." I waved a hand to dismiss him. "We'll talk about this once the audit is done."

"Call it off."

I tipped my head to the side, trying to figure out what the man hoped to gain by starting an argument with me. "I won't be doing that, Mr. Tulloch."

He stabbed a finger at me. "You will, or you'll regret it."

"Leave my office, or you'll be getting your head in your hands to play with."

Tulloch snorted. "You can't punish me without cause."

"Your behavior right now is cause enough to fire you."

"Fire me?" He swung his fists up. "You bleeding scunner, ye willnae get away with this. I'll tell the board how you've been trotting your American whore out for the whole company to see."

"Instead of blaming everyone else, maybe you should've been taking a tumble to yourself and getting your department in order."

"What would you know about working hard?" he snarled, spittle spraying from his lips. "You'd rather shag your American whore."

Heat erupted in my chest, burning out reason and self-control. I stormed around the desk to him and seized him by the throat. "Say that one more time and see what happens."

Tulloch sneered. "American whore."

I towed him across the office by his throat. He stumbled, sputtered, and cursed at me until we reached the open door. His eyes widened. His crimson flush began to pale.

"You don't work for me anymore," I said and pitched him out the door.

Tulloch landed in a heap on the other side of Tamsen's desk.

"Call security," I told Tamsen, "and have this man removed from the building. His employment has been terminated."

Her eyes were almost as wide as Tulloch's, but she picked up her phone and made the call.

Tulloch scuttled backward until he bumped the wall, as far away from me as he could get.

"Don't move," I said in a tone that assured him I meant it.

He cringed.

Security arrived shortly, and once they'd taken Tulloch in hand, I rushed back to my apartment to pack. Getting away from Scotland appealed to me even more after my confrontation with Tulloch. The thing I hated most about running this company was dealing with disgruntled employees. Tulloch's tantrum had been the last straw. I was escaping to America.

How long would I stay there? I had no idea. Whatever it took to convince Keely we belonged together, I would do it. However long it took, I would wait. My company had been my mistress for six years, and it was about damn time I took a holiday abroad.

Chapter Fifteen

Keely

Soft music murmured in the background, tunes culled from the Top 40 charts, designed to be unobtrusive and make our customers feel relaxed. I knelt in the corner of the store nearest to the main doors rearranging the audio accessories and found myself humming along to the song currently playing. I didn't know the words, I'd never heard the cheery song before, but it had gotten into my brain after the third time in a row it played.

Over my shoulder, I shouted, "Paige, take that song off repeat, please. We don't need to become known as the earworm store."

Paige Dawkins, the perky eighteen-year-old manning the customer service counter, feigned a pout. "You're so mean, Keely. This is my anthem song."

"It's nice, but we can't play the same song all day. Go back to the approved station."

"But satellite radio is so boring."

She reached under the counter to switch from CD to the radio feed.

"Thank you, Paige."

She saluted.

Returning to my task, I moved a package of corded earphones to the correct hanger and a set of Bluetooth ones to their appropriate spot. Customers had a knack for putting things back in the wrong place.

The automatic doors swished open and shut.

"Hi," Paige said in an oddly breathy voice. "Welcome to Vic's Electronics Superstore. How may I help you today?"

Was that a touch of awe in her voice?

Focused on moving another pair of headphones to the right hanger, I decided to ignore it. She probably thought the customer was cute. Paige had a habit of going dreamy-eyed whenever a good-looking boy her age walked into the store.

"I'm looking for Keely O'Shea."

My spine snapped straight at the sound of that familiar, sexy voice. Awareness tingled over my skin, hot and shivery. I was too damn old to react to a gorgeous man the way Paige did, yet here I was clutching a blister-packed set of headphones to my chest like a life preserver while my heart raced and my mouth went dry. It couldn't be him.

Right. Tons of men with Scottish brogues walked into this store in the middle of Utah every day.

I rotated my head, though the rest of me refused to budge, and peered in the direction of the customer service counter twenty feet away.

Evan stood there with one arm resting on the high counter, one hip cocked, and one ankle crossed over the other. And he was wearing a kilt. Well, it was Monday after all.

Paige had gone blank-faced, her mouth partly open.

For once, I could not blame the girl for her reaction. Evan looked deliciously ready to nibble in his long-sleeve, powder-blue shirt that matched his kilt. The shirt collar was stiff, most likely starched, and he had the top two buttons undone. The glare of the overhead fluorescent lights reflected off his glasses, making it hard to see his eyes. My memory filled in the visual of those blue eyes so pale they seemed silver and the dark rims that reminded me of the rings of Saturn. He was like a kilt-clad angel from another world, an incredibly hot and insatiable angel.

Paige, still speechless, raised a finger to point at me.

Evan's gaze swiveled in my direction, and he smiled. "There she is."

A giant rock got stuck in my throat. There *he* was. I'd said goodbye to him in Scotland. Why was he here? I'd told him I didn't want a relationship with him or anyone. How much clearer could I have been?

Evan flashed his disarming smile at Paige. "Thank you for the help, lass."

She blushed and hunched her shoulders.

He sauntered toward me.

I jumped up. The headphone package tumbled from my hands.

"Keely," he said, his voice turning sensual.

"Evan," I said crisply. "What are you doing here?"

"I'm not ready to give up on you."

My tummy fluttered. It seemed to have no idea I was a mature woman in her forties who did not get a fluttery tummy when a man said something nice.

No matter how sexy his voice was or how earnestly he gazed at me.

"You should've called first," I said.

"If I had, you would've told me not to come."

"Because you shouldn't have come here."

He took off his glasses, tucking them in his shirt pocket. "I'm going to kiss you."

"Absolutely not."

Evan took one step closer. "I will. Right here, right now."

My gaze darted around the store. Paige was watching us. Three cashiers were checking out four customers. He couldn't kiss me here. He wouldn't dare.

Of course he would. This was the man who had traipsed in front of floor-to-ceiling windows in the nude. And then he had…Oh, what he'd done to me next.

He slanted in.

I flung a hand up to stop him. "Not in front of my employees."

"Thought they were Mr. Bazzoli's employees."

"Yes, technically. But I'm in charge of human resources, so Vic says they're my employees."

"More people to command, eh? You must love your job."

"I'm not a dictator."

"No, you always say please when you order people around."

Paige was still watching us. She'd braced her elbows on the counter with her hands linked and her chin resting on them. A dreamy little smile curled her lips.

"Come with me," I told Evan.

"Anywhere you want."

I spun on my sensible heels and headed for the door marked "Employees Only." The hems of my pants swished around my ankles where they flared out. The way the rest of my pants hugged my figure seemed to fascinate Evan.

Fishing my keys out of my pocket, I unlocked the door.

Evan peeked over my shoulder, his expression faintly amused. "A key lock? That's quaint, but not the best security." He rolled his eyes up to indicate a gray box affixed to the wall ten feet up. "Your surveillance cameras are dummies, aren't they? They don't do anything."

"We don't have the budget for fancy doohickeys. Besides, we don't get much crime in this town."

I pushed the door inward and held it open while Evan entered the hallway beyond it, then I shut the door. It clicked shut, the lock engaging automatically. I led Evan to the first door on the right and opened it.

"Not locked?" he said with raised brows.

"We've got the outer door locked. I don't need to lock my office too."

He clucked his tongue. "Keely, I'm surprised someone as professional and precise as you would leave your door unlocked. It's a good thing you met me. I can help."

"Thank you, but I don't need your help. I do fine on my own."

I wondered if "professional and precise" was code for "uptight and inflexible." And then I wondered why I cared about the answer.

We walked into my office, and I shut the door.

Evan reached for me. "Now I can kiss you."

I shuffled backward two steps and raised one finger. "Behave, Evan."

He smirked. "You know how I love it when you say that."

"Not interested in being your schoolteacher fantasy."

"You aren't a fantasy." He moved closer, the scent of his spicy aftershave tickling my senses. "You are a real woman, the kind a man wants to keep forever."

"Also not interested in dating or relationships. I told you that."

"But you spent five and a half days with me. That was dating, Keely."

"Go home, Evan."

"Afraid I can't, not without you."

We assessed each other in silence, two pigheaded people who wanted polar-opposite things. I wanted to stay away from romance. He wanted to woo me. What had he expected? That I would leap into his arms the instant I saw him? He'd known all along how I felt about relationships.

He placed his hands on my upper arms and aimed that heartbreakingly earnest look at me. "I missed you."

Oh God, his voice. Soft and tender, filled with longing. He had genuinely missed me.

If I was honest with myself, I'd missed him too.

He coasted his hands up and down my arms. "I missed you very much, Keely. Couldn't work because I kept thinking about you, about how I let you walk away, and then Tamsen gave me a kick in the erse. That's when I realized I couldn't let you go without a fight. Even if you punch me in the face and call the police to drag me away, I have to try."

"Evan…" I shook my head, having no clue what to say.

"Keely, I missed you," he said, this time with a fervency that roughened his voice.

I threw myself at him, locking my arms around his neck, my feet off the floor. "I missed you too."

Well, at least I hadn't leaped into his arms the instant I'd seen him. I had waited a respectable minute or so before doing it.

Our mouths crashed into each other. He slung his arms around me while his tongue thrust deep, coiling around mine, and our teeth gnashed. We consumed each other like we'd been apart for years, not nine days, like we'd die if we couldn't merge in every way imaginable. I tore my mouth from his only long enough to nod toward the sofa along the wall, across from my desk.

"Sofa," I mumbled right before I mashed my lips to his again.

He staggered backward until we tumbled onto the sofa. I wound up underneath him with the full weight of his big body pressing me into the cushions. I lashed a leg around his while I shamelessly groped every part of him I could reach. His kilt had gotten pushed up, leaving nothing at all between my hand and his cock when I closed my fingers around its thickening length. He groaned into my mouth, fumbling for the button on my slacks.

I pushed on his chest and gained enough space to speak. "We can't do this."

He was breathing hard, and his cheeks had turned pink. "Your employees are on the other side of two doors and a hallway."

"Not the point. This is my workplace."

"You let me feast on you in my office."

Good point, but I had to stop this before he got the wrong idea. What was the wrong idea again? I'd flung myself at him and initiated this frantic make-out session. So what idea was the right one? The answer had flown out of my brain the second he'd said he missed me in that heartfelt voice.

He moved to kiss me again.

I blocked him with my hand. "No, Evan."

With an annoyed sigh, he slid off my body to lie on his side wedged between me and the sofa's back. "It's not fair to tell me to stop in that bossy tone, the one you know makes me crazed with lust."

"You'll have to get used to it. I talk that way a lot."

"I'll need to get used to it?" He perked up. "That sounds like you won't be ordering me to leave."

Damn. That wasn't what I'd meant to say, but my subconscious seemed to have other ideas.

"We would never work," I told Evan in my calmest, least schoolteacher-like voice. "Two stubborn, demanding people used to doing things our own way? That's why they say opposites attract. You and I are too much alike."

"That's nonsense."

"Face facts, Evan. It would never work out between us."

He studied me for a moment like he was trying to figure me out. "You're wrong. We're not that much alike."

"We both got where we are by being stubborn and determined."

"I got where I am by taking big risks without knowing whether they'd pan out." He bent his head close to mine. "When was the last time you took a risk? You're so afraid of getting hurt again you won't take any chances."

Once again, he made a good point. All my excuses seemed to be crumbling to dust. The last time I'd taken a risk, Evan had dragged me into an alley for a quick hump and then he ran away. I couldn't blame him for my anxiety, though. My exes had gifted me with all the shit I needed to justify my fears.

Evan stroked my cheek with one finger. "Do you really want to miss out on something that could be good because you're afraid? Give us a chance. Please."

I'd gotten lightheaded and realized I'd stopped breathing. Pulling in slow, deep breaths, I considered his request. Take a risk on him? It scared the hell out of me. Evan was nothing like any man I'd ever known, so maybe...

"I don't know," I said. "You show up out of the blue and ask for things I don't want to give. But I like you, Evan, I do. Give me time to think about this."

"All right. Take time." He looked and sounded disappointed.

"Where are you staying?"

"The Carrefour Motel. It was the only room available."

"Summer is tourist season." I fingered a button on his shirt, focusing my attention on it. "I'll stop by your motel this evening. We should talk. There are things about me you need to know before we do anything as drastic as dating."

"Drastic? I've never heard dating described that way." He touched his lips to my forehead. "I can be patient. I'll look forward to seeing you tonight."

Two knocks rattled my office door.

"Keely?" Vic said. "You in there?"

"Yes, I am. Just a minute." I wriggled away from Evan and clambered off the sofa. Straightening my clothes, I approached the door and grasped the knob. My gaze wandered back to Evan lying on the sofa with his kilt lumped around his waist. "Could you try not to look like we just enjoyed heavy petting on the sofa in my office?"

He winked. "Aye. Anything for you."

I waited until he'd gotten up and sorted out his clothes before I swung the door inward. "Hi, Vic. What is it?"

"Heard you've got a 'total hottie from another country' in your office. Those are Paige's words."

Evan strolled up beside me. "Mr. Bazzoli, it's a pleasure to finally meet you in person. I'm Evan MacTaggart."

He held out his hand.

Vic shook it and smiled warmly. "Great to finally meet you too. Keely, why didn't you tell me Evan was coming for a visit?"

"Well, I—"

"It was a surprise," Evan said as he retrieved his glasses from his pocket and slipped them on. "Keely didn't know. I had an opening in my schedule and decided to pay a visit to my newest business partners."

"That's terrific," Vic said, beaming. "Let me show you around. Unless Keely wanted to do that."

"No," I said, grateful for an excuse to get some time away from Evan. Time to think clearly. I had trouble doing that when he was nearby. "You two go ahead. I have paperwork to catch up on."

Vic stepped backward, away from the door, waiting for Evan to follow.

Evan commandeered my hand and kissed it. "Looking forward to seeing you again later."

My boss slapped Evan on the back and led him out onto the sales floor.

I had agreed to meet Evan later. At his motel. Alone. Just me and a bed and the sexiest man I'd ever known. Maybe I wanted to be tempted. Maybe I longed to take a risk.

Maybe I liked Evan a lot more than I wanted to admit.

Chapter Sixteen

Evan

After a long and fruitful conversation with Vic Bazzoli, I took him up on his offer to let me wander around the store and talk with any of his employees I bumped into along the way. Everyone who worked here seemed happy, and everyone raved about their assistant manager. Keely was, according to her employees, tough but fair and always available for a chat whenever one of her people needed it—a chat about anything, from their jobs to their personal lives. I wasn't surprised to learn Keely cared about her employees as more than workers, but as human beings too. She had a nurturing nature.

I couldn't understand why she didn't have any children.

For the entire morning, I pretended to explore the store while in reality I was observing Keely. She bustled around like a mother hen, making sure her people did what they were meant to be doing and sorting out any problems that arose. She also seemed to have a minor obsession with straightening the shelves. I watched her move from aisle to aisle, display to display, reorganizing things that must've gotten disorganized by customers. Twice, she retreated into her office for a short period. The woman seemed incapable of leaving the floor for more than fifteen minutes at a time. No wonder she worked late every day to get her managerial tasks done.

No one I'd ever met deserved a holiday more than Keely O'Shea. How could I convince her of that?

Setting aside that question, for the time being, I considered how to tell her about the plan Vic and I had come up with earlier. Keely wouldn't like it, I was sure, not at first. She would recognize my ulterior motive for suggesting it. The woman had left me no other options.

At noon, I resolved to take her away from the store for lunch whether she wanted to go or not. She needed a break, though Paige had assured me Keely never left the premises for lunch. She ate in her office. *Not today, Miss O'Shea.* I gave up the pleasure of watching her trousers stretch taut over her bonnie erse every time she knelt down or reached for something further down a shelf, and I walked up beside her.

She paused in sorting a rack of DVDs. "I thought you'd be gone by now."

"Not leaving the country until we're sorted."

"I meant I thought you would've gotten bored with exploring the store and left to find something better to do."

"There is nothing I'd rather be doing than watching you bend over repeatedly." I gave her rump a pat. "The view from behind is spectacular."

"Please do not fondle me in front of my employees."

Despite her firm tone, I knew she wasn't annoyed. The way her lips twitched gave it away.

"It's the lunch hour, Miss O'Shea."

Keely sighed and gave me her standard reprimanding look, softened with what I hoped was a hint of affection. "I eat in my office. But feel free to toddle off and entertain yourself somewhere else for the rest of the day."

She flapped her fingers in a go-away gesture.

"Afraid I can't." I leaned against the shelves next to the DVD rack. "Your newest employee needs your personal attention."

Her brows cinched together, and she glanced around the store. "I haven't hired anyone new. What are you talking about?"

I clapped a hand on my chest. "Your new hire is right here."

She blinked once slowly. "Excuse me?"

I couldn't help the self-satisfied smile that stretched my lips. "Vic and I came up with a dead brilliant plan to help me get to know the company I've just signed to a distribution deal. I'll work here for two weeks."

"You—Huh?" She blinked furiously, her delicious lips parted in an accidental invitation. "I hope you're joking."

"Haven't you seen the television series where managers and CEOs go undercover in their own companies?"

"You are not the CEO of me or my company." She started as if she'd realized too late what she had said. "I meant you're not the CEO of this company. Vic's business. His company."

She gave up floundering for a way to cover her original misstatement, shaking her head and pressing her thumb and forefinger to her forehead.

"Relax," I said, stroking her arm with my hand. "This will be a perfect opportunity for us to get to know each other better and for you to boss me around. We both enjoy that."

"You're impossible."

"To quote my cousin Rory, the lawyer, I'll stipulate the fact."

"I'm still not going out to lunch with you."

"Not even to welcome your newest employee?" I slid my hand up to her shoulder. "It would be the professional thing to do."

She puckered her lips, but it seemed less like annoyance than an attempt not to smile. "Fine. Your boss will buy you lunch as part of your orientation. It's not standard procedure, but then you are no average employee."

"True."

"Luckily, nobody around here knows who you are."

"Vic and I decided I should be called Evan Fraser while I'm undercover."

"Sure, whatever." She sounded dubious, but she took a deep breath and exhaled it in a rush. "I'll get my purse and meet you by the main doors in five minutes."

"Two minutes."

"Honestly, Evan. Is everything a negotiation with you?"

I pretended to consider her question for two seconds. "Not everything. Only the things involving a stubborn, beautiful woman who drives me mad with lust."

"Better learn to keep that in check while you're working here. There will be no hanky-panky in the workplace."

"Give me all the rules you want, *leannan*. I'll have fun breaking them just to make you chastise me."

Keely sighed again, more heavily, her shoulders slumping. "You are going to be a handful, aren't you?"

"No more than you are." I slanted in so I could gaze into her beautiful eyes. "For the record, I know I'm not the CEO of you. Wouldn't want to be. Breaking the spirit of a wild mustang is nowhere near as satisfying as taming her with tenderness."

She didn't move for several seconds, and neither did I, our gazes bound to each other.

"I'll wait for you by the doors," I said and headed in that direction.

Only I knew the full extent of my plan. Working here gave me an excuse to be around Keely every day. I needed time, lots of it, to complete the rest of my plan.

Taming Keely O'Shea.

Chapter Seventeen

Keely

Evan hadn't been kidding when he said he wanted to have lunch with his new boss. We talked about work the whole time. While the waitresses and other customers gawked at the man in a kilt, I explained our rules and procedures and made him promise to read the employee orientation manual once we got back to the store. When I escorted him into my office and handed him the manual, he smirked.

"Will there be a test later?"

"No, but you still have to read it." I wagged my finger at him. "Actually read it. No pretending to pay attention to the manual while you're ogling my ass."

"You'll be here while I'm reading the manual?"

"Of course. Do you think I'd leave you alone in my office? Who knows what you'd get up to."

His smirk slanted downward into a frown. "You think I'll steal from you."

My thoughts rewound to when I'd met Evan at the main doors and we had walked out into the parking lot. I'd suggested we each drive our own cars, and he could follow me to the restaurant I'd chosen. When I'd waved toward my car, a fifteen-year-old Ford Taurus, he had made a mildly disgusted face.

"No, Keely," he'd said in a patient tone. "We will take my car, and I will choose the restaurant."

"Have you forgotten? I'm the boss of you now."

"Only while we're in the store." He'd pulled a key fob out of his shirt pocket. "Besides, my car is nicer."

"Fine, have it your way." I raised a finger. "This one time."

Evan's car turned out to be a red Lexus that looked like a sports car masquerading as a sedan. While he swung the passenger door open for me, I admired the vehicle.

"Where on earth did you find a luxury rental car?"

"I didn't rent it. I bought it."

My legs refused to move one more inch. "You bought a car? I thought this was a two-week vacation in America, not a long-term stay."

"That has yet to be determined." He placed a hand on the small of my back and gently urged me to get into the car. "How long I stay depends on you."

I had decided to save that discussion for later when I would set him straight about a lot of things. However, he blindsided me again once he got behind the wheel.

Starting up the vehicle, he'd said, "I plan to give you this car once I'm done with it."

"That's not necessary." I'd wanted to tell him no way, no how would I accept a luxury car as a gift from anyone, but especially him. That was another discussion we would have later, once I figured out how to pound the facts into his steel-reinforced skull.

"I want to give you the car," he'd said.

"No, Evan."

Our conversation about the car had ended then.

Here in the present, I sat down at my desk. "I'm not worried you'll steal from me. But if I leave you alone in here with a phone and a computer…" I made a sweeping gesture to indicate both of those things on my desk. "I'll probably come back to find you've bought me a house. Or maybe the whole town. You have an inappropriate need to give me extravagant things."

He dropped onto the sofa and propped his feet on the table that separated it from the two chairs opposite it. The employee manual lay on his lap. "Buying you a car is not extravagant. You won't let me do it, anyway."

"I don't want to be beholden to anyone."

"Getting fair sick of hearing that word. Beholden." He linked his hands over his belly. "I don't want to own you, Keely. I want to take care of you."

"I don't need a man to take care of me."

"Don't want to control you. Let me help, that's all."

My mouth opened, determined to announce I didn't need help, but I clapped it shut. Evan meant well. I believed that. He went overboard, though, and I needed him to understand it wasn't necessary. Even if I dared to date him, I wouldn't want extravagant gifts.

"I appreciate your generosity," I said, "but I'd rather you be yourself and stop trying to impress me. I realize you haven't dated much, so please take some advice from a battle-scarred veteran. Flashy gifts and grand gestures are not the way to forge a genuine, lasting relationship."

Not that I had a clue about how to do that, but I did know grand gestures wouldn't do the trick. All I had to do was convince Evan of this.

He absently toyed with the corner of the employee manual, though his attention stayed on me. "Battle-scarred? Christ, Keely, what did your exes do to you?"

"That's not the point. I'm saying you need to stop going overboard."

"I understand that, but you haven't answered my question."

When I'd suggested this morning that we should meet at his motel this evening, I had intended to tell him about my exes. Not this afternoon. Not here in my office. Maybe I was being a coward, delaying and delaying in the hopes he might give up wanting to know. I couldn't help it. No one knew the whole story. Sharing it with Evan would make whatever this was between us real.

"Tonight," I said. "I'll tell you all about that tonight."

"When you come to my motel room." He imbued those words with a sensuality that made a delicious warmth rush through me. He caressed the employee manual with his long fingers. "I'll be dreaming about this evening for the rest of the day."

I leaned back in my executive chair with its cracked leather upholstery. "For the rest of the day, and every workday for the next two weeks, you are my employee. That means no daydreaming. Focus on your job, young man, and do as I say."

His fingers massaged the manual in slow, sensuous strokes. "I will obey my beautiful, desirable boss during the workday. But after hours, you'll be begging for the chance to take orders from me."

"Are you sure you don't have a BDSM fetish?"

"I've told you before, I have no fetishes. But we both know you like it when I tell you what to do—while we're having sex."

Earlier, he'd compared me to a wild mustang and implied I needed taming. Tender taming. I would've loved to be able to honestly tell him I didn't want that, but part of me liked the idea.

He watched me for a moment, though I couldn't see past the glare on his glasses from the overhead light. He flipped open the employee manual and turned his attention to it. "You can tell me everything later, in my motel room."

"And you will tell me everything too."

Without looking up, he smiled. "Yes, ma'am, Miss O'Shea."

"You are completely impossible." Remembering something I'd meant to give him, I opened a desk drawer and pulled out the item. "Almost forgot your uniform."

"Uniform?"

I tossed the plastic-wrapped shirt to him.

He caught it. "Ah, yes. I did notice all your employees wear these shirts."

"You'll need to wear beige pants, but we don't provide those." I eyed his incredibly muscular arms. "Hope the shirt is big enough. It's the largest size we have, but we've never hired a brawny Highlander before."

"No kilts allowed, I'm guessing."

"Sorry, no. Beige pants only."

He tore open the plastic and brought out the uniform shirt. The wrapping fluttered to the floor. Whipping off the shirt he was wearing, he donned the royal-blue one emblazoned with the store logo and spread his arms wide. "What do you think?"

The fabric of the shirt stretched taut when he flexed all those muscles. I forgot what he'd just asked me, too distracted by thoughts of those arms belted around my naked body.

"How do I look?" he said, pronouncing each syllable with extreme precision.

"What? Huh?" I ripped my focus away from his chest. "Looks like it fits okay."

He linked his hands behind his head and leaned back. "Think I'm going to like working under you, Miss O'Shea."

Ignoring the innuendo in his voice, I rolled my chair closer to my desk and opened the accounting software on my computer. For ten minutes, I tried to concentrate on entering yesterday's receipts. After the fourth time I screwed up and had to start over, I gave up.

Rising, I cleared my throat to get Evan's attention. "Can I trust you to behave if I leave you alone for a while?"

"Behave? Me?" He pointed at his chest, his expression one of faux innocence. "I'll be the best employee you've ever had under you, Miss O'Shea."

"Making a suggestive statement is not behaving, Mr. MacTaggart."

"Is it my fault you have a dirty mind? I meant I work under you because I'm your employee. You are my superior." He tsked. "Try to keep your mind on business. I wouldn't want to have to file a sexual harassment complaint."

"Uh-huh." I laid a hand on my computer monitor. "Do not use my computer or the phone while I'm gone. If I come back to discover you have ordered me a yacht, I will fire you no matter how cute and sexy you are."

He grinned. "I'm cute and sexy? That's definitely harassment. Shame on you, Miss O'Shea."

"I will be on the floor if you need anything."

The infuriating man made a hungry noise deep in his throat. "Haven't had ye on the floor yet."

"The sales floor. It means I'll be walking around out there." I made a vague gesture in the direction of the main store area if we could've seen it through the walls. "Read the manual while I'm gone."

"Aye-aye, Miss O'Shea."

"Be—" I'd almost told him to behave again, but he would've liked that. "Just read the damn manual."

He skated his hands down his thighs and back up to his groin. "I'm looking forward to being under you all day long, but you'll be under me after hours."

Maybe he was the one in need of taming.

With that thought in my mind, I headed for the door. As I closed my hand around the knob, Evan spoke.

"Don't eat before you come to me this evening. I'll buy you dinner."

I walked out the door.

Chapter Eighteen

Evan

Keely had canceled our date last night, the one she wouldn't call a date, claiming she was too tired. I'd been a little jet-lagged myself, despite sleeping during the entire flight, so I let her get away with canceling. She probably needed time to come to terms with the fact I was not giving up on her. I'd give her one more night alone before I started my campaign to tame her fears and win her heart.

How did a man do that? My cousins were the only examples I had, but each of them had taken a bumpy road to happiness. Bumpy? Their roads had been full of land mines they planted in their own paths. They might not be the best role models for my relationship with Keely.

Tuesday was my first full day as an undercover agent. Spending eight hours working under Keely made me want to get under her in other ways too. Nine days without touching her, without feeling her naked skin on mine, had threatened to turn me into a bampot of the first order. Never before had I craved a woman the way I craved her. It was more than sex, though. I wanted to devour her because she was the most stubborn, intelligent, and exciting woman I'd ever met.

I liked seeing other sides of her. The assistant manager who treated her employees like her own brood of chicks enchanted me as much as the bossy woman who loved to tell me to behave. I looked forward to experiencing every side of her, and I suspected I had a lot more to learn about Keely O'Shea. I understood I'd have to tell her about myself too. She wouldn't open up to me unless I did the same.

After work, I drove back to my motel. My cousin Iain called, distracting me from my preparation for Keely's arrival. He teased me about my new "girlfriend," and I let him. Sometimes it was easier to accommodate my cousins than to try to make them stop harassing me. I considered tormenting Iain in return but decided I hadn't reached that level of family engagement yet.

I had just stepped out of the shower when someone knocked on the door. Wrapping a towel around my hips, I hurried to the door and swung it open.

All the blood rushed to my cock.

Keely wore the dress from Paris, the deep-green one that made her creamy skin look creamier and her stunning eyes seem an even more intense shade of green. The low neckline and spaghetti straps left large expanses of her soft skin exposed. The high hem brushed her thighs. She'd worn the same stiletto heels she'd had on in Paris. I wanted to grab the knot that nestled between her breasts and yank it hard to tear the dress from her body.

Like I had back then, I imagined pinning her to the wall and lifting one of those slender ankles to hook her leg around my hip while I thrust into her.

Keely swept her gaze up and down my body. "I thought you'd be dressed."

"You caught me getting out of the shower."

"I can see that." Her attention shifted to the towel covering my hips and part of my thighs. "Guess the motel doesn't have Scotsman-size towels."

"No, they don't." I stepped back. "Come inside, Keely."

Ahhh, but I did mean that in every way.

She sashayed over the threshold and leaned back against the wall beside it.

I shut the door and caged her with my arms, my hands on the wall at either side of her head. "I'm glad you're here."

"You're having inappropriate thoughts, aren't you? I'm here to talk and have dinner with you. It's not a date, simply a get-together."

"It's a date, Keely." I fingered one of her spaghetti straps. "You're wearing the Paris dress, which means you came here to defile me."

"Oh please. I was not looking for sex the first time I wore this dress."

"Maybe not, but we did have sex. I don't believe you have no idea what message this dress sends." I hooked my finger under the strap and skimmed it up and down her skin. "You want me to take your body, then take you to dinner."

She lifted her chin. "You can think what you like, but for me, this is not a date. Do you want to talk or not?"

"We usually talk after sex, but I'll let you have it your way this time."

"There is no usual between us. We are not a couple."

I couldn't help laughing softly. She was the most obstinate woman. "Already agreed that we can have a conversation first. You don't accept victory well, do you?"

"Never can be sure I've really won an argument with you. You're sneaky."

"I'm not sneaky. I'm clever and a master negotiator."

"And oh-so-humble too."

"Where's the value in being humble? Nobody knows how good you are unless you tell them."

She must've guessed based on my slight smirk that I was having her on because a slight smile of her own tightened her lips. With one finger, she gestured toward my towel. "Are you going to put some clothes on?"

"After we talk." I stepped back and dropped the towel. "Unless nudity bothers you. It didn't back in Scotland, but maybe you've gotten uptight since then."

She waved a hand in a negligent gesture. "Stay naked. I like ogling you."

I ambled to the bed and hopped onto it, bouncing and making the frame creak. Shifting sideways, I made room for her and patted the mattress. "Come, Keely."

"Now you're talking to me like I'm a dog?" She kicked her shoes off and climbed onto the bed beside me. "Woof."

She panted loudly with her tongue hanging out.

I slapped her thigh. "Behave, Keely."

Her lips quirked into a sly smile. "I will if you will."

"Let's both misbehave. Often."

Her smile faded. "I've already misbehaved with you in ways I never thought I would do with anyone. Not sure if that's a good thing."

Disappointment erased my smile too. She wasn't sure if I was a bad influence on her, that's what her statement implied. I wanted to be good for her, good to her, but she couldn't seem to shake her fears of getting hurt again. "Tell me what your exes did to make you so afraid."

Her head fell back against the wall, and her whole body wilted. "Guess I better start at the beginning."

I slipped my hand around hers on her lap.

She curled her fingers around mine. Her gaze was aimed at the far wall, but her focus seemed to have retreated into a place only she could see. "In my junior year of college, I met David. He was beautiful and sexy and the guitarist for a local rock band. I went to college in Albuquerque, so this was the glamorous big city for me, and I was in awe of everything metropolitan. Like a silly little groupie, I followed David to all his gigs to scream and clap. I was head over heels for him. When he asked me to marry him after two months together, I said yes. My parents were not thrilled, but they let me make my own mistakes. His parents hated me."

"How could anyone hate you? They must've been eejits."

"They weren't idiots, but they were snobs."

I was impressed she'd figured out "eejits" without asking, but then, she was an incredibly clever woman.

She sighed and closed her eyes. "David's parents thought I was trailer trash, told me so to my face. I pointed out I have never lived in a trailer in all my life, but they didn't care. I wasn't good enough for their little darling. David married me anyway. Everything was good for a few months—until he changed."

Keely lapsed into silence for several seconds.

Though I wanted to ask questions to prod her along, I held myself back. She needed to tell me in her own time.

"He wanted to be a rock star," she said. "When he announced he was moving to LA to pursue his dream, I assumed he would ask me to go with him. Instead, he announced he wanted a divorce."

"The *bod ceann* abandoned you?" I wanted to hunt down her first ex-husband and throttle him.

"What did you call him?"

"A dickhead, in Gaelic."

Her mouth started to tick upward, but the expression faltered. "I should've known better than to marry a guy for sex and rock 'n roll."

"You must have loved him."

"It's pathetic but true. I loved the *bod ceann*." She pulled in a long breath, blew it out, and sat up straighter. "A year later, I found out he'd married someone else and they had a baby. Last year, after my second divorce, I got maudlin and googled David. Turns out he and his wife own a music school and have three children. Sounds like they're happy."

Her tone was so miserable I longed to drag her into my arms and kiss her until she stopped thinking about the past. "You don't know how happy they are. What you've seen is the surface, the bits they choose to share with the world."

"I know, but it's not like I want David to be unhappy."

"Of course you don't. You're a kind person."

"Kind of bossy, you mean."

I hooked a finger under her chin and turned her face toward me. "I like your bossiness, you know that. It's not a fault. It's part of what makes you Keely O'Shea."

"My parents made me Keely O'Shea. They picked the name."

"Be quiet. I'm trying to pay you a compliment."

Her lips twitched, but she seemed unwilling to smile yet. "Go on, Mr.

MacTaggart. Pay me a compliment. Make it a good one, though. As soon as you're done, I'm going to tell you another pitiful story."

"Well, in that case, I'm thinking actions might do better than words."

I caught her face in my hands and gazed into her green irises, wondering if she might understand how much I thought of her if I stared long enough and deep enough into her eyes. The tension in her body eased, and she angled in a touch. I brushed my thumbs over her lips. They parted in response, and she angled in more, her eyes fluttering half closed.

"Keely," I murmured, "you are the most enchanting woman I've ever met. And I've traveled the world, met more kinds of women than most men will see in their lifetimes. You are exceptional in every way, far more than any of the silly girls who want to bed a billionaire or the married women who think they can make me their sex toy. You have a keen mind, a loving heart, and a strong will. You know who you are and what you can offer, and you never try to be something else. That's what makes you Keely O'Shea, the most incredible woman in the world."

Her lids popped open. "Holy shit, Evan."

"What? Did I say something wrong? I'm not the best with words, at least when it comes to expressing feelings. I'm sor—"

Her delicate fingers sealed my lips, silencing my apology. Her mouth curved into a sweet smile that made my chest ache in the strangest way.

"Don't apologize," she whispered. "What you said was perfect. Nobody has ever described me that way before, and I can't even think of words strong enough to express how much it means to me that you feel that way." She removed her fingers from my mouth. "Thank you, Evan."

"I spoke the truth, nothing more."

"Oh, it was a lot more." She crawled onto my lap, straddling me, and splayed her hands on my chest. "You are much more than a billionaire CEO. You are hands-down the smartest man I've ever met, you're sweet and thoughtful, sexy and demanding, but most of all you are one of a kind. I want to know you better. Considering the story I shared with you, I think it's time you shared something of equal value with me."

I had agreed to talking, and if I wanted her to trust me and concede we were dating, I had to share my past with her. I cleared my throat and tried to sit up straighter, but that only rubbed her body against parts of mine that wanted more of her.

She poked my chest with one finger. "Speak, Evan. I can't read your thoughts."

I groaned. "You know what that tone of voice does to me. How am I meant to reveal painful secrets when I'm hard as steel?"

"No more procrastinating. Tell me." She raked her nails down my skin. "If you answer one question for me, I'll do you right here and now." She curled the tip of her tongue over her front teeth, gliding it back and forth. "I'll do it with my mouth."

Keely's mouth. Around my cock. As if I hadn't been hard enough already, my dick shot stiffer than a flagpole.

I dug my fingers into the covers. "What's your question?"

"Are you ever going to tell me about your secret project?"

"Eventually."

"But not tonight." She analyzed me in silence, tapping her fingernails on my chest. "Okay, we can shelve that question for later. Here's another one. Why don't you get along with your mother?"

Though in my head I snarled a slew of Gaelic curses, I managed to stay calm on the outside when I answered. "My mother has been keeping a secret from me all my life. Even though I'm a grown man, she still won't tell me."

"How do you know there's something to know if it's a secret?"

"It's simple." I exhaled a long, heavy sigh. "I have no idea who my father is."

Chapter Nineteen

Keely

I searched his eyes for some clue to his mood since his expression had gone flat, but I couldn't find anything in his silvery irises either. At last, he'd shared something with me, but I sensed there was a lot more to the story. I itched to ask more questions. I didn't want to be too nosy. Since I had him talking, I needed to let him continue at his own speed the way he'd done with me. Tonight, here in this motel room, I felt closer to Evan than I ever had with anyone.

The hairs on my arms lifted, prickling my skin. I could not be falling for him. I didn't want to. Feeling close to him didn't mean I'd gotten attached to him. Still, the idea of getting attached to him didn't frighten me as much as it had a week ago.

Evan's expression softened, and he touched my cheek. "Go on. Ask your questions. I know you're dying to interrogate me, and I never want you to hold back because you're afraid I won't like it. Even if I don't like the question you ask, I always want you to feel free to ask it. Understand?"

"I think so. Thank you."

He settled his hands on my hips. "Ask away."

"Why won't your mother tell you who your father is? Isn't his name on your birth certificate?"

"There is no father's name on my birth certificate. My mother claimed she didn't know his name, but I realize now that was a lie. She knows. She doesn't want to tell anyone, not even me."

"I can't imagine not knowing something like that. It must be awful."

He shrugged. "It's been this way all my life. Other children cared more than I did about my family situation."

"What do you mean?"

"They taunted me. Called me names, all the things children do to be hurtful. It wasn't so much that my parents didn't marry, but more that I had no father. They called me an alien and said I was strange because my father came from Mars. That was the kindest thing they said." He rubbed his eyes with the heels of his hands. "It's part of why I was quiet as a lad. I still don't speak unless I have something worthwhile to say, though my cousins have been doing their best to cure me of that habit."

"You talk about your cousins a lot."

"They've become an important part of my life over the past year. I wish I hadn't waited so long to get to know them better."

"Better late than never." I paused to consider how to ask my next question. "Did your mother know other kids harassed you?"

"Aye. Teachers told her."

"What did she do?"

He scrunched his face into a pained expression. "Aileen MacTaggart is not a brazen woman. She's soft-spoken and kind, not inclined to confrontations. She spoke to the parents of the children who'd been taunting me the most, but the best thing she did for me was to give me advice."

"What did she say?"

"My mother told me to stop caring what others think of me and remember that the mean things they say come out of their own fears and insecurities. It has less to do with me than their own self-doubt. As long as I remember that, no one can hurt me." He smiled faintly. "She is clever, my mother. Almost as clever as you are."

"You love her, don't you? In spite of being angry with her for keeping a big secret."

"Of course I love her. She's my mother."

I let my hands fall to my thighs. "I guess I can't understand why a parent would refuse to tell their child anything about their father. It clearly bothers you, and that's why you have a strained relationship with your mother."

"Yes, but she's not a bad person. She was always a good mother." He leaned his head against the wall, his gaze retreating into the past. "She worked hard to support us both, doing all sorts of jobs until she settled on wool processing. Local farmers pay her to clean and spin the wool and even knit clothing from it, which they sell. She encouraged my interest in electronics and technology, even though she didn't understand it. When I went away to university, twice a week she would send me packages filled with things from home. At my graduation ceremony, she cried."

Aileen MacTaggart loved her son, and he loved her. That much I could tell not only from what he said but also from the way he said it. His tone of voice attested to it. The tension between Evan and his mother must've hurt all the more because they'd had a good relationship until recently.

"Do you get along with your parents?" he asked.

I knew he was trying to change the subject, to avoid the painful subject of his mother and his mystery father, but I took pity on him and answered the question. "Yes, I get along great with my parents. They got divorced when I was twenty-four, but there was no acrimony involved. They still talk on the phone once a week even though Mom moved to Seattle."

"If they like each other, why did they divorce?"

This would take a bit of explaining. "I was born in Philadelphia, Pennsylvania. My dad was a cop. It was very stressful for all of us knowing he might be injured or killed at any moment, but it was the worst for my mom. She stuck it out until my brothers and I all graduated from college, then she and Dad agreed to split up. Mom said she needed to be on her own, to find out what she wants to do with her life."

Evan did not speak, though he kept his steady gaze on me.

"I was upset about it at first," I said. "Eventually, I made peace with it. If my parents are happy, I'm happy. We had moved to Utah when I was fifteen. When my parents divorced, they told me the move had been for my mom's sake. Dad hoped Carrefour, Utah, would be a less dangerous place to be a cop."

"The move didn't ease your mother's worries."

"No, but it did make it easier for her to stay until my brothers and I finished college. It was important to her that she not split up the family before then. I respected her choice."

"My mother made different sorts of choices. You might say I had an unusual childhood."

"In what way?"

He twined a lock of my hair around his finger, around and around and around, concentrating on the task. "For one week every June, she would send me to stay with one of my uncles while she went on holiday. Whenever I asked where she was going, all she would say was 'abroad.' I learned to stop asking. There were rumors about where she went and why, but I also learned to stop listening to the gossip."

"Did other kids harass you about that too?"

"Aye. They liked to say my mother couldn't stand me because I'm strange and have Martian eyes, so she had to get away occasionally."

"I'm so sorry, Evan."

"Not your fault." He released my hair, letting it fall away from his finger. "Being with you is the first time I feel like I belong in this world."

My heart ached for him, for the lonely boy who'd been harassed and dismissed, and for the man who still couldn't figure out where he belonged. He'd built a business from the ground up and found incredible success, but finding his place in the world eluded him.

After everything he'd told me, I had to share more of myself. "Guess I should tell you about my second ex-husband and the in-between man."

"Not tonight. We've both opened up enough old wounds."

"You don't mind waiting for the rest?"

"I can wait as long as you need. You're being patient about my secret project, so I'll be patient too. Have to admit I'm curious about how an intelligent woman like you wound up with such bastards."

"I keep picking the wrong men," I said. "I fall for a pretty face and try to make it work even when it's obvious the relationship is doomed to fail. I am foolish and stupid."

"Keely, you are not foolish or stupid," he said in a tone so fierce I had to look at him. "Everyone makes mistakes."

He was forgiving me for my bad judgment. If only I could forgive myself so easily.

"Let me take you to dinner," he said. His mouth stretched into a wry smile. "Donnae worry, I won't call it a date."

Gazing into his eyes, I couldn't remember any of the reasons why I'd refused to get involved with him. He was kind, intelligent, considerate, passionate, determined, sexy. Evan didn't care about my terrible judgment concerning men or my pigheaded insistence we weren't dating. Maybe I could tell him everything—but not tonight. We needed time to decompress, time to get to know each other.

"Yes," I said, "we should go to dinner. It's our first official date."

"Are you sure? Dating is drastic after all."

"We both know I said that because this scares me. But I want to try. I think you're worth the risk." I picked up his hand, clasping it to my chest. "Evan MacTaggart, will you date me?"

"Yes, Keely O'Shea, I will date you."

"Whew," I said, sagging and sarcastically swiping a hand across my forehead. "I was afraid you'd turn me down."

"No you weren't." He took hold of my chin and touched his lips to mine. "I've been all but begging you to date me since the day you first walked into my office."

"Yes, but I've refused to call this a relationship. You must be annoyed about that."

"I could see you had reasons for your fears." He threw his arms around me, hugging me tight, and jumped off the bed with me still caged in his arms and my feet dangling in the air. "I knew you'd come around to my way of thinking eventually."

"You are so arrogant."

"Not arrogance." He set me down. "It's unwavering faith in you."

His words left me speechless. Unwavering faith? We'd known each other for two weeks. Yet somehow, those two words spoken by Evan made sense. He'd told me he believed fate brought us together. I didn't believe it, but it made sense that he did. This man had faith in everyone who mattered to him.

That meant I mattered to him. With a start, I realized he mattered to me too.

"While we're dating," he said, "I think we should have no distractions."

"Okay. What does that mean exactly?"

"Let's not have sex for two weeks."

"No sex?" I drew my head back, utterly confused by his proclamation. "You love sex. You're the man who couldn't keep your hands off me in Scotland."

"We couldn't keep our hands off each other."

"That's true, but it doesn't explain your celibacy idea."

"I want us to get to know each other without the distraction of sex."

The idea did make a certain kind of sense, an Evan kind, but my body rebelled against the idea of going two more weeks without feeling him inside me. "One week."

"Ten days."

"Deal. Should we sign a contract?"

"I don't have a pen or paper."

"No problem." I thrust a finger into my mouth, getting it good and damp, then signed my name on his bare chest with that finger. "There. Contract signed."

He wet his finger and signed my chest. "Now it's fully executed."

"No sex for ten days. Sure you can handle that?"

"Better than you will." He tapped a finger on the tip of my nose. "You're the predatory cougar who's determined to ravish a poor, defenseless thirty-year-old man twice your size."

"Ha-ha. You're not twice my size, anyway. One and a half times, maybe."

"One point one, to be precise."

"I'll take your word for that." I gestured at his body. "Better get dressed. I don't think there are any nudist restaurants in this town."

Evan nabbed the towel he'd discarded earlier and snatched up a stack of neatly folded clothes from the dresser. He carried all of it into the bathroom and shut the door.

I watched his fine behind until the door got in the way. That man did have the best ass I'd ever seen. And the best arms, the best legs, the best chest...and the best cock.

Sighing, I resigned myself to ten more days without my favorite part of his body.

I was dating again. How on earth had this happened? Evan tempted me to give up celibacy within minutes of meeting him. Tonight, he'd tempted me to try dating again. Whatever the circumstances, I never could resist him.

And I loved it.

Chapter Twenty

Evan

*A*fter our first official date, I said good night to Keely outside my motel room and watched her drive away. The next day, I started my employment at Vic's Electronics Superstore. Working under Keely proved to be a stimulating experience since she conducted my training herself and I got to admire her luscious body all day long. Her breasts bounced when she hopped up on her toes to reach a high shelf, giving me a chance to lend a hand and get an excellent view down her blouse. Whenever she crouched down, I wanted to reach out and lay my hands on that erse of hers. I knew she wouldn't appreciate me doing it in view of her employees.

Then again, I would enjoy having her discipline me. *Behave, Evan.* I loved the way she said that.

Every evening, we had another date. Sometimes we went to a restaurant and other times we curled up in my motel room to share a meal. On Saturday, the fourth full day of our fledgling relationship, Keely invited me to her home for dinner. We were strolling through a park in the city when she hit me with the suggestion.

"Is your father going out for the evening?" I asked, not joking at all since I assumed she wanted me nowhere near her family.

She surprised me with her answer. "No, Dad will be joining us. Serena would like to come too if you don't mind her fourteen-year-old son being there. When she told Chase you're Scottish, he apparently begged to join our little dinner party."

"Are you sure your father wants me there?" I couldn't believe he did, but maybe Mr. O'Shea planned to have the immigration authorities arrest me at the doorstep. Not that I was breaking any laws by being here.

"It was his idea," she said and nudged me in the side with her finger. "Nervous about meeting my dad, huh?"

"Aye. He was a police officer, which means he probably knows many different ways to murder me and dispose of the body without getting caught."

"You don't need to worry about that unless you criticize his choice of beer."

I must've looked worried—and I was, considering I'd never met a lass's family before—but instead of pitying me, she laughed.

"Relax," she said. "Dad is looking forward to meeting you. My mom wants to meet you too, but she can't get away from Seattle right now. She's an interior designer, and she's got a big project to finish up."

Her mother? I wasn't sure I'd survive meeting her father and already her mother wanted to come for a visit. "I've never met the parents of any woman I've dated or, ah..."

"Had a poke at?"

"Yes."

She hooked her arm under mine and rested her cheek against my shoulder. "Don't be nervous about it. I know you haven't dated much, so it's natural to feel anxious about this. My dad is not a cop anymore. He's a retiree whose favorite pastime is poking his nose into my love life. He's thrilled I'm dating you."

"In that case, I'd be happy to dine with the O'Sheas."

She pulled us to a halt and turned her face up to me. "There's one thing. My dad is in a wheelchair. He was badly injured in a car accident three years ago. A drunk driver hit him head-on."

"Is he all right?"

"The only lasting damage is the paralysis. He can't use his legs."

"Are you afraid I'll be disgusted because he's in a wheelchair?"

"No, but—" Her expression turned pained. "My ex-husband, the second one, hated living with a disabled person. He kept pushing me to put Dad in a nursing home, but I refused. It's part of why we split up."

Though I wanted to know all the reasons why, everything that scunner had done to her, I wouldn't push for more than she wanted to share. "Your father's medical condition doesn't bother me. And if we should ever live together, he's welcome to live with us too."

A relieved smile softened her expression, and her eyes glistened almost as if she were on the verge of crying. "I'm glad you feel that way. For some reason, I want you to meet my dad."

I supposed that was her subconscious way of admitting she cared for me.

The next evening, I pulled into the driveway of the O'Shea home on the outskirts of town. The white house was rather small but charming and well kept, with two stories and a neatly mowed lawn. Along the front, flowers in various shades of red, pink, and purple nestled against the house. A basket of yellow flowers hung on the stoop beside the door. As I climbed the steps, I heard muted voices inside followed by laughter.

I knocked on the door.

Keely pulled it open and smiled, her entire being seeming to glow with the expression. "Right on time. Come inside and meet the gang."

"Gang? Should I have brought a bodyguard?"

"Chill out." She slipped her hand into mine as I crossed the threshold into the vacant entryway. "They're going to love you."

"I was thirteen seconds late."

She pinched my cheek. "You're very cute when you're being precise."

Keely shut the door and guided me through an interior doorway into a cozy little dining room. A gray-haired man with green eyes slightly darker than Keely's occupied a wheelchair at the head of the table. A woman about Keely's age, with brown hair and gray eyes, had taken the chair directly to his right. A teenage boy sat beside her. The laddie had hair a shade darker than his mother's and he squirmed in his chair like he couldn't wait for dinner to begin.

"Hey," Keely's father said, smiling at me. "Welcome to the O'Shea homestead. Hope you like hot wings because we've got the extra spicy ones. That'll test your mettle for sure."

"Dad," Keely said with a tone not unlike the one she used to chastise me, "don't scare Evan away before he even sits down. Let him acclimate before you start ribbing him."

"Oh, don't worry," I said. "The MacTaggarts love to harass each other. I'm already acclimated and desensitized."

When I moved to sit in the chair second from her father's, Keely gave me a wee shove in the direction of the chair closest to him. I raised my brows. She pointed at the chair while making a stern face. The bossy lass wanted me to sit beside her father. Smiling, I took my seat next to the man of the house.

Keely settled into the chair beside me. "Evan, meet my father, Gary O'Shea."

The older man held out his hand to me. "Pardon me if I don't stand for the introductions."

A twinkle in his eyes assured me he was joking.

I shook his hand. "I'm—"

"This is Evan MacTaggart," Keely interjected before I could speak my own name. "He owns the company that's selling us all those spiffy doohickeys I told you about."

She glanced at me when she said the word doohickeys, and her lips kicked up slightly at one corner.

"What's your company called again?" the elder O'Shea asked. "Keely told me, but when you get old, stuff starts to fly in one ear and out the other."

"Dad remembers," Keely said. "Don't believe a word he says. His memory is like a steel trap."

Her father's smile turned mischievous. "Anything I do remember is still in there only because Keely ordered me to remember. In case you hadn't noticed, my daughter is kind of bloody-minded."

"Bloody-minded?" I said. "I didn't think Americans used that term."

"Most don't, but Keely makes me watch PBS shows about British people. Pretty soon I'll start talking with an accent."

"Try for a Scottish one. Women love it."

Gary O'Shea shot his daughter a meaningful glance. "Keely sure seems to like it."

I swore Keely blushed, not much and only for a split second, but I was sure I'd seen it.

She lowered her head, focused on unfolding her napkin and draping it over her lap.

Her father leaned back in his wheelchair. "So, what's the name of your company again?"

"Evanescent Security Technologies Limited."

"And what kind of whatsits do you make?"

"Surveillance and security devices for personal and business use." Since he looked confused, I added, "Spy gadgets. That's what your daughter calls them, Mr. O'Shea."

"Call me Gary." His lips curved into a crafty smile. "Maybe soon you'll be calling me Dad."

Keely blustered out a breath. "Honestly, Dad, we only started dating a few days ago."

"I thought you met in Scotland weeks ago. What were you doing if you weren't dating?"

Keely froze, her eyes wide and unblinking.

She didn't want her father to know we'd been shagging relentlessly and that she had refused to date me.

I laid my hand over hers on her lap, under the table where no one else could see. To Gary, I said, "We weren't calling it dating, officially. At first, we were sightseeing together. I was Keely's tour guide, showing her the city where I live."

He nodded slowly. "Okay. But why did it take you so long to show up here? I mean, if you really like my daughter you should've come home with her in your jet."

Keely tensed even more, her fingers crooking into her thighs.

I squeezed her hand and caressed it with my thumb. "Keely was anxious to come home, and I had business to finish up before I could follow."

Keely's friend Serena shook her head, a slight smile on her lips. She must've known Keely had refused to get involved in anything more than a fling with me.

Serena's son lodged his elbow on the table and propped his head on his fist. "Are we gonna eat this century? I'm starving."

His mother shot him a chastising look. "Chase, don't be rude. And get your elbow off the table. We're guests, and we'll eat when our hosts are ready for us to eat."

"We eat here all the time. Since when are we guests?"

"Since tonight. Apologize to our hosts for being disrespectful."

The boy bowed his head, seeming well chastened, and mumbled, "Sorry, Keely. Sorry, Mr. O'Shea."

Gary made a dismissive noise.

"Oh!" The word burst out of Keely. "I didn't finish the introductions. Evan, this is Serena Carpenter and her son, Chase. Serena is Dad's home care nurse, but we've been friends since high school."

I half rose and leaned across the table to shake Serena's hand. When I offered my hand to Chase, his eyes widened.

The laddie gawped at my hand for a moment, then gingerly shook it. "Nice to meet you."

"Pleasure to meet you, Mr. Carpenter."

"Mister? Nobody's ever called me that."

"You seem mature enough to deserve it. Formality is a show of respect."

He gawped again, fleetingly this time. "Thanks, Mr. MacTaggart."

"Since I'd like us to be friends, maybe we should be less formal. You can call me Evan."

"Cool. You can call me Chase."

With the introductions done, we all settled in for a dinner prepared by Keely. Back in Scotland, she had cooked for me once. Tonight's feast outdid our picnic along the River Ness, at least in terms of the food.

After sampling all the offerings, I leaned in to tell Keely, "This is the best food I've had in years."

"Thank you. I don't do fancy stuff, but I manage with the basics."

"Basics? This is a feast fit for kings. You are a superb cook."

"You're only saying that because—" She noticed her father watching us and wriggled, clearing her throat. "Because we're dating."

I suspected she'd been about to say something inappropriate for a family gathering.

After dinner, I tried to help clean up but was summarily informed by Keely that guests did not have to pitch in. Serena insisted Keely should stay with the "guest of honor" while she and her son handled clearing the table and washing the dishes. When Gary excused himself to "hit the head," Keely jumped up, determined to help him.

He waved her away. "I can get myself to the bathroom, kiddo. Been doing it all day every day while you're at work. Haven't needed help for a long time."

The man did have well-developed arm muscles that strained his short-sleeve shirt. I had no doubts Gary could take care of himself.

Keely seemed doubtful, though. "You might fall."

"For Pete's sake, Keely, I don't need a mother hen." He cast a sly glance at me. "Why don't you see if Evan needs help? I'm sure he'd appreciate your nurturing instincts."

"Aye, I would."

"There ya go." Gary slapped his hands on the wheelchair's arms. "It's settled."

Keely's shoulders sagged. She had apparently realized the futility of arguing with her father, who seemed as stubborn as his daughter. She returned to her chair and slumped onto it.

Gary rolled out into the hallway.

I draped my arm over the back of Keely's chair and slanted in to whisper in her ear. "You can nurture me all ye like."

"Uh-huh."

"What were you about to say before you stopped yourself? After I said you're a superb cook."

Keely eyed me sideways, her frown twisting upward. "I almost said you're only saying that because you want to get laid."

"Love to get laid, but we have an agreement. Our ten days aren't up yet."

"Unfortunately." She sank back into her chair, letting out a long breath. "Thank you for being so gracious with my dad, and with Serena and Chase. They like you a lot."

"I like them too. Thank you for inviting me to dinner."

She laid a hand on my leg, sliding it down to my inner thigh, and massaged my flesh with her delicate fingers. "Couldn't we forget the ten-day agreement? You look so good tonight, I've been incredibly horny all through dinner."

Gary wheeled back into the dining room.

Keely's cheeks turned pink. With a nervous little laugh, she said, "Dad, I didn't hear you coming. Must've gotten those wheels greased, huh?"

Gary took his position at the head of the table. "I heard a rumor there's dessert."

Keely gave me a questioning look.

If she'd hoped I could clear up the mystery of whether her father had heard our discussion a moment ago, I had no help to offer. The man seemed to have a wheelchair equipped with stealth technology.

Serena and Chase returned then, carrying plates loaded with cake and ice cream.

The next evening, on our sixth date, we ordered pizza and had it delivered to my motel room. We sat on the floor eating, joking, and generally enjoying each other's company. Keely told me funny stories about her family, and I told her about some of the crazy antics my cousins had gotten up to over the years.

"Why don't you talk about your childhood?" she asked after wolfing down a large bite of pizza. "I know all about your cousins, but I'd like to know more about you. What did little Evan do for fun?"

"He played with broken televisions and radios. When I was ten, my aunts and uncles banded together to buy me my first computer since my mother couldn't afford it. That's when I started trying to write code. I've never been adept at it, though."

"Didn't you ever have fun?"

"Creating something new out of something old was fun for me."

She set down her fourth slice of pizza. "Come on, Evan. You must've done something other than writing computer code and tinkering with dead electronics."

"I never had any real friends, but my cousins would invite me over to play games with them." I bit off a mouthful of my food, the cheese stretching instead of breaking. I snapped the cheese string with my finger and slurped it into my mouth. Keely smiled and laughed. I loved making her smile. After consuming the bite of pizza, I said, "My cousins tried to teach me to play shinty, but I never took to the game. They still keep trying to get me to join their matches when they play against the Buchanans."

"What is shinty?"

"It's similar to lacrosse and field hockey, but not exactly like either. We carry sticks called camans and try to knock a ball around and stop the other side from getting it."

"You don't like the game."

"The game is fine. What I don't like is how inept I am at it."

"But you're supposed to be having fun with your cousins." She tipped her head to the side. "Or do they razz you about not being a star player?"

"No, they never do that."

"Then stop worrying and just enjoy it."

While I gnawed on another slice of pizza, I considered Keely. "When was the last time you did something purely for fun?"

"I took a vacation in Scotland."

"You started it as a business trip. Your holiday was a second thought, and you only had a good time because I forced you to."

"Forced me?" She snatched up her pizza slice and shoved it into her mouth, tearing off half the slice and chomping on it. Her voice was muffled by the enormous chunk of food in her mouth. "I know how to have a good time, with or without you."

"Name one thing you've done strictly for the fun of it without me."

She gulped down her food and ripped off a much smaller bite. While she chewed, her eyes narrowed as if she were pondering her response. She raised a finger. "I went to the Louvre when I was in France last year."

"A museum?" I said in a mock scoffing tone. "That's not real fun."

"You love museums."

"That's irrelevant."

She devoured the last of her fourth slice of pizza and wiped her hands with a napkin. "Okay, Mr. Smart-Ass MacTaggart, tell me one thing you've done strictly for fun without me."

"That's easy. I let my thirteen-year-old cousin, Malina, teach me how to use a pogo stick."

"You played with a teenage girl?"

"She's my cousin, and she insisted I had to learn to bounce around on a small stick."

"But did you enjoy it?"

I contemplated the pizza slice in my hand. "Yes, I did. Donnae go telling my other cousins I liked it, or I'll never hear the end of it."

"You're implying I might meet them sometime."

"Would you want to meet my family? It's a bit larger than yours."

She picked up a napkin and dabbed at her mouth, though she had no food there. "How do you think your mother would feel about you dating an older woman?"

"My mother does not choose my girlfriends for me."

"Thought you'd never had a girlfriend. I'm too old to be called that, anyway."

I dumped my pizza slice back into the box, my appetite gone. "You are the first woman I've genuinely dated, the first I've been interested in dating. But you are not too old to be anyone's girlfriend. What would you rather I call you?"

"Not sure."

"How about Mrs. MacTaggart?"

"Oh please. We've known each other for a couple of weeks." She waved a hand as if to shoo away the idea. "I know you're not serious. You're teasing me again."

I hadn't been serious at first, not until she'd dismissed the idea like it was pure nonsense. "What if I am serious?"

"You're talking to someone who's been divorced twice. What makes you think I ever want to go through that again?"

"Maybe I could understand better if you told me about your second ex-husband."

"Not now."

"When?"

She got up and brushed off her pants. "I should get home. It's late."

I realized she wasn't going to tell me anything tonight. My pseudo-proposal had knocked her off balance, and considering her two failed marriages, I couldn't blame her for being uneasy. Maybe tomorrow she would tell me about scunner number two.

She let me kiss her good night—a relatively chaste kiss by our standards—and then she left.

I lay awake for a long time wondering if I had been serious about wanting to marry her. Did I love Keely? We'd known each other for such a short time. All I knew for certain was that I wanted her in my life for longer than a few weeks. She meant more to me than a sexual partner or even a casual affair.

About time I proved that to her.

Chapter Twenty-One

Keely

On the tenth day since we'd made our no-sex pact, Evan clomped into my office, shut the door, and flopped onto the sofa. He spread his arms over the sofa's back, plunking his feet on the table, and crossed his ankles. "Tonight, we're fucking."

I spun around in my desk chair to face him. "We are at work. No sex talk in the office."

"Maybe we should do it right now." He made a deep growly noise in his throat. "Not sure I can look at you for much longer without shoving your skirt up and having ye on that desk."

And of course, my body sizzled to full awareness of him. Memories of all the times he'd taken me rushed through my mind, and wetness blossomed between my thighs. My gaze gravitated to his groin and the swelling bulge that stretched his tan slacks. My mouth watered. I'd wanted to take him in my mouth on that first night after he showed up in town. There in his motel room, I'd promised I would do it if he talked to me. We'd gotten distracted by our emotional confessions and I didn't get the chance.

He was right here. Aroused. Hardening. His gaze burning into me like he wanted to devour every inch of my body.

I couldn't. Not in my office.

Evan wet his lips with one long, slow glide of his tongue. "You're wearing the outfit you had on the first day you walked into my office. That blouse gets tighter when you move or when you lean forward like you're doing now. Almost looks like the buttons will pop loose and the fabric will fall open. Makes me want to go over there and suck one of your stiff little nipples into my mouth."

I glanced down to see I had tilted forward just enough to make my shirt tighten. My nipples had gone hard, and my breasts ached. I longed to rip off my shirt and bra, to let Evan do whatever he wanted to me.

"We're at work," I said. Why did my voice sound husky? It was inappropriate. At work, I maintained my boss-to-employee demeanor.

Except with Evan. He made me want to be inappropriate anytime, anywhere.

His phone jingled. He dug it out of his pocket, checked the screen, and frowned.

"Bad news?" I asked.

"No, it's nothing." He stuffed the phone back into his pocket, and his sensual smile returned. "What were we talking about? Oh yes, how I'm going to ravish you."

"You should get back to work."

"Come over here and I'll gladly get to work—on removing your clothes."

"I have a better idea." I walked to the door, engaged the lock, and ambled over to the sofa to stop in front of Evan. Inch by inch, I lowered myself to kneel between his legs with my hands spread on his thighs. "Remember the first night in your motel room?"

"Yes."

"Remember what I promised I'd do if you answered my questions?"

"Aye." His gaze was locked on mine, and his chest rose and fell with breaths that grew heavier by the second. "I remember."

"It's about time I fulfilled that promise."

His brows rose. His lips kinked into a smile of anticipation and surprise.

"Don't look so shocked," I said as I unhooked the button on his slacks. "I'm an older, experienced woman."

"That does have its benefits, eh?" He rested his hands on the cushions at either side of his thighs. "You're not shy about anything, are you? That's part of what makes you a fantastic lover."

"Only part of it?" I took hold of his zipper. "What's the rest?"

"Your enthusiasm, your energy, your bossiness." He exhaled a long, groaning sigh while I eased his zipper down. "And I love how wet you always are for me. But my favorite part is the way you come, like it's the first time you've ever had an orgasm and you can't believe how good it is. You abandon yourself to the feeling and let it take over. Keely O'Shea in the throes of a climax is the most erotic thing I've ever seen."

I paused in pulling down his zipper and rolled my eyes up to see him. "You mean that, don't you?"

"Do you think I'd lie?"

"No, but—" I swallowed against a constriction in my throat. "Other men haven't been as complimentary about having sex with me."

"I'd like to know more about that. Your relationships with those other men, I mean. Every one of them sounds like a *bod ceann*."

Bod ceann. What a strange and endearing term for a dickhead. I couldn't help smiling. "Think I'll be using that word a lot. I can insult people and they won't have a clue they're being insulted. But let's save the discussion of my exes until later."

"Keely—"

I flattened the heel of my hand over the firm bulge of his erection trapped inside his pants. I rubbed up and down until he winced. "Talk later."

"Aye," he hissed. "Later."

With my thumb and forefinger, I grasped his zipper again and pulled it down, revealing his beautiful, naked dick. "Thought you ditched the underwear only in your off hours. You're at work today."

"Needed to feel you around my cock as soon as possible. Shorts get in the way."

"Damn, I wish this was Monday so I could lift your skirt for a change."

"The only time I wear a kilt on a day other than Monday is when I'm at home with my cousins."

I wanted to know more about that, about why he'd called the place where his cousins lived "home" instead of Inverness. He lived there almost exclusively as far as I knew. I didn't know as much as I wanted to know about him, considering I'd agreed to this dating thing.

At the moment, I had a more pressing task that demanded my full attention.

Taking his cock in my hand, I blew a breath across the head and curled my fingers around its impressive girth. His head fell back against the sofa. I slid my fist up and down his length. His mouth was open, and his eyes were half closed. I pumped slowly, methodically, watching his every reaction. My nipples pushed against my bra, their tips so rigid they ached, the friction arousing me even more. His fingers clenched the cushions. His breaths grew uneven, coming faster and harder.

A drop of moisture poised on the head of his erection. I licked it away and sealed my mouth around the tip.

He made a choked noise.

"Mmmm," I purred, "you taste better than an ice-cream sundae."

I cupped his sac with one hand, holding the base of his shaft with the other, and took his length deep into my mouth. His back arched. I moved my mouth up and down, alternately licking and sucking, loving the taste of him and the firmness of his erection, the velvety smoothness of his flesh and the way he hissed in each breath through his gritted teeth. I rubbed the flesh between his sac and his ass. His entire body jerked. His mouth open, he hauled in heavy breaths and bucked his hips every time I sank my mouth over his cock. When I began to glide my hand up and down in time with the thrusts of my mouth, he flung a hand up to grip the sofa's back and plowed the other hand into my hair.

"Christ," he spluttered. "Keely, I—*bod an Donais.*"

Pulling my mouth away, I milked him with my hand.

His cheeks had gone ruddy. His gaze was glued to me, his chest heaved, and I knew from the tension in his body that he was on the edge.

And I burned to push him over it.

I raked my tongue over his head.

His fingers in my hair crooked into my scalp, scraping it, the action enough to expose his need but not enough to break the skin. "Keely, I cannae—ye donnae have to—ahhh."

A knock rattled the door. "Keely? A shipment arrived. I know you like to unpack those yourself."

What were the odds? The one time I was going down on a man in my office somebody had to interrupt.

Though I stopped working his shaft, I kept my hand around it. "Be there in a minute, Paige. Get back to the counter, please."

"Okay."

I waited several seconds to make sure she'd left the vicinity before I gave Evan's cock a long, slow lick from the base to the head. He squeezed his eyes shut, his features contorted with need. I flicked my tongue over the slit on the underside, again and again, while I pumped him with my hand.

His body went rigid, frozen with his back bowed and his mouth open.

With one final flick of my tongue, I swallowed his shaft.

Evan exploded. He choked back a cry.

I grabbed a tissue off the box on the table and wiped him down with it. "Sorry I don't have a damp towel to clean you off with. I wasn't expecting to do this, but the mood struck and..." I wiped my mouth and smacked my lips. "I couldn't resist."

He gaped at me, struggling to catch his breath. "Keely, you are incredible. The best lover I've ever had."

"The best ever?" I smiled and parked my bottom on the tabletop. "That's quite the compliment, Mr. MacTaggart."

He ran a hand through his hair and did up his pants. "You've earned the compliment. I was right, you do have no shame at all."

And he liked that about me, which made me like him all the more.

Evan squinted at me, his head tipped to the side. "Those erseholes made you feel ashamed of your enthusiasm for sex, didn't they?"

"They weren't adventurous." I clasped my hands on my lap. "They all liked getting blow jobs, but apparently I was too enthusiastic about it. Bryce, my second ex-husband, said it was unseemly for a woman to enjoy giving a man oral sex. I asked him how exactly he thought I should act about it, and he told me I should be more demure."

Evan twisted his face into a look of sheer disgust and disbelief. "The scunner had an incredible woman in his bed, and all he could do was suggest you be demure? *Mhac na galla.*"

"What does that one mean?"

"Son of a bitch." He shook his head. "Cannae believe these bloody erseholes you were involved with. Didn't even one of them appreciate you the way you are?"

"No, not really."

He sat forward and grasped my hands. "No wonder you're afraid to get involved with me. I'd like to know more about the second ex-husband."

"I have to get out there and check that shipment."

"That's what employees are for. Delegate, Miss O'Shea."

I lifted my head to aim a sarcastic look at him. "Right, you know all about delegating. You're so skilled at it that you have to go to the factory when somebody orders the wrong part."

"That was different."

"Sure it was." I jumped up and patted the top of his head. "You scoot on out of here like a good little employee and get back to work or else I'll have to reprimand you."

A sly grin spread across his face. "I'd love that."

I smacked his arm with the back of my hand. "Go, Evan. You're supposed to be working here like everybody else."

"Do all your employees get serviced by the assistant manager?"

"Oh sure, I go down on everybody." I grabbed his arm and tugged. "Get up. Go. Pronto."

He rose in a leisurely manner, stretching and yawning. "My boss wears me out."

I pushed him toward the door. "Shoo."

"Aren't you coming? You have that important shipment to unpack and verify like the bossy wee boss you are."

"Be there in a minute. Scoot."

I waved for him to leave.

He slung an arm around my waist and dragged me into his body for a kiss. The second our lips met, I melted into him. He didn't thrust his tongue into my mouth, though. He held the kiss for a long moment, our lips fused, my heartbeat accelerating with each passing second. Then, he walked out the door.

For the next hour, I unpacked the shipment and verified every item on the purchase order matched the contents of the three boxes. After that, I recruited Evan and Paige to help me carry the boxes into the back room where we kept our inventory that wasn't out on the floor. I'd already selected the items to put on the shelves and left them on the customer service counter. We stowed the boxes and returned to the floor to put the new items out on the shelves and racks.

Every time I knelt down or bent over, I caught Evan admiring my ass.

And every time he knelt down or bent over, I ogled his ass.

I ate lunch alone in my office since Evan had told me last night he had an important errand to run today. For the rest of the afternoon, I slaved over spreadsheets and purchase orders while Evan stayed out on the floor. When I went to the restroom, I came back to my office to find a package awaiting me on my desk. The slim, rectangular box was white and held shut with a satin ribbon.

Plopping into my chair, I rolled it forward and untied the satin bow. I removed the box's lid. Inside it lay a black garment, folded neatly. I lifted the garment out by its straps.

A halter dress, a short and sexy one.

I noticed a small card inside the box and picked it up. A note written in Evan's hand said, "Wear this tonight. Meet me at my place at seven."

After that, he'd scrawled an address. It was not the address of his motel.

What on earth was he up to this time?

I returned the dress to its box and tried to focus on work, but my gaze kept wandering back to the box and my mind kept wondering what he had planned.

Chapter Twenty-Two

Evan

At precisely seven o'clock, I watched from the porch while Keely pulled her ancient car into the driveway of the house on Elm Avenue. As soon as her car had come to a stop and she'd shut off the engine, I trotted over to open the driver's door for her. Her closed lips curled up in a sweet smile. I offered her my hand, and she laid her elegant one in my palm to let me help her out of the vehicle. In her other hand, she grasped what looked like a small briefcase.

I kissed her cheek. "Good evening, Keely. What have you brought with you?"

"Good evening," she said carefully as if she expected a terrible surprise at any moment. She held up the strange little case. "It's my overnight bag."

"Planning to stay the night, then?"

"Absolutely."

I took half a step backward to admire her outfit. "You are breathtaking in that dress. You're always breathtaking, of course, but you make that dress more than a piece of fabric. It's a masterpiece on you."

"I never know how to respond to your over-the-top compliments. 'Thank you' doesn't seem like enough." She swept her gaze up and down my body. "You are breathtaking too. I love the suit. It shows off all your gorgeous muscles. I have to admit I'm a little disappointed you didn't wear a kilt."

"Next time I'll get out the kilt."

She glanced around. "What is this place?"

"A house." I spread one arm to indicate the entirety of the large, two-story structure. "Welcome to my new home."

"Your what?" She tipped her head to the side and squinted her eyes. "You rented a mansion?"

"No, I bought a house."

"Why?"

Did she have to sound so baffled by the idea? I'd hoped she might be happy I was planting roots here in America, hoped she might see it as a commitment to our relationship. Instead, she acted like I'd done something insane. Again.

"I'm tired of the motel," I explained. "Since I'll be here for a while, I thought buying a house would be the best option. Financially, it's a better investment than renting."

"How long are you planning to stick around? I thought this was a brief stint undercover at the store so you could learn about our business."

For pity's sake, she wasn't that dense. Was she? I'd thought only men misunderstood things that were obvious, but Keely was proving me wrong. An intelligent woman like her couldn't fail to see the truth. With an inward groan, I realized she would. Keely had called dating "drastic." She wouldn't want to admit what we both knew because she was afraid.

Taming Keely might take longer than I'd anticipated.

I ran a hand over my jaw, trying not to get annoyed. "We both know bloody well why I'm here in America and why I wanted to work undercover at the store. You are the reason."

"But I didn't think…I mean, I assumed you would get bored and go home."

"Ah, Keely." I rubbed my hands up and down her arms. "I'm not like those other men. You are my priority, above business, above everything else. I want us to work. No matter how long it takes, I will prove you can trust me."

"I'm your priority? But you're obsessed with work."

"I was. Not anymore." I dug my phone out of my pocket, turned on the screen, and aimed it at her. "Here's the proof. Have a look."

Keely squinted at the screen, reading the words on it. Her gaze flew to me. "You have ten missed calls from Tamsen Spurling and a dozen texts from her."

"Aye."

"Why are you ignoring her? She says you need to call her ASAP."

"I'll call her when I'm good and ready." I returned the phone to my pocket. "Tonight, I'm focused on you, on us. Work doesn't seem as important anymore."

"But your company. What if it falls apart without you?"

"Thank you for assuming I'm indispensable, but I've got a company full of well-trained, intelligent, resourceful men and women who are thoroughly capable of running Evanescent without me."

"You're the CEO."

For the moment. I was considering retirement or at least a severe cutback in how much time I spent on the company. Telling her that tonight would only escalate her anxiety. I suspected she'd never been with a man who'd valued her above everything else.

I placed an arm around her shoulders and guided her toward the porch. "Let's forget about work for tonight. I have a surprise for you in the backyard."

"Do I want to know what surprise you have up your sleeve this time?"

"It wouldn't fit up my sleeve. It's in the backyard."

We strolled through the house, pausing so Keely could set down her overnight bag. She turned in a circle to take in the high-ceilinged entryway and the curving staircase that led to the second floor. I would show her the rest of the house later. Right now, I guided her past the staircase and through the large kitchen and walked us out the back door into the yard.

Keely froze, not even blinking. "What is this?"

"What it looks like. A special setting just for you."

I watched her while she absorbed the scene I'd created. Her shock gradually dissolved into a smile of pure delight.

The patio housed a glass-top table that I'd outfitted with a white table-cloth, and I'd set out all the dishes and silverware we might need along with the appropriate glassware. Two candles occupied the center of the table, their flames flickering gently. All around the spacious yard, I'd set up torch-es to light the surroundings with a romantic, golden glow. A cart held all the foods I'd prepared, hidden under half-dome covers, and an ice bucket held a bottle of champagne.

I escorted Keely to the table, pulled out her chair, and pushed it back in when she sat down.

"Thank you," she said, still with a hint of disbelief in her voice.

"You're welcome." I moved to the cart and plucked the metal cover off one plate, then carried it to the table. I placed it in front of Keely. "Your meal, prepared by me."

"Wow. This looks delicious. Is that salmon?"

"Yes, with a butter sauce and served on a bed of wild rice and with garlic potatoes on the side."

"Mmm," she hummed, dipping her head to inhale the scents of the food. "This smells heavenly."

She took a deep breath, drawing in more of the scents. The halter dress plunged low over her chest, giving me a breathtaking view from this height. When she'd inhaled so deeply, her full breasts had lifted—and all the blood had evacuated my brain, pouring straight into my groin.

I rushed back to the cart to give Keely my back, so she wouldn't notice the erection growing inside my slacks. My suit jacket didn't extend low enough to hide my response to her sensual body. I'd wanted tonight to be about getting to know each other better, with sex afterward. My cock had a different plan, but I meant to hold it back as long as possible.

After popping the cork on the champagne, I poured some into each of our glasses. I settled into my chair and held out my glass. "A toast to us. To the future, whatever it may hold, and to the bonnie woman sharing an evening with me."

Keely hesitated but finally raised her glass to clink it against mine. "To a lovely evening."

We sipped our champagne and set down our glasses.

Keely speared a bite of salmon and slid the fork between her lips. She withdrew it slowly, moaning with satisfaction as she consumed her food.

"This is so good," she said, her voice sultry. "You are an amazing cook, Evan."

I shifted in my seat, but instead of alleviating my discomfort, it made my dick go harder. "Glad you like the food."

"The setup is gorgeous too." She took in the torch-lit scene. "You sure know how to romance a girl."

"You're a woman, Keely, and this is all for you. Only you."

"Are you saying you've never gone all out like this for anyone else?"

I shook my head, tore off a chunk of fish with my fork, and jammed it into my mouth. Focusing on my food gave me an excuse to look away from her and to try to forget, for a moment, how stunning she was in that dress. But I couldn't forget. "I'd like us to talk more."

"We are talking." She took another bite of salmon.

"I meant we should get to know each other more. Talk about our pasts."

She swallowed a mouthful of rice and pointed her fork at me. "You have mommy issues, I have man issues, end of story."

"There's more to us than that." I poked at my fish but couldn't get interested in eating it anymore. "You haven't told me about your second ex-husband or the man in between husbands."

Keely set down her fork, leaning back in her chair. "Not much to tell. Wes, the man in between, convinced me living together was better than marriage. We didn't need a piece of paper to prove our commitment to each other, we had real love, blah, blah, blah. I went along with it because my first marriage had gone bust. Maybe Wes was right. Who needs marriage?"

I regarded her in silence, her face lit by the golden glow of the candles and torches. The lighting imbued her face with an ethereal quality that didn't match her melancholy expression. "A relationship like that might work for other people, but you don't seem like the sort of woman who believes marriage is a sham. Since the night we met in Paris, I've known you're a woman who needs a serious commitment, the sort a man wants to marry even if he didn't believe in marriage before."

She fiddled with her silverware. "That's the problem. I was trying to be what Wes wanted because I wanted him. Once again, I fell for a pretty face and expected to find a lasting relationship at the end of the rainbow. All I got was a downpour. After four years and eleven months together, I cautiously suggested maybe we could get married after all."

"I take it he didn't react well to the suggestion."

"Nope." She smacked her knife down on the table and met my gaze head-on. "He summarily dumped me. Two weeks later, Wes moved in with a twenty-year-old college student. I was twenty-nine, about to turn thirty, and no longer a hot property."

Not a hot property? American men were bleeding morons if they dismissed a beautiful, sensual woman like Keely as being too old at twenty-nine. I couldn't accept all American men held that opinion about women, but Keely seemed to attract erses who did.

"He was an eejit," I said. "You are a hot property even today. That *bod ceann* has no idea what he lost."

She picked at the tablecloth, her gaze downcast. "After Wes, I realized I shouldn't try to be what a man wants. If he can't love me the way I am, we don't belong together."

"Dead right."

Her lips twitched upward. "Thanks for the vote of confidence, but I haven't exactly found relationship bliss by being myself either. Men don't like a bossy woman, particularly in the bedroom. I'm overzealous and domineering, that's what other men have said."

"About sex with you?" I grunted. "Donnae believe a word any of those other men said. You are the most passionate, exciting woman I've ever taken to bed. You are not domineering. You know what you like and speak up about it. I love those qualities. I love everything about you."

I realized I'd said too much the instant her demeanor changed. Her back went straight as a pole, her shoulders rolled back, and her chin lifted. Whether she was upset about my compliments or about my use of the L word, I couldn't tell for sure.

"That's nice," she said, her tone far too even, "but you would probably say anything to make sure we have sex tonight. You've gone without for weeks."

"It's been twenty days. And yes, I'm looking forward to making love to you tonight." I was fighting back the stiffest erection I'd ever had but keeping that fact to myself didn't seem like lying. It was self-preservation. "You did take care of my needs in your office this afternoon. It wasn't making love, but it eased the pressure."

"I wish you wouldn't call it that."

"Making love? That's what it is. Why does the term fash you?"

"Because men like to say they're making love to me, say they love me even, but they don't mean it." She picked up her champagne glass and swigged the bubbly liquid. "Words are empty."

"You're trying to end the conversation so you won't have to share anything else with me. I don't give up that easily."

"I'm all too familiar with your pigheaded nature."

"Tell me about your second husband."

She downed the rest of her champagne in one gulp, smacking her glass down on the table. "This is turning into a one-sided conversation. I rip open my old wounds so you can gawk at the blood while you sit there safe and sound, not sharing anything."

Was I doing that? I supposed so. The only things I hadn't told her already involved the worst mistakes I'd made, but none of them involved romantic relationships. I had nothing of equal value to tell her. It was no excuse, and I knew it. Her pain centered on the men in her life, while my secrets centered on my business.

If I didn't open up to her soon, I'd lose her. She was already upset over my reticence. Here, tonight, I had to take a chance on whether she could understand the things I'd done.

"You're right," I said, slouching into my chair. "I'm sorry. You know I don't have past relationships to tell you about, but there are things I've done. Things I'm not proud of. You might not want to be with me once you know what I'm capable of."

"You're a good man. I don't believe you have ever done anything so bad I can't get past it."

I rubbed the bridge of my nose, making my glasses jump. "I hope that's true."

"Trust me."

Her words, spoken with conviction, made me raise my eyes to look at her. "Do you trust me?"

"Yes, I do."

An odd pain ached behind my ribs. I scrubbed at my chest with the heel of my hand, but the sensation wouldn't go away. "I trust you too, so I'd better tell you everything."

"Take your time. I'm not going anywhere."

I emptied my entire glass of champagne in one swallow. I laid my hands on my lap. Folded my arms over my chest. Rested my elbows on the table. Deep under my skin, an itch started. I couldn't scratch it away. The itch was in my mind, in my soul, and nothing could get rid of it.

Unless...Would telling Keely everything banish the itch?

I loosened my tie and unhooked the top button of my shirt. "I need to start at the beginning. At university, my focus was on electronics, but I dabbled in computer programming. I was approached by a security company that wanted me to test their systems for vulnerabilities. I'd shown an aptitude for finding the holes in software and security systems, and the job paid very well, so I took it. After that, word got around that I was the man to call if you were concerned about your system being compromised. I would ferret out the weaknesses and correct them. I made a good living at it, enough to pay for my education."

"That's amazing. I already knew you're a genius."

Her tender smile made my chest ache again. "That was the start. After university, I tried working for other companies in regular, salaried jobs. I hated it. I'd gone from deciding which projects to take on and doing the work on my own to answering to superiors who knew less than I did. They got their jobs because of connections, not based on merit. Finally, I'd had enough and decided to go out on my own."

"I've been wondering how you got so rich so fast."

"You're about to hear the answer." I reached for my champagne glass, realized it was empty, and grabbed the bottle to slosh more into my glass. When I lifted it to my lips, I noticed Keely watching me with that schoolteacher look. I set the glass down. "Getting drunk won't help, I know. I have never told anyone what I'm about to tell you."

She got up and walked around the table to me. "I get that you're anxious about telling me. It's okay. Nothing you say will change my mind about us."

"You haven't heard it yet."

"Don't need to." She perched her bottom on my lap with her legs draped across my thighs and looped her arms around my neck. "I trust you, so stop worrying and spill your guts."

I did feel a bit like I was slashing my stomach open with a machete. A moment ago, she'd described our one-sided conversation as ripping open old wounds so I could gawp at them. It was my turn to do the same for her. Not that I believed she would gawp. No, Keely would want to heal those wounds, the way I wanted to heal hers.

Sighing, I hooked my arms around her waist. "When I decided to start my own company, I told my cousins about it. Didn't ask for money. I was just talking. We weren't close back then, but they still wanted to help me. I didn't want them to do it because I was afraid I'd lose everything they'd invested, considering that most new businesses fail. Lachlan, Rory, and Iain insisted on giving me the money outright as a gift. They're wealthy and very generous to everyone, not only to me."

"But you're family. They wanted to help you more than they do strangers."

"I didn't understand why at the time. I've never had close family other than my mother."

"You said you played with your cousins when you were a kid."

"Aye, but we weren't close. Most of them were much older than I was." I felt my forehead tighten as I thought back on those days when I'd been the odd boy no one wanted for a friend. "Iain is twenty years older. Lachlan is fourteen years older, and Rory has eleven years on me. They were adults before I reached puberty. Aidan and Jamie were around the same age, so I did spend time with them. I wasn't good at sports, though, and my interest in math and technology didn't appeal to them. It wasn't until last year, when Iain and his new wife made me their project, that things changed. That's when I finally started to understand why my cousins gave me their money and expected nothing in return."

"And what did you realize?"

"Even back then, when I was more of a recluse, I was their family and family is very important to the MacTaggarts."

"They love you. That's why they gave you money."

"And they felt that way even before I made an effort to be a part of the family." I gazed into her green eyes, seeing reflections of the flickering torches in them. "The idea of unconditional love has always confused me. Being with my cousins, being with you, I've realized it makes sense. When you trust the ones you love, you'll do anything for them whether it benefits you or not and no matter what mistakes they might have made. That's why my cousins gifted me with their generosity."

Was that why Keely stayed with me? She'd said she trusted me. Could she be falling in love with me? I had a feeling deep in my chest, a strange kind of pressure that somehow felt good, that made me wonder if I was falling for her.

Her emerald eyes captured my focus, spiraling me down into their spellbinding depths.

No need to wonder. I was falling, and I loved the way it felt.

She laid a hand on my cheek. "Are you okay? Seems like you went somewhere else for a minute."

Maybe I had. I'd never known this kind of love before, and it did feel like I'd been transported to another planet where the usual laws of nature didn't apply and nothing made sense without her beside me. I didn't like going there alone.

At present, she was on top of me. I liked that a lot.

"Iain gave me two hundred thousand pounds," I said. "Rory and Lachlan gave one hundred thousand each. Technically, they each owned one share in the company since I could only accept investments from shareholders. I paid them back three years later, with interest, and bought back their shares. It's what they wanted. Their gifts were enough to give my company a solid start, but when I was almost finished designing and building my first surveillance system, I got an unexpected influx of cash from an angel investor."

"I've heard of those, but I'm not sure how it works."

"An angel investor buys an interest in a new company based on the business owner's proposal. They provide upfront cash, betting they'll earn that money back from the company's dividends. I suppose that makes my cousins angel investors too." I stifled a grunt when Keely wriggled her erse on my lap, and my cock roused again. "My official angel investor insisted on being anonymous, communicating through an investment broker. There was no negotiation of terms, no request for a proposal or to see prototypes of my devices. The money came out of the blue, an offer to provide three-quarters of a million pounds in exchange for a five-percent interest in the company."

"You accepted the offer."

"Seven hundred and fifty million pounds was an unusually large amount for an angel investment. I was going to reject it, but the broker convinced me. The money was more than enough to do anything I wanted with my new business."

"Sounds like there's a 'but' coming."

"There is." I focused on the table while I considered how to explain. Maybe I was delaying because I worried she wouldn't like the rest. "Once the business was up and running, and I had a small but loyal clientele, another broker brought me an offer from another anonymous angel investor. This time, I'd get four hundred thousand pounds."

"But..."

"The investor wanted a controlling interest in my company."

"You said no."

"Why do you think that?"

"Because it's your company—your baby, your life's work, your reason for living."

I pulled my head back. My reason for living? Did she honestly believe that? I supposed I had acted like it was, but tonight I'd told her she was my priority. When she'd first come back into my life, maybe I'd said or at least implied that my business mattered more to me than anything else. At one time, it had been everything I needed or wanted. Work no longer came first, not since I'd realized how much she meant to me, since I'd forsaken business in order to win her heart. Getting Keely to love me had become my sole purpose in life.

Business had slipped to number two on my list of important things in my life. Maybe it had slipped to three, after my family and the newfound bond I'd forged with my cousins.

"It's not my reason for living anymore," I said, brushing a hair away from her face. "Other things matter more to me these days."

She fidgeted on my lap, her gaze aimed past my shoulder. "Go on with the story, please."

"Not yet." I grasped her chin with one hand and forced her to look at me. "Business isn't the most important part of my life anymore. I told you that earlier, but you still don't believe me."

"I don't want to hear this." She tried to turn her head away, but I wouldn't let go of her chin.

With both hands, I cradled her face and waited until her eyes swerved to mine again. "I abandoned my company and moved here, bought this house, so I could be with you. Because you, Keely O'Shea, matter more to me than anything else in the world."

I couldn't say I loved her yet. She would panic for certain if I did.

And now, all I could do was keep my focus squarely on her beautiful eyes and pray she wouldn't run away from me.

Chapter Twenty-Three

Keely

I couldn't look away from Evan. He wore that earnest expression again, the one that always made me want to cuddle up with him and forget all the reasons why I'd given up on dating and relationships. We were dating. This was a relationship. He vowed I meant more to him than the business he'd devoted all his energy to and spent years building up. A billion-dollar empire, and he'd walked away from it.

No man had ever given up so much to be with me. Nobody had given up much of anything for me, certainly not without making me feel like I'd stolen something from them. For how long would Evan renounce his business? Eventually, he'd go back to work—on another continent, far away from where I lived and worked. All of this brought up another question, one I didn't want to think about tonight.

What would I give up for him?

I tried to get off his lap, but he shackled his arms around my waist again. "Let me go."

"Never."

"Let me get off your lap, that's what I mean."

"Can't do that either." He tugged me closer, our faces inches apart. "I won't let you run away. Not this time."

I smacked my palms on his chest. "Let go of me, Evan."

"There you go with that schoolteacher voice." He slid a hand under my bottom and pulled my right leg over his lap so I straddled him. Both of his big hands coasted up my bare back, eliciting a tingle that swept down my spine and straight between my legs. He nuzzled my nose. "A wild mustang wants to run away, but sometimes she needs to be penned."

"Stop with the horse metaphor, please. I'm not a mustang."

"But you are skittish and used to having your way in a relationship."

A wave of cold gushed through me, lifting every hair on my arms and at my nape. "Are you implying it's my fault every relationship I've had ended in disaster?"

"No, *leannan*. That's not what I'm saying at all." He roved his hands down my back. "From what I've heard so far, your exes were weak men who resented a strong woman. You had your way because they let you, because they liked being told what to do but resented it at the same time. Even when you tried to change yourself to please them, they resented it. Weak men are often that way. Afraid to go after what they want, so they blame everyone else for their failures."

My mouth opened, but I couldn't summon any words. Evan had described my exes to a tee. How had he known? Oh, I knew the answer. He'd listened to everything I'd said. More than that, his brilliant mind had analyzed the facts, considered the possibilities, and deduced the truth. His ability to understand my life better than I did, to understand me better than anyone ever had, both excited and frightened me.

He tugged closer until my groin rested over his hard-on. "I love your bossiness, and I will never resent you for it. I love your strength and your vulnerability, I love it when you're all business and when you misbehave. You never need to change yourself for me. I want you, Keely, that's all. I want *you*. Do you believe me?"

"Yes." It was barely a whisper but all that I could manage to say.

"Taming you isn't about making you change who you are to please me. It's about helping you move past the pain other men have caused you."

He *was* helping me. For the first time in years, I felt like I could be myself with a man, like he wouldn't punish me for it later. Evan would always be honest with me. I knew that. He might've kept secrets, but I believed he had reasons for that and would tell me the truth. If he didn't tell me everything soon, I'd need to reevaluate our relationship.

Just thinking about ending things made me feel cold inside.

"I need your help too," he said. "I've done things I'm not proud of. I told you part of the story about my company, but there's more."

I sealed two fingers over his lips. "Tell me later. Right now, I want to misbehave with you."

A smirk tightened his lips under my fingers. "Misbehave how?"

"In the way where your cock is inside me, thick and hard and hot, and you're making me come like a bomb going off."

"Love to do that." He slipped his hands under the hem of my dress and up to my naked ass. One of his brows rose. "No underwear? I thought you only did that in Paris."

"Why would I need underwear? I'm alone with you tonight."

He moved one hand to my mound, teasing the damp hairs with his fingertips. "Yer already wet."

"I'm perpetually turned on ever since you walked into my life."

"You walked into my life, in point of fact, on the day you first walked into my office."

"Mm-hm. But you flew thousands of miles to barge into my world here in Utah."

He slipped one finger between my folds, petting me casually. "Let's agree we've both invaded each other's lives."

And I loved the way he'd invaded mine, just like I loved the way he invaded my mouth with his tongue and my body with his dick. I rocked my hips to move his fingers closer to my entrance, to make those long and strong fingers stroke me. "Oh Evan, yes."

I fumbled with his jacket and shoved my fingers into his shirt pocket.

"What are ye doing?" he asked, pressing his fingers more firmly against my flesh, whisking them back and forth along my cleft.

"Looking for a condom. You always have one."

"Try the inside pocket."

I thrust my fingers into the inside pocket of his jacket and pulled out a condom packet. "Thank goodness. I can't stand it much longer, not having you inside me."

"Neither can I." He plunged two fingers into my sheath.

A long, low moan escaped my lips. I tore open the button on his slacks and yanked the zipper down, shoving my hand inside to cup his erection and ease it out of his pants. My fingers trembled thanks to the buzz of adrenaline and the wonderful torment of his fingers gliding in and out of me the way I wanted his shaft to do. I ripped the condom packet open with my teeth and rolled it onto his length.

He winced, hissing in a breath.

"Did I hurt you?" I asked.

"No, but I'm fair near to my own bomb going off."

"What would you like me to do?"

He swirled his fingers inside, the motion lazy and wickedly erotic. "Show me your breasts, Keely."

That commanding tone. God, it flooded heat through my entire body. Dizziness spun through me from the staggering need to take him inside me, and I couldn't move, could barely breathe.

"Do it," he said and thrust his fingers deeper.

I gasped.

He dived his fingers deeper to pet a spot that made me squirm and gasp again. "Show me, or I'll do it for you."

I made a hungry noise, somewhere between a grunt and a whimper, and reached behind my nape to untie the bow that held up my halter dress. The long, thin ties fell away. The night air cooled my skin, and my nipples stiffened.

His fingers caressed me deep inside in a way no one else had ever touched me. He lifted his other hand to close it around my breast and flicked his thumb across the nipple, back and forth, until I sucked in a breath and grasped his shoulders. He caught my taut peak between his teeth and tugged. I dug my fingers into his shoulders. He nipped and suckled, blew air over my nipple until I shuddered, and all the while kept moving his fingers inside me.

"More," I breathed. "More, please, more."

He shifted his hand until the heel pressed against my clit even as his long, dexterous fingers caressed me deep inside. The heel of his hand chafed my swollen nub with every stroke of his fingers. The need to climax built inside me like a rubber band stretched to its limits, about to snap any second. I rocked my hips, desperate to take his fingers deeper, to speed up his intimate massage, to reach the limit and blast through it. He kept me on the edge, his mouth tormenting my nipple, his hand kneading my breast. A cry burst out of me when he pushed a third finger inside me.

The rubber band snapped. An orgasm barreled through me, so hot and hard and inescapable that I lost my breath, unable to even moan at the unbridled pleasure of it. I threw my head back, my mouth open, tiny staccato gasps the only sound I could make.

Evan withdrew his fingers. He whisked his hands under my dress to grip my hips. "Fuck me, Keely. Now."

I rose up on my knees and sank my body onto his cock, moaning at the sensation of his length consuming me, the heat of his skin, and the incredible firmness of his shaft. He groaned and tugged my hips forward, deepening the connection of his body to mine. Oh, it felt wonderful. I moved up and down, rolling my hips into every downward thrust, loving the friction of his slacks against my thighs, but I needed more. I needed his skin on mine.

With shaky fingers, I undid his tie and got to work on freeing the buttons of his shirt.

He grunted every time I plunged onto his length. His hands pressed down and forward, intensifying the contact and driving him deeper inside my body.

I fumbled with his shirt buttons, buzzed by my orgasm and sensing another one mounting, that band tautening again little by little. My breaths came in sharp gasps. I needed his skin, but the damn buttons seemed to be secured with superglue. A frantic moan voiced my frustration, and his grunting breaths cranked up my own need. I gave up on the buttons. With both hands, I grasped his shirt and tore it open.

Buttons spewed everywhere. One clinked on the glass tabletop. Another landed on my breast only to tumble off when my tits bounced upward and back down in time with the quickening pace of our movements. I splayed my palms on his chest, reveling in the sensation of his skin on mine.

He bucked his hips up and yanked mine down, over and over, harder every time.

I crushed my chest to his, my arms latched around his neck. My harsh breaths gusted over his ear, each punctuated with a soft grunt when he slammed his cock up into the downward push of my hips.

His lips mashed to my ear, he wrapped his arms around me and growled, "Come for me, Keely. Come for me now."

As if by his command, my release thundered through me. I clutched him with my arms, my legs, my sex, with every inch of me that could cling to him. Sounds spilled from my lips, words without meaning, noises of sheer pleasure, his name again and again.

With two more thrusts, violent and all-consuming, he came apart inside me. His strangled cry filled my ear, and my name tumbled from his lips.

For a moment, we stayed there not moving, just holding each other in the aftermath until we each caught our breath. I combed my fingers through his hair. He ran his palms up and down my back. When we'd touched down on planet Earth again, I pulled back so I could see his face.

"Oh Evan, that was amazing." I traced my fingertips down his cheek to his mouth. " I love everything you do to me."

"You have a fetish for tearing my shirt off."

I splayed my hands over his bare chest. "Sorry, can't help it."

"Not complaining. I've developed a fetish for carting you off to the nearest bed."

"Don't stop doing that. I love it when you carry me away like a medieval warlord."

He clasped his hands at the small of my back. "What should we do now? Eat?"

I glanced over my shoulder at the food. It had probably gone cold. "Well, I hate to waste your delicious meal…"

"Hell with the meal. I'll cook another one for you. Better yet, I'll buy you a fishery or an entire ocean so we can have fish anytime you want."

"Thank you, but that's not necessary." I peeked at the house behind me. "Does this place have a bed?"

"Aye, it's fully furnished." He slid a hand around my side and up to palm my breast. "The bed is large and soft, perfect for pinning you to the mattress while I'm slamming my cock into your sweet body."

"Take me to your bed and make love to me all night."

He stared at me.

"What is it?" I asked.

"You called sex 'making love.' It's the first time you've said that."

He had said it before, more than once. A little while ago, when he'd referred to sex with me as making love, I'd told him not to call it that. Yet here I was asking him to take me to his large, soft bed and make love to me. Something had shifted between us or maybe inside me. Evan liked the parts of me other men had tolerated. He liked everything about me, he'd said.

No, he'd said he loved everything about me.

A shiver sidled down my spine, not a chill of anxiety, but a shiver of anticipation. Those words, the ones he'd spoken with such conviction, implied so much more. For the first time in more years than I cared to count, I wasn't afraid of what that meant. I wasn't afraid at all.

"Maybe it is the first time I've said it," I told him. "But it's not the first time you've made love to me. Not even the first time I've felt that's what you were doing and let myself enjoy it. I'm not afraid anymore, Evan, and that's because of you."

He grasped my waist and hoisted me off his lap, onto my feet.

I wobbled a little on my high heels. My legs hadn't fully recovered from our rockin' sex in the patio chair.

Evan swept me up in his arms. "I'm taking you to bed, Miss O'Shea, and I plan on commanding you to come for me over and over and over."

I twined my arms around his neck. "Let's go."

"Feel free to tell me to behave. You know how I feel about that."

"Can't do that tonight, Mr. MacTaggart. The teacher is taking the night off."

Chapter Twenty-Four

Evan

Something tickled my nose, making it itch, something that felt like a feather. I opened my eyes. While I lay flat on my back, Keely straddled my thighs with her lovely erse between my knees. She wore my shirt, the one she'd torn all the buttons off of last night, with the sleeves rolled up enough that they didn't hang past her fingertips. The shirt looked much better on her, especially with the way it revealed a strip of her body from her slender throat all the way down to the curly hairs between her thighs. With her legs spread to sit astride me, I got a glimpse of her luscious pink flesh.

Keely held the feather near my nose again. "Time to rise and shine, Mr. MacTaggart."

I glanced at the clock on the bedside table and blinked several times, struggling to accept what the digital display told me. "It's eight fifteen."

"Bet you've never slept this late, have you?" She tickled my nose with the feather. "I haven't slept this late in years and years and years."

The way she was speaking, with a light and playful tone, made her seem younger. In the time I'd known her, I'd never seen Keely like this.

"I'll make you breakfast," I said and tried to sit up.

She flattened one hand on my chest and shoved me back down. "Uh-uh-uh. Stay put or I'll have to make you do it."

One side of my mouth curled upward. I couldn't help it. The playful lass holding me down with her sumptuous body was a new side of Keely, and I loved it. Then again, I loved everything about this woman.

Her challenge that she would make me stay put if I tried to move again made me want her to do that.

I pushed up on my elbows. "Let me up or I'll have to fuck you senseless."

"Is that supposed to be a threat? Sounded more like an offer."

"Well, it's true I will fuck you senseless either way."

I stretched out a hand to touch her.

Keely seized my wrist. "I said no getting up. Behave, Mr. MacTaggart."

She held my wrist while she dropped the feather on the bed and leaned over to grab something off the floor. She straightened and held up a pale-pink scarf made from semi-transparent material. While keeping my wrist in her grip, she dragged the scarf over my belly.

I hissed in a breath. "Where did you get a feather and a scarf?"

"Brought them in my overnight bag. Just in case." A naughty smile curved her mouth, and she dragged the scarf over my skin again. "Will Evan behave? Or does Keely need to make him do it?"

Talking about us in the third person should've seemed silly, but when she spoke those words in her schoolteacher voice, darkened with a hint of sensuality...I wanted to flip us both over and drive into her so hard she'd gasp.

"Cannae behave," I said. "Not when I can smell how excited you are."

"I am turned on," she said, rotating her wrist to coil the scarf around it. "But I want something else first."

She moved my wrist to the headboard, between two of the slats, and tied one end of the scarf around it. I twisted my head around to watch her movements. She threaded the scarf behind the slats and back out on the other side of my head. I didn't need to wait long to find out what she was planning. Keely grasped my other wrist, forcing me to lie back, and moved my hand between the slats where she secured the scarf around that wrist too.

"There," she said breezily. "You're all set."

"For what?" I hoped to heaven she was about to fuck me because my cock was as hard as an iron rod.

Her smile was enigmatic.

I gave my bindings a light tug, not really trying to escape. "Thought you didn't like this sort of thing."

"Oh, I don't mind at all when you're the one who's bound." She sat back, her bottom cradled between my knees. "I've got you tied up and turned on, so you won't be able to resist answering my questions."

"Questions? Havenae ye noticed the flaming-hard cock waving at ye?"

"Yes, I noticed." The saucy lass closed her fist around my erection. "This is for later, after you've been a good boy and told me everything I want to know."

"Are ye planning to torture me?"

"Only in the best way." She bent to lave the head of my erection with her tongue. "Ready to talk yet?"

"I was talking last night. You ordered me to stop."

"Tell me later, that's what I said. It's later." She straightened again, sliding her hands along my thighs. "Besides, I wanted to hear the rest of the story and you said 'not yet.' I said 'tell me later' only after you had me on your lap, right before you started petting me."

"Donnae care who ended the conversation first." I tried to reach for her, but the scarf restrained my hands, so I tried to raise my knees and move her body closer to where I wanted her. I couldn't get enough leverage with her sitting on me. "Need sex, Keely, not talking."

"No, Evan. There will be talking." She grabbed the blasted feather and skimmed it down my chest until it grazed my groin. "Tell me the rest of the story. You turned down a shitload of money and then…"

Christ, the woman was determined to have her way. If she'd wanted to shag me while I was tied to the headboard, I would've loved it. Tying me up to make me confess everything was not what I wanted.

I grumbled out a sigh, resigned to giving in to her. "A few weeks after I turned down the four hundred thousand pounds, I got a text message. It said, 'Saying no was your first mistake. Don't make another.' I thought it was a prank or had been meant for someone else, and I deleted the message. An hour later, another one arrived. It said they had a job for me."

"Who's 'they'?"

"No idea. Still don't know." I wanted to focus on the ceiling while I told her all of this, but I forced myself to look her in the eye. "Since I thought it was a mistake, I replied and told them they had the wrong person. The response came seconds later. 'We have the right person, Evan. Instructions will follow.' A few seconds after that, I received a text file followed by another message that told me I had twenty-four hours to complete my task."

"What did you do?"

I shrugged, and the knotted scarf tightened around my wrists. "I ignored it."

She nibbled on her lower lip.

That should've made me harder, but instead, my erection flagged. Bad memories had sapped my lust.

"Something happened, didn't it?" she asked.

"Aye." A coldness trickled through me at the thought of explaining the rest. I'd known one day I would need to tell her everything. The words wouldn't come out of my mouth, though. They were caught in my throat, caught under the lump that had solidified there. Why was it so hard to tell the truth? She was the only woman who had ever wanted me, understood me, and made me feel like a human being instead of a Martian. If she left me…Maybe part of the truth would do for today. "I did what the thugs wanted. I wrote a program that would disable one particular security system in one particular building in downtown London."

"Did they break into the building?"

"I don't know. If they stole something, the theft didn't make the news. If they'd killed someone, that would've been reported. Whatever they did, I should never have given in to their blackmail."

She studied me for a moment, though her expression gave away no hints to how she might react to what I'd done. Bile burned in my throat. My mouth went dry.

"Why did you give in?" she asked.

"I had no choice. They have…ways to force me to do what they want."

"What ways?"

I glowered at the ceiling for a minute or more. Hard to gauge the time when I was struggling with the opposing needs to tell her everything and to protect her from my mistakes.

"Did you try to figure out what they'd done?" she asked.

"I assume they disabled the security system in that building. The information they provided told me all about the system, but I had no idea which building it was in." I snarled a Gaelic curse under my breath. "Later, I realized the code they had me work on was familiar. It had been written by someone at my company, and I had approved it. I went through the records of where we had installed security systems and eventually figured out what building it was. Only one client had ordered the precise configuration the software was designed for. That's all I know."

"There's more, isn't there? Tell me. Please."

Her polite command didn't make me smile this time. I groaned and shut my eyes, knowing what I had to tell her next. "For the past year, these anonymous criminals have made me do three more jobs for them. All of it involved disabling security systems I had designed, and always I had no idea what they were after. I didn't hear from them for eight months after the fourth job." I forced myself to look at her. "Until the day you came back into my life."

She puckered her lips in the manner I'd come to know as Keely thinking. "Was that the top-secret project you had to work on? The one Tamsen knew nothing about?"

"It was."

"Why do you keep doing what these creeps say? Hire a private investigator, hunt them down, turn them over to the authorities."

"I can't. I've aided criminals, and that's a crime in itself."

"But you are the victim."

I shifted uncomfortably, though it wasn't the scarf binding my wrists that bothered me.

Keely slid off my legs to sit on the edge of the bed. Though she still faced me, her legs hung off the bed like she wanted the option to run away. I couldn't blame her for that. A quick getaway might be the safest option for her. I'd brought her into my tangled life knowing it might lead to this moment, this choice, all because I needed to possess her. Things had gone too far, and I'd fallen in love with her.

"Couldn't you find out who's behind it all?" she asked. "Hack their phone when they text you or something?"

"I've told you I am not a hacker," I said too harshly. Taking a deep breath, I tempered my voice. "I design security and surveillance devices for—"

"For personal and business use. I know, I'm sorry. Guess I don't understand what hackers do."

"It's nothing I can do, that's for certain. The only reason I could write code to disable that security system is because I designed the system in the first place and what they wanted me to do was fairly simple. I'd done similar work at university when security companies hired me."

"Right. I guess that's why they picked you." She spread her hands on her thighs. "There has to be something we can do."

"We? This is my problem." I shut my eyes. "I should never have pushed you into a relationship with me. The only excuse I can offer is that I believed they'd given up. Honestly, I'm sure I would have pursued you even if I'd known they would call on me again. I wanted you, I needed to possess you, and so I did whatever it took to get you—like the selfish ersehole I am."

Chapter Twenty-Five

Keely

"You haven't possessed me." I swung my leg over him to straddle his thighs again. "You showed me what it's like to be with someone who appreciates me the way I am. My second ex-husband, Bryce, convinced me I was lacking in every way, as a wife and as a lover and as a human being. He did it slowly, a little dig here and there, nothing overt that I could've reacted to the way I should have. On the day he announced he wanted a divorce, he told me I'm too assertive, that I emasculated him in bed and out and I would never find a man who would put up with me."

Evan's mouth flattened into a line. The glint in his eyes was cold and sharp. "He's the one nobody should put up with."

"The point is, you taught me a real man doesn't resent a woman because she has a mind of her own." I picked at the sheets, staring down at them, searching for answers in the faint pattern of lines in the fabric. "Bryce would never tell me what he wanted, but he resented it if I took charge, whether that was during sex or at the grocery store. When we got married, he had a dream to start his own business making custom motorcycles. He got a loan from the bank, using our house as collateral. My contribution was to handle the business side of things—I had an MBA after all—so Bryce could do the fun part. I built his business for him. Every client he had came to us because of the advertising I crafted or the word of mouth I built up for him. When the chamber of commerce honored him with an award for being a great entrepreneur, he took all the credit. Didn't mention me once in his whole ten-minute acceptance speech."

"He definitely needs a good skelping."

"What does that mean?"

"Means he needs to be smacked around."

I rested my hands on his thighs and leaned into them, leaned into his body. "I love that you want to beat up my ex-husband, but he's not worth it."

He grimaced. "Beating someone isn't an admirable act."

"Sometimes it's warranted. Not in Bryce's case, though. I'm done with him."

"Believe me," he said with a fierceness that roughened his voice, "if anyone tries to hurt you, I will beat them bloody."

A tingle swept down my spine. He would do it. I had no doubts about that. No man had ever cared that much about me.

I gazed into his silvery blue eyes, overcome by an emotion so strong it gripped my heart and penetrated down into my soul. The room seemed to spin around me, the whole world seemed to have tilted on its axis, and I struggled to keep steady in the aftermath. Warmth bloomed in my chest, spreading outward until my entire body, my entire being tingled with the realization of what I was experiencing. I'd fallen for him. There was no going back, no easy way out, nothing I could do except let myself drown in the euphoria of loving the only man who had ever accepted me for who I was.

I couldn't catch my breath, but neither could I tear my focus away from his eyes. This was the turning point that would change everything between us irrevocably. If I told him how I felt, and he didn't feel the same way…But he'd said I mattered more to him than anything else in the world. He must share this feeling, this head-spinning, world-altering sensation of falling down and down and down into the sweetest unknown.

Take a risk, my heart screamed. *Be careful*, my head warned.

I started to speak, to share my epiphany with him, but rationality slammed down around me like a steel coffin. Three times in my life I'd told a man I loved him, and all three times it had ended in catastrophe. My pulse slowed. The whirling freedom of realization settled down. I couldn't dive into that deep abyss yet. It might take me to a marvelous new world, or it might suffocate me.

This was cowardice, a land I knew all too well. I owned a resort here.

Evan had shared his secrets with me, but had he shared all of them? I'd let him into my life completely, and yet I knew so little about his world.

I climbed off his body, untied the scarf to free him, and sat down beside him. "We have another problem."

He pushed up on one arm, twisted at the waist to look at me. "What is it?"

"My mom flew in last night. My dad and Serena picked her up at the airport, and she's excited to meet you."

"I can handle your mother."

"Well, there's more." I made a sheepish and slightly pinched face. "My twin brothers are coming too. They're flying in later this morning with their wives and their kids."

"Are your brothers identical twins?"

"Yes. Even though Ryan and Grady are younger than me, they act like they're my big brothers."

"Overprotective, eh?"

"Exactly. I'm too old to have my brothers smothering me with their good intentions, but they do it anyway. My whole family wants to spend the weekend with both of us. There will be lots and lots of questions aimed at you. If it's too much family time for you, I'll understand."

He stretched toward the bedside table to pick up his glasses, bending forward enough to bring his face within inches of my breasts. He smirked.

Slipping his glasses on, he said, "I have a horde of cousins, Keely. They poke their noses into my business on a regular basis. I think I can handle your family."

"Good, because I promised we'd be there for brunch this morning. It's at eleven o'clock."

"Are we all squeezing into your house? Sounds like a large gathering for such a small space."

"Where else would we gather?" The instant I'd asked the question, I regretted it because I knew what he would say.

"Have the brunch here."

"At your house? I don't know about that."

Evan hopped off the bed and spread his arms wide. "This is your house. I bought it for you, not for me. I've even arranged to have the place made wheel-chair friendly with a stair lift and other enhancements to make it comfortable for your father."

"Last night you said you bought this house to live in."

"That's true."

"You expect me and my dad to move in with you? I don't think we're at the living-together stage yet."

"This house has five bedrooms. Pick one for yourself."

"Separate bedrooms? Not sure how I feel about that either."

He flapped his arms. "What do you want? I buy you a house, but you don't want to live with me. I offer to sleep in a different room to make you comfortable, but you don't like that either. You've never had trouble saying what you want before, so tell me."

What on earth did I want? Evan, that's what. But living together? I loved him, or I thought I did, but when I considered living with him all my old doubts came crashing through the gates of my heart.

"It's too much too soon," I said. "I need time to get used to, um, the way things are progressing. Dad and I will stay put, but we'll have the brunch here. Okay?"

"That's acceptable."

He didn't sound like he thought it was acceptable, but I decided to take him at his word. I had bigger issues to deal with, namely organizing a brunch in two hours, a brunch for everyone in my family. Impossible tasks were not my forte.

"We can't move the brunch," I said. "Serena and Chase are coming too. That means there will be nine adults and six children. We don't have time to get everything set up."

"There is time." Evan grabbed his phone off the bedside table. "If you have enough money, you can do almost anything in no time at all."

I didn't get the chance to protest.

He dialed a number and walked out of the room to arrange, or rather rearrange, our brunch plans. He hadn't bothered to even pull his pants on and instead exited buck naked.

I rushed to get my overnight bag. Evan had carried it upstairs last night while he was carrying me. The man had strength and coordination, high-level skills that let him do all sorts of things to me. Last night, we'd enjoyed each other in creative ways and in mundane ways that proved no less hot than the more inventive positions we'd tried.

I'd packed the basics I would need this morning—a T-shirt, jeans, underwear, socks, and a pair of sneakers. The clothes were wrinkled from being in the overnight bag, but I'd expected to go home to get ready for brunch. Evan had changed the plan. I'd need to adapt. So, I wandered into the en suite bathroom and splashed water on the shirt, stretching and smoothing it with my hands until it looked less wrinkled. My family would have to accept I wasn't as put together as usual today. I decided against a shower, refreshing my hair the way I'd done with my clothes. I washed off my makeup—it had smeared anyway—and opted for the au naturel look.

Should a forty-something woman go without makeup? Evan had seen me without it before, and he clearly didn't care. My family wouldn't either. I frowned at myself in the bathroom mirror. Since when did I care what other people thought of my appearance? Hooking up with a younger man had made me want to look perfect for Evan all the time. I took a deep breath and let it out gradually, releasing the anxiety.

As I crossed the threshold of the bathroom door, Evan was standing beside the bed zipping up the khaki pants he'd pulled on. He was shirtless, though.

I leaned against the doorjamb, admiring the view of his sculpted chest and six-pack abs. "Have you rearranged my whole life or just the brunch plans?"

"Only the brunch," he said as he slipped into a golden-tan, short-sleeve shirt and began buttoning it up. "Your life I'll work on later."

I wagged a finger at him. "No more buying things in hopes of talking me into accepting them as gifts."

He hooked the last button and held up one hand, palm out. "I swear on the lives of my children I will never do that again."

"You don't have children."

"I hoped you wouldn't notice that." He pushed his glasses up with one finger. "Should've known I can't fool a clever woman like you. Why don't you have children? You never told me."

"Wes wanted kids, but I wasn't comfortable having them unless we were married. Bryce claimed he didn't want children, but after he dumped me, he married his twenty-two-year-old mistress. And now they have a baby."

He sat down on the bed, socks in hand, his gaze traveling to me. "I'm sorry, Keely. You've had a bad run, haven't you?"

I hiked up my shoulders.

"Well, that's over now." He put on his socks and shoes, smiling at me with a heartbreaking sweetness. "You're with me, and I appreciate every-thing you are."

What could I say to that? He meant it, that much I knew.

Forty-five minutes later, we were in the backyard watching six people hustle around setting up the buffet for our brunch. Evan was consulting with the leader of this catering crew. I got the impression he had thrown a boatload of money at the problem of how to move the brunch here because I'd never heard of emergency catering before. Plus, the owner of the catering company seemed awfully happy about doing a rush job for "Mr. MacTaggart, sir" as the middle-aged man had called him.

The spry young men and women setting things up wasted no time and made no mistakes. I was impressed, but what impressed me more was that Evan wanted to meet my whole family and cared so much about making them comfortable. He'd ordered chairs, the kind with plush cushions, and a table long enough to accommodate all of us.

My family arrived an hour later.

Ryan and Grady marched straight up to Evan and shook his hand, then introduced their wives and children. Grady had two daughters, and Ryan had three boys. Evan greeted everyone in a calmly cheerful way. My mom hugged him. Dad displayed a bit less enthusiasm since he'd already met Evan.

Brunch turned into a boisterous occasion with everyone chatting and getting to know Evan. He didn't bristle at the questions Ryan and Grady asked him, not even when Grady asked if Evan was using me for the thrill of scoring an older woman and would dump me soon. Evan had replied, "I respect and care for your sister too much to treat her that way."

My brothers had been satisfied with his answer.

After everyone had left, Evan gave me a curious look. "Doesn't it feel odd to have your oldest friend taking care of your father? She's your employee."

"Technically, yes. I've known Serena for twenty-five years, and she loves Dad almost as much as I do. Who better to trust with his medical care?"

"I suppose it does make sense."

Our conversation ended there because we were wiped out. After a nap and a shower together, we lay down on the huge sofa in the living room to watch TV. He cooked me dinner and took me home, assuring me he didn't mind sleeping alone tonight so I could hang out with my family.

Evan and I spent the next day with my family too. He entertained my nieces and nephews, playing games like hopscotch and tag, then heading indoors for three rounds of Go Fish and a half-hour-long princess tea party with my nieces. I couldn't help laughing when I saw Evan MacTaggart wearing a pink, feather-laden tiara on his head.

By the time we got back to his place Sunday night, we were wiped out. In the high-ceilinged entryway, he pulled me into his embrace.

"You'll want to go home soon," he said, "so I'd better kiss you good night."

"I'd rather not go. Unless you'd prefer to sleep alone."

Evan picked me up. "Not a chance in hell of that."

He grinned and carted me up the stairs, taking them two at a time.

Chapter Twenty-Six

Evan

Monday morning after breakfast, Keely rushed home to change clothes before work while I hung around my new house wondering what to do next. Keely trusted me. She'd stayed the night because she wanted to be with me, even without sex, and she'd introduced me to her entire family. Should I do the same for her? My family life was far more complicated than hers. I wasn't sure how my mother would react to meeting the older woman I'd fallen in love with after a month together. Aileen MacTaggart had a traditional outlook on dating in spite of the fact she wouldn't tell me anything about my father.

A knot twisted in my gut. I didn't want to think about that today.

But I did need to check in with Duncan Hendry. A quick exchange of text messages assured me all was well at my mother's house.

By the time I arrived at the store, Keely was busy in her office. I wanted to go in there and talk to her, but the always-cheery Paige waylaid me. She needed help restocking the DVD racks, and after that, she asked for my help with other tasks around the store. Technically, the eighteen-year-old was my superior since she'd worked here longer and had earned the title of shift supervisor. It seemed odd to have such a young lass telling me what to do. I'd gotten used to being the CEO, the one who told everyone else what to do and made the final decisions on everything.

Until I met Keely. For her, I ignored calls and texts from Tamsen.

Which reminded me I ought to call my executive assistant.

By the time Paige released me from my enslavement, I wanted nothing more than to see Keely. Maybe it was a sorry excuse for not calling Tamsen, but I didn't care. I told Paige I'd be conferring with our boss in her office, and I clomped into Keely's office a few minutes later. I shut the door and headed straight for the sofa. When I dropped onto it, the sofa thumped into the wall.

Keely rotated her chair halfway toward me. She had a stack of papers on her desk and held one sheet in her hand. Her reading glasses perched on her nose, but that only made her more attractive and even sexier. The loose-fitting pants and blouse she wore couldn't temper her sensual appeal either. When she picked up a pen and delicately chewed on its end, I felt the blood rushing straight to my cock.

I laid my arms across the sofa's back and braced my ankle on the opposite knee. "You look ravishable this morning."

She pursed her lips as if she were annoyed, but the way one side of her mouth ticked upward gave away her game. "I wore the unsexiest, but still work appropriate, clothes I own. Guess I should've picked the baggy, faded sweatshirt and the schlumpy jeans with paint stains on them from when I repainted the bathroom."

"Wouldn't matter. I'd want to ravish you anyway." I let my gaze travel over her from head to toe and back again. "Why did you want to be unsexy? You can't pull that off no matter what you do."

"I had hoped to discourage you from seducing me in my office." She dropped her pen and flapped the paper she held. "I've gotten behind on going through the job applications. We've had a flood of them, and it's all your fault. You ought to feel guilty enough to stop teasing me."

"My fault? What did I do?"

She snorted, and even that turned me on. "All you had to do was walk around where people can see you."

"I don't understand. Is that a strange American saying?"

"No, it's the plain truth. Let me share some choice excerpts from these applications. Every one of these is an answer to the last question about why the applicant wants to work here." She snatched up a handful of papers and flipped through them one by one as she spoke. "I want to work with the hot Scottish guy. May I please have all my shifts scheduled with Evan. I want to learn about electronics from the mega hottie with the swoon-worthy accent. I would do anything to work with that gorgeous Evan." Keely shook the papers in her hand, but her slight smirk told me she wasn't angry. "See? All your fault."

"Can't help it if women find me attractive."

"The last comment was from a man."

"Don't be jealous. I'm interested in only one woman." I paused for one point five seconds to be melodramatic. "Is Paige seeing anyone?"

Keely tossed the papers onto her desk. They scattered, but she didn't bother straightening them. "Sorry, but Paige has a boyfriend."

I stretched my legs out to set them on the table. "I want you, Keely. No one else. I'm sorry if my presence here has caused you trouble, but it won't be a problem anymore. I hereby resign from my employment at Vic's Electronics Superstore."

She plucked her glasses off her nose and tossed them onto the desktop. "You don't have to quit because of these applications. I was being sarcastic."

"I know that, but I was planning to quit anyway. I've left Tamsen to deal with the company alone for too long, and I have personal issues to handle. It's time for me to go back to Scotland."

Her shoulders caved in, and she slumped back in her chair. "Already? I mean, I knew you'd leave sometime but…"

I dropped my foot to the floor and leaned forward. "Will you miss me?"

Her head jerked as if I'd surprised her. "Of course I will."

Next came the part where I took the biggest risk of my life. It felt like the biggest risk, that was for certain. Denying the thugs who'd been black-mailing me was more dangerous and a bigger threat to my business and the safety of the ones I loved, but what I was about to ask Keely had my stomach twisting and my throat going dry.

I sat forward and cleared my throat. "Will you come with me?"

She straightened, tugging on the hem of her blouse. "I'd love to, but I can't. Got too much to do around here."

"Vic told me you have six weeks of vacation time saved up."

"Yes, but the store needs me."

"Maybe it does." I rose and approached her desk, kneeling in front of her. I settled my hands on her knees. "But I need you more."

Her mouth opened, but she said nothing.

"Please, Keely." I grasped her hands. "Please come with me."

"Evan, I—" She swallowed hard enough I saw the movement in her throat. "I want to, I do. But my dad…the store…"

"I spoke to your father this morning. Your mother decided to stay in town for a few weeks, which means both she and Serena will be around to help your father. When I told Gary my plans, he thought it was a wonderful idea to take you with me." I lifted her hands to kiss the knuckles one by one. "Let me show you my real home in the Highlands, Ballachulish and Loch Fairbairn."

"You're going *home* home? Where your mother lives?"

"Aye. She'll be wanting to meet you."

My mouth had turned to cotton—bone-dry, scratchy cotton. A pain started in the back of my throat while I waited for her response. Never before had I wanted a relationship with a woman, much less to take her home to my family. My cousins would love Keely. My mother might be prickly about it.

Keely nodded once. "Yes, I would love to go with you."

A smile broke across her face like a sunrise on a clear spring morning, bright and full of life. It lit her up like a sunrise too.

I couldn't resist. I threw my arms around her waist and stood up, carrying her with me, and hugged her so tight she must've had trouble breathing. She looped her arms around my neck, holding on to me just as tightly.

She was going home with me. It wasn't as if we were getting married, but when she'd agreed to go with me, I had felt like she'd offered herself to me in a commitment almost as strong and meaningful as marriage vows.

"Thank you," I said, kissing her cheek, her mouth, her chin, her nose.

"You don't have to thank me. I'm getting a free vacation with the sexiest tour guide on the planet."

"Is there any chance you'll let me spoil you? Or should I rent a dilapidated car to drive you around in?"

Biting her lip, she pretended to consider the problem. After a brief length of time I didn't bother to count, she tickled my cheek with her fingers. "You can spoil me. I will not complain even if you buy an entire town for me."

"Good." I squeezed her bottom. "I sort of do own a town, or at least a large part of it."

"Are you serious?"

"Yes. Does that bother you?"

"No." She smiled. "It doesn't fash me at all."

"I'm glad." I set her down on her feet. "But I can't promise not to buy the whole Highlands for you."

"That's a risk I'm willing to take."

I pretended to be shocked. "Keely O'Shea taking a risk?"

"Tease me all you want, I don't mind."

"You know what this means." I smacked her erse. "I've tamed you."

She leaned in, tilting her head back to expose her throat, and placed her hand over my cock. "I've tamed you too."

The heat of her hand penetrated my trousers, and things started to rouse down there.

She removed her hand. "I should get back to work. Got an employee to replace."

"I suppose it was too much to hope I'm irreplaceable."

"You are." She drew a heart on my chest with her finger. "To me, anyway."

Anything I might have thought about saying was trapped in my throat. I took several steps toward the door but stopped halfway there. "You're irreplaceable to me too, *leannan*."

"You keep calling me that. What does it mean?"

"It's Gaelic for sweetheart."

"You've been calling me that all this time?"

I shrugged one shoulder and shuffled to the door, grasping the knob.

"I love you, Evan."

Her words stopped me. Everything inside me froze like someone had punched the pause button on a video recording. I couldn't move, not even to hand off the doorknob or to turn my head to look at her. Had she said what I'd thought I heard her say? Had I imagined it? I had to know for sure.

"What did you say?" I asked, glancing at her over my shoulder.

She laughed softly, sweetly. "I love you."

With her emerald eyes locked on me, I lost my breath. She meant it. Keely loved me. I took two deep breaths before I could speak again. "I love you too."

She ran toward me and threw her body at mine. We collided, our arms lashing around each other and our hands groping for skin-to-skin contact. My lips found hers, and though I kissed her, I didn't deepen it. Just her lips on mine, that was all I needed.

"Have I ever told you," she said against my lips, "what an amazing man you are?"

"You're the amazing one, a dirty lass disguised as a proper businesswoman."

"What you said earlier is true. You've tamed my fears and freed me." She loosened her grip on me, sliding down my body until her feet hit the floor. "I love you for that and so much more."

And that was all I'd wanted since the night we'd met, for this woman to want me and need me the way I wanted and needed her. She had changed me too, but I didn't know how to tell her that. No words I could think of seemed like enough.

"Your holiday starts now," I said. "Let's get you home. You'll need to pack."

She looked at the papers on her desk.

"Forget work," I said. "If I can do it, so can you."

"Oh, what the hell." She threw her arms up. "I'm taking a vacation."

"About bloody time."

I hooked my arm around her waist, leading her toward the door. We made it out into the main store area and almost to the sliding doors before she stopped us.

"Forgot my purse," she said. "Wait here while I go grab it."

She jogged off before I could say anything, so I did as she'd commanded. I loitered by the doors waiting for her to come back to me.

My phone chimed.

I pulled it out of my pocket and checked the screen. A chill whispered over my skin like a ghost had walked right through me. It was a ghost, in a way. The message came from my invisible masters.

We have another job for you, it said.

A pain stabbed through my jaw. I was grinding my teeth, of course. Messages from these villains always made my body tighten as if I'd been hit with a jolt of electricity. I typed my response: *I'm done.*

Not until we say so.

The last time I'd denied them, they threatened my mother. I shouldn't say no, but I could no longer say yes, not with Keely in my life. Duncan's men were watching over my mother. I would watch over Keely.

Another text appeared: *Do the job.*

My finger hovered over the screen, and a reckless impulse pushed me to type one word: *No.*

I waited for a response, but several seconds ticked by with no new messages. Maybe they'd accepted my answer. Right, and maybe I'd grow a pair of wings.

Had I just made the worst decision of my life?

Keely trotted up to me, smiling, her purse slung over one shoulder. "Ready to go. You can follow me in your car."

"Ride with me. We can pick up your car later."

She gave me a look I knew well, the one that meant she was not giving in this time.

I waved for her to go. "I'll follow."

By the time I started up my car, Keely was already pulling out onto the road. I drove a bit too fast to catch up to her, but she waved at me when she spotted my car behind hers. I waved too. Soon, she would be with me in Scotland. My family would meet her. We had crossed a new threshold. This woman was in my life for good—forever, I hoped—and whatever happened, I would never let her go without a fight.

My phone chimed again.

I held the wheel with one hand while I picked up the phone. A new text glared at me from the screen.

You will regret this.

Muttering an oath, I tossed the phone onto the passenger seat. I couldn't do what they wanted, not anymore, but I was risking more than my own safety. My invisible masters didn't know about Keely. How could they? Unless they'd been watching me. Watching us.

The minute we got to her house I would make the call to arrange for security for Keely.

And I would pray it was enough.

Chapter Twenty-Seven

Keely

The next morning, I reclined on the sofa inside the Gulfstream jet exactly the way I had a few weeks ago when I flew home from Scotland. This time, though, I wasn't missing Evan and wondering what to do about him. No need for that. He was sitting at the end of the sofa with my feet on his lap, massaging my soles with deft strokes of his fingers. My lids partly closed, I watched him through my lashes.

"That feels good," I said. "You should've been a masseur."

"How would you feel about a full-body massage?"

"Yes, please."

Evan patted my leg. "You will have to get up for that, so we can go to the bedroom. Not stripping you here where the pilots might see you."

"We had sex in front of a window."

"No one saw us, though." He threw a sharp glance at the door to the cockpit. "Those pilots were a little too attentive when you came on board."

"They were not hitting on me." I nudged him with my foot. "Besides, I'm not interested in anyone but you."

"I feel the same way about you." He pushed my feet off his lap. "Get up. We're going to the bedroom so I can rub you all over and then do filthy things to that body."

"Sounds good." I yawned and stretched. "But I'm too comfy to move."

"Not a problem." He surged up from the sofa, swept me up, and strode down the short hallway to the open bedroom door. "Here we are."

He walked inside and kicked the door shut.

"You can put me down," I said.

"All right." He tossed me onto the bed, making me bounce and yelp. "How's that?"

"You have fetishes for kicking doors shut and tossing me onto beds along with your fetish for carrying me." I scooted forward so my feet hung off the bed. "Guess we're skipping the foreplay this time, hey?"

"Never." He knelt at my feet and tickled the soles. "I took care of your socks and shoes. You get the rest off."

"You'll need to be more specific. I might think you mean I should get myself off without you."

"Maybe I'd like to watch you do that." He sat on the bed next to me. "Undress, Keely."

"I let you be the boss earlier today. It's my turn."

He considered me for a moment, probably thinking about how to negotiate this deal with me. "You'll do as I say until after the massage, then I will follow your commands."

"I can accept those terms."

"Get up and strip for me."

The very idea made me wet. I rose and turned to face him.

A knock rattled the door.

"Mr. MacTaggart?" the man said in his Scottish brogue. "You left your mobile out here and it keeps ringing. Thought I should let you know."

"Thank you, Martin," Evan said. "I'll take care of it."

"Must be Tamsen," I said. "The poor woman has been trying to get you on the phone for days."

"Aye, it's probably her." He moved to the door but hesitated with his hand on the knob. "Wait here. This shouldn't take long."

"I'll get naked while you're gone."

"No, you will not. Wait for me." He narrowed his eyes with feigned annoyance. "That's an order, Miss O'Shea."

His commands never failed to make me hot in all the right ways.

"Okay, I'll stay dressed." I stroked my sex through my pants. "Can't promise I won't slip a hand inside my panties, though."

"Guess I'd better hurry."

He rushed out the door, shutting it behind him.

I lay back on the bed, staring at the ceiling. Though I was aroused, I didn't want to get off without him. We enjoyed teasing each other, and he knew that's what I'd been doing. No other man I'd been with liked to play. Evan excelled at it. He'd opened me up in ways I'd never imagined possible. Back in the store yesterday, I hadn't meant to say I loved him. The words would not be contained any longer, especially after he'd told me I was irreplaceable and that *leannan* meant sweetheart. So often he gazed at me like I was the answer to his prayers, like he cherished me more than anything in the world, like he loved me as much as I loved him.

How could I not say the words?

And he'd said them back to me.

The joy I had experienced at that moment made my heart swell and my spirits soar straight into outer space, spinning and spinning with the life-altering realization I loved a man who loved me in return. He didn't expect me to change to please him. Evan wanted me as-is. Of course I loved him. How could I help it? Despite our age difference, he was the most mature man I'd ever known. My husbands might have been closer to my age, but Evan was the first real man in my life.

The door opened.

I sprang up into a sitting position.

Evan shut the door but wouldn't look at me. "Afraid I'm not in the mood anymore. We'll have to delay the massage until later."

The tension in his body matched the tension on his face. He seemed like a string stretched to its limit, being pulled even tauter until it might snap at any second.

I went to him, taking his hands in mine. "What's wrong?"

"Nothing you need to worry about."

"Bullshit. Anything that worries you is my concern too." I laid a hand on his cheek and made him turn his face toward me. "We're in a relationship, Evan. The L word has come into the picture which means this is a serious thing between us. Tell me what's going on."

His features twisted into an expression somewhere between pain and anger.

I knew he wasn't angry with me. Whatever that phone call had been about, it was the trigger.

"Talk to me," I said. "Please."

He peeled my hand away from his face and stalked to the bed, dropping onto it with a *whump*. "It's better if you don't know."

"Did you not hear a word I said?" I stomped to the bed and sat next to him, turning sideways to see his profile. "Serious relationship. That means you don't get to keep secrets from me anymore."

"I know." He braced his elbows on his thighs and let his head fall into his raised hands. "I shouldn't drag you any deeper into my mess."

"Too late for that. I'm already in it with you."

"I've been selfish and reckless." He took his phone out of his pocket and turned it over in his hand once, twice, three times. "My phone wasn't ringing. It was chiming because I've received three texts in the last five minutes." He pushed a hand into his hair, head bowed. "It's the blackmailers."

That word made me shut my mouth when I'd been about to speak.

He winced and thumped his phone against his forehead. "I did a very stupid thing."

"What did you do?"

"I told them no."

His words came out harsher than ever before, much sterner than my schoolteacher voice that he loved. This time, I spoke with a conviction that if he didn't tell me the truth right now, everything we'd built together might crumble into dust around us.

"Tell me what's going on," I said. "Tell me everything. You gave in to the blackmail before, so what's changed?"

"You." He kept his head down, the phone clutched in his hand. "I can't go on being an accessory to their crimes, whatever those crimes might be. How can we have a life together unless I stop giving in to them? Yesterday, I told them no. They said I'd regret it."

"It's time you told me what hold they have on you."

He stuffed the phone in his pocket. "After the first time they contacted me, I ignored it because I thought it was a mistake. I told you that bit. A few days later, I was visiting my mother when I received a text telling me if I wanted to keep her safe I'd better do what they say. I couldn't believe it was a serious threat, but I went to the police station in Loch Fairbairn to report their harassment."

I didn't speak or touch him. I waited for him to tell me more, knowing he needed to do this in his own time. Had I made the right choice by waiting for him to explain everything? Maybe I should've broken things off with him when I first heard about the blackmail, but I'd gotten in too deep by that point. I loved him, and I had to find out what all of this meant for him and for us.

"While I was waiting for a constable to speak to me," he continued, "I got a call from my Uncle Angus. My mother had nearly been struck by a car while walking down the main street in the village. The driver had swerved onto the pavement, clearly aiming for her, but missed. She tripped and fell trying to get out of the way. She wasn't injured, only frightened, but I got the message. My anonymous masters texted me a picture of my mother lying on the ground."

"Oh God, Evan." I gripped the edge of the mattress. "I can't imagine how terrifying that must've been."

"I should've stayed in the police station and filed a report, but instead, I did what the blackmailers wanted. I became a criminal like them." He got up and paced the width of the room in front of me. "That's not the worst thing I've done."

"What else did you do?"

"My mother's near miss happened two blocks from the police station where I was when I received the picture of her. I rushed to the scene." He grasped the back of his neck with both hands. "My mother swore she was fine and didn't need to go to the hospital. I wanted to call for an ambulance, but she wouldn't hear of it. My Uncle Angus was with her, so he drove her home. I said I'd follow in my car, but then a bystander came up to me and said he'd seen the car that nearly hit my mother. It had sped off down the main street. The witness described the car in detail including the make and model and part of the registration plate number. I saw a chance to catch up to the car and...I don't know what I thought I'd do."

I wanted to get up and wrap my arms around him, but I didn't think he would want that.

"At the time," he said, "I was driving a Jaguar F-Type I'd borrowed from my cousin Rory—from his wife, actually. I drove as fast as the car would go, as fast as the terrain allowed, and I caught up to the swine who'd aimed for my mother. I ran him off the road to make him stop."

"That's not so bad," I said cautiously.

"I did more than that," he said. "I hauled the man out of his car and tried to make him tell me who he worked for. He had an English accent, that's all I found out. He wouldn't tell me his name or whether he was working for someone else. All he would say was that he'd missed on purpose and next time he would kill my mother."

"Jesus, Evan, that's awful. But that's a horrible thing he did, not something you did."

"At first, I was shaking him and shouting. When he stopped talking..." He halted directly in front of me, wincing. "I beat him."

No matter how hard I concentrated on him I couldn't get a read on his state of mind. He seemed agitated and ashamed, based on his movements.

"When I finished with him," Evan said, "his lip was split, his nose was bleeding, and he had bruises forming all over his face. I don't think I cracked his teeth, but his nose might've been broken. I realized what I'd done, the brutality of it, and I let him go with a warning for his cohorts. If they touched my mother or anyone I cared for ever again, I would hunt them down and kill them."

I clamped my teeth over my upper lip, restlessly moving my hands because I didn't know what to do with them. Didn't know what to do with him either. "I'm sure anyone would've said that in the same situation."

"I meant it. If they hurt anyone I love, I will murder them."

"You don't know who or where they are. Why didn't you tell the police about the man you caught? You knew his license plate number, or part of it."

"How could I report him? I doubt he was the one in charge of the blackmail scheme, and I didn't know whether he would follow through on his threat to kill my mother. I couldn't risk anyone getting hurt." He shook his head. "I have hurt you, though. I've lied to you and brought you into a dangerous situation. I'm a bastard, Keely."

"You are not a bad person. Beating up the guy who almost ran down your mom is understandable." I rose and took his face in my hands. "I understand why you've been afraid to tell me about the threats to your mother. You've always been different, an outcast. You're used to being self-contained and taking care of everything yourself because you can't trust other people."

He moved his eyes to look at me but kept his head down.

"The other night you said you trust me. Has that changed?"

"No." He lifted his head. "You are the only person I've ever trusted completely."

"I knew from the start you had secrets, and I realized you kept them because you don't know how to let somebody in and ask for help. It's time to learn, Evan."

What are you doing? part of me asked. *Can you trust a man who keeps secrets?* I'd considered the answer to that question ever since the morning when I'd tied him to the bed and made him talk. He'd refused to tell me why he went along with the blackmail. Today, I finally understood why he'd done it and why he'd been so reluctant to tell me. I'd had friends growing up and parents I trusted. He'd lived with not knowing who his father was, lived with a mother who kept a huge secret from him, and he'd had no friends or close family to rely on when things got tough. He hadn't developed real relationships with his cousins until recently. I was his first real relationship with a woman.

Of course he'd panicked. Of course he'd believed he had to deal with the blackmailers alone. And of course he suffered from intense guilt about pursuing me without letting on about his problems.

Maybe I should run from him. I couldn't. I didn't want to. If my father could be happy again after a devastating injury, if Serena could get back out there after losing her husband, then I had to stick with Evan through this ordeal. He'd been alone in this for too long.

"I've done it again."

His statement pulled me out of my thoughts. I withdrew my hands from his face. "Done what again?"

"Lost my temper, lost control." He shut his eyes briefly. "The day I left for America, Ron Tulloch burst into my office in a rage because I'd ordered an outside audit of his department. It's clear someone is embezzling. He didn't appreciate the implication it might be him."

"He was angry, not you."

"At first. When he called you my American whore, I lost my mind. Threw him out of my office, literally, with my hand around his throat."

"I'm sure he had it coming. That guy gives me the creeps. And what's his deal with you?"

"He blames me for the failure of his company." Evan took off his glasses and rubbed his eyes. "He tried to start up a computer programming firm, even though he's much better at accounting than programming. The company never got off the ground. At the same time, my company was gaining ground. I don't know why he thinks his failure is my fault. I gave him a job when Evanescent got big enough to need a full-time accountant and now he's the head of his own department."

"Maybe he's not grateful because he's jealous of your success."

"It's possible, I suppose."

"You think you're the villain because you lashed out at the man who hurt your mother and because you want to hunt down the people responsible for all of this. That's bullshit."

"I am a villain." He jammed his glasses onto his nose again and shoved his hands in his pants pockets. "That day, I learned what I'm capable of. No one should forgive me for it. I had no right to drag you into my life and into this mess I've made."

"Sorry, but you're stuck with me." I rubbed my arms, suddenly cold. "Should I be worried the blackmailers will come after me?"

"I don't know. As long as I do what they want, they have no reason to go after you." A muscle in his jaw jumped. "I will never let anyone hurt you."

"Don't do what they say anymore."

He shuffled backward a step. "I have to."

"No. You can't keep giving in to their demands. It isn't right."

"I know, but…" He bowed his head, scrubbing the back of it with both hands. "Maybe you're right, but it's too big a risk. I made this mess, and I have to end it."

The hard tone of his voice and the look in his eyes spoke to the part of himself he feared, the part that had driven him to beat a man. Despite what he seemed convinced of, I did not hate him or fear him for what he'd done. If anyone had threatened somebody I loved, I might've taken drastic action too.

He grimaced. "You're worried. You should be. I've had bodyguards protecting my mother for a year without her knowing. I can hire more men to guard you, but I can't promise you'll be safe."

Yesterday, I'd realized I loved him. Today, I'd found out criminals might come after me to get to him. How did a person react to something like that? I had no frigging idea. "Do you think they would hurt someone? If they missed your mother on purpose, maybe all they wanted was to scare you into giving up."

"Maybe." He plowed a hand through his hair, frowning. "Run, Keely. Get away from me as fast as you can. I've been selfish and reckless, and you should hate me for what I've done to you, not to mention what I did to that man."

"What you did was understandable considering the circumstances. I don't condone violence in general, but what those assholes did to you and your mother is the real crime. I don't think any less of you, though I'm sure you believe I should." I moved closer, tipping my head back to meet his gaze. "You pursued me because I wanted you to do it. I wanted you, period, but I was afraid to feel this way again. You changed my mind, you changed my life, and I am not running away because you punched some guy who deserved worse than what you gave him."

He flopped backward onto the mattress. "I'm sorry, Keely. I'm so sorry."

"Sorry for what? Telling me the truth?"

"I shouldn't have pushed for a relationship you didn't want. I shouldn't have pursued you. I shouldn't have—" He shut his eyes. "Shouldn't have made you fall in love with me."

"Do you honestly think I fell for you because you made me do it? Nobody controls my emotions or my choices. I chose to be with you, and I fell in love with you because of who you are."

His laughter had a bitter edge to it. "You must have a fetish for criminals."

I kicked his foot. "Don't get cute about this. I am not running away, but we need to deal with the situation. Together. As a couple."

"That could make you an accessory." He covered his face with both hands. "I need to think."

"We need to figure this out together."

He heaved his body up off the bed like he had a boulder strapped to his chest. "Give me time to think. Please, Keely, that's all I'm asking for."

I wanted to complain, but the desolation on his face changed my mind. I would give him the space he'd asked for and keep my mouth shut. "Okay."

He shambled out of the bedroom.

I trailed after him, my thoughts spinning with questions I wanted to ask him but couldn't and with imagined scenarios of what the blackmailers might do next.

While he collapsed into a chair by the windows, I lay down on the sofa. No matter what, I had to trust my instincts about him. Since the moment we'd crossed paths in Paris, I'd known he wasn't like any other man I'd ever met. Today, I had gotten what I'd wanted all along—a peek behind the curtain of his secrets.

Careful what you wish for, my rational brain warned. My heart had a different opinion. I loved him, for better or worse.

Even if the truth about him destroyed us both.

Chapter Twenty-Eight

Evan

Our jet landed at the Inverness airport late in the evening. Keely and I drove back to my apartment and fell into bed. She slept. I lay awake for hours thinking about what I'd done and how it would affect her. I'd done plenty of thinking on the jet, but none of it helped me figure out what to do. I had called Duncan to check on my mother and ask him to provide a security detail for Keely. Since I would be with her every minute, bodyguards weren't strictly necessary. I wanted the extra layer of protection in case I overlooked something.

I'd made too many mistakes already.

Shortly before we'd touched down at Inverness, I had gotten another text from the invisible masters who'd been pulling my strings for a year. *Remember the cost*, the message said. It included a photo of me and Keely in the park in downtown Carrefour. The floor had seemed to disintegrate under me, sucking me out into the atmosphere, spiraling me downward toward oblivion.

I could not let them hurt her. Whatever I had to do I'd make certain she was safe.

By the time I fell asleep, it was nearly dawn. In the morning, we stopped in at my office so I could reassure Tamsen and take care of a few business matters. After that, Keely and I drove to Ballachulish. When she noticed the large, metal suitcase I loaded into the car, she seemed confused.

"What's in there?" she asked. "Your entire billion-dollar fortune?"

"No, I brought extra security." I opened the case to show her. "Doohickeys."

She bumped her shoulder into me. "You mean security and surveillance devices for personal and business use."

I winked. "Aye, isn't that what I said?"

"What's that thing?" She pointed to a small black bag.

"A drone. It has onboard thermal and motion sensors, plus a high-definition camera."

"Are you planning to spy on me everywhere I go?"

"These are precautions, that's all."

She seemed to accept my explanation, and we didn't talk about it again.

Keely enjoyed the scenery during the drive, asking me questions about the places we passed by and the history of everything. We stopped occasionally to stretch our legs and get some fresh air, and we decided to have a picnic on the shores of Loch Linnhe, not far from North Ballachulish. I couldn't enjoy the journey the way she did. I knew these places too well, had too many memories of my childhood here, memories good and bad. I did my best to set aside all of that and focus on giving Keely a good impression of my home.

She hadn't noticed the car following us at a discreet distance. The security men knew how to blend in.

I let my gaze roam around the view. This was a beautiful place, especially the spot we'd chosen for our picnic. Trees screened the road from our view where we relaxed on a plaid blanket along the rocky shores of the loch. Across the water, we could see the Ballachulish Bridge with its elegant metal frame stretching across the invisible boundary between Loch Linnhe and Loch Leven. The dark waters of the lochs glistened in the sunshine, but the scenery paled next to the woman sitting beside me. Keely wore a green dress that accentuated her stunning eyes and made them stand out like jewels in a field of bare earth. Her raven hair cascaded over her shoulders and blew into her eyes now and then, thanks to a mild breeze. Every time she swept strands away from her face, she gazed out at the loch like she'd just seen it for the first time, her eyes clear and bright, her lips curving into a faint smile.

How she could be relaxed and happy knowing the dangers around us, I couldn't understand. Maybe she was happier because I'd told her everything. Or because we had a drone.

Our lunch was laid out on the blanket—fish and chips that we'd bought in Fort William, along with a bottle of Ben Nevis. We hadn't sampled the whisky yet.

Keely touched the bottle with two fingers. "Should we be drinking when we're on a road trip?"

"I brought that for you." I picked up a chip. "Since I'll be doing all the driving, you can feel free to enjoy the whisky."

"Oh no you don't." She flapped her wedge of fried fish at me. "I will take my turn at driving after we eat."

I stuffed the chip in my mouth. "If you insist."

She took a bite of her fish and ate it, eying me curiously. "We're going to the place where you were born and raised, where your mother lives. You are taking me home, but only once or twice have you called it home. Why is that?"

"I've told you about my childhood and my relationship with my mother. You know why I don't often say the word home."

She set down her food and wiped her hands with a napkin. "That's baloney, Evan. There's some other reason why you don't call this place home even though you clearly feel like it is."

This woman understood me better than anyone. I loved that about her, and the way she wouldn't let me get away with avoiding my problems. Most of the time I loved it. Today, I wished to hell she'd give up on this line of conversation.

I consumed three more chips, shoving them into my mouth one by one and gnawing on them like a starved animal.

Keely watched me, her gaze sharp and her posture stiff.

She didn't like it when I refused to talk. The lass had tied me to a bed to force me to confess a few of my sins to her. But that had been in Utah, a world away from my world. I'd brought her to my home, and I owed it to her to explain. She wouldn't risk imprisonment by hearing this truth.

"I don't belong here anymore," I said. "My life is in Inverness. My company is there. I come back to Loch Fairbairn to visit my cousins, but otherwise, I stay away from this area. Eighteen months ago, my mother and I had an argument and I walked away from her. I've barely spoken to her since. She wouldn't answer my questions about my father, and I was angry about that."

Keely's stern expression softened into an empathy I didn't deserve. She reached across the blanket to touch my arm. "Evan, you are not a bad son or a bad man. I know what you've done, and I still believe you are the best man I've ever known."

How could she say that about me? I'd kept secrets from her from the beginning.

"I need you with me," I said, "and I don't think I can ever make myself give you up. I've tried to be the sort of man you deserve, but I'm not."

"Aren't you the man who said fate brought us together?"

"Yes, but..." I groaned, and my eyes lifted to look at her even though it was the last thing I wanted to do. She was everything I'd never known I wanted in a woman, and she loved me. I ought to set her free, but I couldn't do it. "I believe we were meant to find each other, but I think fate has a bloody awful sense of humor. It gave me you, and at the same time it sent my worst mistakes crashing down on my head."

Had I spoken those words out loud? I hadn't meant to. With Keely looking at me that way, like she honestly would love me no matter what, I'd let the words come out. I shifted my gaze to the loch, to its dark and deep waters, the depths cold and impenetrable. That's what I'd been before Keely—a fathomless abyss no one could penetrate. She knew everything and hadn't run away from me.

Keely crawled across the blanket on her knees and pressed her warm body against mine, slipping an arm around me. "What we have is not a sick joke fate played on you. It's real. It's complicated and crazy, and I don't know where this will lead, but it is real. Even if fate put us in each other's orbits, we made the choice to be together. You chose me, and I chose you."

"Are you saying you believe in fate?"

"Let's say I'm on the fence."

"That sounds dangerously close to a yes."

She rested her head on my shoulder. "Maybe it is."

I wrapped my arm around her waist and pulled her snug against me. "I'll take that as a yes."

"Think whatever you like." She nuzzled my neck, her soft lips grazing my skin. "How far is it to your mother's house?"

"Not far."

Movement caught my attention out of the corner of my eye. The car the security men were in was parked a short distance away from our vehicle, but the movement hadn't come from that direction. A strange sensation, something between a tingle and a shiver, slithered up my spine. Someone was watching, my instincts told me. I couldn't see anyone.

My anonymous masters had followed me to America. They could easily have followed us from Inverness to Ballachulish.

I jumped up so fast Keely almost fell over at my feet.

She gave me an annoyed look. "Where are you going?"

"We are going back to the car."

I grabbed her arm and urged her to get up.

"What's going on?" she asked as she stood and brushed crumbs off her dress.

"It might be nothing, but I want to check in with your security detail."

She dug in her heels when I grasped her hand and tugged. "My what?"

"Your security detail. Bodyguards. Did I forget to tell you?"

"Uh-huh." She gestured at the picnic blanket and food. "Are we coming back for this stuff? Or will I be locked in the trunk for safekeeping? You might've forgotten to tell me about that plan too."

"Not locking you anywhere. We can collect the picnic things after we check in with your—"

"My personal secret service detail. I'm starting to feel like I've hooked up with a world leader."

"Come with me, Keely. Now. Please."

Her lips twisted into an expression halfway between a frown and a sardonic smile. "You're learning from me, eh? Polite and demanding at the same time."

"Will you come with me?"

"Yes, Mr. MacTaggart, I will obey."

Christ, I wanted to drag her into my arms and kiss her until she'd lost her breath and couldn't speak or move, until she went boneless against me with her eyes half closed in that sweet and sensual way I loved.

Instead, I stalked up the gentle slope of the beach towing her along with me. We went through the trees to the road. I checked left and right but saw only the security men's car. Squaring my shoulders, I marched us up to their vehicle, a nondescript beige sedan.

When the two men inside caught sight of me, they exchanged confused looks with each other.

I knocked on the driver's window.

The sandy-haired driver rolled down his window. "Yes, sir?"

"Have you seen anyone else in this area in the past few minutes?"

"No, sir."

Keely glanced around. "I don't see anything either."

I scanned the surroundings but couldn't make out any shapes among the trees or hidden vehicles along the road. "Search the immediate area. I thought I saw someone watching us."

Sensed someone watching. I'd never placed much faith in human instincts. Electronics, yes. People, no. Suddenly, I believed in instincts as well as fate.

"What about watching Ms. O'Shea?" the security man asked. "We were told that's our primary job."

Keely waved her hand. "I'm right here, boys. Everyone is watching me at the moment."

Ignoring her, I told the security man, "Protecting Miss O'Shea is your priority, but I will take care of her while you lot look for whoever was watching us."

"Yes, sir."

I turned to leave, hesitated, and looked back at the security man. "What are your names?"

The sandy-haired man pointed at himself and his partner in turn. "I'm Randall, and that's Howard."

"Aren't you meant to blend into the background?"

"Mr. Hendry instructed us to be inconspicuous but to stay within sight of Ms. O'Shea at all times."

I had told Duncan the security men didn't need to be in full-on stealth mode, so I shouldn't have been annoyed with these blokes for sticking close to us. Maybe if the person watching us knew we had bodyguards, they might think twice about trying anything.

"Keep to your orders," I said. "Thank you both. And she's Miss O'Shea, not Ms. O'Shea."

"Yes, sir. Thank you, sir."

These men, or at least Randall, must have been former military. He said "sir" a fair sight more than the average Scotsman. Good. Ex-military men knew how to handle rough situations.

Keely and I walked back to the beach to collect the remains of our picnic.

"On a scale from one to ten," she said, "how terrified should I be right now?"

"Honestly?"

"Yes."

"Between five and eight."

She snatched up the blanket and began folding it. "The man who's always specific to the fourth decimal place is being vague. This sounds very bad, Evan, and I'm not being sarcastic."

"You might be right about this being very bad, but there's nothing we can do about it this afternoon."

Keely stayed quiet while we tramped back to the car. I hadn't meant to frighten her so much, but I had needed to convince her there might be danger. She would be cautious if she understood the risk.

The security men were already in their car.

I kept Keely's hand in mine when I approached the sedan. She might as well hear whatever the security men had to say. When Randall rolled down the window, I asked, "Did you see anything?"

"Marks that might have been footprints, but we couldn't say for sure. If there was someone watching, they've probably left the area."

"All right. Stay a little closer behind us on the road."

"Yes, sir."

Keely leaned around me to smile at Randall. "Thank you."

"It's our job, Miss O'Shea."

When we got back to our vehicle, Keely held out her hand. "Keys."

"No."

"You've been driving for hours, and you're anxious about these threats." She wiggled her fingers. "Hand over the keys or I'll dig them out of your pocket myself."

Since the keys were in my trouser pocket, the last thing I wanted was Keely thrusting her hand inside to probe around for them. I needed to stay alert and vigilant. Her fingers that close to my cock would not help me focus.

"Okay," she said, "here I come."

She slanted toward me, her hand moving down, aiming for my pocket.

I grasped her wrist to stop her. With my other hand, I fished the keys out of my pocket and dangled them in front of her.

She grabbed them. "Thank you."

While she settled in behind the wheel, I climbed into the passenger seat. My knees hit the dashboard. I adjusted the seat and buckled up.

"Don't worry," she said. "I'll keep to the left side of the road."

If only that were the worst of my fears.

Chapter Twenty-Nine

Keely

Evan gave me directions as I steered the car down the tree-lined road toward North Ballachulish. The trees gave way to open road when we got within sight of the town, and I navigated over the Ballachulish Bridge, trying to safely admire the view of the conjoined lochs without driving us off the bridge. On the other side of the water, we took a right toward the village of Ballachulish. He instructed me where to make turns after that, and I focused on keeping to the left side of the road.

When we made the last turn, onto a dirt road, I was gripping the wheel firmly with both hands. Evan's anxiety seemed to have infected me. He had the security situation in hand, and I trusted him to watch out for both of us. Meeting his mother was a different story. What if she hated me? I was a dirty cougar after all.

I guided the car around a curve, and his mother's house came into view.

The home was a modest-size, one-story structure painted white with blue trim. Flower boxes lined every window on the front side, their cheerful colors bright in the sunlight. An older-looking car was parked in front of the house.

Evan told me to park behind the other vehicle.

We had barely gotten out of the car when a woman rushed out of the house. She seized Evan in a bear hug and kissed his cheek.

"*Gràidh*," she said, a hint of moisture glimmering in her eyes. "I havenae seen ye in so long."

Evan's face was pinched, but he put his arms around his mother.

She pulled back to study her son, her hands clasping his arms. Her gray hair hung in loose curls, framing her lovely face. Despite the wrinkles that lightly lined her face, deepening around her eyes and mouth when she smiled, the woman didn't seem all that much older than I was. Evan had never told me her age. He hadn't wanted to say much of anything about his mother.

"Oh dearie," his mother said, clasping her hands to her breast. "Ahm so happy to see ye."

"Aye, Ma," Evan said, his mouth quirking into an affection expression. "I gathered that from the way you were suffocating me with a hug."

She sniffled. "It's been so long."

He snared me around the waist and hauled me against his side. "This is Keely O'Shea, Ma. Keely, this is Aileen MacTaggart, my mother."

Aileen's joyous expression crumbled. Her lips cinched into a pucker.

"Say hello," Evan said to his mother. "Keely has come a long way to meet you."

"Could've come before you left the country instead of spiriting my son away to America." Aileen squinted at me. "How old are you, Miss O'Shea?"

An explosive breath burst out of Evan. "For Christ's sake, Ma, what does that matter? I love Keely, and you will be kind to her or I will never come back here again."

I believed him about that, but I didn't want to be the latest reason he shunned his own mother. I had no illusions I could mend the rift between them. Still, maybe I could ease the tension of this moment.

"Ms. MacTaggart," I said, offering my hand to her, "it's a pleasure to meet you."

She accepted my hand, barely shaking it, her gaze wary. "You can call me Aileen."

"Thank you, Aileen." Peripherally, I noticed Evan's attention shifting back and forth between me and his mother. "I'm forty-one, by the way."

Aileen froze. Her eyes flew wide. She acted like I'd announced I was an alien from a distant galaxy who enjoyed interspecies orgies.

Evan held me a little tighter, his body tensing.

I was about to speak—to say what, I had no idea—when Aileen snapped out of her shock and squared her shoulders.

"Pleased to meet you," she said to me. "Come into the house and we'll have a piece. You must be hungry after your long drive. Do you like tea, Keely?"

"Yes, I do."

Our picnic had been a few hours ago, and I was getting hungry again.

Hand in hand, Evan and I followed his mother into the house, down a short hallway, and into the kitchen. A small, round table occupied one corner of the space. Aileen invited us to take a seat while she organized a quick snack. I took the chair next to Evan, settling a hand on his thigh under the table and giving it a light squeeze. He smiled tightly.

Aileen brought us plates, smiling almost as tightly as her son had, and set one plate in front of each of us. "Hot cross buns. The tea is steeping, but you can start on the buns."

Evan eyed the food, his mouth twisting like he couldn't decide whether it was safe to eat. He pushed his plate with one finger, then pushed it the other way.

I leaned in to whisper, "Don't like your mother's cooking?"

"She's a fine cook. I used to eat these buns by the dozen."

"Why aren't you eating, then?"

He grumbled.

I decided that meant he was stressed about the mother-son reunion. While Aileen fussed with teacups, I pulled a piece off my hot cross bun and popped it into my mouth. It tasted faintly of lemon and had bits of dried fruit mixed into it. The top of the bun seemed to have been glazed with fruit jelly or jam.

Swallowing the food, I told Evan, "Your mom is a great cook. The buns are delicious."

Aileen returned to the table with a tea tray. As she set it down in the center of the table, she offered me a cautious smile. "Keely, I'm sorry for being unfriendly to you. I had no idea Evan was seeing anyone. I was surprised and let it show too much. Please accept my apology."

Shifting in my chair, uncomfortable despite the cushioned seat, I smiled at Aileen. "It's okay. I understand I'm a bit of a surprise."

"Aye, a surprise for sure. But a good one." She shot her son a look of disapproval tempered by affection. "You didn't need to keep your lass a secret, *mo luran*. She's lovely."

Evan studied the bun on his plate, picking at it with his thumb and forefinger.

"I donnae even mind," Aileen said, "that she's almost the same age as I am."

His hand coiled into a fist on the table as he looked straight at his mother. "Keely is not almost the same age. She's eight years younger than you and eleven years older than me. That's nearly even between us."

Aileen held up her hands. "Didnae mean offense. I'm trying to make conversation."

"Then ask Keely something other than her age."

Was he sensitive about our age difference? Since I'd first told him how old I was, he had insisted it didn't matter to him. This was his mother, though, and everybody got a little anxious about introducing a new girl-friend or boyfriend to their parents.

I squeezed his hand where it lay on his lap. His other hand stayed fisted on the tabletop.

Aileen turned to me. "Tell me a bit about yourself. I want us to get ac-quainted, especially since it's clear you mean more to Evan than any other lass he's…um…dated."

"It's okay," I said. "I know Evan hasn't had any serious girlfriends. No need to dance around it."

"Aye, he shags lasses and willnae even tell me their names."

Though she had a teasing slant to her lips and a teasing tone to her voice, it seemed lost on Evan. He scowled down at his hot cross bun.

"*Mo luran*," she said, reaching out to touch his hand, "I meant it as a joke. I'm glad you found a woman who makes you happy, and the fact you brought her here means it's more than a passing fancy."

His fisted hand relaxed, but he hunched his shoulders, his whole face pinched. Peeking at me sideways, he muttered, "She's calling me *mo luran*, a darling boy, like I'm a wee bairn."

Embarrassed? Evan? I hadn't known it could happen. I peeled his hand away from his thigh and threaded my fingers through his.

"Tell me about yourself," Aileen said to me. "Where did you grow up?"

For the next fifteen minutes, I told Aileen all about my childhood in Penn-sylvania and Utah and my current job working at Vic's store. When she asked if I'd ever been married, I hesitated only for a second. I was involved with her son, in love with him, so I figured I owed her the whole truth about me. I left out the details I'd shared with Evan, giving his mother the abridged version. The longer we chatted, the more comfortable she seemed to become with the reality of her son's relationship with me and the less she seemed to care about my checkered romantic past. When she called me "*gràidh*," I had the feeling it was an endearment, an assumption Evan confirmed when he leaned close to whisper in my ear.

"It means darling," he said, "in Gaelic. Until now, she's only called me *gràidh*. She likes you."

His mother liked me. I got a strange thrill from knowing that.

Aileen got up from her chair. "I'll wash the dishes."

"I can do the dishes," I said. "You should sit and catch up with Evan."

"Oh no, you're a guest."

"Please," I said, getting up. "I insist. You welcomed me into your home and fed us a delicious snack. The least I can do is pitch in with the dishes so you can chat with your son."

Aileen sat back down. "You are a good woman, Keely. It's no wonder Evan loves you."

I patted her shoulder as I walked past and headed for the sink. While I washed the plates and teacups, Evan and his mother talked. I didn't intend to eavesdrop, but it was hard not to overhear when they were ten feet away. Evan updated his mom on his business activities and answered her questions about Tamsen and her family. Apparently, Aileen knew Tamsen because she had visited her son's headquarters quite often before the argument that had driven a wedge between them.

When Aileen asked how Evan and I had met, I stopped in the middle of drying a plate off with a dish towel. No way could Evan answer the question honestly. Nobody told a parent they met their significant other when they had sex in a Parisian alley.

Evan cleared his throat, squirming in his chair, making it creak a little. "I met Keely when she walked into my office a month ago. Her employer had sent her to negotiate a business contract with me."

Aileen smiled over her shoulder at me. "Evan has to do everything himself, doesn't he? Cannae let anyone else handle things that no other man in his position would do."

"I know," I said. "Evan's a control freak, but it's cute."

He narrowed his gaze on me in mock censure. "Keeping the reins in my hands does not make me a control freak. It's my company, in case the two of you have forgotten."

"Aye," his mother said, her eyes twinkling. "It's your company, but it seems like you've walked away from it lately. Keely must be the one for you if she can pry your fingers off those reins."

"Yes, Keely is the one."

He looked at me when he said it, and I got a little shiver from hearing the words. No man had ever called me "the one" before. Evan believed in fate, and maybe I was starting to believe in it too. He was definitely the one for me. I'd never felt that way with my exes. I'd loved them, but not like this, not so much that I got a warm shiver from hearing him say I was the one for him.

"When will ye marry?" Aileen asked.

I dried off another plate and set it on the counter. The mention of marriage didn't bother me the way I'd expected it would.

Evan went motionless, unblinking, his expression blank. He scratched his neck. "We, ah, haven't discussed it."

Well, that wasn't entirely true. Weeks ago, he had jokingly called me Mrs. MacTaggart and then asked how I would feel about it if he wasn't joking. The night I went to his new house, the one he'd bought for me, he had said I was the kind of woman a man wanted to marry. He hadn't popped the question. Other than those two passing mentions of marriage, we had not talked about it.

Did he want to marry me? Did I want to marry him?

I got out of needing to think about it, at least for a while.

Aileen stood and said, "Your room is ready. I thought Keely would be sharing it with you, but if she'd rather not, I have the guest room ready too."

"Keely's with me."

Aileen led us upstairs. She gave me a quick tour of the room where she processed the wool she got from farmers and promised to show me the clothing she knit from it in the morning.

Once Evan and I were in the bedroom with the door shut, I set my hands on my hips. "You didn't ask me where I wanted to sleep."

"With me. That's where you want to sleep." He pulled the quilt off the bed and tossed it over a chair in the corner.

"You made a decision for me. You know I don't like that."

"I apologize." He pushed the covers back and sat on the bed. "Where would you like to sleep, Keely?"

He gave me a pleasant smile.

I moved in front of him so only a few feet separated us. "I want to sleep with you. But it would be nice if you asked me before assuming you know what I want."

"But I do know what you want." He grasped my hips and hauled me closer. "Took me a while to learn what you want, but I've always known what you need, *mo leannan*."

"It's polite to ask first."

He tugged me down to straddle him on the edge of the bed. "Keely, may I please have sex with you?"

"Your mother is sleeping two doors down."

"We had sex in your office. You weren't concerned about anyone else then."

"Your mother wasn't there."

"Ah, I see." He glided his lips up my throat, flicking his tongue out along the way to coax me into melting against him. "I can keep anyone from hearing the noises you make."

"I just met your mother. Don't want her thinking I'm a dirty cougar who has to seduce her son five times a day."

He picked me up and plopped me onto the bed on my back without even getting up. My legs wound up draped over his lap.

"All right," he said, patting my thigh. "We'll abstain as long as we're in my mother's house."

"Thank you." The last thing I wanted was to abstain, but I also didn't want his mother to get the wrong impression of me. My age had bothered her at first. How would she feel about me and Evan getting it on under her roof?

He crawled across the bed to lie down beside me. "We'll be staying at Iain's house after this. It's very large and has a guest room on the first floor, away from the other bedrooms upstairs."

"Doesn't Iain have a teenage daughter?"

"Yes, but I'm sure Malina has heard her parents having a poke. She won't be horrified if she overhears us." He rolled onto his side, slinging an arm over my midsection. "But I'm sure Rae will lock Malina in her room."

"How long are we staying with your mother?"

"A few days. She'll be coming with us to Iain's house after that." He gave me a sly look. "Don't worry. Ma will be upstairs with everyone else."

"Good."

"Hard to believe you're the same woman who let me have my way with you five minutes after we met."

"I want your relatives to like me." I hunched my shoulders. "Especially your mother."

"Relax. She likes you."

"Sure hope so."

He moved his hand up and down my belly. "Once the shock has worn off, my mother will be falling in love with you. She already called you *gràidh*."

That was true, and Aileen had been much friendlier after she recovered from being told I was eleven years older than Evan.

While he made his way to the bathroom down the hall, I walked to the window and gazed out at the darkening sky and the wooded landscape. I glimpsed the figures of the security men patrolling the property. A different kind of shiver, the cold kind, raised the hairs on my arms whenever I thought about the situation with Evan's blackmailers. Tomorrow, I would talk to Evan more about that and convince him we needed more than a security detail. We needed serious help.

Chapter Thirty

Evan

Three days after introducing Keely to my mother, the three of us drove from Ballachulish to Loch Fairbairn. My mother and Keely had become friends, fortunately, but I still had the rest of my family to deal with. We pulled into the driveway of Iain and Rae's home half an hour later, and I expected to see only Iain, Rae, Malina, and the baby. Instead, we walked into a full family reunion with seven of my cousins, their spouses, and their children along with my uncles Angus and Niall and their wives. My extended family had, of course, turned this into a bloody family reunion.

Iain was behind this. I was certain of that.

My plans for easing Keely into the MacTaggart clan evaporated the instant we stepped out of the car.

First, Aidan whooped and shouted, "Evan's finally caught a girl!"

"She caught him is more like it," Iain shouted in response. "Must've needed a bear trap to hold him down."

The crowd descended on us, an army of well-meaning but loud and boisterous Scots determined to welcome another American to the family. Keely wasn't quite family, not yet, but my cousins and aunts and uncles treated her like she was. Somehow, Keely managed to avoid being trampled or suffocated by too many fierce hugs. The rapid-fire introductions must've left her confused, but she kept up a calm and composed demeanor throughout the assault of the MacTaggarts.

I loved my family, but honestly, they all needed tranquilizers.

My thirteen-year-old cousin Malina stayed behind the others, shy as always when meeting new people. Malina was relatively new to the family since Iain hadn't known he had a daughter until last year. When I'd first met the lassie, she'd stared at me with eyes so large I thought they'd pop out of her head. Since then, she'd gotten used to me and I had trouble stopping her from blethering at me about my lack of a girlfriend.

Sometimes I swore Iain was a closet sadist and left me alone with his inquisitive daughter purely to torture me.

When Malina finally approached us, after the others had retreated, she bit her lip and stared at Keely the way she'd stared at me on our first meeting.

"Hi," Keely said, offering Malina her hand. "I'm Keely O'Shea. Evan tells me you're Malina. It's very nice to meet you."

Malina hesitated, then took Keely's hand. "Nice to meet you too."

Her voice was barely a whisper.

"No need to be shy," I told her. "Keely doesn't bite."

She wouldn't bite Malina, at least. As for me, I enjoyed the occasional nip from Keely.

"It's okay," Keely said. "I know how overwhelming it can be to meet new people. Malina and I can chat later when it's quieter."

My cousin nodded.

Keely touched Malina's arm. "I hear there's a big kitchen. Maybe us girls can whip up something gooey and delicious later with your mom's help. I love chocolate. How about you?"

"I love chocolate too."

"Bet your kitchen has all the coolest gadgets."

"Yeah, it does." Malina grinned. "We have the hugest mixer you've ever seen. Dad says it's a MacTaggart-size model."

"Can't wait to see it." She glanced my way. "Is the mixer as tall as Evan?"

Malina pretended to size me up. "Not quite, but it is pretty huge."

I half listened while Malina and Keely discussed what type of "gooey" dessert they would bake later, but I had trouble concentrating on their words. I couldn't stop looking at Keely, marveling at the way she had charmed my entire family including the shyest member. I'd fallen under her spell in Paris, but today she had my cousins and my mother enthralled too.

Keely put an arm around Malina, and they followed the group into the backyard. I trailed behind them, partly so I could admire Keely's erse and partly to give the two lasses time and space to get acquainted. I wanted my family to love Keely. I'd never introduced a woman to any of them, never talked about the women in my life because all I did was have sex with them. I had a real woman in my life, and I planned to keep her.

Malina said something that made Keely laugh. Her eyes sparkled in the sunshine like brilliant green jewels, their brightness matching her expression. When she tipped her head back, laughing harder, her hair spilled down her back.

She was the most beautiful thing I'd ever seen.

I rubbed at my chest with the heel of my hand. My chest felt tight, constricted by an emotion I'd never experienced before. I rubbed harder, struggling to name this alien feeling. I went stone still when I realized what it was.

Joy.

Most people smiled when they felt this way, but I couldn't move any of my muscles, not even the ones in my face. I stayed paralyzed, watching Malina and Keely walk away, until a large hand landed on my shoulder.

"Evan, laddie, you look stunned," Iain said. "Never been in love before, have you?"

"Is that any of your business?"

"Aye, it is. My daughter says I'm to be your fairy god-cousin who helps you find your happily ever after."

"I don't need any kind of fairy god-thing."

He clapped my shoulder. "No, you've found your true love all on your own."

True love? I had told Keely I believed fate brought us together. I supposed true love wasn't out of the question either.

"Rae was right," Iain said. "She told me you'd find your woman soon enough, and you did."

Yes, I remembered what Rae had said several months ago. *One day you'll fall in love and then everything will make sense.* I'd fallen for Keely, but I was still waiting for the moment when everything would make sense.

I also remembered what Iain had once told me. *When you meet the right woman, you'll gladly do anything to make her smile.* That was true. I loved making Keely smile. If my cousin had been right, his wife might've been right too. How "everything" would become clear, I had no idea.

"We'd best catch up," Iain said, "or we'll miss the big moment."

"I don't want a big moment, Iain. This was supposed to be a quiet meeting."

"Ah, but you know the MacTaggarts." He winked. "We never do anything small or quiet."

His reminder of that fact triggered a sinking feeling in my gut. "What have you lot been plotting?"

"Come and see."

Iain kept his hand on my shoulder while we trudged behind the house to the expansive yard and flower garden. My cousin had bought this overly large house last year when he decided to hire a private investigator to find Rae, his lost love. She loved the house. I'd bought Keely a house and she wouldn't accept it. My cousin Rory had given up his medieval castle and bought a smaller home for his wife. Which was it, then? Large house or smaller house? Maybe I shouldn't look to my cousins for all the answers, but I had no bloody idea how to manage a relationship with a woman.

"Stop thinking," Iain said. "This is a party."

"Where are the bairns? I see their parents, but not the burping, drooling babies."

"You'll like babies when you have one." Iain tilted his head to indicate the house. "Mrs. Darroch and Tavish are caring for them inside with the help of the aunts and my mother. They're taking turns."

"How did you convince Tavish the gardener to play nursemaid to bairns?"

Iain smiled knowingly. "If Mrs. Darroch is there, Tavish will be too. She's a widow, you know, and very bonnie."

And Tavish Brody was a bachelor. I supposed that solved the mystery.

I surveyed the area until I spotted Keely. She and my mother stood near the flower-covered arbor in the garden talking to the American Wives Club—otherwise known as the wives of Lachlan, Rory, Aidan, and Iain. Jamie's husband, Gavin Douglas, had been named an honorary member of the club and the Original American Husband. So far, he was the only American husband in the family. The husbands of the American Wives Club loitered a short distance away talking to my cousins Catriona and Fiona while my uncles Angus and Niall talked to Matthew Buchanan and his two brothers.

Buchanan? I threw Iain a sideways glance. "Why are the Buchanans here?"

"For shinty," Iain said as if I'd asked a ridiculous question.

"Shinty? Iain, you know I hate sports."

"This isn't a competition. It's a friendly match."

Yes, I knew how friendly matches between the MacTaggarts and the Buchanans went. Lachlan would end up wrestling with Matthew, and they'd both be reprimanded for violating the rules. Rory and Aidan would join in along with Matthew's brothers, and soon the friendly match would become a friendly brawl.

I had to talk Iain out of this nonsense. "You need twelve men for a shinty match. I count four of you, five if you count Gavin Douglas. I can't play since I'm bloody awful at it."

My cousin squeezed my shoulder. "Friendly match. Do try to grasp the concept, Evan. This is for fun and to impress our lasses."

I doubted Keely would be impressed by watching me fall on my erse repeatedly and whack myself in the shin several times.

"Even if you drag me onto the field," I said, "we still don't have enough men."

"The official rules say we need at least eight but not more than twelve."

"You have six if you're conscripting me."

"Oh ye of little faith." Iain gave me a light push, urging me to approach the crowd. "Have you forgotten how many cousins we've got? It was easy to find a few more who are willing to show up simply to watch Evan MacTaggart play his first shinty match in nine years."

I didn't play because I hated the game. All that running and swinging the caman. The MacTaggarts and the Buchanans played dirty too. If I were going to play dirty at anything, it would be in the bedroom with Keely.

My gaze traveled to her like a magnetic pull had drawn it there.

She spotted me and waved, smiling broadly. The expression lit up her entire face, her entire being, and my chest tightened again. I waved to her, though my smile wasn't as bright or as broad as hers. At least that was what I thought.

Iain chuckled. "You're grinning at Keely like a laddie who's just seen his first naked lass. Told you one day you'd meet a woman who would make you want to do anything to see her smile."

She had made *me* smile, apparently like a euphoric idiot.

But I would do anything to see that glorious smile on her face again.

"All right," I said, half groaning the words. "I'll join your friendly match. Donnae blame me if we lose. You know how awful I am at sports."

"Relax. Have fun."

Aidan threw his arms up and shouted, "They're here! The game is on!"

Four more of my cousins, ones I hadn't seen since Iain's wedding last year, jogged around the end of the house toward us. Among them, I spotted Logan, but his sisters had not arrived yet. They hated shinty as much as I did, so they might not come at all.

Aye, Logan and the others gave us plenty of men for a shinty match.

Was that a good thing?

Keely sashayed up to me, her hips swaying and her breasts bouncing just enough to make me smile. Through a miracle of willpower, I resisted the impulse to throw her over my shoulder and cart her into the house to find the nearest private room where I could make her come.

"Your laddie's worried," Iain said to her. "He thinks he can't handle a shinty match. I'm sure all he needs is a wee bit of womanly inspiration."

My cousin walked away, heading for his wife and the other American Wives.

Keely sidled up to me, slipping her arm around mine. "Do you need womanly inspiration?"

"That sounds like a sexist comment. You'd better file a harassment claim against Iain."

"Uh-uh-uh. You can't quip your way out of this one." She raised my arm and ducked under it, placing my arm around her shoulders. "Come on, you're a tough guy. You can handle a piddly little game of...whatever it is."

"Shinty. I told you about it before. We have sticks called camans that we use to bash the ball around."

"Erica told me these matches usually end in a brawl, but nobody gets hurt."

Lachlan's wife had been the first American in the family, but she'd only seen a few shinty matches. The MacTaggarts had been busy with other things and hadn't pulled together a team in quite a while. I'd hoped my cousins had given up on the idea of getting me into the sport again.

"Why don't you like shinty?" Keely asked.

"I told you I'm terrible at sports."

"But this is for fun, to spend time with your cousins."

"The last time I played shinty, I wound up with more bruises than the entire opposing team combined. I fell repeatedly." I winced, remembering the doomed match. "We lost, and it was my fault."

"Baloney." She reached up to lay a hand on my cheek. "You like to blame yourself for everything, but you are not responsible for every wrong thing that goes down in the entire universe. Your cousins want to hang out with you."

"They'll lose the match if I'm in it."

"What happened to the man who takes big risks without knowing whether they'll pan out?" She moved in front of me and linked her hands behind my neck. "Take a risk, Evan. Have fun with your cousins, win or lose, and make them happy."

"Better write my name on my shirt in case I'm battered beyond recognition after this."

Keely rose onto her toes to peer at me. "That won't be so bad. You'll have me to tend your wounds. I'll kiss them and lick them and make sure you feel all better."

My cock liked the idea, but I wasn't sure an erection was appropriate during a shinty match.

I cupped her erse. "All right, you've convinced me."

"Good." She waved to Iain. "Evan's in."

My cousin grinned. "Good show, Keely. You're an angel and a miracle worker."

I tried to frown at Keely but couldn't manage to be annoyed. "Did Iain get you to talk me into this?"

"He mentioned they wanted to play shinty today and that you haven't been willing to participate for nine years." She clucked her tongue. "Really, Evan, you need to take more risks."

"Cheeky woman." I peeled her away from my body reluctantly and walked toward my cousins. "If we lose the match, don't blame me. I warned you."

Lachlan punched my arm. "Take it easy, laddie. We haven't hanged anyone for losing a match in at least fifteen years."

"And Rory survived it," Aidan said with a smirk.

Rory rolled his eyes. "Don't listen to them. My brothers are bloody liars."

I looked back at Keely.

Surrounded by the American Wives Club, she pumped her fists in the air. "Go, Evan!"

I could hardly believe she was the same woman who had walked into my office dressed like a librarian and behaving like a proper businesswoman, the woman who had reprimanded me for flirting and told me to behave. Pumping her fists and grinning at me, she looked younger and more beautiful than ever.

"Blame Emery for that," Rory said. "My wife insisted on initiating Keely into the American Wives Club, which means agreeing to be silly and loudly supportive of their men."

"Keely is not my wife."

"Not yet." Rory's smile was enigmatic as if he knew the future.

Aidan smacked my arm. "Donnae worry. If ye marry her and she leaves you, Rory can handle the divorce. Maybe you should get him on retainer today."

"I haven't even proposed to her. It's rather early to be hiring a solicitor."

Fortunately, my cousins left to set up the playing field in the open area beyond the garden, and I was left alone. Keely had won over all my relatives—and the Buchanans too, considering the way they kept smiling and waving at her. Were they being overly friendly? Maybe I should go over there and remind them Keely belonged to me.

What sort of jealous eejit had I become?

I forced myself to look away from the friendly Buchanans, instead gazing out across the fields that surrounded Iain and Rae's home. Sheep grazed in one of several fenced areas. I turned around to look past the house toward the drive where everyone had parked their cars.

A beige sedan was parked among the throng.

The security detail. I'd forgotten about them for a while. The men would be patrolling the area, discreetly enough not to disturb our family gathering but carefully enough to keep Keely and my mother safe. I hated that they needed protection. I hated that I was the reason they needed it.

Fifteen minutes later, after talking to my uncles and Gavin Douglas, I followed the crowd out to the makeshift shinty field.

Iain handed me a blue sash. "Suit up, Evan."

"We used to have blue shirts."

He chuckled. "It's shirts off for this match. Ladies' choice."

"The women want us to play without shirts? Why?"

"If you think about it, I'm sure you can figure out why."

My cousin left to give instructions to our goalie, who was another of my cousins.

Keely rushed up to me and kissed my cheek. "Good luck."

I held up the blue sash. "I'm meant to take off my shirt and wear this."

"Yes, I know. Emery suggested the idea, and the rest of us agreed whole-heartedly."

"Why would you do that?"

"Sweaty, shirtless men on display. What red-blooded woman can say no to that?" She took hold of my shirt's hem and slid it up, her fingers grazing my skin. "Don't worry. The only shirtless man I'll be drooling over is you."

"I think you've spent too much time with Emery."

"Don't tell me you're shy about taking off your shirt. The man who walks around buck naked in front of floor-to-ceiling windows in his apartment."

"That's different."

She smiled, her cheeks dimpling and her eyes sparkling. "How, exactly?"

I opened my mouth only to realize I had no idea how to justify my statement. I groaned out a sigh, handed her my glasses, and pulled my shirt off over my head. "Have it your way."

Catcalls erupted from the American Wives Club.

Emery cupped her hands around her mouth and shouted, "Woo-hoo, Evan!"

"About time we saw some skin!" Erica called out.

I didn't even try to understand these women. They were insane.

When I glanced at Rory and Lachlan, they were smiling and laughing at their wives' statements. It seemed they didn't mind their women sexually harassing me.

"Can you see without your glasses?" Keely asked.

"Well enough. All I need to do is avoid getting smacked in the head."

"Everyone on the field," Iain shouted.

I slung the sash around my neck, letting it drape diagonally across my chest, and marched off to my doom.

Chapter Thirty-One

Keely

For an hour, I occupied a folding lawn chair alongside the wives of the MacTaggart men and watched them playing shinty. I'd never heard of the game before I met Evan, and I'd certainly never witnessed a match. Shirtless men dashed around the field carrying camans, which reminded me of field hockey sticks, and bashed the ball around with those sticks. Since this was a lawn and not an official shinty field, they'd drawn chalk lines in the grass—a circle in the middle and two semicircles at either side of it. They'd also created goal posts out of saplings that had their limbs sheared off. The nets attached to the goal posts looked well-worn.

The men moved so fast I had trouble following the action. Sometimes they would whack the ball while it was on the ground. Other times, they would send it flying through the air. Lachlan grabbed the ball and tossed it in the air, swinging his caman to send the ball sailing. Its arcing trajectory slammed it into the ground halfway across the field. Evan got hit in the shin twice but kept going without a pause. At one point, Rory tackled a Buchanan, the two rolling around on the ground like Greek wrestlers until Lachlan and Iain pulled them apart.

Rory and his opponent grinned and slapped each other on the back.

The match kept going.

I didn't know if wrestling was a regulation shinty tactic, but I had my suspicions these families liked to play rough and break the rules. Evan got tackled twice and later jumped one of the Buchanans, the two wrestling even more roughly than Rory and his opponent had done. Despite his reluctance to take part in the match, Evan gave as good as he got. He made two goals, inspiring raucous cheers and whoops from the crowd. I screamed louder than I ever had in my life. Evan noticed and gave me a thumbs-up sign, then blew me a kiss.

Logan MacTaggart, another in Evan's army of cousins, scored a goal by leaping in the air and whacking the ball. It barreled into the goal net, tearing a hole in the flimsy thing. Everyone cheered, even the opposing team. We ladies agreed that Logan was one tough player and, as Emery phrased it, "too hot to have been hidden from our view for so long." Apparently, none of my new friends had met Logan before Iain's wedding last year. He laughed and joked with his cousins during the game, but when he had the ball, he got a deadly glint in his eyes.

By the time the match ended, no one could remember how many goals either side had scored. They decided to call it a tie. Winning or losing was not the objective here.

Logan ambled past the ladies, smiling and nodding to acknowledge us. Sweat dampened his dark hair, and I could barely see his hazel eyes with the sun making him squint.

Evan sauntered up to me, his body covered in splotches of dirt and grass. Sweat dribbled down his temples. He had shed the blue sash but still wore no shirt. I'd never seen him rumpled and filthy. It was amazingly hot.

"I did all that for a bleeding tie," he said.

"You had fun, didn't you?"

He screwed up his mouth, trying not to smile, but finally gave it up and grinned. "Aye. Never knew getting dirty without a naked woman under me could be fun."

"Oh, don't worry. You'll be getting dirty with a naked woman as soon as possible."

"Yes, I will." He threw an arm around my waist and hauled me into his sweaty, filthy body. "Did I impress you with my athletic prowess on the field?"

"Definitely. But I already knew you're powerful and agile and have incredible stamina." I pulled his glasses out of my shirt pocket. "You'll want these."

He slipped them on and feigned surprise. "I thought I was holding Mrs. Darroch."

I punched him in the arm.

Just then, Iain approached us and slapped Evan on the shoulder. "Good show. We would've beaten the Buchanans if Matthew hadn't cheated on that last goal. It's all for fun, anyway."

"Yes, it is," Evan agreed.

His cousin gaped at him with sarcastic shock. "Evan MacTaggart is admitting shinty is fun? I think I hear the Four Horsemen of the Apocalypse riding up the driveway."

"Don't tease him," I said, "or you'll never get him on the field again."

"Oh, he's in the cult already," Iain said. "There's no way out."

Evan shook his head at his cousin's comment. "Do cult members get to have showers? I'm covered in dirt and possibly spittle."

Iain looked at me. "There's a very large shower in your room. Malina put a sign on the door so you'll know which room it is."

"You'd better be giving us the downstairs bedroom."

"Aye, Evan, we know you'll want your privacy. Your room is at the back of the house away from the common areas. So go on, take your woman and enjoy the amenities. You've earned it."

I swore Evan blushed the tiniest bit, but he grasped my hand and guided me toward the back door of the house. We said goodbye to his family along the way. Most of them tromped around to the driveway to find their cars and leave. The Three Macs—which was, I'd learned, what Iain called his three cousins Rory, Lachlan, and Aidan—hung around to chat with Iain and Rae and Evan's mom. Malina, who had cheered and screamed for her dad during the shinty match, lounged in one of the folding chairs while her parents gabbed.

The teenage girl had marked the door to our room all right. It sported a bright pink cardboard sign with gold glitter lettering on it and puffy lavender stuff glued around its edges. The sign read, "Keely and Evan 4ever." A red glitter heart surrounded the words.

"Well," I said, "we certainly won't get confused about which room is ours."

"I'm familiar with Malina's love of glitter and the color pink." He pushed the door inward. "Welcome to your suite, Miss O'Shea."

He threw me over his shoulder.

I yelped. That fact he wanted to carry me wasn't a surprise, but the over-the-shoulder treatment was new. My hair fell around my face so I couldn't see anything when he strode into the bedroom and, as usual, kicked the door shut. He laid me down on the bed. I pushed my hair away from my face, spitting out strands that had gotten into my mouth.

"Take your clothes off," he said. "We're having a shower together."

I got undressed in record time, hurling my clothes across the room in my haste to get naked for him. Once I was nude, I jumped to my feet. While I'd been focused on my own clothing, he'd shed his too.

He crooked a finger at me. "Come, Keely."

"I think you're confusing me with a dog again."

"Not that kind of 'come,' Keely."

"Oh." I trotted toward the door of the attached bathroom. "I like the sound of that."

He slapped my bottom as he sprinted past me.

We got the water good and steamy and stepped inside the glass-enclosed shower. Iain had not exaggerated. This was a MacTaggart-size shower. It featured five heads each pulsating water over our bodies, and even a bench seat.

I poured soap into my hands and lathered it up. "Time to get you clean."

He lifted his arms and spread his legs. "Have at it."

I started with his face. He shut his eyes and lowered his arms, letting me wash the grime off. He sighed, relaxing as I stroked his cheeks with my fingers and ran my palms over his forehead. Since I had him alone and in no condition to run away, I decided this was a good time to talk.

"Why don't you ask your cousins for help?"

"In what way?"

Done with his face, I squeezed shampoo out of a large bottle and began to work it through his hair. "You know what. The blackmail problem."

"There's nothing they can do."

"Oh come on." I massaged his scalp with my fingers, spreading the shampoo suds, gratified when he moaned and the tension in his muscles slackened. "Rory is a lawyer and the others have skills too. You could talk to them."

"No. This is my problem to solve."

"And you've done such a great job of that for the past year."

"Yes, I'm a raging eejit. We've already established that fact."

"I would never say you're an idiot." I touched my fingers to his forehead to encourage him to tilt his head back and smoothed my fingers through his hair to rinse out the shampoo. "You have been very self-contained, though. And you still think you have to deal with everything on your own, won't even let me help. The DIY method is not working, and you know it."

He groaned, a miserable sound rather than an erotic one. "Could we talk about this later?"

"Nope." I grabbed a big sponge from a little shelf and poured liquid soap onto it. "While I bathe you, my lord, you can explain to me why the hell you won't ask anyone for help."

"I asked Duncan Hendry to send a security detail."

"Mm-hm." I squeezed the sponge until the milky soap turned into white suds. "I bet you paid him for that and didn't share all the details about what the problem actually is. Right?"

"Well, I—" He scrunched up his face. "Yes, right."

The water had rinsed off most of the dirt, but that didn't stop me. I skated one hand over his skin while with the other I glided the sponge in big, slow circles. The suds dribbled down his chest, inching their way toward the trail of hairs that led to his groin. I let my hand follow the path of the soap, swirling my palm and caressing his flesh with my fingertips.

His cock began to stiffen.

"You like your cousins," I said. "I know that, but I guess you don't trust them—or me. Not enough to let us lend a hand."

He let his head fall back, his eyes half closed. "You're currently lending two hands, and I have no problem with that."

"Do I have to tie you up again to get a straight answer?"

"Wouldnae mind if you did."

My breasts brushed against him as I smoothed the sponge over his neck and shoulders and down again to his rippling pectoral muscles. I took my time, exploring his skin with my fingertips and laving him with my tongue when the steaming water had rinsed away the soap.

"I trust you," he said. "And I trust my cousins, but I don't know them very well and they don't know me well either. It's my fault."

"You have to stop blaming yourself for everything." I moved the sponge to his hips and slid it around to his ass. "Your cousins love you. I could see that from the moment they greeted you today. I get that you've always felt like an outsider, but it doesn't have to be that way. You are not a bullied kid anymore, and your family will not hate you for what you've done. Give them a chance to do something for you."

When I finished washing his tush, I couldn't resist giving his erection the same treatment. I squeezed the sponge to drizzle suds onto his length. He groaned again, this time a deep and resonant sound of pure pleasure. I stroked him lightly, grazing his balls with my fingers.

"Keely," he said, his voice huskier.

I gave him a nudge, and he turned to the side enough that the water cascaded down his torso and spilled over his dick, rinsing away the soap. Kneeling, I got to work cleansing his legs. The feel of his hair-dusted skin and those powerful leg muscles had my body awakening with a tingling warmth that suffused my body and a slickness that gathered between my thighs.

"Ask your cousins for help."

"I will consider it."

"Uh-huh. I know that's Evan code for 'no bloody way.' If you don't ask, I will." I pushed on his hip, waiting until he leaned back against the wall. I picked up one foot and bathed it too, massaging the sole until he was breathing hard, every muscle taut from his mounting desire. "Last chance. Ask them or I'll do it."

"Ordering me to—" He hissed in a breath when I accidentally grazed my hair against his erection. "I'll do it if and when I decide it's necessary."

So damn stubborn. I'd known this about him from the start, but never before had his pigheaded streak resulted in a potentially dangerous situation. Bodyguards were nice and all, but we needed to root out the cause of our problem.

Done with his feet, I poised my face in front of his cock. "Would you like me to relieve your pain?"

"No," he growled, his eyes blazing with unrepentant hunger. "Prepare for a good, hard fucking."

He grasped me around the waist and hoisted me up and off my feet.

I latched my arms around his neck. "Oh yes, please."

"You're always wet for me, but this time you're drenched all over." He pushed me back against the wall with his hard body pinning me there. His cock was trapped against my belly. "I will think about what you said—once I'm capable of thinking again."

That was good enough for me, for now.

Chapter Thirty-Two

Evan

In the morning, I brought Keely breakfast in bed. She was still sleeping when I sneaked back into our room carrying a tray of food, so I set the tray down on the bedside table and sat on the edge of the bed to marvel at the woman I loved. She looked so peaceful and happy when she slept. Her lips had curled up slightly at the corners, making me wonder what sort of dreams she had. Her hair had fallen over half her face. I swept it back, tucking it behind her ear.

She stirred but didn't wake up.

I kissed her cheek.

A breath whispered out of her.

"Wake up, Keely," I said, touching my lips to hers.

Her arms came around my neck, and she pulled me in for a deeper kiss. When she let me go, she smiled sleepily and stretched. "Good morning."

"Aye, good morning." I couldn't help admiring her breasts when she stretched again and the sheet slid off them. "I made you breakfast."

"Mmmm, yum. I'm starved from all that exercise last night."

"I did work you rather hard. Are you sore?"

"No, Evan, I'm fine." She sat up and draped her arms around my shoulders. "I'm no delicate virgin. I can handle you just fine, Mr. MacTaggart."

"Likewise, Miss O'Shea."

She traced the seam of my lips with her fingertip. "I do love it when you call me Miss O'Shea. Reminds me of the day in your office when you ordered me to hike up my skirt."

"You like it when I command you."

"Can't deny that."

I smacked her bottom. "Sit back. It's time for breakfast, Miss O'Shea."

Keely shimmied her hips as she backed up to the headboard. The sheet had slid away from all of her body except her calves and feet. Her stiff little nipples jutted out like signposts guiding me to my destination, but I needed to feed her, not fuck her.

"Ready to eat," she said, her gaze flicking to the lump in my trousers.

"Food, Keely, that's what you'll be eating." I grabbed her robe off the bedpost where she'd hung it last night. Handing it to her, I said, "Cover up. Can't have my woman catching cold."

"You weren't calling me your woman until after we came here." She slipped the robe on, covering her edible body. "I think you got the 'my woman' thing from your cousins."

"If you don't like it, I won't call you that again."

"Never said I don't like it." She fingered the collar of my shirt. "Actually, I love it. And for the record, you are my man."

"Yes, I am." I picked up the food tray and set it down on her lap. The legs of the metal tray rested on the bed at either side of her hips. "I could feed you."

"That's what you're doing. You made me breakfast."

"No, I meant—" Giving up on explaining, I lifted the half-dome lid that covered the plate of food and set it on the table. I picked up the fork. "I meant I could feed you."

"Oh." She folded her hands on her lap beneath the tray. "Go on. Serve me."

"Anything for you." I pointed at the items on the plate in turn while I listed them for her. "Lorne sausage, link sausage, bacon, fried eggs, tattie scones, fried tomatoes, black pudding." I lifted the lid off a smaller plate. "Buttered toast."

"Holy cow, Evan. I hope this is for both of us because I cannot eat this much food and still be able to walk afterward."

"I thought we could share, yes." I tapped the teapot seated beside the larger plate. "I also made you some tea, Highland blend."

She bent forward to kiss me, nearly toppling the tray. "Thank you."

"Better wait to thank me after you've tasted the food." I glanced at the plate. "I should warn you black pudding is sausage made with pig's blood, with oatmeal as a filler. When Lachlan and Erica first met, he fed her black pudding without telling her it has blood in it until after she'd eaten it. She didn't appreciate that."

"Erica told me that story. She laughed about it."

"Today, she does. At the time, according to Lachlan, she screamed and punched him in the arm, then ran for the nearest sink to wash her mouth out."

"And Erica told me that's a myth. She did not scream, she yelped and slapped his arm."

"Either way, I don't want you to be shocked. You can eat the black pudding or not."

She leaned back against the headboard. "I'll try it."

"You will? Even Rae won't try it, and she's not at all squeamish."

"A month ago, I probably would've said no thanks. But you have opened me up to all sorts of new experiences and you've shown me the value of taking risks." She straightened and adjusted her robe. "I'd love to try black pudding."

I picked up a fork and speared the sausage in question, broke off a bite, and raised it to her lips. "Open up."

She closed her lips around the fork, drawing the sausage bite into her mouth. Her brows drew together, and her lips puckered a wee bit as she chewed. Once she'd swallowed, her expression smoothed out. "It does have a lively flavor."

"Erica called it the most disgusting thing she'd ever put in her mouth."

"I've tasted much worse things." She flapped her fingers to gesture at her mouth. "Give me another bite."

"You don't have to eat it."

"Need at least two bites to decide how I feel about it."

I speared another bite and slid it between her lips.

She chewed, her eyes half closed. After swallowing, she took a few seconds to consider her opinion. "It's okay, but I won't be begging you to cook it for me."

"Fair enough." I picked up a tattie scone and tore off a piece. "You'll like this. It's made with potatoes, not blood."

She opened her mouth, and I placed the scone bite in her mouth. She closed her lips around my fingers, licking them before letting go. After she'd swallowed her bite of scone, she hummed her approval. "Very good. Did you make all this food from scratch?"

"Yes."

"Impressive, Mr. MacTaggart. Feed me more."

After I'd finished feeding her, and she'd fed me, we dressed and left the privacy of our room to find Iain and Rae. They were in the kitchen—kissing, as it turned out. Iain had his wife backed up to the island, his hands on her hips. When Keely and I walked into the room, they stopped kissing but didn't move.

"Good morning," Iain said. "Thought you two would sleep later."

"We're well rested, thank you," I told him.

Keely raised onto her toes to whisper in my ear. "Ask him."

I knew what she meant, of course. She wanted me to ask Iain for help with the situation I'd gotten us both involved in, the blackmail and the threats to our safety. After sleeping on the problem, I'd realized she was right. I did need help. Understanding the need and speaking the words proved to be very different things. It had taken a year for me to see I couldn't let this go on any longer. I'd needed Keely to show me that. Asking my cousin for help...

A cold sweat broke out on my brow just thinking about it.

"You can do this," Keely whispered.

And if I didn't do it, she would. She'd told me that last night. I understood why she felt that way. I'd let the problem fester for much too long, all because I was too damn stubborn to let anyone see my weaknesses and my mistakes. I'd never been good at swallowing my pride. It always got stuck in my throat.

Iain leaned against the island next to his wife. "Evan, you look like you've got something on your mind."

"Yes, I do." I tugged on my collar, but my throat still felt tight. "Could we go into the sitting room? The kitchen is rather...open."

"Rae," Iain said, "why don't you show Keely the rest of the house?"

"The women should come too," I said. "Keely already knows what I need to tell you. Rae should hear it too."

Iain nodded again and led the way out of the kitchen, down the hall to the sitting room. Keely and I sat on the sofa while Iain and Rae took the chairs by the fireplace. Outside the windows, clouds began to overtake the sun, painting the world in shades of gray.

Everyone was waiting for me to speak. How was I meant to explain this? I'd been a bloody-minded moron driven by pride and my inability to trust anyone completely.

Keely touched my knee and offered me an encouraging smile.

Trusting her had been the most intelligent decision I'd ever made. She believed Iain would understand. Maybe he would, maybe he wouldn't. I had to try.

Iain crossed one ankle over the opposite knee and laid his hands on the chair's arm. "Whatever it is, you'll feel better if you say it."

Though I had my doubts about that, I cleared my throat and started. "I'm being blackmailed by people I've never met or seen or spoken to. They've made threats against my mother and Keely, though the threats are vague. I need to find these people and stop them." I hauled in a deep breath and blew it out. "I need help."

"You shouldn't have been afraid to tell me. I understand your situation better than most people would."

Rae gave her husband a knowing look. "You can say that again. I seem to recall a certain MacTaggart man who was afraid to tell me he was being blackmailed by a Welsh asshole."

Keely's gaze flickered between me and my cousin. "Iain was blackmailed?"

"Aye," Iain said. "Long, long ago during a regretful time in my life, I let Rhys Kendrick push me into authenticating a forged artifact. I'm an archaeologist, in case Evan didn't mention that. Kendrick threatened to send my father to prison. Da used to, shall we say, appropriate possessions that didn't belong to him in order to make ends meet. He only took from wealthy people and never more than he needed."

Rae shook her head and sighed. "Poor Angus, that sweet, deluded man."

Keely stared blankly at Iain for a few seconds. "Your father is a burglar?"

"A well-meaning and misguided one, yes," Iain said. "He only stole as much as he needed to keep our family from starving, and he was in and out of prison for most of my childhood. My father is retired these days."

"The point," Rae said, "is that Iain knows very well how a good but stubborn man can get tangled up in unsavory things. He's the right one to help you, Evan."

Iain leaned forward, his elbows on his knees. "Evan needs more help than I can give. Let me call in reinforcements before we get into the details. Everyone should be here."

"Everyone?" Keely said.

I settled my hand on her knee. "He means Rory and Lachlan, and possibly a few other MacTaggarts. I imagine their wives will want to be here too."

"Only if you consent to it," Iain said. "This is your show, not mine. But we do have a large pool of talent in the family, including the American Wives Club."

"We should bring Emery in on this. I'm an expert on security and surveillance systems, and I'm involved in creating the software for my devices, but I am no hacker. Emery knows more about computer systems than I do. Maybe she could trace the text messages I've been receiving."

"If she can't, I'm certain she knows someone who can." Iain trained his gaze on Keely. "Did Evan tell you how he helped solve my problem with Rhys Kendrick?"

I snorted. "That was all your wife's doing."

"Not all," Rae said. "Your devices helped us get the proof we needed to have Kendrick locked up for a good long time."

Keely smiled—at me. "That doesn't surprise me at all. Evan is a genius."

I contemplated my feet, scratching the back of my neck.

"He's a little shy about accepting credit."

"We've noticed," Rae said.

Once they'd finished making me uncomfortable with their praise, Iain called Rory. When my other cousin picked up the call, Iain said, "Rory, my man. We've got a code-red situation here. Evan needs our help with something that's not unlike my problem last year. Yes, bring Emery. All right, you call Lachlan and Aidan. We need all hands on deck for this one."

After saying goodbye to Rory, Iain dialed another number.

"Who are you calling?" I asked.

He gave me his casual smile, the one Rae called his Buddha smile. No one could understand what Iain meant when he smiled that way, no one except his wife most likely.

"Logan," Iain said into the phone. "We need your special expertise with a situation Evan's gotten into. Aye, right away. You're a good man."

Once he disconnected the call, I squinted at Iain. "Logan? What's his special expertise? The man works as a bricklayer. Are we planning to build a fortress?"

"You haven't gotten to know Logan yet, have you? He used to be MI6."

Keely looked confused, so I explained. "It's the Secret Intelligence Service or SIS, commonly known as MI6."

Her eyes widened. "Your cousin Logan was a spy?"

"This is the first I've heard of it."

"Most of the family knows," Iain said, "but Evan's been a bit standoffish with his cousins. Rae and I had to all but kidnap him to get Evan to come to our house for dinner the first time."

Keely's lips cinched together, a clear sign she was trying not to laugh. "I'm familiar with his extreme need for privacy."

Rae smiled. "At least he finally found a good woman."

"What every man needs," Iain concurred. "Being a billionaire doesn't hurt either."

His wife squeezed his knee. "Poor Iain has to settle for being a multi-millionaire."

"At least I have more money than Lachlan and Rory."

I dropped my forehead into my palm, suddenly exhausted from listening to the people I loved making jokes and plotting how to get me out of the mess I'd made for myself. They shouldn't need to do this. I shouldn't have let things spiral out of control. I managed an entire company, a billion-dollar corporation, but I couldn't manage my own life.

Keely settled a hand on my back, moving it in circles, trying to soothe me.

ANNA DURAND

221

I shouldn't be soothed. Solving the problems I'd caused should've been my top priority, not pursuing a woman who hadn't wanted a relationship. What had I done to her?

She stood up. "While we wait for reinforcements, Evan and I will take a walk."

"Good idea," Iain said. "Fresh air will make the obstacles seem less insurmountable."

I raised my head to frown at Iain. "Something is either insurmountable or not. There's nothing in between."

Keely tapped one finger on the top of my head. "That's the attitude that got you into trouble in the first place. You need to develop a positive attitude, like you did when you decided to win me over."

I grumbled.

She seized my hand and tugged in an attempt to make me get up. When I didn't, she planted her hands on her hips and drummed her fingers. "Will you stand on your own or do I have to get Iain to pick you up?"

Iain jumped out of his chair as if preparing to do just that.

"Fine," I said and pushed up off the sofa. "Take me for a walk, Miss O'Shea."

"Behave, Mr. MacTaggart."

My cousin and his wife seemed mildly confused by our interchange, but I had no intention of explaining why Keely and I called each other by our last names. "Because I love fucking her while she's telling me to behave" wasn't the sort of thing I would ever share with anyone.

I let Keely lead me out of the house.

Chapter Thirty-Three

Keely

I rested my head on Evan's thick bicep while we ambled around the outside of the fenced pastures. The sheep grazed, occasionally baaing, and the llama grazed too while sticking close to her charges. Malina had told me all about Lily the llama, who guarded the sheep from predators, and her infatuation with Iain. He had, Malina said, gotten used to being the object of a llama's affection even when Lily nuzzled and licked his face. Two horses also hung out in the pasture.

The green grass and rolling terrain dotted with wildflowers created a beautiful picture. I would have enjoyed it more if not for the danger looming over us and Evan's need to take sole responsibility for everything. If we found out where the blackmailers were, would he take off on his own to confront them?

I asked him that very question.

He halted us on top of a little rise. His gaze went distant, not like he was admiring the landscape but as if he were brooding about the past. "Maybe I will. Maybe I should."

"Take off after the bad guys all alone? No, Evan, you should not."

"It's my fault this is happening."

"Promise you will not go lone wolf on me."

"Do you want me to lie?"

"No, I want you to see reason." I searched his face for some clue to his mood, but he wasn't showing me anything. His self-contained persona had taken over again. "Maybe you could get away with this before, but you are no longer alone and you no longer get to make decisions alone. You wanted a relationship." I spread my arms to indicate myself. "Well, here it is. We do this together, all the way or not at all."

"Am I meant to include you in every decision I make? Should I consult you about the specifications for all my devices?"

"You know that's not what I meant."

He scowled at the lush, green fields around us. "I understand what you meant, but you don't understand what I've said."

"Explain it to me. I'm listening."

"It's not about me." He took his glasses off, like he intended to clean them, but frowned and put them back on. "Everything I'm doing, everything I might do, will be to protect you. I will do anything it takes to keep you safe."

A note of desolation colored his resolute statements, and I resisted the urge to hug him. I didn't want to feel this way. I wanted to be angry and clobber some sense into him. How could I? He'd sworn he would do anything to keep me safe. If he ran off on a lone-wolf suicide mission, it would be to protect me. I couldn't change his mind. I'd known from the start he was the most stubborn man on earth.

Since I had no chance of talking him out of his decision, I switched tactics. "At least promise me you won't take off on your own without talking to me about it first."

He looked me straight in the eye. "I promise I will not do anything without telling you."

At least he had agreed to one concession, but his phrasing left me uneasy. I knew he would never make a promise unless he intended to keep it, but I'd said he shouldn't do anything without talking to me first. He had said he wouldn't do anything without telling me. The slight difference in meaning made my skin itch.

We walked for a bit longer, without talking, and returned to the house to find the cavalry had arrived. The sitting room had gotten too cramped, so they'd moved into the larger dining room. I met Mrs. Darroch, the housekeeper who looked after the homes of two couples, Rory and Emery and also Gavin and Jamie. I also met Tavish Brody, who served as groundskeeper at the castle Rory and his wife had turned into a museum. Today, Tavish was helping Mrs. Darroch wrangle all the kids with assistance from Malina. The trio had taken the tots outside for some playtime. Seven toddlers and infants? I didn't envy their babysitting duty.

Evan and I joined the rest of the gang, taking the seats they'd saved for us around the long wooden table. The others seemed to have been discussing Evan's dilemma for a while before he and I arrived. When we walked into the room, everyone stopped talking. Once we'd sat down, Rory rose to speak to us.

"We've been tossing ideas around," Rory said. "I can help with any legal issues, and I have a connection at the Home Office who would be more than happy to lend a hand if there's anything he can do. Lachlan also has a connection at the Home Office, and he has a large group of former clients with varying levels of influence and connections that may be of help to us."

Evan had told me Lachlan used to work as an independent financial consultant before he met Erica and retired to raise a family. He'd earned a small fortune from his job and even more when he sold his company.

A blonde woman seated beside Rory got up. It took me a moment to remember this was Emery, Rory's wife. I'd met so many people since yesterday that I had trouble keeping the right names with the right faces. Evan had jokingly told me he could give me a cheat sheet with photos.

He hadn't cracked a joke, or a smile, since we'd left the bedroom this morning.

"I have connections too," Emery said, "but not in government or MI6."

Aidan craned his neck to see the whole room. "Where is Logan, anyway? Didn't someone call him?"

"Yes," Emery said. "Rory called him, and Logan will be here soon. He had a job to finish first."

"Is that a bricklaying job?" Aidan asked. "Or a James Bond job?"

Rory rolled his eyes. "Logan is an ordinary citizen these days."

Emery waved her hands to regain everyone's attention. "As I was saying, I have connections. I'll take a look at the texts Evan has received, but I'll probably need to bring in reinforcements on the tech front. I've already called my friend Sabri in America. He's a wiz at deconstructing stuff like that, so I'm sure he can help us track the messages. If not, he knows even more people, the type with mad skills when it comes to hacking. Strictly for legitimate reasons. Some of them work for the US government."

"What about the angel investors?" I asked. "Evan thinks the money is related to the blackmail somehow."

"It's not."

Though Emery had opened her mouth, those words had not come from her.

Aileen MacTaggart had stepped into the dining-room doorway. A determined expression had replaced her normally pleasant one, and she held her shoulders back, her chin lifted.

Evan's entire body went rigid.

I laid a hand on his arm, but my attention stayed glued to his mother. Everyone else's did too.

"No one thought to invite me to this discussion," Aileen said, her tone revealing no anger about that fact. "Mrs. Darroch told me what was happening in here. It sounds like you have a plan."

"We do," Rory said.

"Then I need to talk to my son in private." Aileen met my gaze. "And Keely too."

She had included me, planned to tell me whatever she needed to say to her son. I should've felt pleased by this development. It meant she accepted, or at least had come to terms with, my role in Evan's life. I couldn't muster any feelings beyond anxiety for the future.

Evan and I rose and followed his mother to the sitting room. She shut the door. Evan and I sat on the sofa again while Aileen perched on the edge of a chair, hands clasped on her lap.

"How do you know," Evan asked, "the angel investors are not connected to the blackmail?"

The flat tone of his voice and his stony expression made my skin crawl. He'd pulled back into himself, retreating into his persona as the stoic CEO. Even when I'd watched him performing his CEO duties, he hadn't been like this. It was worse today. Much worse.

I placed my hand on his, but he pulled away.

Aileen studied her hands. "I don't know about the second one, but the first angel investor was your father."

Evan went so stiff, his back ramrod straight, that I expected to see a steel rod jutting out of the top of his spine. "That is not possible."

His mother nodded gravely, keeping her head down. "Evan, I'm sorry I've lied to you all these years. Please believe everything I did was to protect you."

"Protect me?" he said with a flinty edge to his voice. "I have a right to know who my father is. You swore to me you had no idea where he was."

"No, I always said you would never find him."

A muscle twitched in his jaw, and I could see him grinding his teeth.

His mother lifted her head, gazing at him with a pleading look in her eyes and tears gathering there. "Please let me explain. I love you, *mo luran*, and I would never have hurt you this way without a reason."

Evan shot to his feet. Through clenched teeth, he snarled, "Tell me the truth. Now, Aileen."

Chapter Thirty-Four

Evan

I shouldn't have sounded so angry. I shouldn't have called my mother by her first name. No matter what I felt inside, I always kept my anger tempered on the outside. How was I meant to react to what my mother had confessed? Thirty years of thinking my father hadn't known about me, hadn't cared about me, ended right here in this room—and I wanted the goddamn truth. I deserved it, didn't I? My father had provided the largest single investment that made it possible for me to start my company.

My father. He'd always been a ghost to me.

Keely slipped her hand into mine, squeezing lightly to get my attention.

I looked down at her, and the love and worry on her face doused my anger in an instant. She had never seen me this way. Only once before had I gotten this upset, and that instance had been with my mother too, on the day last year when I'd demanded she tell me something about my father. She'd refused.

"Sit down," Keely said softly, tenderly. "Let your mother explain."

I love you, mo luran, my mother had said. She'd never spoken those words before. We weren't the sorts to express our feelings that directly. I'd always believed my mother loved me, even when she refused to answer my questions. Looking at her this morning, with tears rolling down her cheeks, I knew I still believed it.

Sighing, I dropped back onto the sofa.

Keely rested her head against my shoulder and slipped her hand into mine, lacing our fingers.

I wrapped my arm around her, taking more comfort from the warmth of her body than I'd ever taken from anyone else. I would never let anyone hurt her.

Calmed by the woman in my arms, I spoke to my mother in a neutral tone. "I'm listening."

She dug a tissue out of her pocket, sniffled, and dabbed at her eyes. "I met your father when I was eighteen. I'd begged my parents to let me go to Rome for a summer course in painting. I had wanted to be an artist when I was younger. Since I earned enough from a part-time job to pay for the trip myself, they let me go. I was eighteen after all and very levelheaded."

I fought the urge to tell her to speed up the story. She needed to tell me in her own time, in her own way.

Her eyes took on a dreamy softness, and her lips curled up at the corners. "I met him on my second day in Rome. We bumped into each other at an outdoor market. Samuel Drake was the best-looking man I'd ever seen, charming and clever, more attentive than any of the lads I had known at home. He was seven years older than me and had gone to Rome for his work on a temporary assignment for a few months. We became lovers, and by the summer's end we were engaged to be married."

"Married?" I said, somehow staying calm. With Keely pressed against me, I couldn't hold on to anger for more than one second. One point two seconds at most.

"Aye," my mother said. "We decided to fly to America before going to Scotland to tell my parents. Sam planned to quit his job and move to Ballachulish to be with me. His mother had passed away years earlier, and he didn't get along with his father, so he had no reason to stay in New Jersey. We were going to make a life together in Scotland, for us and our child."

"Did your parents disapprove?" I couldn't imagine my kindly grandparents slamming their collective foot down and refusing to let my mother marry the man she loved.

"No, they never found out about Sam."

"Why not?"

Keely elbowed me in the side, a silent command to be quiet and let my mother finish her story. I took a deep breath, exhaled it slowly, and waited.

My mother wrung her hands, her gaze downcast again. "During our second week in New Jersey, I wasn't feeling well. Sam went out one night to buy dinner for us and get some medicine for me. He never made it back to me. He was arrested walking out of the grocery store."

"Arrested?" I said. "My father was a criminal?"

"No, Sam is a good man. It was a mistake. The police thought he resembled the police sketch of a man who had raped and murdered a woman. There had been a witness who saw the man running away. It was night, but the witness swore he could identify the murderer. The jury believed him."

I sank back into the sofa, keeping my arm around Keely, feeling suddenly exhausted and numb. My father had been wrongfully imprisoned. If I had known all these years…What could I have done? Nothing. Other children might have harassed me even more if they knew my father was a convicted rapist and murderer.

"We didn't have the money for a lawyer," my mother said. "Sam's father refused to help or even speak to him. I was ashamed to tell my parents the truth, so I said I was in America studying art when I was actually working as a waitress while we waited for Sam's trial. His court-appointed lawyer was very young and inexperienced. Sam was convicted and sentenced to life in prison without parole, and he was ordered to pay restitution to the victim's family. He had no money left after that."

"You should talk to Rory. He might be able to—"

"Let it be, Evan." She raised her head to look at me. "Your father will never be released. We both made peace with the situation a long time ago."

I couldn't help thinking back on my childhood, remembering the children who had tormented me and called me an alien and all the times I'd wondered who my father was. A secret agent had been at the top of my wish list. But no, my father was a convicted murderer.

An innocent convicted murderer.

Thinking about the past brought up another question and a possibility I had never considered because I had no reason to think it was possible. "Your annual holidays abroad. Have you been visiting my father in prison all these years?"

She nodded. "Sam told me not to do it. For the first three years, he wouldn't see me. He finally realized I would keep coming back no matter what, and he gave in. I wished I could visit him more often, but once a year was all I could afford."

"Why have you never told me any of this? I'm thirty years old, Ma, not a bairn. You could have told me a long time ago, should have told me."

"I know. I'm so sorry, gràidh, but Sam insisted you should never know." She blew her nose delicately. "He didn't want you to be the son of a murderer. I wanted us to get married even after he was in prison, but Sam wouldn't hear of it. He wanted both you and me to have a normal life untainted by what he'd done. I've told him all about you through the years, showed him pictures and videos. He knows what you've accomplished, and he's very proud of his son."

Proud. My father. The ghost who'd haunted me all my life was a real, living man. He knew me, but I knew only his name and I hadn't known that much until a moment ago. How should I respond to these revelations? How should I feel?

I rolled my gaze toward Keely. How would she feel about being with the son of a murderer who had committed crimes of his own? She deserved better than the melodrama my life had become.

She touched my cheek, smiling with a tenderness that stabbed a pain through my heart.

"There's more," my mother said. "About the money. Sam's mother died when he was young, and his father passed away seven years ago. Sam inherited all his father's assets, but he refused to touch it. When you started your company..." She wrung her hands harder, then tucked them under her thighs. "With Sam's permission, I gave you the full amount of the inheritance, three-quarters of a million pounds, to help your company get a good start. I found a broker who would let me give you the money anonymously as an angel investor. I didn't care about owning a part of the company, but the broker insisted that legally I had to accept shares in exchange."

I searched my mother's face, speechless and unable to move a single muscle. Who was this woman? I'd thought I knew her, but she seemed like a stranger. My mother had made it possible for me to create the company I'd dreamed of having. She owned five percent of Evanescent.

"Did your broker offer me four hundred thousand pounds later on?"

"No. There wasn't any more money to give." My mother fidgeted in her seat. "I know I've kept too many secrets from you. I understand if you can't have me in your life anymore."

Tears streamed down her cheeks. She stood and wiped away the tears with her tissue.

I hadn't seen my mother in eighteen months until I brought Keely home to meet her. Why shouldn't she expect I'd cut her out of my life after hearing the truth? I'd stayed away because of an argument. Today, she had answered all my questions.

She took a step toward the door.

This was the woman who had raised me. She'd looked out for me all my life and kept secrets only to protect me.

I heaved myself up off the sofa, crossing the distance to my mother in two steps. I grasped her shoulders to stop her from walking out the door. "Ma, you are in my life. I've been a selfish fool, refusing to speak to you for so long. You've taken care of me all my life and done what was best for me even though I couldn't see that's what you were doing."

She had protected me the best way she knew how to do it. I believed that. My childhood would've been rough even if I'd known my father, even

if he hadn't been serving a life sentence, because I was different from other
children. I'd always been different, and I always would be. Keely loved me
for that. So did my mother.

I took her hands in mine. "It's all right. I understand why you never told
me about my father."

She bowed her head, her tears dripping onto my hands. "You are a good
man, and I am so proud of you."

To hear my mother say that, it robbed me of words. How could I thank
her for everything she'd done for me? I couldn't. She had looked after me,
and I had harassed her for not telling me everything I wanted to know. What
a selfish bastard I'd been.

I peered over my shoulder at Keely.

She smiled, her eyes glistening with emotion.

"Would you like to meet him?" my mother asked.

I swung my attention back to her. "What?"

"You should meet your father, Evan. It's time."

Chapter Thirty-Five

Keely

I sat up straight on the sofa in the sitting room with Evan slouching into the cushions next to me, both of us listening while his cousin Rory and Rory's wife Emery explained what had been found. They'd sent their twins to Lachlan and Erica's house. Aileen was helping Malina babysit her infant brother elsewhere in the house. Four days had gone by since everything turned upside down, since the MacTaggart family had convened to help us and Evan's mother had dropped her bombshell. Ever since Aileen's suggestion that he should meet his father, Evan had said not one word about the offer or about his father. Whenever I asked, he avoided answering.

"We were able to narrow our search," Rory said, "once we knew the original angel investor had nothing to do with the blackmail. We hired an investigator and tapped into our connections in government. Em took another route."

He looked at his wife.

"My friend Sabri got in touch with his connections," Emery said, "and all of us worked together to sort out the mystery of the text messages. Turns out these baddies aren't as badass as they think. They sent the text messages via an anonymous email account. They weren't super clever about it, though. We were able to hack into the email account and find the IP address of the person who signed up for it."

Whatever that meant. I didn't pretend to grasp the technical aspects of what Emery and her friends had done, any more than I could understand how Evan did what he did at his company.

Though he sat beside me, he hadn't glanced in my direction since we came into the room. He'd barely spoken five complete sentences today, and that was an avalanche of words compared to the past few days. Every night and at least once every day we'd had sex. He seemed to need it for reasons beyond physical satisfaction or even stress reduction. He needed the closeness with me, and so I'd let him make love to me without speaking to me.

"What does all this mean?" I asked Emery. "What did you find?"

"The location they sent every text from. It was always the same place, so it must be their hangout or their lair of evildoing or whatever."

"And that's where?"

"Inverness."

Evan bolted upright, his hands on his knees. "They've been in my city all this time?"

"Yep," Emery said. "Once we cracked the email account, it was pretty simple to get the IP address. The geolocation for an IP address isn't exact, so I can't promise they're in the city itself, but it seems likely."

I raised my hand like I was a dopey schoolgirl. I'd begun to feel like the class dunce since I was apparently the only one who didn't get the intricacies of computer speak. "How do you know all the texts came from Inverness? They started a year ago."

"Evan saved them. Even the old ones."

Of course he had. Evan might not have believed he would ever track down the culprits, but he was too smart to not save the evidence.

"But we don't know exactly where these people are," I said.

"We didn't yesterday," Rory answered. He held up a file folder. "Today, we do. I contacted Stephen Beckham at the Home Office and called in my last favor with him. He used his influence to get the address of the person who opened the anonymous email account."

"What's our next—" I didn't get to finish my question.

Evan leaped up and snatched the folder from Rory's hand. "Thank you for your help, but I will deal with this myself."

Rory met Evan's gaze head-on, unflinching, evincing a calm and cool demeanor worthy of the man even his loved ones called a steely solicitor. "You have no idea what you might be walking into. Let's think about this first."

"Done enough thinking."

Evan whirled toward the door.

Rory surged up from his chair and ripped the folder away from Evan. "You haven't asked the right question yet."

"And what precisely is the right question?" Evan glared at his cousin, but Rory was unfazed.

The solicitor tapped the file folder on his palm. "Who has a grudge against you?"

"No one."

Rory rolled his eyes. "Come off it, Evan. You aren't that naive."

Evan's focus retreated from this room, from this place and time, and I could almost hear the engine of his mind revving up.

"You are the only one," Rory said, "who can answer that question. Until you do, best not take off on a mission alone."

I went to Evan, angling my face up to his. "You know, don't you? You figured it out a second ago."

"So did you." He touched my face with his fingertips, but then pulled his hand away. "It can't be. He doesn't hate me this much."

"Are you sure about that?"

Rory waved the folder at us. "You both know, eh? Care to tell the rest of us who don't share your telepathic connection?"

Evan ran a hand over his face. "It might be Ron Tulloch. He had tried to start up his own company but failed and wound up working for me. I never realized he was jealous of my success until recently." He groaned, shutting his eyes briefly. "Ron works in my accounting department, but he also studied computer science in college."

Rory pulled his phone out of his pants pocket. "I'll ring my investigator and see what he can dig up on this Tulloch man."

Evan held out his hand. "May I have the file, please?"

"If you promise not to do anything rash. We'll come up with a plan once we know more about Tulloch."

"Do I ever behave rashly?"

Rory studied Evan for a moment, then handed him the folder.

Evan stalked out of the room.

Oh, I didn't like this at all. He hadn't sworn not to do anything rash. He'd asked if he ever did behave that way. After spending four days with the Mac-Taggarts, I'd gotten to know them a little, so I knew Rory was smart enough to have noticed Evan's careful wording. None of us could stop Evan from doing something crazy if he got it into his head it was the right thing to do to protect his loved ones.

"Don't worry," Rory said. "He'll wait until we have a plan."

I wasn't so sure about that, but then, I knew Evan better than anyone else.

"Thank you," I said. "For everything."

"You're welcome." He nodded toward the door. "Best catch up to him. He needs support right now or perhaps to be shackled to the wall until this is over."

I heeded Rory's advice and took off after Evan.

He had turned left out of the sitting-room door, most likely headed for our room. I sprinted down the long hallway.

Thick, strong arms seized me around the waist from behind.

I swallowed a yelp.

Evan pressed his mouth to my ear. "Where are you going?"

"To find you."

He slid a hand up to palm my breast. "I found you."

"I'm glad you did."

"Are you planning to shackle me to the wall?"

His fingers massaged my breast, and I had trouble focusing on what he'd said. "Were you listening at the door after you left the room?"

"Aye. How else will I know what you and Rory are plotting?"

"I'm not plotting. But you haven't promised not to run off half-cocked and do something reckless."

"Wasn't eavesdropping. I happened to overhear your conversation." He ground his hips into me, rubbing his erection against my back. "And I'm fully cocked at the moment."

"Mm, I can tell."

If I got him relaxed and well sated, he might confide in me why he'd been so quiet for the past few days. Sure, that explained why I'd suggested sex. It had nothing to do with how much I wanted him every minute of every day and even while I was asleep and dreaming. His voice, his body, his tongue, every part of him had invaded my dreams since the night we'd met.

He nuzzled my cheek and groaned. "How badly do ye want me?"

"I'd let you push me up against the wall and take me right here in the hallway."

A chuckle, deep and dark, resonated inside his chest. "That's why I love you, Miss O'Shea."

He dragged me to the end of the hall and into the bedroom, slammed the door, and backed me up to the wall. With his entire body molded to mine, he caged me against the wall. My pulse accelerated, excitement zinging through me. He collared my wrists in one hand and pinned them above my head.

"Yer a drug," he rumbled. "Cannae get enough. Ahm addicted to yer scent, yer flavor, the feel of yer body around me."

My breaths shortened into gasps, and I couldn't tear my gaze away from his. Even the glare on his glasses couldn't dampen the fire that raged deep within his eyes. The silvery blue blaze made me ache all over, from my breasts to my rigid nipples straight down my belly and into the cleft between my thighs. The intensity of his need tightened his body and throbbed in his cock where it pressed into my belly. That same intensity infused his voice with a rough, carnal tone.

He unzipped my jeans and shoved them down until they slid down to pool around my ankles. His lips twitched upward. "No panties?"

"You've been insatiable lately. Had to be prepared."

"What about your bra?" He thrust his hand under my shirt and up to my breast, squeezing it before moving his fingers until he found the front clasp of my bra. His smile was wicked. "I love it when you wear this one."

He freed the clasp one hook at a time, grazing his fingertips along my skin as he worked to free my breasts. When he undid the last hook, my tits spilled out. He caught one in his hand, rasping his thumb back and forth over the nipple.

My back arched, my neck too. My mouth fell open, but the only sound I made was a breathless little "uh."

While his hand kneaded my breast, he kissed me. Hard. Rough. Demanding. I gave him what he wanted, what we both wanted, with my tongue and my teeth and my lips. He scraped his thumbnail across my nipple at the exact moment he flicked his tongue across the roof of my mouth. I moaned, but he swallowed the sound. Prevented from touching him by his hand around my wrists, I tried to hook one leg around his hip but tripped over the denim lumped around my ankles.

His hands kept me from falling.

"*Bod an Donais*," he hissed and dropped into a crouch to rip my shoes off, followed by my socks and jeans.

My tennies whacked onto the floor on the other side of the room. My jeans flumped onto the bed.

He sprang up, released my wrists, and tore my shirt off over my head. His toss sent it flying, and my bra went sailing a second later. While I leaned against the wall totally naked, he unzipped his pants to liberate his cock.

"On your knees," he growled.

Without a second's hesitation, I dropped to my knees.

He knelt behind me and shoved my legs apart with his knee. "Hands on the floor."

I obeyed.

He rubbed his erection along my cleft and groaned deeply. "So hot, so soft, so wet."

"Oh God, please."

"I need ye so much." He bent forward, his shirt tickling my naked backside, and sealed his mouth over my throat in an open-mouth kiss, nipping lightly at my skin.

Someone knocked on the door. "Keely, are you in there?"

I muttered something very unladylike under my breath before calling out, "Yes, Iain."

"We have news. It's urgent. Meet us in the dining room."

"Shit," Evan snarled.

"Be right there," I told his cousin.

Footsteps assured me Iain had left the vicinity.

I ground my ass against him. "Please hurry."

Evan pulled his hips back and impaled me with his cock. "Yer driving me mad."

He grasped my hips and thrust with frenetic need, pounding into me again and again, our bodies slapping and instigating a wet sound every time he drove into me. I dug my nails into the rug and let him do whatever he wanted with me. We both needed this release and the deep connection only sex could give us right now. Stress and fear had merged into a desperation that kept us both on edge all the time. But when he took me, when our bodies merged and the pleasure blanked out everything else, nothing mattered except the love that intensified every sensation.

Evan latched his arm around my waist and pulled me up, clasping me to his body. Even as he kept thrusting, he slid his hand down my belly to slip his fingers between my folds and find my rigid nub. His fingers rubbed and pinched it.

My climax struck like a lightning bolt from a clear blue sky. I threw my head back, about to unleash a wild cry.

He slapped his hand over my mouth.

I screamed against his palm, the sound muffled.

A second later, he blew his top. I cradled his head with my hand when he buried his face against my neck to muffle his own agonized shout.

We huddled there for another few seconds, panting, needing a moment to regain our wits and our breaths.

At last, he pulled away from me.

"Well," I said, "I think we're ready to go."

I heard the sharp, metallic sound of him zipping up.

He patted my bottom. "Might want to dress first."

"Right." I scurried around the room gathering my clothes and shoes. Once I'd gotten them on again, I kissed his cheek. "Feel better?"

"Aye, much better."

Hand in hand, we hurried down the hall to the dining room where Rory, Emery, Iain, and Rae waited for us. The women had taken seats at the table. Iain leaned against the sill of the tall window, half sitting on it. Rory stood between the window and the table, arms at his sides, shoulders back, a look of stoic resolve on his face.

"You might want to sit," he told us.

I took his advice and pulled out the chair beside Emery's, settling onto it with a growing sensation of acid burning in my gut.

Evan positioned himself behind my chair with his hands on its back.

Rory looked me square in the eye for a heartbeat before he switched his attention to Evan. "The situation has changed. The IP address from the Internet provider proves it's Tulloch. Emery and her friends got into the GPS on his phone. He's left Inverness."

"Where is he?" I asked.

"In Loch Fairbairn. And he's on the move, traveling in this direction."

Evan moved his hands to my shoulders, his fingers tensing. "You think he's coming here. How could he know where I am?"

"He's not working alone," Rory explained. "We know he has at least one accomplice, the man you battered last year. It's safe to assume that man still works with Tulloch. You noticed someone watching you and Keely on the beach last week. I think Tulloch's man has been keeping an eye on you, to let the mastermind know where you are at all times."

"They knew when I was in America, took a picture of me with Keely there." Evan's fingers tightened over my shoulders. "Tulloch must have sent someone to America to track me. Why is he going to so much trouble? It seems excessive for a wee bout of jealousy."

"It's more than jealousy, Evan. Tulloch wants revenge for whatever imagined wrong he blames you for. Vengeance can be a powerful motivator."

Evan pulled his hands away from me. "If he's that powerfully motivated..."

"We need to take defensive action."

"He must know I'm here at Iain's house. What do you suggest we do?"

Iain slid off the windowsill. "Batten down the hatches and prepare for the storm."

"Thank you for the vague suggestion," Evan said through clenched teeth.

I didn't need to see him to know his jaw was tightly clenched. I heard it in his voice.

Rory waved toward the table. "The women will go to Lachlan and Erica's house where they'll be safe."

I shook my head. "I am not leaving Evan."

"Go, Keely," Evan said.

"Not following your orders this time. I stay. No arguments."

I craned my neck to look up at him. He was, of course, giving me a tight-lipped expression that told me he did not approve of my decision. I raised my brows at him. "Want to argue right here in front of your family? Besides, Tulloch might track me down wherever I go in hopes of using me as leverage. I'm safer with three brawny men around."

He mumbled something that was probably Gaelic but caved with a sharp nod, then surveyed the room. "Where is my mother?"

Rory answered. "In the kitchen with Malina. We haven't told Aileen about the danger yet."

I got up. "Aileen should stay with us too. Tulloch already used her as leverage once. We're safer together."

"Then may I suggest," Iain said, "we relocate to Dùndubhan. It is a fortress after all. And that ought to give us time to prepare while Tulloch realizes we've gone somewhere else and reassesses his next move."

Evan grunted. "If he reassesses. Clearly, the man is delusional."

Rae and Emery rose from their chairs. Rae said, "We'll get Malina and head to Lachlan and Erica's."

"Yes," Iain said. "I'll send Aidan there too. We'll need Gavin and Logan with us at Dùndubhan. An ex-Marine and a former spy could be useful in a situation like this."

The plan sounded good, but the acid in my gut had spread up into my throat. Swallowing twice did nothing to rid me of the sour taste in my mouth. We had no choice other than to confront Tulloch and his cohorts. Calling the cops wouldn't do. Evan had broken the law to comply with the blackmailer's demands, and we had hacked the bad guy's phone and probably broken several more laws in the process. Besides, if we called the police Tulloch would know about it. He'd known when Evan went to the police station in Loch Fairbairn.

"Do you think the phones are bugged?" I asked. "Will Tulloch hear us sharing the plan with the rest of the family?"

"No," Rory said. "We haven't discussed our plans over the phone. At most, Tulloch would have overheard us asking various people for their assistance. All reports were sent via Emery's secure email account and everything was encrypted. Trust me, she knows how to protect her data."

Emery approached her husband but spoke to me. "We checked for listening devices and other types of surveillance, anyway. Evan let us borrow his equipment."

Ah, yes. The suitcase of spy gadgets he'd brought with him.

Logan might have been the official James Bond of the family, but Evan had all the toys a spy needed.

"All right," I said. "Off to the castle."

Chapter Thirty-Six

Evan

I leaned against the windowsill of the sitting room in Dùndubhan and gazed out at the forbidding gray clouds that threatened to close in around the house as fog. We wouldn't see much through the soup if it descended on the castle. Were the elements conspiring with our enemy? It seemed like an idiotic thought, but then, I had started to believe in fate since meeting Keely. Maybe karma existed too, and the weather was my punishment for being arrogant and self-contained, refusing to ask for help when I needed it because I was too proud to admit I couldn't do everything on my own.

Keely walked into the sitting room and stopped beside me. "Are your security men settled in at Lachlan and Erica's place?"

"Yes, they texted me using Emery's secure method." I held my arm out, and she moved under it so I could hold her against my side. "I asked Duncan if he could send more men to guard Dùndubhan, but he has no one available—at least not for three hours or more. I doubt we have that much time. I don't trust anyone else to supply security for us."

"You have trouble trusting people. I get that." She laid a hand on my chest. "You've always felt like you had to be in control of every situation since other people let you down too many times. When that happens to a child, it leaves bigger scars."

Sometimes I wondered how anyone could know me so well after such a short time together. My mother had been with me all my life and didn't know me half as well. Before Keely, I'd never let anyone get close enough to understand me.

Keely managed a small smile. "At least Aileen agreed to go to Lachlan and Erica's too. She'll be safer there."

"I hope so." I rubbed my eyes. "I've made a right mess of things. You wanted to know what was happening, but I refused to tell you, refused to trust you. How can you trust me after everything I've done? Too many mistakes, too much pride, not enough good sense."

"That's crap, Evan." She aimed her emerald eyes at me, and they were full of love and determination. "How could you trust me with a secret like this when I wouldn't even admit we were dating? I told you I wanted your body and nothing else."

"I pushed you into a relationship. I brought you into the disaster I've made of my life. You deserve better."

Her lips crimped at one corner, a sign she was chewing the inside of her cheek. I'd seen her do that before when she was anxious. Another thing I'd done to her.

"If we hadn't gotten together," she said, "would you have ever confided in your cousins? Would you have ever tried to get someone to help you? Or would you have bumbled along on your own?"

"Bumbled? I suppose that's an accurate assessment." It was what I'd done all my life. Getting by but never overcoming the fear of losing everything.

She raised a hand to my cheek. "I'm worried about you. About what you'll do to stop these creeps. You've got a lone-wolf complex, and you haven't promised not to go off on your own to deal with Tulloch and his men."

"Don't worry." I pulled her closer. "No one will hurt you. I won't allow it."

"Not concerned about my own safety. I'm afraid for you."

Of course she would be. I'd been a selfish bastard yet again, seducing her at every opportunity to satisfy my own desperate need to keep her close in any way I could. I should've been comforting her instead.

I studied her face but couldn't find the answers I needed there. "Why did you let me keep using your body for my own selfish needs? I've barely spoken to you, much less anyone else, for days. You should've castigated me for the way I was behaving."

She fiddled with my shirt collar, her attention riveted to the movements of her fingers. "It's not as much fun to chastise you when I can tell you're desperate for sex because you're in pain."

"That's no excuse. I'm sorry, Keely."

"For having sex with me?" She clearly aimed for a playful smile, but her lips couldn't quite achieve it. "In case you haven't noticed, I love making love with you."

"But I used you to—"

"You have never used me, not even in Paris. I understand that now. We had this instant connection that shocked us both, and we each reacted to it differently. You ran because you were scared, not because you had used me to slake your lust."

She believed that. I could tell by the way she looked at me, by the tone of her voice, by the way her fingers had stopped their anxious movements. If she believed I wasn't selfish…

A figure stepped into the open doorway.

"Is there news?" I asked Iain.

"Yes. Tulloch is close, possibly at the end of the drive. We can't pinpoint it too closely, but we need to assume he could be here at any moment."

"Then we move to the main hallway and wait." I pulled my phone out of my pocket and called up the app that let me monitor the cameras, motion detectors, and infrared devices I'd set up all around the castle, as well as the drone that was ready to take off whenever necessary. "It's time to assume battle stations. Full red alert."

"You've been talking to Emery too much. You're starting to sound like Captain Kirk."

No one was in the mood for much joking, so the conversation dwindled as Keely and I followed Iain down the hallway of the guest wing, through the dining room, and out into the main hallway of the ground floor. The castle featured four levels and a tower, not to mention windows designed for easy defense. It made the structure darker inside but safer during a battle.

Dùndubhan hadn't seen a battle in centuries. I had brought danger and violence back to the building that had been peaceful for a very long time.

No, Ron Tulloch had brought this to Dùndubhan. If any blood was spilled today, it would be his.

We met the others in the main hall. Rory, Gavin, and Logan had taken up positions on the three sides of the castle's front walls, each staring out at the darkening weather. Gavin had brought a baseball bat, which leaned against the wall beside him. Rory had a cricket bat he held in his hand.

A display along the rear wall featured replicas of medieval weapons of various types. Glass cases enclosed them—everything from daggers like the *sgian dubh* and the dirk to a pair of swords, one a claymore and the other a basket-hilt sword. This was a working museum after all.

"Where's Lachlan?" I asked.

Logan turned his head and shouted, "Are ye done in there, Lachlan? Evan thinks you're lying down on the job."

A toilet flushed further down the hall.

Lachlan emerged from the bathroom. "I was sitting down, not lying down. Nature doesn't wait for a good time to issue the call."

Keely glanced at Lachlan, her brow furrowed. "Who's taking care of the ladies and the babies? I thought Lachlan was staying with them. Not that women can't take care of themselves, but…"

I pulled her against my side and kissed the top of her head. "Relax, *mo leannan*. Randall and Howard, the security men, are there. Lachlan made his own arrangements too." I gave him a sharp look. "Right?"

"Aye," he said. "Tavish, Angus, and my da are on duty at the farm."

"That would be Lachlan and Erica's farm," I told Keely. Then I realized what my cousin had said and snapped my attention back to Lachlan. "A gardener, a former inept burglar, and a retired butcher? Where's Iain? I thought he was doing…something."

"And an archaeologist is more qualified than my father?" Lachlan pretended to take offense, but I knew he was really trying to distract me from the reason we had all gathered here. "Iain is watching from the walls."

Keely's brow furrowed even deeper. "He's hiding in the walls?"

"No, love," I said with a chuckle. "Lachlan means the wall around the castle. It has a walkway on top of it, though nobody's dared use it for a very long time."

She rubbed her arms. "Never thought I'd be in a castle fending off villains with a bunch of Scottish knights."

"Hey!" Gavin said. "I'm American, you know."

"Sorry, I forgot about you."

Lachlan strode over to Logan, who had taken a position at one end of the hall, watching out the window. "You're up, laddie. Don't let us down."

Logan gave one sharp nod, his expression deadly serious. "I'm on it."

"You're on what?" I asked.

"Grounds patrol."

I had no idea what Logan meant by "grounds patrol." Was that spy jargon?

He moved toward the doorway that led into the vestibule. "I'll be patrolling the grounds around the castle. Since the target seems to be coming down the roads, I'll head in that direction."

"Tulloch will see you."

"No, he won't."

"The woods aren't that dense. You won't have cover."

Logan's smile was not cheerful. It was pure arrogant certainty with a hint of excitement. "No one will see me. I'll be belly-crawling the whole way."

I tried to picture him doing that, but I couldn't comprehend anyone moving through the woods on his belly, crawling through the grass and weeds and mud and whatever else. That was when I realized my family had not been pulling my leg. Logan had been a spy. Who else would seem excited about rolling in the muck? Or hunting a *bod ceann* who'd blackmailed me.

Why would he do that for me? We hardly knew each other.

Logan exited out the vestibule and disappeared around the corner of the house.

Gavin, Lachlan, and Rory held their positions and monitored the grounds outside with unswerving focus. When we had all met up here, Logan had handed out two-way radios for us to communicate with, ones we felt certain Tulloch and his gang could not infiltrate to listen in to our conversations. I pulled my radio out and called Iain to check in. He reported nothing unusual.

"Don't you want to check in with Aidan?" Rory asked.

"What the bloody hell is Aidan doing here? I thought he was at the farm with the others."

"Aidan didn't want to miss any blood and gore, his words exactly."

I rubbed my forehead, but the headache starting behind my eyes had no intention of surrendering. "Why did no one tell me the plan was changed? And where is Aidan?"

"He's watching from the tower," Rory said. "And we didn't tell you because we forgot. You were, ah, busy with Keely at the time."

Busy with Keely. I supposed that was Rory's polite way of describing what she and I had done earlier.

I checked in with Aidan, who reported nothing amiss. Getting out my phone, I opened the tracker app. It showed Tulloch approaching Dùndubhan, not quite to the driveway yet.

With nothing else to do, I paced the length of the hallway, my hands linked behind my back, thinking more than was probably healthy in a situation like this. My mind conjured all the possible scenarios, or at least the ones I was capable of imagining, everything from Tulloch arriving armed and shooting us all down where we stood to Tulloch hurling bombs at the castle. For a few seconds, I even entertained the idea he might arrive in an alien spaceship.

Keely sat on the floor with her back to the wall watching me pace.

"Go into the kitchen," I said. "Grab a piece. We could be here a while."

"You think I can eat right now?"

I shrugged and kept pacing, spinning on my heels at the end of each circuit. I wished Keely had gone with the other women. Here, I had to worry about her and remember that I'd brought this danger into her world. If Tulloch laid one finger on her—

All our radios beeped at the same time. Iain's voice crackled through the speakers. "There's a car coming."

Logan replied from wherever he was outside. "I'm on it."

I decided not to question what Logan meant to do. His MI6 training must have equipped him for worse situations than this.

"There's some sort of activity," Iain said, sounding a bit confused. "Even with the binoculars I can't quite make out what's happening. Is that Logan? Or Tulloch? They might be wrestling."

I pressed the button on my radio. "I'm going out to see."

Keely leaped to her feet. "Not alone you aren't."

"You are not coming with me. It's dangerous."

"And you are not going out there alone."

I scowled at her. "Logan did."

"He's trained for this stuff."

Part of me needed to be angry at that statement, but I knew she wasn't insulting my manhood. She was afraid for me, which was the same reason I would never let her go out there. Besides, Logan was trained for "this stuff," as she put it.

"Gavin," I said, "you're with me."

He thumped his baseball bat on his palm. "I'm good to go."

To Rory, I said, "You and Lachlan watch out for Keely."

She gave me a tight-lipped look. "You expect me to cower in the corner while you're off catching the bad guy? You should know me better than that."

"I do." And her determination scared the hell out of me today. I grasped her shoulders. "Please stay here. I'll be distracted by worrying about you unless I know you're safe."

Her lips twisted as if she were trying not to scowl at me or scold me. She huffed out a breath and relaxed. "Fine. I'll be a good girl and stay put."

"Thank you." I handed her my phone. "Keep an eye on the thermal imaging app. The trees make it more difficult to spot heat signatures, but it's the best we've got."

She accepted the phone.

I kissed her forehead. "Be right back."

Gavin and I stalked through the vestibule and outside into the gloomy daylight. By the time we'd exited the castle compound, I could see two figures moving around within the shadows in the trees near a vehicle, their motions swift and jerky. When we reached Logan and his opponent, the battle was well and truly done. Logan had a slender, dark-haired man by the throat, the man's back flattened against the tiny car he'd driven here. Based on the way the car was angled across the gravel drive, I suspected Logan had leaped out in front of it like a human roadblock.

That's when I noticed the knife sticking out of the right front tire. How on earth had Logan hit a moving target with a knife? I didn't ask because it didn't matter. He had gotten his job done.

Unfortunately, it wasn't the result I'd hoped for.

I frowned at the stranger who was literally quaking in his boots, his lower lip quivering. "That's not Ron Tulloch. It's the English shit who ran down my mother."

"Aye," Logan said, his voice and his expression sharpened with a deadly edge. "We've been having a good blether. Tell Evan all about yourself."

My cousin shook the stranger's throat.

The pale man went paler. "I'm Bert Stamp."

"And what have you done?" Logan said, his words less a question than a command.

"I'm a messenger, that's all." Stamp cringed when Logan raised his other hand in a fist. "I've been spying on Evan MacTaggart and his lady friend for Ron Tulloch."

"How much is he paying you?" I asked.

"No payment. Tulloch said he'd help me get revenge on anyone I wanted."

Revenge as a form of payment for services rendered was a new one on me. Tulloch had found a kindred spirit to aid him in his quest for vengeance.

I scanned the trees around us and the section of the lawn I could make out from here. I couldn't see anyone else, but Tulloch had to be around here somewhere.

Logan pulled his hand away from Stamp's throat. "Where is Tulloch?"

The scunner seemed to have recovered a bit of his nerve, what little of it he possessed. He lifted his chin and did not answer.

Logan smacked him. "Next time I'll skite my fist on your face and dislocate your jaw."

Stamp's eyes bulged. "Tulloch went through the wood to get where he's going. All he said was I should keep you busy out front while he gets his hands on the leverage."

I grabbed Stamp's shirt and leaned in close enough I could smell his sour breath. "What leverage, you pathetic wee toad?"

"He wants the one thing you care about most." Stamp's gaze darted to the house. "He's after your woman."

Chapter Thirty-Seven

Keely

I squinted out the window trying to make out what was happening in the driveway. The shade of the trees, deepened by the near twilight of this dark day, made it impossible to sort out what was going on over there. They must've been a hundred feet from the house. What if Evan lost it like he had when his mother was injured? What might he do this time? I wouldn't blame him for pummeling Ron Tulloch. The asshole deserved it.

But I did not want Evan to get hurt or to get arrested for assault.

"Should we go out there?" Lachlan asked Rory. "Looks like they might need a hand."

"It's three against two. They'll be fine."

"Unless Tulloch brought more friends."

More evil cretins? I clamped my fingers over the window frame, leaning forward to peer out at the shapes in the woods. What if Tulloch had too many men? What if...*Shit*. I didn't even know what else he might have or do.

"I'll get Aidan down here," Lachlan said. "He can watch Keely while you and I lend a hand out there."

Lachlan gestured at the window and the outdoors beyond it.

My gaze ricocheted around the hallway and landed on the display cases. Weapons. Lots of them. I could grab one and run out there to—Gah, I had no clue what I'd do to help. I was not built for being the damsel in distress who waited in an ivory tower while her man battled the enemy. *Do something*, my inner voice urged. What could I do?

I picked up Evan's phone from where I'd set it down on the windowsill. The screen had turned itself off, so I punched the button to wake it up. The thermal-sensing map appeared on the screen. A white spot blipped into and out of view so fast I couldn't be sure of what I'd seen. Was it a genuine heat signature? An animal? Nothing at all?

"What is it?" Lachlan asked.

"The thermal sensors are...I don't know. Maybe it was nothing."

Lachlan trotted over to me and peered over my shoulder at the phone. "I don't see anything now. It might've been a false positive or an animal."

"Yeah, I guess." What I'd glimpsed a moment ago niggled at me, though.

"I'll get the drone in the air so we can get a better look."

"Be careful."

He told Rory, "Toss me your bat."

Rory tossed his cricket bat end over end through the air. I would've been impressed if I hadn't been biting my fingernails and worrying about what was going on outside.

Lachlan caught the bat. He marched down the hall to the dining room and disappeared through the doorway. He must've been heading for the side door in the guest wing. It led into the courtyard.

I fiddled with Evan's app. He'd shown me how to switch from the sensors outside the castle compound to the drone feed. Which button did I tap for that? I saw two of them, one blue and one red. I hit the red one.

Nothing happened.

I tapped the blue one. The feed switched from infrared to a camera feed inside the house. It showed the guest-wing hallway and Lachlan turning down a shorter hall toward the door to the outside.

A figure lunged at him, whacking him in the head with the butt of a handgun.

"Rory!" I shouted. "Someone's in the house and they've got Lachlan."

He took off, unarmed, for the guest wing while barking orders into his radio. "Aidan, Iain, get down here. We're under attack."

Rory froze at the dining-room door, his gaze swiveling to me.

"Go," I said. "Nobody can get from the guest wing to this hallway without going through the dining room. I'll be okay."

He raced through the doorway and out of sight.

My gaze flew to the display cases yet again. Knives. A mace. Two swords.

Screw this. I was not standing here doing nothing while someone assaulted the men who'd volunteered to protect me.

I shoved Evan's phone in my pocket and approached the display case. Covering my face with one arm, I kicked the case.

The glass shattered.

My shoes crackled on the shards as I retrieved a good-size knife from the display case. Its blade was long and tapered, its handle round and perfectly shaped to fit in my hand. This was a dirk, the sign in the case told me, a medieval dagger.

I gripped it and jogged toward the dining room.

A gunshot detonated inside the house.

My ears rang, and the shock of the blast left me paralyzed for a second too long.

Ron Tulloch barreled through the dining room toward me, his face wild and his gun raised. He slammed his entire body into mine, tackling me to the ground. My head smacked into the wood floor. Stars flashed in my vision.

The dirk skittered across the floor.

A door banged elsewhere in the house.

Tulloch seized my throat in one hand and rammed the gun into my temple with the other. "I've got him now. Evan willnae do a bloody thing if yer in danger."

An unholy roar reverberated through the hall.

Ron Tulloch was yanked off me, his feet flailing in the air above my face.

I blinked rapidly, struggling to sort out what I was seeing.

Evan had Tulloch by the collar of his coat, but I couldn't get a good view of his face what with Tulloch's flailing body in the way.

"Watch out!" someone shouted from the direction of the guest wing, the voice muffled by the walls between us and them. "There's another one!"

Everything seemed to happen in fast forward, the movements a series of blurs. A figure rocketed into the dining room. Tulloch did something to Evan, and Evan hollered in pain. The newly arrived figure dashed past me right as Tulloch hit the floor on his knees. I couldn't tell what happened next, but there was a lot of scuffling and grunting and wordless shouting.

I clambered to my knees, snagged the dirk, and staggered to my feet.

Tulloch raised his gun at Evan, who was busy fending off another man. Gavin had just come through the vestibule door, but no one was near enough to Tulloch to stop him.

Except for me.

Gavin shouted a warning.

When Evan turned his head toward me, the man attacking him landed a nasty blow to Evan's chin. His head snapped back. Blood spattered from his mouth.

I rushed at Tulloch.

He saw me too late.

I howled like a banshee as I slammed the dirk into his shoulder.

Tulloch dropped his gun.

Yanking the knife free, I staggered backward.

He crumpled to the floor, landing on his side.

Gavin snagged Tulloch's gun and trained it on the man. "I know how to use this, asswipe, so don't move a muscle."

Evan punched his attacker. The man collapsed to the floor with a thud, unconscious.

Lachlan and Rory jogged through the doorway to the guest wing toward us. Rory sported a darkening bruise around his left eye. Lachlan had scratches on his face and, I suspected, a lump emerging on his head that his hair concealed. He looked more haggard than his younger brother, but Rory hadn't been struck on the head with the butt of a gun.

"Is everyone okay?" I asked.

A round of "ayes" from the Scots and one "yeah" from Gavin assured me they were. Evan hadn't spoken. He hadn't moved, staring at me from the other side of Tulloch.

"You sure you're okay?" I asked Lachlan.

He gingerly touched his head. "Not bleeding, so aye. Never got the chance to use the drone, though. This one jumped me." Lachlan nodded toward Tulloch. "Luckily, he's a poor marksman and hit the wall with his only shot."

"Is there anyone else?" Rory asked Tulloch.

The villain shook his head.

Gavin nudged Tulloch with his foot. "If you're lying, I won't hesitate to take you down. I served in a war zone, jackass, which means I've shot people before."

"No one else," Tulloch said, his voice shaky and laced with panic. "I swear it. Only me, Stamp, and Wasserman."

I'd started to shake, though not from fear. The adrenaline rush that had fueled me throughout the castle-storming incident had evaporated. I was experiencing the flip side of it when my body needed time to readjust.

Evan's brows tightened the slightest bit.

I set the blood-stained dirk on a nearby table, atop a pile of brochures, and hugged myself. "Should someone call the police?"

"Already on the way," Rory said. He glanced at the shattered glass on the floor. "When you broke into the display case, it triggered the silent alarm. Evan installed the security system for us, so we have real-time monitoring of any alarms. His people will have called the police."

"I have the proof of what MacTaggart did," Tulloch whined. "You cannae bring the police in. I'll give it to them, and he'll be arrested."

Evan crouched beside Tulloch and roughly dug around in the man's pockets until he found Tulloch's phone. "Everything's on here, I'd wager."

The look on Tulloch's face, a mixture of fury and defeat, answered Evan's question.

Evan tossed the phone to Rory. "Have Emery and her friends take care of that."

"No one will care about the code you wrote for them," Rory said. "Not after what Tulloch's done today. But I'll use the app or whatever it is Emery gave me to demolish any files on his phone."

"It's called shredding."

Rory made a dismissive noise.

Tulloch tried to sit up but fell back down. "It's on my computer too. You'll never find it before the police do."

Rory laughed with menacing glee. "My wife and her friends had no trouble hacking into your system to delete anything that implicated Evan. You took more care with your phone than your computer." He clucked his tongue. "You ought to have better security if you're going to blackmail people."

Gavin planted his boot on Tulloch's chest. "Hear that, asswipe? A woman outsmarted you." Gavin threw me a smug smile. "Two women, actually. You're a real limp dick, aren't you, Tulloch?"

Evan came to me and held me against his side. I tried to figure out his mood, but he'd retreated behind a stony facade.

"Why did you do it?" I asked Tulloch. "What was the point of making Evan write code for you?"

Tulloch glared at me for a moment, then seemed to reach a decision. He lifted his chin as much as he could with Gavin's foot on his chest. "I proved I'm smarter than the great Evan MacTaggart. Took him down a few pegs, I did. The code was a lark. I wanted to see if he would do what I said, and the dimwit did. Everyone knows he's unfit for that sort of work. Watching him squirm was the best part."

"What about the four hundred thousand pounds?" I asked. "I assume you were the one behind that attempt to take over Evan's company, but I doubt you have fifty pounds, much less four hundred thousand."

"I wanted to see how greedy he is." Tulloch tried to move his arm but winced, most likely from the pain of his stab wound. "The blackmail was strictly to humiliate him. I was going to leak it to the media that he had written code giving himself a back door to his clients' security systems. His business would've been finished."

We each questioned him a bit more, but Tulloch refused to say anything else until he got a lawyer. We handed Tulloch and his cohorts over to the police when they arrived. Logan had held Stamp in the driveway to guard the only viable exit available to the villains. The constables who answered the alarm call seemed to know Logan and respect him, so they accepted his version of events. We had all agreed to leave out any mention of the code Evan had written and the blackmail. What Tulloch had done today, not to mention his histrionics in Evan's office, was enough to put him away for a good long time. Each of us had to go to the station in the morning to give our statements, but the constables decided we'd earned a night's rest first.

All of us watched the three blackmailers get handcuffed and stuffed into the backseat of one police car.

Logan clapped a hand on Evan's shoulder. "Don't worry. The constables let me have a private word with Tulloch in the back of the police car. He won't be mentioning anything about the programs you wrote for him."

Though he spoke the words casually, his voice had a lethal undercurrent.

I didn't doubt for one minute Tulloch would fear getting on Logan's bad side.

"But he will be confessing," Logan said, "to everything else, including threatening your mother's life and getting his cohort to almost run her over. The embezzlement too."

Who was this man? Solving the mystery of Evan's cousin would have to wait for another day.

Night had fallen over the landscape by the time we returned to our respective homes—or in the case of Evan and me, back to our guest room in Iain and Rae's home. We undressed and got into bed without saying a word, too exhausted for anything more taxing than a quick good-night kiss before we fell asleep in each other's arms.

I realized something was wrong the second I woke up in the morning.

Before I'd even opened my eyes, I sensed a lack of bodily warmth pressed against my back and an emptiness in the room. A chill swept over my skin. I sat up and blinked to clear my vision. What I saw did not change no matter how many times I blinked. I was alone in the room, and Evan's things were gone.

A piece of paper lay on the bedside table, folded in half with my name written on it in Evan's handwriting.

I picked up the paper, my eyes stinging as I unfolded the sheet. Somehow, I knew what I would learn from his note before I read it. I felt the truth. Knowing him the way I did, I'd been worried he might do something reckless like going after Tulloch alone, but I hadn't anticipated this.

"*Mo chridhe*," the note began, "I have to leave you. I need to sort things, and I can't do that with you here making me forget about all the mistakes I've made and the way I've pushed you into a relationship you never wanted. You could have died yesterday, and it would have been my fault. Please forgive me. *Mo ghaol ort*, Evan."

I crumpled the paper in my hand. Those strange phrases must've been Gaelic. Was it a code? He knew I didn't understand the language. Why begin and end his dumping-Keely note with something that made no sense to me?

Tears pricked at my eyes. I wiped them away with the heel of my hand, but my nose didn't get the message that I did not want to cry. I sniffled and crushed the paper harder. The tears ignored my command, rolling down my cheeks. I wrapped my arms around myself and rocked in place, helpless to stem the salty tide. My head hurt, my heart hurt, my soul hurt. How could he do this to me? Make me love him and then leave me.

I hurled the crumpled paper across the room.

Once the tears subsided, I went into the bathroom and washed my face before pulling on some clothes.

He'd left me in his cousin's home. I didn't belong here without Evan.

I caught sight of the crumpled paper on the floor.

My eyes stung again, but I banished the tears by sheer force of will. No more crying. So he'd abandoned me. I would not crumble into a pathetic mess on the floor. Men had tossed me away before, and I had survived. This was no different.

Except I loved Evan so much more than I'd loved the others.

No, I would not dwell on it. Go home, get on with my life, pretend this had never happened. That was the only way to get through it. I packed up my bags and dragged them into the hall. The crushed paper caught my eye again, and I couldn't stop myself from picking it up, smoothing it out, and tucking it into my purse.

I found Rae and Iain in the kitchen. Smiling and laughing, they seemed to be having a good time cooking up a breakfast feast.

Two people in love. I remembered how that felt.

Rae noticed me, and her smile faltered. "Keely, what's wrong?"

"Evan left. Thank you for your hospitality, but I think it's best if I go home right away."

"No," Iain said, "you shouldn't go anywhere when you're upset. Have a seat. You'll feel better after a good breakfast."

Rae gave her husband an annoyed look. "Bangers and mash won't fix a broken heart."

"Whose heart is broken? She said Evan left." He gave me a questioning look. "How long will he be gone?"

His wife elbowed him in the gut. "Evan didn't go to the store. He's gone for good. Can't you see that on her face?"

I tried not to cry, tried so hard, but the damn tears had a mind of their own. I shielded my face with one hand so at least they might not see me bawling. I didn't sob, though. The tears streamed down my face in silence.

Rae pulled me into a hug. "I'm so sorry, honey. Men can be such idiots."

"He'll change his mind," Iain said. "Lachlan and Erica broke up for two months before they got married. Evan will come around eventually."

"Iain, you are not helping," Rae said.

"Doesn't it help for her to know breaking up isn't the end?"

"Not right now. She's hurting too much."

I pulled away from Rae. "I need to go home. Please, I just need to go home."

"Take the jet," Iain said. "Lachlan, Rory, and I share it. You'll be home in no time."

Rae squeezed my arm. "Have something to eat first. I'll whip up some French toast for you. It's the best comfort food."

I let Rae guide me to the island and perched my butt on a stool. The French toast turned out to be delicious, but nothing short of a drinking binge would've been enough to soothe me. Since I didn't want to get drunk, I had no choice but to push through the pain the best I could.

Half an hour later, I stood at the front door with my purse over my shoulder. Iain had already carried my bags out to the car and insisted on driving me to the airport. The private jet he shared with his cousins waited for me there.

Rae kissed Iain on the cheek. "Don't say anything to upset her."

"I won't, *gràidh*."

His use of a Gaelic endearment made me think of Evan's note. I pulled it out of my purse and held it up so Iain could see. I pointed at the words *mo chridhe*. "Do you know what this means?"

"Yes, it means my heart."

"What about this?" I pointed at the phrase *mo ghaol ort*.

"That means I love you." He smirked. "I don't love you, the man who wrote that does."

"I get the picture. Thanks for the translation."

All the way to the airport and on the plane ride home, I wondered why Evan said he loved me in the note he used to break up with me.

Chapter Thirty-Eight

Keely

I propped my feet on the desk in my office, reached down to unlock my chair, and leaned it back as far as it would go without me tumbling over backward. My arms hung off the sides. My gaze was aimed at the ceiling, but I couldn't focus on it. Six weeks had gone by since Evan dumped me with a handwritten note. I hadn't seen or heard from him since, though I'd called him often—a dozen times a day at first, then dwindling down and down until I gave up. My voicemails, texts, and emails went unanswered. Iain and Rae called, Rory and Emery called, and even Evan's mother called me. Aileen wouldn't tell me where Evan was or what he was doing because he'd sworn her to secrecy, though she mentioned he'd needed time to adjust to the changes in his life.

Why did I care where he was? He'd moved on. For all I knew, he had another woman warming his bed these days. Maybe several women.

No, I couldn't believe that. His misplaced guilt and too many revelations about his family had knocked him off balance, and he needed time to get his bearings again.

Someone knocked on the door to my office.

I jumped and almost fell out of my chair. Scrambling to get upright again, I thumped my feet down on the floor. "Come in."

Serena waltzed inside and shut the door. "You look awful."

"Did you stop by to insult me or is there a reason for this visit?"

"You've been grumpy for a month. Getting dumped does not agree with you."

"My employees haven't complained."

"Like they would tell their boss she's being annoying. Besides, you're nice to them and only get snippy with the people who love you." She pointed a finger at herself. "That would be me, your parents, and your brothers."

"I'm fine." I held up a hand, palm out. "I swear to control my grumpiness from now on."

Not sure how I'd do that. With a choice between being grumpy or weeping uncontrollably, I'd chosen the option least likely to make my eyes red and puffy. What good did it do to feel heartbroken? I'd gone through this enough times to make me an expert on repressing my feelings and pushing through it all.

"The way he left doesn't make sense," I said, more to myself than to Serena. "He's not a coward. Why wouldn't he say goodbye in person? He disappeared."

"What makes sense to a man usually doesn't make sense to a woman. It's not like you haven't heard from him at all."

"Yes, it's exactly like that. No contact."

"That's not true."

I rolled my eyes. "Sending me a car is not contact. It's more like a payoff for giving him great sex."

"Evan also gave you a house, one you refuse to set foot in."

"Another payoff, or maybe a guilt trip." I remembered the night we'd spent in that house and how much closer we'd gotten because of it. How could I walk into that house ever again? Driving past it made me queasy. Maybe I'd sell it.

But the idea of that made me queasy too.

"He loves you," Serena said. "We all know that."

I didn't want to talk about this anymore, but Serena wouldn't give up unless I changed the subject. "I have work to do."

"Oh no, you're coming with me," Serena announced. "I talked to Vic, and he agrees that you need to take the rest of the afternoon off. We're having a high-calorie, carb-loaded, totally decadent meal. Right now."

"Did I say you could have the afternoon off?"

"Technically, I work for your father. But not anymore."

I snapped upright, the momentum pushing my chair backward. "What? Since when?"

"Since your parents—" She waved a hand. "Never mind. They want to tell you themselves."

"What will you do? You're unemployed."

Her smile was cryptic and a touch mischievous. "I've got a new job. It starts in a week, and no, I will not tell you about it yet. Get off your butt and let me kidnap you."

"I don't need an afternoon off. Work keeps me going."

"No way." She seized my wrist and pulled, leaning back into the pull for better leverage. "Get off your stubborn ass this instant."

I gave in and had lunch with her. Serena offered to trash talk men with me, but I declined. Bashing Evan wouldn't make me feel better and neither would bashing any of my other exes. After lunch, she insisted we go to a day spa for facials and a massage. The experience failed to relax me.

On the drive home, I passed the newest building site in Carrefour. The construction company had put up a sign advertising it was their project, but nothing indicated what the building would house. They seemed to be whipping it together in record time. We didn't get a lot of new construction in this town, so I'd asked around to see if anyone knew what the structure would be. Nobody had a clue. Apparently, the construction company had signed a nondisclosure agreement that barred them from discussing the project.

Maybe it was a government building. Those guys loved secrets.

Early in the evening, I arrived home and walked into the living room but nearly tripped over my own shoes in an attempt to halt abruptly. My purse fell out of my grip and whumped onto the floor.

My parents stopped making out and aimed cheery smiles at me.

"Keely, there you are," my mom said. "We were wondering when you'd get home. Have fun with Serena?"

"What are you two doing?"

Dad waggled his eyebrows. "What does it look like we're doing?"

"Something you're way too old for."

They both laughed.

I stood there dumbfounded. My parents had been divorced for a long time. Never had they mentioned reconciling, so I had to assume this was a casual thing. My parents having a casual affair? That just wasn't right.

"We are not too old," Mom said. "And you are not too old for Evan. He's such a sweet boy."

"Calling him a boy doesn't convince me I'm not too old for him." I rubbed my temples, but the headache threatening to start ignored my command to stop that shit. "This isn't about me and Evan. I'm trying to wrap my head around whatever you two are doing."

Dad looked at Mom. "It's time to tell her."

I glanced from one parent to the other. "Tell me what?"

Mom smiled. "We're engaged."

"To do what?"

"Get married, of course."

I opened my mouth but needed several seconds before I could speak. "When did this happen?"

Dad brushed hair away from Mom's face just like Evan used to do with me. My throat hurt watching it.

"It started right after you went back to Scotland with Evan," Dad said. "Your mom and I spent a lot of time together, and things sort of happened. We realized there's never been anyone else for either of us. We belong together, so I'm moving to Seattle to be with your mother." He winked at Mom. "And it's been fun doing the dating thing again."

Mom giggled. She *giggled*, like a teenage girl.

"Oh yes, it's been lots of fun," she said. "I sneak into your dad's room after you go to bed so we can make love."

Her statement left me slack-jawed and speechless.

"Keely," Mom said, "you are a mature woman who shouldn't be shocked to find out her parents enjoy sex. We may be senior citizens, but we're not dead."

I was acting stupid. Maybe it wasn't their renewed relationship that bothered me as much as it was my failed relationship with Evan. He'd meant more to me than anyone.

And I had no clue what happened to us.

My parents had divorced, believing their marriage couldn't work anymore. Seventeen years later, here they were in love again and starting over in their relationship. If they could come back from a failure, maybe Evan and I could too.

If he would ever answer his damn phone.

There was an alternative way of finding him.

"What are you thinking?" Mom asked. "You've got that squinty look on your face that means you're chewing on a problem."

Yes, it was hard to fool people who'd known you since birth.

"I was thinking about Evan," I admitted. "I'm suddenly wondering if I made a mistake by letting him dodge me all this time. Not even sure whether he really dumped me."

"You seemed sure before tonight," Mom said. "What changed your mind?"

"Weirdly, it was you guys. Seeing my parents get back together after being divorced for so long makes me wonder."

"Go find him, Keely. You'll never know the answers unless you dig them up yourself."

Dad scoffed. "She's been calling him fifty times a day for over a month. If the guy doesn't want to be found, she can't hunt him down."

"Sure I can." Did I want to? Was this a wise decision? Probably not, but Mom was right. I needed answers, and I'd waited long enough for him to come crawling back and offer up the solution to the mystery. "I have to go make a few calls. Good night."

I rushed upstairs to my bedroom, intending to call Tamsen—until I realized it was seven hours later there and too early for her to be at the office. I changed into my nightie and tried to sleep but succeeded only in tossing and turning for nearly four hours before I gave up and dialed Tamsen's office number.

"Evanescent Security Technologies. Tamsen Spurling speaking. How may I help you?"

"That's quite a mouthful to say every time you answer the phone. Oh, this is Keely O'Shea."

"I know. My telephone tells me." She paused. "That is a right awful litany to repeat with every phone call. But you didn't ring me to suggest a shorter greeting. What can I do for you, Miss O'Shea?"

"Call me Keely. I'm looking for Evan."

"Afraid he's not here."

"I've been calling him for weeks, but he doesn't pick up and never calls me back. Where is he?"

She harrumphed. "I wish I had a bloody clue. He left weeks ago saying he'd be spending a good deal of time out of the country. He comes back occasionally and gave me permission to handle matters in his absence."

"Absence? How long is he planning to be gone?"

"Don't ask me. I think Evan's gone insane." She lowered her voice to a conspiratorial whisper. "Or perhaps he's simply insane for you."

Was it my fault he'd taken off? How long did it take a man to sort out his problems? And why did he need to get away from me to do it?

"Please let me know if you hear from him," I said. "I'll do the same for you."

"Of course."

We said goodbye, and I dialed Aileen MacTaggart's number. She answered with a cheerful greeting, and I said, "It's Keely O'Shea."

"Oh dearie, I'm so happy to hear from you. Evan talks about you every time he calls."

Then why the hell didn't he call me? I wouldn't ask his mother that. She'd been so kind to me since her son vanished from my life. "He's not there, I take it. I was hoping he might be since he's not at his office."

"No, he hasn't been home lately. He's not with his cousins either."

"Tamsen told me he's been out of the country a lot."

"Yes, he has," she said carefully. "Evan misses you, and I'm sure you'll hear from him soon."

We talked for a little longer about nothing of any importance. I asked about her flower garden, and she asked after my family. Eventually, we said goodbye.

I went to work and tried not to think about Evan.

Two weeks dragged by with me failing to not think about him. On the afternoon of the fifteenth day, Paige knocked on my office door. She'd brought today's mail for me to sort and handle as appropriate. I'd just begun to flip through the mail, setting each envelope on the correct pile for its category, when I discovered a pale-blue envelope with no address on it. Instead, handwritten letters spelled out "Keely."

The room swayed around me for a moment. I recognized the handwriting. It was Evan's.

How had he slipped this into the mail?

Paige had been smiling rather smugly when she'd handed me the mail. She might've helped Evan get this message to me.

I slapped the blue envelope down on my desk and tossed the rest of the mail aside. The envelopes scattered over the desktop. Why the hell wouldn't he just talk to me? Maybe I should ignore his letter the way he'd ignored all my emails, texts, and voicemails.

My pigheaded side kept me paralyzed for about five seconds.

Then I tore open the blue envelope and unfolded the handwritten note it contained. It consisted of two sentences: "Be at 1025 Main Street at 9:00 a.m. tomorrow. Someone will meet you at the gate."

He hadn't even signed the note. The man had some nerve, issuing a command after disappearing from my life for two months.

I tucked the note in my purse. Later, I would decide whether to obey.

The note made me queasy again, so I got out the package of saltines I'd started keeping in my desk. The stress of getting dumped or possibly not getting dumped but simply being abandoned had left my constitution in a tizzy. While I nibbled on a cracker, I thought about the words Evan had scrawled on a small sheet of blue paper. It had been so impersonal.

Except he'd written it himself. No laser-printed invitation. A handwritten note.

Would I obey his command to appear before the CEO?

I groaned. Of course I would. I wanted to see him if only to slug him and walk right back out the door. But it was more likely I'd throw my arms around him and kiss him.

A hopeless, pathetic romantic. That's what I was.

Chapter Thirty-Nine

Evan

The view out the window of my new office wasn't familiar to me yet, not like the view from my headquarters at Inverness. I knew that skyline by heart. I hadn't quite become that comfortable with Carrefour, but I would. I had one very good reason to get to know this place, and she was about to walk into my office any moment.

I wasn't sure if Keely would kiss me or punch me.

The intercom on my desk buzzed, and my new executive assistant said in her American accent, "Miss O'Shea is here, Mr. MacTaggart."

"Thank you, Serena. Please send her in."

I sat up straighter in my chair.

The door opened. Keely traipsed into the room and shut the door behind her. She wore the same clothes she'd had on the first time she'd walked into my Inverness office, the beige skirt suit that molded to her curves without seeming inappropriate. I knew if she leaned forward, her blouse would tighten over her breasts and the low, but not too low, neckline would give me a tantalizing glimpse of the inner slopes. She wore her raven hair pulled back in a crisp bun, just like before, and she carried the same leather binder.

She halted in front of my desk. "How is Serena your executive assistant? She's a nurse."

"Not anymore. She wanted a position with flexible hours. I was happy to accommodate her. She's good at her job and almost as clever as you."

"I see." Keely bent forward slightly, tilting her whole body so I was robbed of the chance to watch her blouse tighten. "Are you wearing a kilt?"

"Yes."

"It's not Monday."

"I've made an exception for you."

"Hm." She took a seat in the chair a few feet away, crossing her legs and setting the leather binder on her lap. "What business are we discussing today, Mr. MacTaggart?"

She was going to make me work for this. Well, I deserved it. And my pulse accelerated at the thought of flirting with her the way I had the first time she'd stepped into my office.

I'd be less of an eejit this time.

"You're even more beautiful," I said. "Can't describe the difference, but you seem to...glow. Not like a Times Square billboard, but like an angel disguised as a mortal."

"Times Square billboard? That's in New York. You've never been anywhere in America except Carrefour, Utah."

"Ah, that was true. It's not anymore."

Her brows cinched together, and she curled her fingers over the top edge of her binder. "I don't get it. Have you been on an American vacation all this time?"

"Not a vacation." I rocked my chair back a little, taking a moment to decide how to explain this to her. Bluntness seemed like the best option. "I met my father. He's in prison in New Jersey, not far from New York City. I spent time in the city talking to lawyers and investigators. It was not a holiday in any sense of the term."

"Oh." She slouched back in her chair. "How did it go? Meeting your father?"

"Well enough. He's not what I expected, but we're getting to know each other as well as we can while he's in prison."

"He's serving a life sentence without parole, right?"

"Yes." I leaned forward and rested my arms on the desk, studying the calendar that covered a large section of the desktop. "I'm sorry I didn't answer your calls."

"Or the emails, or the texts."

"Yes, I'm sorry for all of it." I traced the lines on the calendar with one finger. "I needed to sort myself, to come to terms with everything that happened and everything I learned about my family and myself. Working to get my father exonerated has helped me work through it all."

"Exonerate him? Can you do that after thirty years?"

"I've hired the best attorneys and private investigators. They've already found evidence the police and prosecutor ignored reports of another man who matched the sketch and who committed similar crimes in New York. They've also tracked down witnesses who saw the other man leaving the scene of the crime my father supposedly committed. The lawyers have filed an appeal to have the conviction reversed. The process will take considerable time. I will see him exonerated, no matter how long it takes or how much money it costs."

Keely slid forward in her chair, her attention riveted to me. "Do you think it will happen?"

"I'm certain of it." I looked into her brilliant green eyes and couldn't believe I'd stayed away from her for so long. "I've spent so much time in this country I've started to think in terms of inches and feet instead of meters. But all I want to learn about is you."

She set her leather binder on the floor and clasped her hands on her lap. "You already know all about me."

"Not the most important thing." I hesitated, swallowing because my mouth had suddenly gone dry as the Sahara Desert. I tugged at the collar of my shirt. "Can you forgive me for leaving you alone for so long?"

"I thought you dumped me."

"Why? I left you a note. Didn't you see it?"

"Yes, I saw it." Her lips puckered, and her eyes narrowed. "It said you had to leave me. Sounded to me like I was getting tossed overboard."

"I said I needed to leave you so I could sort things. I've done that. We can be together now."

"Just like that?" She sat stiff and straight, shaking her head. "You don't get off that easy. If you expected me to throw myself at you and praise heaven you came back to me, think again. I'm not a doormat anymore."

"I've never thought you were a doormat."

"The point is you left without even saying goodbye."

"My note said it."

She bowed her head and exhaled a gusty breath.

"I am sorry, Keely. I missed you, and I love you."

"Yes, I know." She pushed up out of the chair and walked to my desk, leaning her hip against it. "I understand you've never been in a relationship before. This is all new territory for you, and there's no map to show you the way."

"Are you forgiving me?"

She set her palm on the desktop and leaned toward me. "Yes, I forgive you."

I tried not to act like a giddy moron, but I couldn't stop myself from grinning. "I was afraid I'd need to do more groveling before you'd take me back."

"Haven't said I'm taking you back." She leaned in more. Her blouse stretched taut over her breasts, so taut it seemed like the buttons might pop free. "How did you get a building constructed so fast? Is it not up to code and it'll fall down in six months?"

"I never allow anything I do to be less than the best."

"My dad likes to say you can have any two of the following—good, cheap, fast."

"And I agree."

She studied me for several seconds, her expression unreadable. Then she smiled. "You got it done fast and good, but you paid an obscene amount of money to make that happen."

I slanted forward. Her breasts were inches from my face. "I would've given my entire fortune to get you back. The car didn't impress you, I imagine. The house wouldn't have either. I gave you those things because I want to make your life easier."

She twirled her finger to indicate the room around us. "What about this building? I hope you're not planning to pawn that off on me too."

"No, I need it for my new business venture."

"And what is your new business?"

"I'm buying Vic's Electronics Superstore and making it a subsidiary of Evanescent. We will not only design and manufacture the devices, we will also sell them in our own store. Soon it will be a chain of stores across the country."

"Vic would never sell. He loves the store."

"Aye, but he wants to spend more time with his family. He also worries about how hard you work. He will stay on as the president of the new company. You'll be vice president, and I expect you to hire people to help you so you won't be working such long hours."

"What about Tamsen? You've driven the poor woman bonkers with your extended absences."

"Tamsen is now sharing vice president responsibilities with Stewart Atkins. They will each work shorter hours so they can have more time with their families, but they will handle the bulk of the business matters. I'm taking a step back from the everyday operations of the company." I hooked my finger inside the neckline of her blouse, imagining giving it a yank to free those buttons. "I'll need to spend plenty of time with my bride."

She jerked backward. "Bride? You have to propose before you can call me that."

"You know I love heeding your commands." I grasped her hand. "Will you marry me, Keely?"

"I'll consider your offer and get back to you."

The sparkle in her eyes told me she was teasing.

"Maybe I need to tie you up again," I said, "to torture you into saying yes."

"Sounds like fun, but it's not necessary." She waved her a hand in a shooing gesture. "Sit back, Mr. MacTaggart."

"Ahhh, you know I how feel about your schoolteacher voice."

"Sit back," she said more sternly.

I sat back in my chair.

She crawled across my desk and onto my lap, latching her arms around my neck. "Yes, I will marry you."

"Good. But I still might tie your hands behind your back when I have my way with you on this desk."

She kicked off her shoes. "There is one thing I should tell you first."

"You can tell me anything."

"This could be a shocker." She laid a hand over her lower belly. "I, um, took one of those home tests this morning."

"Home test? For what?"

"Pregnancy. It was positive."

I was fair certain my jaw dropped to my chest.

She grimaced. "I know we never talked about kids, and honestly, this is a shock to me too. I'd assumed I was too old to get pregnant the old-fashioned way. But we, well, kind of forgot to use a condom that day when you ripped my clothes off and ordered me to get on my knees."

I muttered an oath. "My fault. I'm sorry."

"Are you upset about this?"

She watched me with a wary expression, clearly worried I might be angry.

"I am not upset," I said, pulling her closer. "This is the best news I've ever heard."

To prove I meant it, I thrust a hand into her hair and pulled her in for a deep kiss. When I finally broke away, her cheeks were pink and her lips were slightly swollen.

"Glad you're not upset," she said. "I hope becoming a daddy won't be too much stress on top of everything that's going on."

"It's not stress. It's a miracle." I ran my thumb across her lips. "You are a miracle, *mo chridhe*, and I can't wait till we have a bairn who's just like you."

"Bossy and polite at the same time?"

"Naturally." I hooked my finger inside the neckline of her blouse and gave it a sharp tug. The buttons broke free, exposing her lacy, front-clasp bra. "Tell me to behave in that voice."

She ran her fingers through my hair. "Behave, Evan."

I growled, unhooking her bra. Those bonnie breasts spilled out, and I caught one in my hand. "What will you do if I don't behave?"

"Tie you to the nearest bed and torture you for hours."

"Afraid the nearest bed is too far away." I stood and set her on the desk. "Ahm needing ye now."

Keely plucked my glasses off my nose and tucked them into my shirt pocket. She lay back on the desk, her arms stretched out above her head, lifting her breasts. "I'm yours to command."

I did just that for the next hour, ignoring the buzzing intercom and the ringing phone. I had people to handle the business for me. My job was handling Keely, something I meant to do for the rest of our lives.

Epilogue

Logan
Four months later

I lingered at the periphery of the great hall in Dùndubhan, watching my relatives dance and laugh and generally have a good time. I enjoyed a party as much as anyone, but I'd had my fill of conversation over the past two hours. The whole clan had gathered to celebrate my Aunt Aileen's birthday. Even the O'Sheas had made the trip to Scotland for this.

Evan, the cousin I'd least expected to walk down the aisle, had married Keely O'Shea three months ago. Today, Keely had a very round belly and Evan looked at her like she was the sun and the moon and Heaven itself all rolled up in one earthly body. I'd always dismissed marriage as an outdated concept, but I couldn't deny my married cousins seemed much happier since they found their soul mates.

There was another term I didn't like. My soul didn't have a mate, and I wasn't completely certain I had a soul, anyway. None of my family knew the things I'd done in the name of Her Majesty's Secret Intelligence Service. Evan had once thought he was a bad man for giving in to blackmailers.

I had killed men.

On the other side of the room, Keely and Evan were sharing some sort of joke with their friend Serena Carpenter. I'd first met Serena at Evan and Keely's wedding—a backyard affair without any of the outrageous things most weddings seemed to involve these days—and I'd seen Serena again when Evan invited me to visit him in America. He and Keely shared the house he'd bought for her back before he'd known if she even loved him.

Serena was laughing, her face alight.

The lass was beautiful. Her slim, sexy body made my cock stiffen. Since she was my cousin's friend, and his wife's best friend, I would never act on the lust she inspired. Besides, I didn't do well with relationships. My past life had a habit of reemerging at the most inopportune moments. Women didn't like to be interrupted during a date by a man carrying a gun under his suit jacket.

More importantly, Serena Carpenter was the most annoying woman I had ever met.

I wandered around the edge of the dance floor, moving closer to Evan, Keely, and Serena—and her son. The laddie was engrossed with the buffet table directly behind his mother. He shoved an entire Scotch egg into his mouth.

Children were disgusting.

I forgot about the boy when I saw Serena's dress. I'd seen it earlier, but now I had the chance to admire it fully. She wore a red dress that clung to her body and ended several inches above her knees. Her stiletto heels matched her dress. Straps held it up, but the neckline plunged very low. Her small but succulent breasts would've fit in my hands like apples.

She noticed me and frowned, then lifted her perfect little nose in the air and turned her head away.

The bloody woman had no manners at all. She behaved politely for everyone else, but whenever she saw me, she turned into a she-devil.

I strolled out of the great hall and down the spiral staircase to the vestibule, continuing into the main hallway of the ground floor. There, I paused to study the glass display cases. Keely had shattered one of the panes during Tulloch's siege, but it had been fixed months ago. Evan had found himself a feisty lass for sure. Lately, he'd started pestering me to "settle down" the way he had.

Not bloody likely.

Sighing, I wandered down the hall and stopped alongside the bathroom door. The party had been enjoyable, but I needed a break from the festivities upstairs. I leaned against the wall, shoving my hands into the pockets of my trousers, and shut my eyes. The faint strains of the music upstairs drifted down to this floor, the subdued song making me want a lie-down. But I'd promised to stay for the entire party. In a minute or two, I'd go back upstairs.

The clacking of high heels on the wood floor roused me.

I opened my eyes.

Serena was sashaying toward me, her hips swaying and her head held high.

Those legs. Those breasts. What had I said about not giving in to my lust? I could have her once, purely to get her out of my system. Once I'd fucked her, she wouldn't seem so enticing anymore. She'd be nothing more than the uppity woman who refused to look at me.

Aye, one good fuck ought to do the trick.

She stopped in front of me. "Guarding the bathroom? Or are you trolling for loose women?"

"Neither. I'm taking a break from the party."

"Yeah, I've noticed you're a real party animal." She set a hand on her hip. "Hanging out in dark corners doesn't count as participating."

"Does fucking you count as participating?"

Her lip curled. "Tell me you didn't say what I think you said."

I waved toward a door down the hall. "Let's go into the cloakroom and have a poke."

She snapped her spine so straight so quickly I wondered if she'd dislocated a few vertebrae. And of course, she lifted her perfect little nose again. "You are the most disgusting man I have ever met."

"But would ye like to fuck?"

Serena Carpenter smacked me in the face. "Go to hell."

The lass stormed into the bathroom. The door banged shut behind her.

I rubbed my stinging cheek. Ah well, even I didn't strike gold every time. Since I would be seeing Serena again, considering she was the best friend of my cousin's wife, I might have another opportunity to shag her and get rid of this craving for her body.

Keely claimed Serena was a sweetheart.

Sweet? That woman was a bitch.

But someday I would get her naked. Someday soon.

Logan MacTaggart returns in *Lethal in a Kilt*.

Love the

Hot Scots

series?

Visit
AnnaDurand.com

to subscribe to her newsletter
for updates on forthcoming books in this series
&
to receive a free gift for signing up!

*A*nna Durand is a bestselling, multi-award-winning author of contemporary and paranormal romance. Her books have earned bestseller status on every major retailer and wonderful reviews from readers around the world. But that's the boring spiel. Here are some really cool things you want to know about Anna!

Born on Lackland Air Force Base in Texas, Anna grew up moving here, there, and everywhere thanks to her dad's job as an instructor pilot. She's lived in Texas (twice), Mississippi, California (twice), Michigan (twice), and Alaska—and now Ohio.

As for her writing, Anna has always made up stories in her head, but she didn't write them down until her teen years. Those first awful books went into the trash can a few years later, though she learned a lot from those stories. Eventually, she would pen her first romance novel, the paranormal romance Willpower, and she's never looked back since.

Want even more details about Anna? Get access to her extended bio when you subscribe to her newsletter and download the free bonus ebook, Hot Scots Confidential. You'll also get hot deleted scenes, character interviews, fun facts, and more!

Made in the USA
Middletown, DE
08 April 2021